Stuck Together

BOOKS BY LILY JOSEPH

The Near Miss

Lily Joseph

Stuck Together

bookouture

Published by Bookouture in 2024

An imprint of Storyfire Ltd.
Carmelite House
50 Victoria Embankment
London EC4Y 0DZ

www.bookouture.com

Storyfire Ltd's authorised representative in the EEA is Hachette Ireland
8 Castlecourt Centre
Castleknock Road
Castleknock
Dublin 15 D15 YF6A
Ireland

ISBN: 978-1-83525-350-2
eBook ISBN: 978-1-83525-349-6

For George and Freya

ONE

In some love stories, the peak moment is a couple standing on a street in the rain, under the orange glow of street lamps, gazing intensely at each other before they passionately kiss. But although my story begins on Grey Street one rainy night, it was anything but romantic. I'd been standing outside for less than a minute, but my hair was already plastered to my head like it had been poured out of a paint can, and the only intense gaze I'd exchanged was with an underage drinker who'd dropped a half-eaten tray of cheesy chips on my shoe. Instead of the dreamy glow of street lamps, hollow plastic Christmas lights hung above my head in preparation for the festive season, grey and miserable in their unlit state.

I should have picked a drier night to get fired.

My shift had started without any sense of foreboding; just a normal night waitressing in one of Newcastle's fancier restaurants. Epicure was the kind of place that had a menu made up of vague descriptions like *Essence of Carrot, Venison Smoke* or *The Souls of All Your Deceased Relatives.* I arrived wearing the staff uniform of a crisp white shirt tucked into jeans and strapped a black apron around my waist.

Grant materialised around the corner of the staff-room door like he was one of the aforementioned deceased souls. Being the maître d', he was dressed in a grey suit, and his blonde hair was quiffed to perfection.

'Annie, we've talked about this.'

'I know, I'm sorry. The bus was late and I got here as quick as I could.'

His smile was reminiscent of a shark circling its next meal. 'Well, maybe you should get on the earlier one from now on.'

The earlier one, if it ran on time, would get me into Newcastle a full hour before my shift, but I smiled and nodded. 'I'll think on that.'

'Best that you do. We can only live up to our guests' expectations if we have similarly high expectations of ourselves.' He disappeared.

'Someone's been given a self-help book for their birthday,' I murmured as I stood in front of the mirror tidying my ponytail. As usual, I needed to stand on tiptoes to see my full face – at just over five feet tall, I found that mirrors often gave me a view of my forehead and little else. My light brown hair, which was exactly the same shade as my freckles, was still slightly blonde at the ends from summer. Now that we were deep into autumn, my next trim would put paid to that and make me mousy again.

This wasn't my dream job; far from it, but it was a damn sight better than some previous jobs I'd had. It was a list that was longer and more varied than I would have liked. But since I'd left school, I'd found it hard to settle on one career. I liked trying new things, and now that I was twenty-eight, I had a CV as long as an epic novel.

The dining room was starting to fill with the first customers, and I tended to my four tables: one family with cute, well-behaved children who also seemed frighteningly cultured; a group of female friends; and two couples – one seemingly on a first date and the other looking at their phones throughout. For all it wasn't the most glittering career, I enjoyed it – talking to people, helping them choose from the baffling menu and making sure they had a great night.

The first few hours passed by under the ever-watchful eye of Grant, who glowered at me in between sashaying from table to table, theatrically unfolding napkins and laying them on people's laps. I just smiled back and remembered to 'forget' one or two drinks on the nicer customers' bills, as a kind of reverse paying-it-forward. I was serving another tray of drinks to the group of girlfriends, who were still there and on their fifth or sixth bottle of wine between them, when Grant escorted three men to one of my tables and nodded at me to take over.

Before I could even whip out my notepad, the biggest, burliest one, who looked like he'd played a lot of rugby in his time, looked past me towards the table of women beyond.

'You all look like you're having a good time,' he said with a wolfish grin. 'I might swap tables – leave these reprobates behind.' He tipped a wink at his two friends. His accent was plummy Southern English on steroids.

The women stopped talking, smiled uncomfortably and subtly turned their shoulders on him. His face fell and his lip curled.

'God, the women up here are as cold as the weather.'

His friends chuckled, and they all checked the menu while I waited, a patient smile on my face. The two other men ordered drinks and then Rugby Wanker said, 'I'll have a Hendricks and tonic. Make sure it comes with cucumber not lime.'

I nodded and walked away, just catching him murmur, 'Can't expect the provinces to be up to speed on how to make a proper G&T.'

Straightening my back, I headed to the bar and passed on their order. 'Hendricks with cucumber and a dash of arsenic,' I said, laughing and shaking my head at the bar manager. 'We've got another one.' Unfortunately, obnoxious customers were par for the course here, although most were perfectly lovely.

When I got back to the table, the three of them were guffawing at something, and one of the women at the next table rolled her eyes at me.

'Here you go,' I said, serving the drinks. 'So, are you ready to order food?'

Rugby Wanker sat back and crossed his arms over his chest, regarding me with curiosity. 'You know, I do love that accent. It's quite sexy.'

'I can recommend the salmon this evening,' I said breezily, ignoring him. 'It comes with a caper foam and dill granola.'

He chuckled to his friends. 'Sexy but indecipherable. Can you say that again?'

Breathing deeply, I repeated it.

'*Dill granola*,' he parroted in a terrible approximation of my Geordie accent, ridiculing my Northern roots. 'I didn't realise people up here really do talk like characters from *Byker Grove*.'

'Do you want to order food or not?' I asked, not bothering to blunt the sharpness in my tone. His friends now looked uncomfortable but stayed quiet.

'Hoo-hoo!' he crowed. 'I heard the Geordies love a fight too. Even the fillies apparently. Now, let's see what passes for good food up here in Newcaaarstle.' His accent mangled the pronunciation of my home town as he lifted the menu.

As he did, I took the opportunity to gently rock his full glass of G&T off the table and onto his lap. He sprang backwards like he'd been electrocuted as the ice-cold liquid poured onto his presumably tiny penis.

'What the fuck?' he yelled, springing out of his chair and grabbing a napkin. 'What did you do that for?'

I looked at him innocently. 'I'm sorry, sir, but I think you caught it with the edge of your menu.'

The women on the next table exchanged expressions of

shock and delight. One by one, their shoulders started to shake with suppressed laughter.

'Get me the manager,' he snarled, but Grant was already scurrying over.

'I'm terribly sorry, sir,' he said in his pretend-posh version of our accent and handed the idiot another napkin. 'Of course we'll be replacing your drink and bringing you another round of complimentary beverages. Annie, come with me.'

He marched me off to the kitchen and rounded on me.

'What the hell was that?' he snapped, his accent now returning to normal.

'He spilled his drink! I can't help it if he's clumsy.'

His eyes narrowed. 'I saw you push it, Annie. I don't care how much of a nightmare some customers are, but that's beyond the pale.'

'Grant, he was bothering the other diners, sexually harassing me and slagging off my accent.'

He sighed. 'Look, I can't be seen to let this go. I'm sorry, but you're fired.'

'What?'

'You heard me. Go and get your things, and I'll send on what we owe you.'

I stood there for a moment, frozen. Then I turned on my heel, grabbed my coat and bag from the staff room, and instead of going out the back door, I stormed into the dining room.

'You know, I'm glad you're wearing beige chinos,' I said, walking up to Rugby Wanker's table. 'Enjoy the rest of your night looking like you've wet yourself. And for the record, it's pronounced New-CASTLE, not Newcaaarstle. Although, coming from you, I suppose you would put the emphasis on the *arse*.'

I stalked off to rapturous applause from the table of women, and that was how I came to be standing on Grey Street on a Friday night, soaked through with rain.

. . .

Despite the weather, I couldn't stand to go home just yet, so I wrapped my arms around my sodden jacket and hunched my shoulders, ploughing through the crowds of glammed up, suited and booted revellers. Compared to my North East brethren, I was overdressed in the sense I was wearing a coat but underdressed in contrast to their smart outfits, so joining them in the queues for the wine bars and cocktail lounges to drown my sorrows was out of the question.

I scurried down a narrow side street and into a more casual pub that seemed happy to allow all kinds of attire, even if it looked like the wearer had done ten lengths in a swimming pool. Happily, it wasn't rammed with people, so I was able to climb onto a bar stool and order myself a bottle of lager without a fuss.

I looked around, feeling the tension drain from my shoulder muscles. The place was dimly lit, and the bar area, which had drinks stocked on reclaimed wood pallets, was backlit in red. In front of a wall cladded with sheets of corrugated iron, there was a small stage where a band played soft rock, guitars balanced on narrow hips, long hair draping over their faces. I tapped my foot to a song I didn't know and watched with vague indifference as I drank.

Then one of the guitarists flicked back his hair and my attention immediately switched from indifferent to transfixed. He was tall and slender, with dark brown hair that was almost black, and had cheekbones you could sharpen a blade on. A girl in the audience whooped, and he flashed her a smile, showing his straight white teeth. It might have looked more cocky if his eyes hadn't crinkled at the sides with amusement, and I kind of envied the girl who had his attention and who was more than likely in gainful employment too.

They played out the rest of their song, and I sat peeling the label off my bottle of beer, becoming lost in my thoughts. Every job I attempted seemed to end in disaster or the realisation that I hated it. Epicure had been a good one, but here I was, out on my ear. In the past, I'd tried being an office administrator (dull – and lots of paper cuts), working at the garden centre (I could kill a plant just by breathing on it) and even a few shifts at a butcher's (the reason I was now a vegetarian). But nothing seemed to stick.

In all honesty, it wasn't just the jobs being boring or too heavy on the animal cruelty. I was starting to wonder if I was incapable of being *managed*. I'd always had an independent streak and immediately felt a pulse of rebellion when I was told to do something, particularly when it wasn't delivered very politely. And that sometimes resulted in situations like the one I'd found myself in tonight.

There was a smattering of applause, and I noticed that the band had stopped playing. A figure came up behind me to stand at the bar, and I realised it was the good-looking guitarist. He ordered a beer in a surprisingly polite voice, his North East accent a little softer than I'd expected, and leaned against the bar rail looking out at the room.

Feeling emboldened by residual adrenaline from my chaotic evening, I said, 'Great set.'

He turned his head and smiled the same way he had at that other woman, but this time it was slower and more wry.

'I saw you come in. You only heard one song. More like half a song.'

I hadn't been aware he'd noticed me come in and felt both gratified and unnerved by the attention. His eyes held mine with complete confidence, and they reminded me of polished mahogany – the way that the burnished wood looked like it had depth. But now I could see him more clearly, I noticed that his nose was slightly crooked, as if it had been broken once or twice.

A small imperfection that somehow made him feel more approachable than his onstage persona.

'I liked it. I would have come earlier,' I fibbed, 'but I had an eventful evening.'

'Riding a log flume?'

'What?'

He gestured to my damp hair and clothes, and I touched my limp locks self-consciously.

'Ha. No. More of an employment rollercoaster than a theme park one. I got fired.'

'Sorry to hear that,' he said laconically, resting his elbows back on the bar. 'Maybe that job wasn't what you were meant to be doing.'

I was fairly sure that being destitute wasn't a great thing to have written in your stars, but I nodded in agreement. 'Yeah. Maybe I can devote time to my more artistic leanings.'

'You're an artist?'

I knitted miniature animals in my spare time.

'Yep,' I replied, deciding not to be bogged down with the homely specifics. 'I work with textiles mainly.'

'Cool,' he said with an upward nod. 'Well, here's to artistic leanings.' He tipped his bottle towards mine with an earnest expression on his face, followed by a smile that mirrored mine. I opened my mouth to properly introduce myself and ask his name, but his eyes flickered away towards his guitar stand.

'Speaking of artistic leanings, I'd best get back to mine. Nice to meet you.'

He walked back to the stage with the slightest suggestion of a swagger and joined his bandmates, who were tuning their guitars for another set. He gripped a plectrum between his lips and studiously tweaked at his strings. *Hot*, I thought. Hot, but a tiny bit pretentious.

Then they started playing, the girls started wolf-whistling and I was just one of the audience again.

. . .

When I got home, the flat was in darkness, except for a pale blue flickering light from under the door of Neo's room. I didn't think that Neo was my flatmate's real name – he had an unhealthy obsession with *The Matrix* and went around wearing a long black coat on the rare occasions he left the flat. I could hear the faint noise of computer sword clashes and the roar of orcs, or whatever mythical creature it was that he was slaying.

I went to the fridge, rummaged past the pots of half-eaten takeaway with Neo's proprietary Post-its on them and pulled out a bottle of beer. Before I took my first swig, I raised an ironic cheers to whoever it was up there that was determined to see me unemployed and impoverished.

The living room was spartan except for Neo's shelves stocked with gaming and film and TV memorabilia. There was a pleather sofa covered in scuffs and one well-established bum-imprint where Neo used to sit, before becoming a semi-recluse who stuck to his room. I sat at the other end and stared at the wall. From the other side came the faint thrum of drill music from the students who lived next door. How was I ever going to get out of this flat and become as financially stable as I thought I would be by my age?

I checked my banking app with the air of someone peeling back the sheet at a morgue, knowing it was going to be grim but having no choice but to look. As expected, there was little in there but a flurry of financial tumbleweeds. I sighed and ground my fists into my eyes. There was only one thing for it, and that was almost as unpalatable as my encounter with Rugby Wanker. With my shoulders slumped, I knocked on Neo's door.

'Come,' said a voice from within.

I pushed open the door and was assaulted by a heady mix of tobacco and Lynx Africa. Neo was just as reluctant to take showers as he was to go outside, and overcompensated with pungent body spray. The room was dark, but I could make out his unmade bed, posters of Princess Leia and She-Hulk, and his desk, which looked like something out of the NASA control room. Three large screens dominated the space, and I saw that he was simultaneously playing *World of Warcraft*, participating in a chatroom discussion and ordering a replica Thor's hammer on eBay.

'What can I do you for, my good lady?' he asked, not taking his eyes off the screens. His long black hair was tethered at the back in a ponytail; its dark colour emphasised the pallor of his skin.

'Um, hi, Neo. How was your day?'

'Successful. I levelled up to sixty on *Burning Crusade* and finished alpha testing and debugging my client's app.'

'I don't know what either of those things mean, but I'm really happy for you.'

'Thanks,' he said, tapping away at his keyboard. 'So. Have you brought me a side quest, or are you just here to make small talk?'

'Er, side quest, I think? I have a favour to ask.'

'Pray tell,' he murmured, still glued to the screen.

'I'm going to come up a bit short on this month's rent. I'm sorry.'

'I see. How come?'

'I poured a drink on someone's lap for being a patronising, misogynistic prick. And then lost my job.'

'No savings?'

I shrugged. 'Waitressing doesn't pay as well as software engineering, I'm afraid.'

He sighed. 'Fine. Leia would have done the same to a misogynist, I suppose. Pay me back when you get a new job.'

'I will. Thanks, Neo. I really appreciate it.'

'No problem. May the force be with you.'

'And also with you.' I left and closed the door.

I stood against it with my forehead rested on the plywood. Thank the lord Neo was a kind-hearted nerd. I felt terrible having to depend on his good nature, but what choice did I have? It was this or be out on the street. I'd need to find a new job, and fast, because I was now even further away from getting out of here. As decent as Neo could be, I didn't think I could bear much more of his spooky presence beyond the bedroom door, or having to tiptoe around the pristine still-unboxed *Game of Thrones* memorabilia.

I headed to my room, ready for the oblivion of sleep, in the hope that I might dream of a solution.

TWO

'Denise. Denise! Have you seen the electric carving knife?'

'It's in the cupboard behind the spiralizer,' said my mam from the sofa, where she was cosied under a blanket. Despite the electric fire being on, she still felt the cold.

'Which cupboard is the spiralizer in then?'

'The one next to the cooker hood.'

'Right or left?'

Mam sighed and tried to get up. 'Hang on – I'm coming.'

I pushed her gently back into her seat. 'No, Mam, I'll go. But is it right or left?'

'Thank you, darl. It's the left one.'

But as I got up, the whirr of the electric knife came from beyond the kitchen door, along with the grating sound of it being dragged across the edge of a plate. My mam shuddered.

'Bless him – at least he's trying!' she said.

I sat back down on the sofa, folding my feet under my legs and snuggling closer to her. My childhood living room had barely changed since I'd moved out – it was small but cosy, with my parents' decorative taste stamped all over it: swirly carpet, a feature wall with bird-print wallpaper, the mantelpiece decked out with quirky vintage-shop finds interspersed with craft projects that I'd brought home from school. There was a photo frame I'd made out of balsa wood flanked by a figurine of a Roman soldier and one of those bottles with a ship inside. Being an only child meant that my childhood efforts were given pride of place.

'Now, what are we going to do with you, eh?' she said warmly. Despite being in an MS flare, she was still cheerful and had her make-up on, complete with trademark red lipstick. Thankfully, her relapses were usually short-lived, and she was on the way out of this one, but they took it out of her.

I gave her a rueful smile. 'I know. Another job bites the dust.'

'You'll figure it out. I have no doubt you'll find your niche soon.'

'I will,' I said decisively, and I meant it. 'And on the bright side, I have twelve years of "wide-ranging experience" under my belt. It has to pay off soon.'

'I'm only sorry we can't have you back home right now. Not until we shift all that rubbish in your old room anyway.'

'Don't worry, Mam – I can take care of myself. Plus Neo's being really decent about it.'

'Good.'

Then the kitchen door opened and my dad bustled through with two plates in hand.

'Get it while it's hot, ladies.' He set the plates on the dining table in the back of the living room, and I helped my mam up to go and eat.

'This looks smashing, Keith,' she said. 'I like what you've done with the mash.'

Since Dad had started taking over some of the cooking, some of his dishes were what you might call 'experimental'. Sitting in amongst the rest of the Sunday roast, mine minus the meat, was a pile of mash that was flecked with little red and yellow bits. On sampling, I discovered these were chilli flakes.

'Delicious,' I said, almost choking, and took a slug of orange squash.

'Bon appétit,' he said with a flourish, looking so chuffed with himself I couldn't help but smile.

He tucked in enthusiastically, wincing as he tried the mash, his tongue running around under his lips, but then shrugged and took another big forkful. Where my mam was slight and small, my dad was built like a tank. Tall and broad, even in his fifties he was fit and strong – when he wasn't at work on the building site, he was in the gym lifting weights.

'Now then,' he said. 'Am I going to have to find you a job on the site, or have you got any better ideas?' He slathered mint sauce over his roast beef and gave me a look that was a mixture of amusement and patience. Thank God my parents were so bloody nice.

'I'm in pretty good shape, Dad, but I'm not sure I can see myself lugging bags of cement around.'

'I've told you, if you put your mind to it, you can do anything.'

'I think I'd draw the line at slipping a disc though. And you've always said that, but when I've tried *everything*, where do I go from there?'

My mam gasped. 'I completely forgot! Your cousin's looking for someone.'

'Kieran? Mam, he's a physiotherapist. I don't think you can just learn that on the job.'

'Very funny. No, they're after a new receptionist. You could apply for that.'

I chewed a piece of carrot that tasted suspiciously of curry powder.

'Yeah, maybe...'

I hadn't seen Kieran for a few years and there was good

reason for that. I'd seen him in town with a woman who was definitely not his wife and who definitely had Kieran's hand placed squarely on her backside, so he'd avoided me like the plague ever since. I was pretty sure he would burn my CV before I even got an interview.

'I'll have a look online after lunch. See if I can get fixed up.'

'Atta girl,' said Dad. 'Now, eat up. I've made sticky toffee pudding with those dates in the back of the cupboard.'

Mam blinked. 'We haven't got any dates, Keith.'

He frowned and went to the kitchen, coming back with an empty jar.

'Sun-dried tomatoes. I'm sure it'll taste fine.'

After lunch, we sat and watched old episodes of *Cheers*, me and Mam tucked under her blanket and Dad in his armchair. I scrolled intermittently through job websites, shortlisting things that seemed okay, like waitressing or admin. I would update my CV that night and start sending it out.

'Annie, pet. You wouldn't pop upstairs and get my readers, would you?' asked Mam. 'I can't make out a thing on this crossword.'

'Yep, no problem.'

Before going to her bedroom, I stopped to look into my old room. In the years since I'd moved out, it had been gradually filled with the remains of my mother's various business ventures. She was a sucker for a home business and had tried her hand at all sorts, mostly through legit multi-level-marketing although some of them seemed suspiciously like pyramid schemes. The room was piled high with boxes containing the most random selection of products, and 'piled high' wasn't an exaggeration. I could barely see the walls for cardboard containers, and the narrow path to the bed would require a contortionist to fit through. Not that the bed was useful, as it was covered with a plethora of promotional materials – posters, leaflets and banners extolling the virtues of an eclectic range of products.

I lifted the flap of one box – inside were dozens of plastic food containers, still wrapped in protective packaging. The next contained herbal remedies for all manner of minor ailments. Another was filled with lipsticks, bronzers and mascaras – all victims of Mam's tendency to flit from one thing to the next. I suspected this was the genetic cause of my similar disposition.

I remembered, when she was well, helping her lug the boxes to and from the car so she could head out to living rooms across the North East. There, she would host parties, selling her wide-ranging wares and getting more and more client recommendations. But illness got in the way, and even though she'd optimistically continued to order the latest products, she'd gradually become less able to sell them. Hence the Aladdin's cave continued to grow, and although she'd insisted she was going to flog it all on eBay, the hoarded goods dropped under the radar.

I retrieved Mam's glasses from her bedside table, but then something caught my eye. An envelope was on Dad's side, the tear at the top revealing a wide red banner across the upper edge of the letter. I felt guilty, but my interest was piqued. Peeling the paper back just enough, I saw their latest mortgage statement. It was in arrears. My stomach clenched; I knew they often found money tight, but I hadn't realised how bad it had got.

Dad was a very experienced builder, and had worked on some big commercial and domestic contracts in recent years, garnering a great local reputation. But business had slowed, and more competition had crept in, and I'd noticed he'd been gradually spending more and more time at home. I thought that might also be partly down to him caring for Mam when she needed him to.

Calming myself, and deciding to say nothing until I'd

absorbed what I now knew, I went downstairs and handed over her glasses.

'Where's Dad?' I asked, seeing his chair was empty.

'He's gone through to the garage. He's working off his sticky tomato pudding. You should go and see what he's done with the place – he's calling it his man-cave now.'

On entering the garage, I could see what she meant. In the centre was a slightly tired-looking weights bench, and to the side was a running machine. Next to the pots of paint and gardening tools on the shelves was a selection of protein powders. This was all amongst his collection of guitars, which was his other obsession – electric, acoustic, you name it, he had it. When he had spare time, he liked to have jam sessions with some of his building-site mates; they'd named themselves The Brick Roses and still enjoyed reminiscing about their single pub gig three years ago.

He got up from his weights bench and gestured grandly to his gym set-up.

'Good, eh?' he said. He tapped the bench. 'I got this off Paul down at the site. And the running machine off Facebook Marketplace.'

'Amazing! Dad, this looks great. But why do you need all this as well as going down the gym?'

He shrugged. 'Ah, I gave that up. Money for old rope.'

I knew this wasn't true. He had a few mates at his gym and it had always been a bit of a social occasion too. My heart sank; it was the money, of course. If they couldn't keep up with the mortgage, then my dad would never be selfish enough to keep his gym membership.

'Well, give us a go then,' I said, wanting to keep myself from blurting out my worries.

So he spent twenty minutes putting me through my paces on the equipment. The radio was on in the background, blaring a Sunday oldies playlist. I was starting to flag under the weight of the dumbbells when Blondie came on – 'One Way or Another'. Suddenly I found a new burst of energy – if there was ever a title that could be construed different ways, it was that one. It might be a slightly concerning song about a stalker, but the beat and the chanting of the song's title was spurring me on. One way or another, I was going to sort this whole mess out. I pumped the weights until my biceps and wrists burned.

Exhausted, I sat up on the edge of the bench, and Dad came and joined me, squishing me a bit with his massive frame. He put an arm around me and squeezed, and it was like I was ten again. No matter how challenging life was, I always felt bulletproof when I was home with my family.

'Listen, Annie. Me and your mam have been talking. We don't feel right about you struggling to pay your rent, especially as we can't offer you anything here except a sofa. So we want to give you some money to tide you over. Just until you get fixed up with a new job.'

If a person could be warm and cold at the same time, this would be how to best describe my reaction. They couldn't afford this, not at all.

'Dad, I can't accept your money. I'll be fine, honestly.'

'Annie... We want to. You're our daughter, and we won't see you struggle.'

'And I won't see you two struggle either.' I pinched my lips together, realising I'd said the wrong thing. My dad was a proud man.

He looked down at his knees and sighed. 'We won't take no for an answer. And we've already sent the money to your account, so you can't refuse now.'

'Dad, you shouldn't...'

He stood up and ruffled my hair. 'Nonsense. That's what families do. We take care of each other.'

I swallowed, feeling my throat grow thick. 'Thanks, Dad,' I managed. I'd send it back at my first opportunity.

'Now, come on,' he said. 'There's a packet of chocolate digestives in the cupboard with our names on.'

Settled back on the sofa, biscuit in hand, I redoubled my efforts on the job search, scrolling through the recruitment apps. *Human Resources Assistant for a Global Hiring Platform* – that sounded interesting. I opened the ad. *Must have working knowledge of Japanese.* Sighing, I opened the next one – *Production Line Operative – Whitley Fisheries.* In spite of my great need for employment, I drew the line at handling raw cod all day long.

I flicked over to Facebook, partly to see if anything was advertised there, partly to torture myself with friends showing off their airbrushed lives. There were a few opportunities for seasonal work with it being late October; Christmas was on the horizon, and there were a few places advertising casual jobs. I added them to my list.

I scrolled on until something else caught my eye. Above some pictures of an empty room with two large windows at the front was a caption: *Pop-up shop space available. Central Newcastle location, established premises with excellent customer footfall and competitive rates. For enquiries please call Mike on this number.*

I sat looking at it for a while, my thoughts racing. Was I on the brink of something that would solve all of our problems, or was I teetering on the edge of being certifiable?

'Mam, you know all that stuff in my bedroom upstairs?'

'Uh-huh.'

'I think I might have an idea.'

THREE

I stood on Pilgrim Street opposite Palmer's Arcade, chewing the skin at the edge of my thumb. Now that I looked at it, I felt daunted. It was a double-fronted building with an ornate arch over the open front door, the hallway beyond floored with black and white tiles. To the right was a window full of books, The Empty Inkwell written in curlicued letters on the glass. It looked classy. The left-hand side was vacant, and the window was wider – a bigger shop space – and it was empty, barring some shelving on the back wall.

Up and down Pilgrim Street were a selection of shops ranging from vintage emporiums to independent clothing stores, and next to Palmer's Arcade was a glossy-looking cosmetics and skincare boutique. Further down the road was the Tyneside Cinema, an arthouse cinema that I'd never been to. It was all very... polished, and I was now not sure at all that stocking the pop-up shop with my mother's eclectic product range would cut the mustard here.

I was just about to scurry away back to the Metro station when a man who looked to be in his sixties poked his head out of the door, peering around like a meerkat. His blue shirt embraced his ample tummy and was tucked into smart jeans. After a moment, he caught my eye and squinted.

'It's not Annie, is it?' he called from over the street.

'Yeah,' I shouted back with a weak wave. Rumbled.

'I thought so. It's Mike,' he said, gesturing to himself. 'I saw you hovering. Come on over and I'll show you around.'

I hurried over the road and shook his hand. 'I was just making sure I was in the right place,' I fibbed. I'd spoken to Mike the day after coming up with this bright idea, and I was now ten minutes late for this appointment.

'Well, you certainly are,' he said, leading me into the arcade and unlocking the door to the shop on the left.

Further down the hallway, I could make out entrances to two more shops, one of which smelled strongly of incense.

'In you come then.'

We went into the shop, which was surprisingly light and airy considering the grey-tinged autumn sky outside. The walls and shelves were painted white, and the floor was honey-coloured polished floorboards.

'So, this space has been recently vacated by a swimwear retailer – not much business for them at this time of the year. That's the beauty of a pop-up shop – we can do seasonal products, limited stock sales, passing trends and so on. Renting short-term means you can commit for as little or as long as you'd like, really. So what kind of thing are you hoping to use it for?'

I thought about the elegant bookshop across the hall, the slick-looking beauty store next door and the painfully middle-class cinema down the road. And then I thought about the mélange of products in my old bedroom; herbal remedies, kitchen gadgets and hand-made fruity soaps.

'Well... it's a curated collection of wellness products, home-wares and artisan skincare.'

It wasn't exactly lying, merely embellishing. And I was desperate.

'Great – that sounds right up our street, Annie. And what would you be calling the shop? Just so I know if it's a good fit.'

I blinked. Why hadn't I thought about this in advance? My mind scanned through various emergency options that would work for a store full of random objects. Objects that I needed to make me fast money.

'Everything Must Go.' It was to the point, and could hopefully pass as ironic and trendy.

'Interesting. But that could work. Now, I must tell you we've had a bit of interest in the space already, and there's another guy coming to see it. He should be here any minute now. So if you want the space, you might have to move quite quick.'

'Right, I see.' Mike didn't seem the type to make that kind of thing up to pressurise me into signing, so I assumed he wasn't spinning me a line. 'Well, it is lovely. And such a great location. And I can be on a flexible lease, two weeks' notice to vacate?'

'That's right. As I said, that's how the business model works. Get in, sell your stuff and be on your way. Of course, we do have more long-standing tenants like Sven and Arthur next door, so you'd be welcome to stay as long as you'd like.'

'Cool,' I said, looking around the room again. I was starting to picture it all. The job lot of paperbacks on the shelves, tables here and there with neat piles of storage boxes and kitchen gadgets on them. I could paint the shop name on the window like they had next door. Or maybe get a sign made up?

I turned on the spot, taking in the airy atmosphere and period features.

Then there was a cough from the doorway.

The first thing I registered was a pair of familiar mahogany-coloured eyes, which blinked in surprise. It was the guy from the bar, the guitarist. Today, his hair was scooped up in a man-bun, which I could forgive him for as it accentuated his cheek-bones. I felt my face heat up, remembering our back and forth, and the way he'd smiled down at me. The way I'd been disappointed when he'd walked back to the stage. He clearly recognised me too, but before we could renew our acquaintance, Mike bounded over.

'Penn, isn't it?' Mike offered him a handshake.

'Yeah,' he replied, his voice almost lazy with nonchalance. He gave me a quick glance, then it occurred to me. This Penn character, despite our friendly exchange the other night and how my stomach had fluttered when he walked in, was now potentially standing between me and my plans. He looked around. 'Looks good,' he said.

'Glad you think so,' said Mike. 'I'm just showing this lovely lady around too. Sorry your appointments have clashed,' he said, glancing at his watch. 'It's just I need to be somewhere. So, are either of you interested?'

'I am,' Penn said smoothly. 'This space is exactly what I need.' He regarded the shelves. 'I can display the vinyl on there, and if it's okay, I'll bring in some display cabinets of my own?'

'Of course – you can use it however—'

'Excuse me,' I interjected, the flutters in my stomach now becoming quivers of panic. 'Um, I'm still here. I was actually thinking the same. I'd supply some tables and benches to display my stuff too.'

Penn locked eyes with me and smiled slowly. 'Sounds like I've got competition.'

'Yes. You have,' I said, looking to Mike with growing anxiety. 'And I was here first.'

Penn laughed and shook his head. 'I don't think it works like that.'

Mike's eyes flicked between us nervously.

'So, let's talk money, Mike,' I said, turning slightly away from Penn, blocking the space between him and the now slightly frightened-looking landlord.

'Yes, let's,' agreed Penn, matching my proximity to Mike.

His elbow bumped against my upper arm, given our difference in height, but I stood fast. 'I'm sure we'll be able to shake hands on it right away.'

'Same here,' I snapped, straightening my shoulders. 'What's the deal?'

'Well, there's a five-hundred-pound security deposit, which is refundable when you vacate. Provided it's all still in good nick, of course.'

'Okay.' I thought of the money that Mam and Dad had given me. With that and a little nudge further into my overdraft to pay Neo, I could stretch to covering the cost.

'Then, ongoing, the rent will be six hundred pounds.'

'A month?' This sounded very reasonable.

He smiled patiently. 'A week.'

I tensed my jaw to prevent it dropping wide open. 'Right,' I said faintly. 'Righto...'

'So, who's shaking hands?' he asked, holding out a palm to each of us.

I looked at his hands, my heart racing, and made a split-second decision.

'So, the boxed baubles go over here on the square shelves, and the loose baubles in these baskets around the Christmas trees. Tinsel is up on the far wall, and door wreaths by the till on that stand.'

A week later, I found myself in a very different kind of pop-up shop – a Christmas tree farm on the outskirts of Gosforth that had a seasonal shop filled with festive decorations and trinkets. Now that it was the beginning of November, they had just started trading and needed staff for the shop right away, and to take payment for the trees when they were ready later. And I'd turned out to be just the person they needed.

I wasn't sure exactly why this was the case but found out

that morning. After looking me up and down in a frankly disconcerting way, Judy, the manager, told me I'd be taking the role of a Christmas elf once December came. The tree farm boasted a Santa's grotto in the run-up to Christmas and apparently I was a similar size and build to last year's little helper.

All I could do was grit my teeth and get on with it. Since Palmer's Arcade was well outside my budget, and I couldn't see a way to make the books balance with the products I'd be selling, I'd been disappointed to walk away. After my frustratingly handsome competitor had emerged triumphant, I'd been honest with Mike that it was more than I could afford. I still felt an idiot for thinking I could breeze in there and sign on the dotted line.

'Here you go,' said Judy, placing a dusty box into my arms. 'These are from last year. Could you get these strung up around the cornices and across the cash desk?'

'Yep, no problem.'

Judy smiled and headed outside with her clipboard.

I opened the box to find several balls of Christmas lights, the cables in horrifying knots. I lifted one monstrosity out and sighed. This was going to be worse than that time I got chewing gum stuck in my hair, and no amount of baby oil was going to help here.

I laid them on the desk, worrying away at the fine cables, trying not to break the bulbs, and thought about Mam and Dad. They'd tried to hide their disappointment about the shop. Dad had already been talking about making some tables to display the stock, Mam had been on standby to help make signs and decorations, and we'd all agreed to split the profits down the middle. But, as ever, they were stoic in the face of adversity and had cheered me on when I got this Christmas gig.

I'd just managed to free twenty centimetres of cable when the door jingled and a woman came in. She was windswept and wrapped up in a patchwork coat with multicoloured evil eyes embroidered here and there. She tugged down her hood and smiled.

'Blowing a hooley out there,' she said, out of breath. 'Oh. Are you open?' She looked around at the boxes that still hadn't been unpacked and the cluster of fairy lights in my hands.

'Yes! We are. But excuse the boxes – we're still finishing off the stocking up. No pun intended,' I said, nodding to the faux fireplace with Christmas stockings hung along the mantelpiece.

She chuckled. 'That pun was a Christmas cracker,' she said, making me laugh in return. She came closer, emanating the faint scent of patchouli. 'So, I'm looking for some Christmas decorations. The vibe I'm going for is kind of organic, things from nature. Woodland, berries, foraged items, that kind of thing?'

'Um...' I tried to draw on any expertise I'd gleaned from my two hours of being in the job. 'Well, it's too early for real foliage. That will be ready in December, I think. But we do have some natural decorations over here?' I led her to one of the fake Christmas trees decked out in a more folksy style. 'These raffia baubles could be good? Or there's some dried oranges and limes, cinnamon sticks, pine cones... Oh, and these.'

I held up a dried brown thing that looked like a wizened shower head, a horn shape with holes in the end. 'I think this is a...'

'Lotus head,' she finished, grinning. 'I love these.'

'Yes. They're... beautiful.' I put the wrinkled cone back in the basket.

She narrowed her eyes at me. 'Do I know you from somewhere?'

'I don't think so.' I looked at her more carefully. Henna-coloured hair in a sharp bob, nose ring. I'd never seen this woman before in my life.

'Oh, I know! You came to see the empty unit at Palmer's. I

saw you talking to Mike as you were leaving.' She held out her hand. 'I'm Christa; I have the unit at the back. Sacred Aura.'

I shook it, thinking that explained the drift of incense down the hallway. 'Annie. It's lovely to meet you. But it didn't work out unfortunately, which is why I'm here.'

'That's a shame. It would have been nice to have another girl on board. The rest of them are all fellas, and the new one's a man too.'

'Yes. We met.' Despite having already drawn a line under my ambitions, my heart still sank.

'Yeah, he's moving in tomorrow. So what put you off?'

I rubbed my thumb and forefinger together and smiled glumly. 'Out of my budget.'

'Ah. Sorry about that. I really am. Listen, I'm having a gem bath tonight, so I'll pop some citrine in there for you.'

'You're having a what, and you'll what?'

She laughed. 'A gem bath is when you put crystals in your bathwater and visualise their energies. Citrine is good for manifesting wealth and success, so I'll send some of that your way.'

'Right!' I said, a little thrown. 'That's lovely. Um, is there some kind of "thank you" bath I can have in return?'

'Well, amethyst would work, but I'll let you off,' she said with a wink. Then she popped outside, returning a few minutes later to bring me a hot chocolate from the festive drinks van, and to pay for her purchases.

'Thanks for the hot chocolate,' I said. 'And also for the citrine spells and whatnot. That's so kind of you.'

'No problem. I like to spread positive energy wherever I can.'

She waved goodbye, and it felt like she really *had* brought some positive energy, with or without the help of crystals. I felt buoyed up and optimistic. Then Judy came back in with the elf outfit for me to try on and the day went downhill from there.

. . .

The next day, I'd just finished my shift and was heading for the bus stop when my phone rang.

'Hello, is that Annie?'

'Yes.' I shuffled to the side of the pavement to let other people past.

'It's Mike. From Palmer's Arcade?'

My brow knitted. I hadn't expected to hear from him ever again. 'Hi! How are you?'

'I'm good, thanks. Listen, are you still interested in the shop?'

'Uh... I'm afraid my circumstances haven't changed, Mike. I can't afford it. Plus, I thought that Penn guy was moving in.'

'Yes, but there's been a change of situation. He's just informed me the unit is a bit on the large side for his stock. It turns out vinyl records stack up quite compact.' He sounded weary and irritated. 'Obviously it's left me in a bit of a situation. So I suggested we could look into a shop-share – two businesses sharing the same space as well as splitting the costs down the middle. I told him about your artisan products and he's keen. What do you think?'

I stared into the distance, my mouth hanging open. What I was thinking was: *That citrine bath worked bloody fast.* But then my mouth caught up with my mind, and I asked, 'When can I move in?'

FOUR

'This is absolutely cracking,' said Dad, standing in the doorway with his hands on his hips – the universal dad stance. He then walked around, assessing the coving, kicking the skirting boards and running his hand over the paintwork. 'A good solid bit of workmanship in here. They knew how to put a building together in the old days.'

He had a point. I loved the period building even more on my second visit; the wood panelling in the corridor, the hardwood doors with a glossy finish. Even the door handles looked like the original brass, the ends of them curled like seashells. It was gorgeous, and I was lucky enough to be working here for the next month or two.

'I'll start unloading the van then, kidda,' he said with a grin and left me to stand there on my own, soaking it all in.

There was quiet acoustic guitar music emanating from a speaker on the other side of the shop, and a sign propped up in his side of the window read 'Uncle Al's Records'. No doubt an ironic name, or a music reference that I didn't understand. Penn himself was nowhere to be seen. I wondered when he'd make an appearance, and if I'd be able to avoid staring into his dark eyes when he did. Since he'd extended the offer to share, my memories of how gorgeous he was had won out over our earlier rivalry.

I wandered over and took a look at my shop-mate's things. On the shelving at the back were rows of albums, mostly with band names that I'd never heard of, and the other walls were decorated with music-related prints and artwork. There were reclaimed wooden crates with more vinyl stacked upon them, a range of CDs and tapes that looked quite old, and some band T-shirts, neatly folded. Then, beside his cash desk, there was a glass case with a lock between the doors, which held a few more records and some signed memorabilia. I touched the glass, peering closer inside – in the middle, standing on its own, was a black LP with a triangle and rainbow, still in its plastic packaging. *The Dark Side of the Moon.*

'Are you into Pink Floyd?' came a voice from behind me.

I spun round. Penn was there, his hair hanging loose this time, dark tendrils framing his angular face. I locked eyes with him, immediately failing in my resolve to avoid doing so. They were just so damn magnetic. As my heart began to pound, I scrambled for something to say. 'No. I'm afraid my tastes run more to Taylor Swift and Beyoncé.'

His lips twitched almost imperceptibly and he nodded. 'Cool. So... moving-in day. I'm glad we were able to come to an arrangement.' He glanced at my side of the shop, and as the eye contact broke, I felt my heart rate slow.

'Me too. And... thanks. For offering to share. Although Mike said you didn't have much stock.' I looked again at the piles of musical junk and it didn't seem that sparse to me.

He shrugged. 'It condenses down. Makes sense to share the space. Maybe we can help generate customers for each other.'

'Maybe.'

My eyes roved over his side of the shop again. The wealth of music-related paraphernalia reminded me of seeing Penn on stage in the bar. We still hadn't spoken about our first meeting, so I thought maybe I should. But he was already looking at me with a knowing half-smile and beat me to it.

'Mike mentioned it's artisanal wellness products that you're selling,' he said. 'I remember you saying that you were into visual arts – are you selling any of your own work?'

'Uh, no. Not at this point.' My little wool animals were very much loved, but only by myself, and I doubted anyone would buy a misshapen harvest mouse or ladybird.

'Shame. I was hoping to see it. But still, artisanal products should sit well alongside my half of the shop.'

'Mmhm,' I said, thinking about the boxloads of silicone muffin tins and electric epilators outside in the van. Maybe they weren't the best conduit to a flow of customers towards Uncle Al's. I felt a prickle of unease. Penn had clearly agreed to this based on our shops complementing each other and seemed pretty set on a certain 'vibe'.

'Is that your van outside?' he asked. 'Do you need any help bringing stuff in?'

'That's okay,' I said. 'I have my A-team with me. We'll try and be quick so we don't get in the way of your customers.' I quickly noted the absence of any patrons. 'I mean the ones that might arrive any minute.' I flashed an awkward grin.

His smile faltered a little. 'It's fine. All good. Just give me a yell if you need anything.' He walked behind his cash desk and started thumbing through his phone, and although he'd been polite, I got the feeling that I'd been dismissed. Business Penn seemed a little more aloof than Musician Penn. Then, just before I turned away, I caught him glancing up at me. Our brief eye contact was like a game of pinball – my gaze flickered up to the thermostat on the wall, as if it was the most interesting thing I'd seen all day, and his returned swiftly to his phone screen. I was surprised to feel a little twist in my stomach, although that could well have been from embarrassment. Dad came in with the first of the boxes, one stacked on top of another, and I rushed to help him set them down. Then my mam walked in, using her stick for reassurance, although she insisted she was feeling better.

'Eeh, this is smashing, Annie. Really lovely.' Then she noticed Penn and lowered her voice. 'He's tasty. How will you keep your eye on the job with him floating around?'

'*Mam!*' I whispered. 'He might be able to hear you.' I gave Penn a nervous glance, but he was still absorbed in his phone.

'All I'm saying is, I wouldn't kick him out of bed for dropping toast crumbs on the duvet,' she murmured. 'If it wasn't for your dad, of course.'

'Delightful,' I said. 'Anyway, I'll help your *husband* with the heavy stuff. Do you want to get started with putting up the signs?'

'Let me at it,' she said, opening one of the boxes Dad had brought in. Inside were some of the merchandising posters that had come as part of the package with her various ventures.

We spent the next few hours bringing in tables, benches and shelves. I had given one of the shelving units from Mam and Dad's garage a lick of paint, and Dad had offered his wallpaper table, which I covered with a spotty tablecloth. He'd set to work hammering up a cash desk – a rectangular counter with a panel on the front and a shelf underneath to hide my money tin. I also had a nifty app on my phone for taking card payments.

Mam was going great guns sticking up various posters for the products, as well as assembling some vertical banners with similar advertising. I looked over at Penn, who'd stayed quiet other than to turn down a cup of tea from my mother, and saw that he was staring at the metamorphosis of my shop. His brow was furrowed as he looked from the sign promoting a herbal weight-loss remedy to another featuring a buy-one-get-one-free deal on camping cookware. Then a customer came in and made a beeline for one of his record stands.

'Alright, mate,' he said and turned his back on me to do business.

It was lunchtime when we'd finished assembling everything and laying out stock, and we stopped for a sandwich, Mam sitting on my chair behind the desk, my dad and I leaning against the tables. Penn had disappeared, maybe out for his own lunch. There was a gentle knock on the door frame and Christa came in, followed by two men who looked to be in their sixties and another younger man with blonde hair in nineties-style curtains.

'Heeeyy,' she said, beaming. 'Welcome to the gang.'

'Hi! I still can't believe I'm here, it's been such a whirlwind. Hello, everyone.' I waved to the assembled group and one of the older men hurried over, taking both of my hands in his.

'A very warm welcome,' he said in a sweet Scottish brogue. His hair was white but full, and he was wearing a tweed jacket and a bow tie. 'It's lovely to meet you. I'm Arthur and this here is Sven.'

The other older man came forward; he was taller, dressed in loose pants and a Nehru shirt, and had a thin, twirly moustache.

'How do you do?' he said with a Scandinavian lilt.

'And this is Jake,' said Christa, presenting the blonde man. He wore jeans and a peacock-blue tracksuit jacket zipped up right under his chin.

'Alreet,' he said, his accent even thicker than my dad's. He nodded over to Penn's side of the shop. 'How are you getting on with Franz Ferdinand over there?'

Christa batted his arm. 'Shush, you. Give him a chance; you don't even know him.'

'I'd have a hard job getting to know him. He never fucking speaks.'

I blinked at him. Penn hadn't been exactly brimming with conversation, but I was surprised to hear the others hadn't warmed to him.

'Mind your language, Jacob,' chided Arthur. 'We don't want to give these lovely people the wrong impression.'

He smoothly introduced himself to my mam and dad, and was joined immediately by Sven, who rested a hand on the small of his back while they all chatted.

Jake came closer to me with a subtle swagger.

'I like what you've done with the place. Annie, isn't it? Listen, if you ever get bored, I'm just down the hall, and I've got better chat than Mr Mysterious.'

I blinked at him, feeling my cheeks grow pink. What did I say to that? Thankfully, Christa intervened.

'Give it five minutes before you hit on our newest recruit,' she said, rolling her eyes, before she turned to me. 'Don't listen to him. I've heard his chat and unless you're interested in football or the highest-rated European lagers, you might be better giving him a wide berth.'

I nodded, unsure of what to say to this, so opted to ask him a polite question. 'So, what kind of shop do you have?'

'Phone repairs, accessories, headphones and that. I do vapes as well – every liquid flavour you can think of. I've got a Christmas range just in, if you fancy a mince pie flavour?'

'Ah, thanks. I don't vape. But it sounds delicious.'

'It is. I'm due a delivery of candy cane ones any time now, so I'll love ya and leave ya.'

'Sorry about him,' said Christa as he left. 'He's harmless really, but he's a cocky little sod. So, do you want to show me around?'

'Sure!' I led her around the various shelves and stands, and she was kind enough to admire everything, even the selection of supportive wrist bandages. We came to a table of natural skincare products, with ingredients like hemp seed oil and chamomile.

'I have these too!' she said. 'Everything in my shop is vegan, cruelty-free and has healing properties.'

'Oh. I hope I'm not treading on your toes.'

'Don't be silly. Skincare's just a tiny bit of my stuff. I'm more into incense, jewellery, crystals, that kind of thing.'

'On the subject of crystals... Your gem bath must have worked wonders. Mike called me the very next day.'

She grinned. 'That and a quiet word in Mike's ear. He really liked you, and when I explained how the universe brought me to the Christmas shop, I persuaded him that it was fate. He's not much of a believer, but I'm very persuasive. And anyway, it looks like I could have saved myself the trouble. Fate's also come in the form of an angsty musician with some room at the inn.'

I nodded. 'Well, thank you for your part. I really need this.'

Christa gave me a sympathetic look; I imagined she was remembering my confession about my money woes. 'I know how you feel. We're all feeling the pinch, I think. Anyway, how *are* you getting on with Penn?'

'It's hard to tell. I've only been here a few hours and he's mostly kept to his side of the shop, but I'm sure he'll warm up.'

'I'm sure he will. He might just be a slow burner. Listen, I've got to shoot, but come and say hi whenever you want.'

'I will,' I said, meaning it. 'And thanks again.'

'No problem. The Christmas shop's loss is our gain.'

After she left, so did Sven and Arthur, and not long after that, Mam and Dad said their goodbyes too.

'I'm proud of you, kidda,' said my dad, pulling me in and kissing the top of my head.

Mam joined in for a group hug, and I felt such a surge of positivity. I had the shop, my family, a potential new friend and, most importantly, a way out of our financial train wreck.

'Thanks, guys,' I said and waved them goodbye as they climbed into the van and drove off.

. . .

I spent some time fussing with the arrangement of my wares and moving some of the product signs into more prominent positions. It was a bit of a jumble; there was no real coherence to the layout, my labels and stickers were a range of neon colours reminiscent of nineties shell suits and there were still boxes lying around that I needed to put away. There simply wasn't enough room to put everything on display, so I would need to keep replenishing things as I sold out.

To the back of the room was a small storage space accessible through a door between our two floor-spaces, so I took some of the boxes through and stacked them neatly next to Penn's. Some of my boxes were still unopened, sealed up with parcel tape and contents unknown, but I'd have to take a look at them another time. Right now, I had a sign to paint or there would be no customers to take any products off my hands when I officially opened tomorrow. I made myself a cup of tea with the shared kettle and grabbed a paintbrush.

When I went back through to the shop, Penn had returned. He was sitting behind his counter, leaning back in his chair with a cup of takeaway coffee in his hand. He looked up and tipped me an upward nod in greeting.

'Hi!' I said, and despite having the sign to paint, I found myself lingering. He sipped his drink, eyeing me over the rim of the cup. I noted how thick his lashes were but then shook myself internally, remembering I ought to speak. 'Did you have a nice lunch break? You didn't have any customers, I'm afraid, but I would have helped them out if they'd come in. It's useful having us both here, don't you think?'

He looked across the vista of my random goods, his expression neutral. 'Sure.'

He seemed to have nothing else to say, so I fiddled with a basket of nail varnishes for a while and then had to break the silence.

'Is it always this quiet?'

He raised his eyebrow.

'I mean customers! Not... you.'

He shrugged. 'It ebbs and flows. Plus with all the... commotion today, it might have put customers off.'

'Sorry about that,' I said, cringing. Of course it would have made his day harder.

He took another drink of his coffee and looked away.

'I could have made you one of those,' I said, pointing to his cup. 'No need to get a takeaway – I do a mean cup of Kenco.' A tinkle of nervous laughter escaped from me. I was clutching at straws to find things to talk about, and he was making me oddly nervous.

'Thanks,' he said with a taut smile. 'But I like the shop up the road. It's the only place I can get Sumatra Lintong coffee in the area.'

'Right. Well... good for you.' I took a deep breath and left him to it, feeling a little disappointed with our latest awkward exchange. Any girl would dream of having a handsome, brooding hero in her life, but this one was proving to be a bit *too* brooding. Maybe he was having an off day. Or perhaps, like Christa said, he was a slow burner. I decided to get on with my jobs and give him a bit of space.

I'd spent almost three hours perfecting the neatest writing I could muster, running outside periodically to make sure I wasn't writing anything back-to-front. Luckily, due to my extremely varied employment history, I'd developed a decent hand for penmanship, mostly through writing chalkboard menus in pubs and restaurants. The overall effect was a slightly vintage-looking script, red with a black outline – a style I hoped would lend the title a kind of edgy, ironic vibe, rather than bargain basement. *Everything Must Go.* Never had a truer phrase been written. Tomorrow I would be doing as hard a sell as I could manage without physically pressing things into customers' hands.

I was standing on the pavement as the sky grew dark, admiring my handiwork, when I saw Penn inside. He wandered over to my tables, looking a little more closely. He stood over a pile of romance paperbacks and I was sure I saw him grimace. Fair enough, probably not his thing. Then he wandered to a shelf stocked with salad spinners and that time I definitely saw him pull a face. Finally, he came outside and looked at my sign.

'Everything Must Go?' he murmured, crossing his arms over his chest. 'Manic Street Preachers fan then?'

I stared at him blankly, and he gave me a smug look. 'It's not a bad album, but it isn't their best. I preferred their earlier work.'

Then he went back inside, and I stood there wondering what the hell I'd let myself in for.

FIVE

It was five minutes past ten on opening day and I stood there, hopefully, watching the door. I'd arrived early to double-check everything was in its place. I'd barely slept the night before, partly through nervous excitement, but mostly because Neo seemed to be taking part in some kind of online gaming event that went on into the early hours. Every now and then, I would hear a triumphant whoop or occasionally a shout of something like, 'For fuck's sake, Aragorn, get your head in the game. Think of the guild!'

Penn wasn't in yet, but there were a couple of people outside, looking in at his side of the shop through the window. I smiled at them, wondering if they might be interested in any of my stuff, but they looked away. Then, across the street, I saw a man leaning against a lamp post, his arms crossed over his chest. He was broad and muscly with a shaved head, and was staring intently at the shop. His expression was stony, so I didn't think he was weighing up a potential purchase. After a minute, he put his hands in his pockets and walked away down the street.

The door jingled, and Penn walked in.

'Morning!' I said with a wide smile. Even though he hadn't

given me the warmest of welcomes yesterday, I was still determined to break the ice. And despite my reservations about our
compatibility, he'd disarmed me again by looking... well, to
quote my mother, 'tasty'. 'How are you today?'

'I'm fine,' he said. 'You?' He quickly looked me up and
down. I was wearing dungarees and a red-and-pink striped top,
at odds with what seemed to be his signature look of black from
head to toe.

'I'm great. Very excited actually. The grand opening of
Everything Must Go!' I waved my hands by my shoulders in an
approximation of Wallace and Gromit then snatched them
down to my sides. He was making me nervous again.

'Congratulations,' he said with a slow smile. Then the two
browsers who had been lurking outside came into the shop and
approached him. It seemed our friendly fresh start was over
for now.

I made myself a cup of tea, rearranged the baskets of
bronzers and toenail clippers on my cash desk, and checked my
phone for messages. There was a text from Mam wishing me
luck for my first day, and I was reminded of how important it
was that I made this a success. Then the door jingled and
someone came in.

It was an older woman, maybe in her seventies, wearing a
beige overcoat and a bobble hat. This could be my very first
customer.

'Hi! Welcome to Everything Must Go! Take a look around
and let me know if you need any help.'

She gave me a funny look and went over to Penn's side of
the shop.

'Excuse me, son. Have you anything by Crosby, Stills &
Nash?'

Great. Even someone in my target demographic was
eschewing my wares in favour of Penn's.

I hovered behind the desk again, and then finally someone

else came in – a woman a little older than me, with curly hair and a friendly face. I welcomed her in the same way as the first customer, and she smiled back and started to browse. On my side of the shop. I tried to control my excitement but couldn't stand still.

'These are lovely,' I said, sidling up to her and nodding at the tray of potato peelers she was looking at. 'They're very good quality, and the non-slip handle is state of the art.'

'Thanks,' she said. 'I'll think about it.'

'Great! You know where I am if you need me.' I backed off and let her carry on.

Then, after a minute of standing behind the desk chewing my fingernail, I went back over.

'These are on three-for-two, if you were interested?' They weren't, but I was hungry for my first-ever sale.

She looked down at the multi-chopper kitchen tools, frowning.

'Why would anyone need three of these?'

'Um... Christmas is coming. They'd make a lovely gift?'

'Right. I think I'll leave them, thanks.' She gave me an awkward smile and left.

I went behind the desk and slumped onto my chair. Then I rested my chin on my hands and watched as a succession of people paraded through the shop, bypassing all my stuff and walking out with records and memorabilia in their arms. Eventually, the shop went quiet, leaving me and Penn sitting behind our respective counters. I was so deflated I couldn't even be bothered to attempt small talk with him again. He seemed quite happy with this and thumbed through a copy of *NME*.

After a while he spoke, not lifting his eyes from the magazine.

'You shouldn't do such a hard sell.'

'Excuse me?'

'I'm just saying. It puts customers off, if you want my opinion.'

'I don't, actually,' I said, stung.

He shrugged. 'I'm only trying to help.'

'Well, there's no need. I know what I'm doing.'

He finally looked up at me. 'If you say so.'

I felt my face growing hot and stood up, almost falling off my chair. Gathering myself, I checked the time. Half past twelve. The perfect time for an early lunch, I thought; and an ideal opportunity to nip this conversational time-bomb in the bud. Without a backwards glance at Penn, I put my 'Closed for lunch' sign on the desk, grabbed my coat and stormed out.

Christa's shop, Sacred Aura, was shadowy, lit with dim orange lights that made it strangely inviting. I walked in to find her extinguishing a set of ivory pillar candles. The room was like a treasure trove: baskets of crystals in all kinds of colours, slender boxes of incense sticks on the shelves, dreamcatchers hanging from the ceiling. There was a small window which had a curtain pulled over it, embroidered with astrological symbols.

'So, how was your first morning?' she asked, coming from behind her counter.

I pulled a face.

'Don't worry. It can take time for things to pick up. Listen, I'm about to go for lunch – do you want to come with?'

I nodded, and she pulled on her evil-eye coat before leading me up the road to a little cafe. We sat down and ordered, and the coffee menu caught my eye – it listed a variety of fancy coffees, and I guessed this must be where Penn had got his achingly hip brew.

'I don't think we're going to get on.' Christa's eyebrows raised. 'Not you and me. Me and Penn. He's... rude.'

'He does seem like a tough nut to crack. Every time I see him, all I can get out of him is a "good morning" or "goodnight".'

'It's not just that. He *is* quiet, but he seems a bit snooty too.

He's a music snob, a coffee snob and gives me the impression he thinks I'm a complete philistine.'

Our drinks arrived, and she took a sip of her green tea. 'Then he's an idiot. I've met that type before; the ones who claim they only liked a band before they got famous.'

'That's pretty much exactly what he said to me yesterday. How am I going to cope with spending the next few weeks, if not months, with him?'

'Maybe he'll give up before you do.'

'More likely he'll sell out of stock. He's doing a roaring trade while I'm sat there twiddling my thumbs.'

'Okay, well, have you thought about making your shop more visible online? Try to draw some customers in? It's only your first day, so you need to let people know you're here.'

'I do have a Facebook page and an Instagram account.' I'd hastily set these up in the run-up to opening. I showed them to Christa.

She winced. 'Give them here. You need to change your settings, lovely. You've got your Facebook set to private, and you've left the shop address off your Insta.' She scrolled and tapped, her silver rings clicking against the edges of the screen. 'Plus, you need to add more content. A photo of a box of squeegee mops isn't going to cut it.'

I watched as she transformed my social media pages, following some accounts that aligned with my business. Within minutes, I'd gathered a small handful of likes and follows in return. 'How do you know about all of this stuff?'

She grinned. 'I don't just rely on manifesting to generate business, you know.'

Our roast vegetable paninis arrived, and we munched quietly for a while.

'So, tell me a bit about yourself,' she said, wiping tomato juice off the side of her mouth.

'Um, there's not a lot to tell. I live with the world's biggest

Star Wars fan. I grew up in Haysworth. No brothers or sisters, and I've had more jobs than you can shake a stick at.'

'Haysworth? I had some friends that went to Haysworth Manor.'

'Yeah, I went there too.' I didn't remember school all that fondly. 'Feels like a long time ago. How about you – where did you go?'

'Northfields.'

'Ooh, posh.'

She shrugged. 'I didn't really fit in. Most of the girls in my class were more interested in make-up and boys than making the world a better place.'

'And that's what you wanted to do?'

'Yep. They thought I was weird – being vegan back then wasn't exactly mainstream, and they weren't keen on my sense of style.' She gestured to her outfit – a flowing skirt and a jumper of coarse wool. 'I haven't changed much. Then, when I started putting up posters about their favourite make-up having been tested on animals, that seemed to be the last straw. I just went it alone after that.'

'I'm sorry,' I said.

'Don't be. Fuck 'em. I'd rather stand up for my principles than try to impress them.'

'Amen, sister,' I said, clinking teacups with her. 'I'm pretty into that stuff too. I went veggie ten years ago, and I try to donate to wildlife charities. When I can afford it.'

'I think we're kindred spirits then,' she said, smiling.

Just then, movement outside the cafe window caught my eye. The guy who I'd seen over the road that morning, the one with the shaved head, had his hands pressed up to the window like binoculars, looking through them directly at me and Christa. We locked eyes, and he marched to the door and came in.

'Neil?' Christa said in surprise. 'What are you doing here?'

He stood by the table and looked down at me.

'I just wanted to say hello. Meet the new tenant.'

I looked from Neil to Christa, puzzled.

'I used to have your shop, until Mike threw me out.'

'He... he said that you moved on, that your swimwear was out of season.' As I said it, it seemed a very odd choice of merchandise for this man to be selling – I would have expected a bubbly, tanned woman.

He gave a nasty laugh. 'Well, he would say that, wouldn't he? It doesn't look good to a new tenant, hearing that he'll throw you out on your ear without warning. As it happens, I was about to start stocking winter stuff – ski gear, puffa jackets and that. But I never got the chance.'

'Neil, I would imagine he had a good reason...' interjected Christa.

'He didn't. No good reason at all. He's just a nasty bastard – I came in to tell you so. You need to watch your back with Mike. Don't say you weren't warned.'

With that, he hulked out of the cafe, his fists balled up tightly.

'What the hell just happened?' I asked Christa, my heart racing.

'Idiot,' she said, staring after him through the window. 'Let's just say that Penn isn't the first dickhead to rent that shop.'

'What happened? Why did Mike kick him out?'

'He never said. But I know Mike, and I know he wouldn't do anything like that unless he had to. I never did get on with Neil either – he was always full of shit.'

I shook my shoulders, trying to expel the adrenaline. Even a restorative slug of tea didn't take the edge off the uneasy feeling that Neil had left in his wake.

. . .

That afternoon, I took my place behind the counter once more. Penn had nodded hello, but I didn't have the energy to try and engage him in conversation again, an arrangement he seemed quite happy with too. He carried on rearranging his stock while I pretended to be busy folding tea towels.

Eventually, I had no more products to rearrange, and the silence was getting uncomfortable, so I distracted myself by continuing my latest knitting project. Penn glanced at me inquisitively as my needles clicked together and I turned the yarn into the final limb of a small purple octopus. I cast off and set it on my desk, giving it a fond pat on the head.

The door jingled open, and a tall blonde woman with exquisite skin, wearing a long-sleeved, maroon body-con dress, came into the shop.

'Hiii!' she said, slinking through the doorway, giving us both a wide smile. I sat up straighter, thoroughly fed up with my lack of sales and Penn's monopoly on the customers, then jumped down off my chair.

'Hi!' I replied. 'Welcome to Everything Must Go. How can I help?'

She cocked her head to one side and pouted. 'Oh, bless you, darling. I'm not here to buy; I'm from the shop next door. I just wanted to pop in and say hello.'

I saw Penn smirk, and my face flamed.

'I had the pleasure of meeting your lovely Penn earlier this week, so I thought I'd drop in and introduce myself to you as well. I'm Melissa Armitage. I own Visage Unique next door.'

She held out her manicured hand, and I shook it. Her lightly lined hand suggested that she wasn't quite as young as I'd initially thought, and I realised she was more likely in her mid to late forties. She looked incredible.

'Annie Wilson. Nice to meet you. And sorry about that,' I said, gesturing vaguely at myself as evidence of my own gaffe.

'Don't you worry,' she said warmly. 'Now, how is it all going?'

'Brilliant, thank you. Off to a great start.'

Penn coughed theatrically, and I glared at him.

'Marvellous. I'm so glad to hear it. We're a supportive bunch here, so if you ever need anything, do shout up. Now, I had another reason for dropping by. I'm having a little drinky-poos after close of play this evening. Just casual,' she said, giving my outfit a subtle once-over. 'You're very welcome to come. Both of you.'

Penn nodded but said nothing, and Melissa's smile faltered. God, he was so bloody rude. I wasn't going to let him show the both of us up, so I said, 'That sounds lovely. I'll be there!'

'Wonderful,' she said. 'No need to bring anything – I've got Prosecco and nibbles all ready to go. See you later, darling.' And she walked out, elegant and poised on six-inch heels.

Penn rolled his eyes and resumed thumbing through his vinyl.

I stood against my desk, arms crossed over my front, brewing a feeling of indignation on Melissa's behalf.

'Is everything alright with you and Melissa?' I asked, trying to keep my tone light.

He shrugged. 'Yeah.'

'I'm guessing you won't be going tonight though.'

Putting down a record, he looked at me for a long moment. 'I'm not sure it's my kind of thing. Besides... I don't really know anyone.'

He said this in a lazy, nonchalant way, rather than self-pitying. I opened my mouth to tell him there was a good reason he didn't know anyone but was stopped in my tracks by the door opening again. A couple came in, cheeks pink from the cold outside, and started browsing around my shelves. My gloomy mood lifted a little. This could be it – my first sale was within my grasp.

I took a step forward to start showing off some of my products, but Penn caught my eye. He gave a subtle shake of his head.

I stopped, my jaw clenched. He really thought he knew it all, didn't he?

I took another small step and then paused again. The couple were holding up a set of steak knives, discussing replacing the ones in their kitchen. The debacle that morning came into my mind, reminding me how I'd scared off that woman with my perky sales pitch. I glanced quickly at Penn again, my lips clamped between my front teeth.

Taking a breath, I slowly, reluctantly went to sit behind the counter then watched surreptitiously as the couple held on to the steak knives and then also picked up a pair of bento boxes. As they made their way to the cash desk, the woman's eye was caught by the display of bodice-ripper novels. She picked up three. All of these were placed on the counter, and I rang them up, exchanging their bag of purchases for two crisp twenty-pound notes. I stared at the money, transfixed by it. I'd done it – I'd made my first sale. If I didn't need the cash so much, I might have framed it.

I looked up to find Penn staring at me, his expression unreadable. For just a moment, I was drawn in to his dark eyes, as if he'd hypnotised me just a little. But then he flashed a smug smile that reeked of 'I told you so'.

He really was an insufferable prick.

SIX

I walked into Visage Unique and immediately wished I'd gone home and changed. Melissa's assurances that it was a casual event suddenly didn't seem very accurate. Around the room, holding flutes of Prosecco and delicately picking at nibbles, were an assortment of well-dressed women in dresses or sleek pantsuits, and men in stylish jackets. Also, the shop was *very* upmarket. It was almost entirely white, with polished, glossy counters and glimmering glass chandeliers. Muted lighting bathed the rows of classy products, which were packaged in a theme of white, soft pink and black. Not a thing was out of place, unlike my stack-'em-high jumble next door.

With a rush of relief, I saw Arthur and Sven over by the perfume counter, and I hurried over, hoping my grubby Converse hi-tops wouldn't leave marks on the gleaming floor.

'Annie, dear, come and have a glass of bubbles,' said Arthur, taking a glass from a nearby tray and pressing it into my hand. 'Tell us about your first day.'

'I made forty pounds!' I said, still buzzing from my first sale, even though it was a pitiful sum.

Arthur and Sven were gracious enough to congratulate me without irony.

'Cheers to that,' said Sven raising his glass, and Arthur and I did the same.

'Swanky in here, isn't it?' I said, looking around. There was no sign of our other shop-mates, and I knew Penn wouldn't bother to show his face. Mike was in the far corner, mainlining peanuts, a row of empty champagne flutes beside him.

'It certainly is,' agreed Arthur. 'I'm trying not to touch anything in case I've got book dust on my jacket.'

At least I wasn't alone in feeling that way. I took another slug of my drink and wrapped my other arm around my middle. Then, through the crowd, Melissa walked over, still wearing the same gorgeous dress from earlier but accessorised with some large gold earrings and a slash of wine-red lipstick.

'Darlings, thank you so much for coming. We're long overdue a catch-up,' she said to Sven and Arthur. 'And I'd love to get to know you, Annie. Tell me, what are your plans for the shop? Such marvellous products – I imagine things are flying off the shelves.'

I wrinkled my nose. I'd said earlier that it was all going swimmingly, but there was something so disarming about her that I told the truth.

'Well, we're very glad to have you, and I'm sure things will pick up. It's such a shame we're going to be losing you two next year though,' she said, turning to Arthur and Sven.

'Oh,' I said. 'I didn't know.'

'We're retiring,' said Sven. 'And making a big move.'

'Sven's whisking me off to his homeland. My Swedish is coming along very nicely.'

Sven grinned. 'We need some more work on it. Yesterday, he said he'd seen a lovely purple dog, when what he meant was a lovely *little* dog.'

'Swedish pronunciation is tricky,' said Arthur, batting his arm.

'We'll miss you very much,' said Melissa. 'Now, if you'll excuse me, I need a quick word with one of my staff. I think we're running low on nibbles.'

'What a woman,' said Arthur as she went. 'Single mother, you know – and putting three children through university. I don't know how she does it.'

I glanced around at the price tags on her beauty products and had a pretty good idea how.

There was still no sign of Christa, and I wondered if she was coming or not. I hadn't seen her since we'd had lunch so had no idea if she'd intended to come. Since Arthur and Sven were now engaged in conversation with another Pilgrim Street business owner, I was hoping for someone else I knew to buddy up with. I wandered around aimlessly, picking up the occasional habas frita or truffle crisp along the way. I ended up hovering around the doorway, nervously draining my drink.

The door swung open, and I turned round to see Penn standing there in a black leather jacket.

'What are you doing here?' I blurted.

'Good evening to you too,' he said.

'I thought this wasn't your kind of scene.'

He shrugged. 'It doesn't hurt to be friendly.' He picked up a glass of Prosecco and surveyed the room.

We stood there quietly for a moment, and I awkwardly sipped my drink, my shoulder brushing his elbow as I raised my glass to my lips. He glanced down at me and gave the tiniest hint of a smile. My stomach turned over.

As well as objecting to the vibe of the party, he'd also said he wasn't coming because he didn't know anyone. But here he was. I felt a little ripple of pleasure that he'd maybe changed his mind because he actually *did* have someone, and that someone was me. After the weird atmosphere in the shop, maybe this was my chance to make it right.

'So, which serum do you think you'll go for?' I joked, nodding towards the pristine displays. 'The hyaluronic acid or the vitamin C?'

He looked at me, momentarily off guard, then laughed. 'I don't know. Which would you recommend?'

It was the first time I'd seen him properly smile since our encounter at the bar. I'd wondered if I'd ever see that smile again, and now here it was, surprising me. What surprised me even more was the attraction I'd felt towards him back then making a solid reappearance, but I extinguished it almost as quickly as it came. *Musician Penn isn't the same as Shop Penn*, I reminded myself.

'You'd have to ask Melissa – this isn't my area of expertise. But I *can* offer you advice on which knitting pattern might best suit your personal style. I'm sure I've got one with an AC/DC logo on the front...'

He sipped his drink and struggled to suppress a smile. 'I think I'm okay for jumpers, thanks very much. Besides, my knitting skills might be below par compared to yours. That little gonk you finished today looked decent actually.'

'That little *gonk* was an octopus.'

'Are you sure? I could only see seven legs.'

It was my turn to suppress a smile. This kind of conflict I could handle – the type with Nerf guns rather than real ones.

'I knew you were interested in my side of the shop. At least you liked the gonk better than the salad spinners.' I gave him an amused side-eye.

He tipped his head back and sighed good-naturedly. 'I'm... acclimatising. When Mike told me you were selling artisan products, I was a bit taken aback when you unloaded the van.'

'You don't like it.'

He screwed up his nose. 'I don't love it. But it is what it is.'

'Huh. How so?'

'It's very... you.'

I paused. What did he mean by that? That I was cheap and cheerful? Suddenly, the Nerf battle felt a bit more combative, and just as Penn caught the change in my expression, Mike came staggering up to us, a glass of fizz in each hand. I was about to decline, assuming he'd brought them for us, but he downed one and then started on the other.

'My newest recruits,' he slurred. 'How are you both getting on?'

'We're getting along great,' said Penn after a moment's hesitation.

I flashed him a look. *Were we?* Considering the tense conclusion to our conversation just now, I would have said we were at least up and down.

'I thought you two would get on like a house on fire,' said Mike, beaming. 'Especially when Penn told me how compatible you two would be.'

'He did?'

'Mmhm,' said Mike, taking another drink. 'Weren't as keen on the other applicants, were you, Penn?'

'Other applicants?' I asked, confused.

'There were other interested parties that hadn't committed. Penn suggested you.'

I looked up at Penn and felt my cheeks warm with pleasant surprise. He smiled uncomfortably, took a sip of his Prosecco and glanced away. But before I could ask any more questions, Melissa glided over and stroked Penn's arm.

'Sweetie, I'm so glad you came,' she purred. 'I was hoping to have a proper chat, not just a quickie over the shop counter.'

Penn flushed as Mike spluttered out a mouthful of his drink. Melissa gave Mike a stony glare, and his face fell. It wasn't just a chilly exchange; it was glacial.

'Come with me, Penn,' she said, taking his arm and leading

him away. She shot Mike a look over her shoulder. 'Come and talk to the grown-ups.' She ushered him over to some stylish guests and made introductions.

'Yikes,' I said.

'Pshh,' Mike said, flapping his hand. 'Mel and I aren't the best of pals. She only invites me to these things to keep up appearances.'

'Riiight,' I said, noticing Melissa flick a glance towards Mike, her nostrils flaring. I looked down into my glass, wondering how much looser Mike's lips might get with the copious amount of alcohol flowing through his veins. As curious as I was, I wasn't about to take advantage of his inebriation and dig deeper about what had happened there.

'Anyway, ignore me. I'm rambling.' He looked at me with a beleaguered, hangdog expression, and I scrambled for something to say before he could tell me his full medical history or the pin number for his bank card.

'Um... I heard about Sven and Arthur retiring! What a shame – they're so nice.'

He ran a palm down his face. 'Don't even get me started on that. The chances of me finding long-term tenants like that are bloody slim. You wouldn't know anyone, would you?'

I shook my head.

His mouth settled into a grim line. 'It's tough in retail. Rising rates, rising prices. I've got to keep those units filled or the books just won't balance. I'm sure it'll be fine though. With you and Penn keeping the lamp alight with your unit, and Christa and Jake doing alright too, we'll keep the ship afloat, eh?'

I forced a smile. After today's performance, I wasn't sure I had the confidence in myself that Mike seemed to.

He tipped his glass towards me and wandered off, almost bumping into Melissa as he went. She looked at him with open disdain then spoke to him tersely. He plonked down his glass, shambled towards the door and left.

Penn, left alone after Melissa had been distracted by Mike, stood against the counter scanning the room with studied indifference. He oozed self-assuredness, whereas if I was left alone, I'd be frantically looking for someone to talk to. We were so unalike.

Why had he picked me to share the shop with, over and above the other options? Maybe the others had been offering goods and services even more undesirable than mine, so it stood to reason that he'd been disappointed with my 'artisan' products, which were apparently *so very me*. And now we were stuck together, he probably bitterly regretted it. But I'd seen a glimmer of common ground when we'd joked together earlier. It reminded me of that easy flirtation in the bar, when I'd wondered if there was something there, and I'd felt disappointed when he'd walked away. Of course, we had to keep things professional now, but if we were going to make this work, I'd need to try and tap back into that relaxed kind of conversation.

I stood up straighter, deciding to just go over there and present Penn with the highest-quality banter I could muster.

Then my phone rang.

'Annie, pet.'

'Hiya, Mam.'

Her voice trembled. 'It's your dad – he's had an accident. Can you come to A&E right away?'

I rang off and bolted for the door.

SEVEN

Dad was propped up in bed in an A&E bay drinking a carton of juice and smiling contentedly. Mam was sitting in a chair beside him, looking haunted. His left leg was in some kind of splint.

'What happened?' I asked, rushing over to his bedside.

'I took a bit of a tumble, pet.'

'Keith, that's the morphine talking. He's had more than a "bit of a tumble"; he's had a compound fracture of his left tibia.'

My jaw dropped. 'What exactly does that mean?'

'It means I've seen more of my skeleton than I bargained on today,' he said. 'The bone popped right through the skin. It stung a bit, let me tell you.'

'He fell off some scaffolding,' said Mam.

'I can speak for myself, Denise, thank you.' He turned to me. 'I fell off some scaffolding.'

'Morphine,' she mouthed at me.

'Ah, Dad, what are we going to do with you?' I took a seat opposite my mam.

He sighed, a cowed expression on his face. 'I'm sorry.'

'Don't be sorry, you dafty.' I rubbed his arm, and he took

another slurp of juice, the remainder rattling in the bottom of the carton. Mam passed him another one.

Between them, one infinitely more coherent than the other, they explained what would happen next. He'd been X-rayed and the fracture was a messy one, so he would need surgery to put his tibia back together and then it would be set in plaster. The recovery time was four or five months according to my mam, and a few weeks in my dad's morphine-addled estimation.

Mam shook her head. 'He's going to be laid up for almost half a year.'

I let this sink in, feeling suddenly nauseous. With her out of work because she was so up and down health-wise, and Dad joining her, they would have no income at all. They still had a mortgage, car payments, all the bills. I didn't imagine statutory sick pay would even touch the sides. Like me, they lived month to month with little in the way of savings. Then there was that ominous red-topped letter from the mortgage company that didn't bear thinking about.

'What are you going to do? For money?' I asked quietly.

'Don't you worry about that,' said Mam. 'I was thinking of getting a little job anyway. Part-time, at home, for a call centre. Fiona next door is doing it, and she says it's not bad.' She smiled weakly.

How was she going to field calls from demanding customers, especially ones with complaints, when she wasn't having a good day?

'And with you doing a roaring trade at the shop, we'll be all set,' said Dad, patting my hand.

My throat tightened. I couldn't speak for a moment, thinking of the forty pounds, an amount so small I'd been able to pop it in my purse and do the button up with no difficulty. I could give them it all, I thought. Take none for myself, just enough to cover the rent on the shop. But then how would I pay

Neo? Or eat? My lip started to tremble, so I bit down on it –
hard.

'That's right,' I managed. 'We'll do this together. As a
family.'

They smiled at each other and then at me, and I tried to
swallow away the lump in my throat.

'Denise,' said Dad, looking sheepish. 'I've had a few too
many of these juices. Would you...?'

She retrieved a cardboard wee bottle, and I beat a hasty
retreat. Standing outside the curtain, trying not to listen to the
sound of my dad's pee stream, I focused my mind elsewhere. I
needed to make this shop work. For my parents, for Mike; hell –
for myself. I had a golden opportunity, with boxes full of stuff
that certainly had value. I just had to find a way to sell it.

After the weekend, I strode down Pilgrim Street with my hands
stuffed in my pockets, my breath making little white clouds in
the chilly air. The pavements were dusted with early morning
frost – winter was truly upon us; that brief, glacial hiatus before
the world was warmed up again with Christmas festivity.

Walking through the shop door to be enveloped in blessed
central heating, I found Penn topping up his stock from the
back room. He nodded good morning, and I did the same, taking
my place behind the desk. After the stress of my dad's catastro-
phe, I didn't have the energy to 'bring the banter' as I'd intended
at the party, or even to ask why he'd chosen me to share the
shop. I knew I was emanating prickly vibes, but I was so worried
about Mam and Dad I couldn't help it. It didn't seem so important to work on mine and Penn's relationship just now, and he
seemed to get the memo that I didn't want to talk – our brief
détente at Melissa's was over, at least for now.

After an uncomfortable half hour pretending to be deeply
absorbed in my little accounts book, I sat restlessly, tapping my

foot on the floor. He glanced over at the repetitive noise, then went to his Bluetooth speaker and turned it up a notch. Soft rock drifted out at a slightly higher volume than before.

I woke up my phone and looked through the social media pages that Christa had souped up for me. I now had a healthy amount of likes and followers, but seeing the steady stream of people walking clean past my shop window didn't give me the impression that it was helping. I remembered what Christa said about adding more content, so I got up and looked about for inspiration.

Keeping Penn's side of the shop carefully out of view, I arranged some of my more aesthetic-looking items, such as the range of pastel-coloured tea and coffee canisters or the rose gold-packaged cosmetics, into neat displays. I took some pictures, messed about with some filters and uploaded them with jaunty captions. They did look better with a Clarendon filter on them actually. Penn looked on with vague interest but was then distracted by a customer.

'Hiya, mate,' he said to a similarly styled man of about his age. They then engaged in a conversation indecipherable to me, but before I had the need to tune it out, another customer came in and started looking at my selection of oven cleaning products. Happily, after a minute's consideration, she came over and bought a few items, and I relaxed back on my stool, feeling buoyed up. So buoyed up in fact that I decided my shop needed a little music too, more in keeping with my style. If Penn could have a soundtrack to his sales then so could I. I scrolled my Spotify playlists and decided to go festive – 'All I Want For Christmas Is You' always got me in the Christmas spirit.

Penn gave me a look but carried on talking to his customer. After a while, the guy walked over to Penn's glass cabinet and pointed to the Pink Floyd album inside. He asked to take a closer look.

Penn hesitated then said, 'Sorry, mate. It's not for sale.'

The guy shrugged, bought a couple of other records and left. Penn followed soon after, leaving his closed sign on the desk, and I narrowed my eyes at his back as he went. What was the deal with that record?

He returned with another of his trendy coffees – of course, he hadn't offered to get me one. I made a point of going into the back room, making an instant hot chocolate and loading it with mini marshmallows. When I came back out, I noticed that the music on his side of the shop was now a fraction louder. Some whiny, mournful sounding singer was drowning out 'Last Christmas'. Indignation rippled through me – my awful weekend had left me with no patience to tolerate his nonsense. I sat at my desk, smiled, took a sip of my confectionery-laden drink and moved my music up a notch too. The playlist shuffled on to 'Santa Claus Is Coming to Town'. I didn't even like that song, but when I saw his nostrils flare, I decided I liked it a little bit more.

He shook his head with a look of resigned amusement and clicked his music up a level again. I was almost distracted by the way his half-smile gave him the slightest dimple in his cheek, but I wouldn't be bested in this battle.

I looked him dead in the eye, and like a cat knocking an ornament off a table, I held his gaze while cranking mine up once more. It was becoming deafening. The competing strains of Radiohead doing battle with The Jackson 5 was like being in a fever dream. Angsty sneering lyrics clashed with seventies merriment until they started to sound like I'd put my head in a tumble dryer.

Penn bit his lip and stared at me intensely. 'Very mature,' he said, having to raise his voice to be heard.

'I could say the same about you,' I shouted.

He smirked in a way that should have enraged me, but there was something about it that made my heart skip. Was he…

enjoying this? The back and forth was starting to remind me of the way we'd flirted in the bar.

Just then, a customer peeped around the door, winced and walked away. There was no knowing which of us he was visiting so we both glared at one another.

'You've just lost me a customer,' I said.

'How do you know he was for you?'

'He didn't look your type! Far too *pedestrian* I'd imagine.'

He rolled his eyes. 'That's very judgemental.'

'Well, you'd know about that.' I looked at the vegetable peelers alongside the packets of clay face masks and remembered him prodding through it all.

'Turn it down,' he shouted.

'You turn yours down,' I replied. 'Or go and get yourself another of your... Kama Sutra coffees, or whatever they're called.'

His jaw tensed, and he opened his mouth to clap back at me once more when the door swung open.

'What the fuck is going on in here?'

Jake stood in the doorway, holding his palms up in question and glaring at us from underneath his baseball cap. 'Are you two for real? I can't hear myself think back there, and I've just lost a sale.'

We immediately switched off our speakers.

'Sorry, Jake,' I said.

Penn muttered an apology too then grabbed his jacket and went out again.

I groaned and leaned on the desk, grinding my palms into my eyes. 'I really am sorry. He's just... argh.' I groaned in frustration. It seemed Penn and I were right back where we'd started, being six feet away and a million miles apart from each other at the same time.

'It seems to be six of one and half a dozen of the other, if you ask me,' Jake said.

'I feel bad. The last thing I want to do is upset everyone else in the building. Would a hot chocolate make up for it?' I asked, daring a smile.

'Aye, go on then,' he said. 'I'll keep an eye on the door for any vapers.'

I brought him his mug, and he leaned against my desk, slurping from it loudly without any self-consciousness.

'You're alright you know,' he said. 'Even with all the racket, you're an improvement on the last one.'

'Yeah, I had the pleasure of making his acquaintance. As well as meeting the vein throbbing in his temple.'

'Aye, he wasn't the most *stable* of people.'

'He tried to warn me off Mike. Should I be worried?'

'Should you fuck. Mike's a top lad. They just didn't get along, and they had a major bust-up in the end.'

'Right. Seems to be a lot of that about. Penn and I are headed that way, I think.'

'He's not your best pal then?' he asked.

I sighed. 'It doesn't look that way. He seems to think I'm the retail equivalent of a weekend at Butlin's. And he's really, really annoying. And rude. And *quiet*. If we aren't having a music battle, you could hear a pin drop in here.'

'He's a pretentious wanker. I asked him if he had anything by The Weeknd and he just laughed.'

'Too mainstream. He looked like he was going to vomit when Katy Perry came on. Here's to liking the things you like.' We clinked mugs, and he held my gaze for a little longer than I expected. We drank our drinks for a bit, while I awkwardly tried to think of something to say to break the tension.

'Um... How's business for you then?' I asked. 'When you're not losing customers to the caterwauling in here.'

'It's canny, thanks. Everyone needs their vapes and their phones.'

I glanced at my wares and wondered how many people

were going to need a desk lamp in the shape of a giant paperclip.

'Yep,' I agreed.

He looked at me furtively. 'I've got a little secret though. I think I can trust you not to break the tenants' code.'

I wasn't aware there was such a thing, but I was intrigued. 'Go on.'

'I'll be packing up in the spring. I'm off to be a holiday rep in Ibiza.'

I stared at him. 'What? You're leaving?'

'Aye. My mate's been doing it for years. Money's just okay, but I'm not gonna turn down sunning myself and hitting the clubs on a night. It's gonna be mint.'

'Yeah, good on you,' I said weakly.

My heart sank. I'd barely absorbed the fact that Arthur and Sven were retiring, and that Mike was going to struggle to keep afloat after that. Now that I knew about this, I felt even more worried for him.

'So Mike doesn't know?' I clarified.

'Not for now,' Jake said, making a buttoning motion on his lips. 'I'll tell him after Christmas. He'll have no bother filling the unit though.'

Knowing what I knew, I wasn't so sure.

'Well, I'll miss you,' I said. I barely knew him, but it seemed to be the polite thing to say.

His face lit up. 'Will you?'

I nodded. 'Of course!'

He stood up a bit straighter, with a slight swagger. 'You know, I've been meaning to ask you...' He flashed a cocky grin.

No, no, no...

'Are you doing anything after work tonight? There's a nice pub up the road. I'll buy you some dinner.'

I tried not to let my mouth drop open and diverted it to a wide smile. 'Oh... I'm sorry. I'm busy!'

'How about the weekend?'

I hesitated. 'I think I'm busy then too.'

He nodded, visibly deflated. 'Right. Well, never mind.' He drained the remains of his hot chocolate in one. 'I'll catch you later, yeah?'

'Yeah,' I said, my voice as limp as a wet flannel.

He smiled tightly, his face starting to glow, and he left.

I cringed, feeling awful. He just wasn't my type. Saying that, I wasn't exactly sure what my type was – my dating history was like my shop: eclectic and with long periods of zero interest. Apart from a couple of doomed relationships with fairly bland men, I'd had the odd date here and there, but that was all.

Suddenly, Penn flashed into my mind – guitarist Penn, charismatic and handsome – and my stomach dropped. Why he was featuring in my back catalogue of boyfriends was beyond me. After all, one brief flirtation in a shadowy bar didn't even come close to a romantic relationship. And knowing what I knew now, it didn't matter how hot he was – we were as incompatible as Michael Bublé and Metallica.

And that was basically it; just like musical tastes, when it comes to romance, you like the things you like.

EIGHT

By the following week, Penn had started to multiply. As I continued to sell modest amounts of my stock, his side was beginning to resemble the backstage area of Glastonbury. Other men in similar costume, who seemed familiar enough with Penn that I assumed they were his friends, were becoming regular fixtures in the shop. Along with their guitars.

I was treated to occasional guitar riffs and regular bursts of laughter at things I had no understanding of. Penn and I had made no further attempt to build bridges, and my exclusion from his gatherings was welcomed on both sides. The shop was becoming more divided than ever, both in vibes and headcount.

My odds and ends still sat forlornly on the shelves and stands, my paper signs starting to wilt at the edges. I'd optimistically continued to forage through the remaining boxes in the stock room, opening one every now and then to replace the more popular items like the romance and children's books, and the kitchen storage. They were becoming my bestsellers, but I was also running out of them. Empty spaces were being filled with lipsticks in weird colours and packets of herbal remedies for constipation.

The natural skincare was selling reasonably well too –
Christa had high-fived me over this. We were becoming a sister-
hood in the banishment of microbeads and palm oil, although
she did sometimes look at my plastic items with faint concern.
Not with as much disdain as she had for Jake though. She
frequently complained about his disposable vapes ruining the
environment, as well as how irritatingly cocksure he was.
Whenever he walked past, she shuddered at his flammable-
looking sportswear and bright-coloured trainers. It meant I got
off lightly for my less-than-eco-friendly items.

That day I was enduring the last strains of a three-guitar
jam session when yet another person came in to ask Penn about
the Pink Floyd album. As with all the other people who'd
shown interest, he shook his head and said, 'Not for sale.'

'Mate, I don't know why you've got that on display if you're
not going to part with it,' said one of the guys, who I'd gathered
to be called Rob.

Penn grinned. 'It's better off here than in the flat, where *he*
can get his hands on it.' He nodded towards the other one,
whose name was Sam. I noticed again that his Northern accent
was slightly smoother and more refined than the thick Geordie
accents of his friends.

Sam, who I recognised from Penn's band, rolled his eyes.
'You've nothing to fear from me. It's the wrong'uns where we
live you need to worry about.'

I'd gathered from previous conversations that Penn and
Sam lived in one of Newcastle's slightly less salubrious areas,
although I wasn't sure which.

'Yeah, when are you two going to get yourselves over to
Forest Grange?' said Rob, referencing one of Newcastle's
fanciest postcodes.

Sam puffed out his cheeks. 'When the band takes off, Forest
Grange'll be in our rear window, pal. We'll be off to London.'

Rob laughed. 'I'll show my arse in Fenwick's window if you lot end up in the Big Smoke. You know, you actually have to write some songs if you want to get anywhere.'

'Fuck off,' said Penn good-naturedly. '"Smoke on the Water" wasn't composed in a day.'

'Aye, it takes time to write a masterpiece,' said Sam, tightening one of his guitar strings. 'Until then we'll survive on Super Noodles and vodka. Rock and roll.'

They all laughed in a self-congratulatory way, and I rolled my eyes, making sure Penn could see. I was getting thoroughly sick of the shop being monopolised by Penn and his crew, but there was little I could do when he had dominion over half the square footage.

Just then, the bell above the door tinkled and my mam walked in, followed by a horizontal leg in plaster before its owner wheeled into sight. Dad looked brighter than I'd seen him in days. I was happy to see that Mam was without her stick – I would have worried myself sick if they were both relying on mobility aids to get around. Dad seemed to be a dab hand with the wheelchair already and manoeuvred expertly into the shop. Penn and his mates said polite but disinterested hellos and went back to tuning their guitars.

'Eeeh, look at this, Keith,' she said, gazing around the room. 'Isn't she doing well?'

'Come here,' he said gruffly. 'Give us a cuddle. We're really proud of you.'

I bent down to give him a squeeze, carefully avoiding his leg.

'How are you doing?' I asked him.

'Canny enough. If it isn't the district nurse bossing me about, it's your mam.'

'If I didn't, he'd stay flat on his backside watching Alison Hammond on *This Morning* and eating Pringles.'

'She's a hell of a woman,' said Dad, rubbing his hands together.

'I hope you mean Mam and not daytime TV's national treasure,' I said, raising an eyebrow.

He slapped my mother on the backside, and she giggled. 'Of course I mean your mam. I don't think Alison could make as nice a brew as our Denise.'

'I'm glad I'm useful for something,' sniffed Mam. 'Ooh, how are these selling, darl?' She grabbed up a duster specially designed for cleaning blinds. 'These used to go like hotcakes.'

'Pretty well,' I said, although I'd only sold one or two. I didn't want to worry them about the cash flow. So far, I'd been splitting the proceeds seventy–thirty in their favour to cover my tracks.

We walked around the shop, chatting about the various products while my mam updated me on all the usual family and neighbourhood gossip, the latter mainly comprising people I didn't really know. Meanwhile, Dad had wheeled himself over to Penn's side of the shop and was flicking through a box of records.

Penn hopped down from where he was sitting atop his cash desk and sauntered over. He greeted my dad politely, and they started to talk – I wondered if my dad might break down Penn's barriers over a shared love of guitars. Silently wishing him luck, I turned my attention back to Mam.

'... so, when she went back a second time, the cage was open and there was only feathers in the bottom.'

'Right...'

'Now, is there anything I can do to help?' she asked, looking around, clearly with the maternal urge to organise and tidy.

'No, honestly, Mam, it's fine! I've got it all under control.' *Except for poor sales and spiralling debts.*

'Oh, this takes me back,' she said, running her hand over a stack of soup containers. 'Sitting in the middle of a room full of people, glasses of wine in hand. I used to do an offer on these – buy one, get a set of travel cutlery free. Those were the days.' She smiled fondly.

Then, like a magpie, she was drawn to the rose gold cosmetic containers. 'I used to love selling these. I'd do a makeover on a lucky volunteer. And these...' She picked up some herbal hangover remedies. 'These used to go down a treat when everyone had had a few drinks.'

'I bet you had a good knack for sales,' I said.

'Not at all. It's not so hard when it's a group of pals, having a laugh, half-cut on Pinot Grigio. When they see everyone else snapping things up, then most do the same. There's psychology to it.'

I blinked. That was it. I couldn't believe I hadn't thought of it before. All of these products had been sold at parties or events, the wheels greased with alcohol and bowls of crisps, in the midst of a festive atmosphere. What if I could do the same?

'What do you think about helping me do something similar? In the shop?'

'Like a party?'

'Kind of.' I paced back and forth, my bloodstream fizzing. 'Like... a Christmas shopping event! I'll advertise it as much as I can – give people some incentives to come. Put on some drinks, nibbles, maybe some entertainment.'

Mam clapped her hands together. 'That's a brilliant idea! Look at you, my little apprentice.'

I grinned. 'I'm learning from the master...'

Before I could say anything else, something bumped the back of my knee and my leg buckled. Recovering myself, I turned to find my dad, pink in the face.

'Sorry, pet,' he said, gesturing to his outstretched leg, which had hamstrung me. 'Still getting used to logistics.' He looked up at me, a wavering smile on his face.

'Are you okay?' I asked.

His eyes flickered towards Penn, who was now back hanging out with his muso mates.

'I'm absolutely fine,' he said. 'Shall we head off, Den? Leave Annie in peace?'

She furrowed her brow at him. 'Are you sure you're alright? You look a bit flustered.'

'I'm fine,' he insisted, his voice edging towards gritty. 'Come on – let's go.'

He wheeled out of the door, Mam following, both saying goodbye over their shoulders. What the hell had gone on there? I turned to look at Penn, who had his back to me, completely absorbed in his conversation. My dad was a weightlifting brickie with a no-nonsense attitude – nothing usually fazed him. I couldn't imagine what could have possibly happened to make him so flustered. Had Penn said something to him?

I marched over and tapped him on the shoulder. 'What happened with my dad?'

He looked at me for a moment, his expression unreadable. Then he spread his palms. 'I don't know what you're talking about.'

'You must have said or done something. He wheeled out of here faster than Lewis Hamilton.'

'Beats me,' he said, glancing at his friends, who were watching with interest.

I widened my eyes at him, spreading my palms too, silently prodding him to elaborate. But nothing was forthcoming. Rob and Sam exchanged a look and tried to conceal awkward laughter. I shook my head and scowled.

'If I ever find out...' I ran out of steam. His friends were biting their lips hard now, so I spun away, my face burning. I went into the back room of the shop and sat on a box, my eyes stinging. How dare he? He'd clearly upset my dad somehow and now had the gall to pretend he had no idea how. I swallowed deeply, refusing to let my emotions get the better of me.

Gritting my teeth, I pulled my phone out of my pocket. The best way I could teach him a lesson was to rise above it and let him watch my business hold its own against his. No, do *better* than his! Instead of the shop being filled with his music-snob mates and his steady flow of customers, it would be brimming with *my* patrons from now on. I'd create an advert for a special event that would put me on the map and kickstart the success of Everything Must Go, so help me God.

I hastily put together an advert for a festive promotional event, choosing that Saturday as the date to give it time to gain traction. There would be drinks and snacks, and everyone who could prove they'd shared the flyer on social media would get a special discount. I put the finishing touches to it – snowflakes, Christmas trees, and Santa with a sackful of presents (subliminal messaging for the pre-Christmas shoppers) – then posted it across all my social media channels, as well as pages for local groups and organisations.

My breathing slowed. Taking back control felt like taking a painkiller – slow relief eased its way through my body. I would make this event, and the shop, a success if it killed me.

I couldn't resist looking to see if anyone had shared it yet, and my heart leaped when I saw it had been reposted a few times already. Smiling, I flicked through some of my previous posts to see if I'd gained any more attention on those as well.

My smile was extinguished like I'd had a bucket of water thrown over me. There, under an innocuous picture of some cleaning cloths, was a comment.

Not my kind of thing. You can get better stuff online.

Then another, below that.

Cheap tat. Not what I'd expect from one of the better shopping areas in town.

My jaw tightened. I flicked to another post. There were more, and they had all been posted over the last few days.

It wouldn't be so bad if it wasn't for the owner.

NINE

I'd never seen the shop so full. My guests weaved through my display tables like shoals of fish, and through the afternoon, as some people drifted away with their purchases, they were replaced by others. There even seemed to be passers-by noticing the festive atmosphere from through the window and coming in to see what was going on. I made a point of greeting every last one of them.

I'd spent the previous day decking the shop out with Christmas decorations – fairy lights, inflatable candy canes, and glittery streamers hanging from the ceiling. There had never been a sharper contrast between mine and Penn's sides of the shop. That afternoon, compared to the riot of colour on my half, his looked like a sepia photograph. He sat there behind his desk, somewhat like Miss Havisham from *Great Expectations*, haunting the room with his dour presence.

'Have another glass of wine,' said my mam, trying to press one into my hand. She'd already embraced the party atmosphere and was on to her third.

'No, Mam! I'm working. I'll have another one later, once it's all done.'

'It's packed!' she said. 'I can't believe it.'

Neither could I. I'd hoped that I could get a handful of people in and flog them a few spiralizers and hand creams, but the event had surpassed even my wildest expectations. Mam was circling with bowls of crisps and nuts, and Sven and Arthur had alternated shifts pouring glasses of wine and handing them around while the other minded the bookshop.

I'd repaid them both by recommending their shop to everyone I sold to, as well as doing my fellow tenants the same favour. It couldn't hurt to spread the goodwill, and I'd even reluctantly nodded towards Penn. Despite how I felt about him and how much I'd wanted to finally outstrip his sales, I'd felt a twinge of guilt seeing the desolation of his half of the shop. Saying that, I was sure that he'd made sales that day off the back of my party, so I felt confident I'd kept a karmic balance. After all, I was capable of rising above our differences even if he wasn't.

'Thank you for this,' said Arthur, clasping my hands in his in between topping up Prosecco flutes. 'We haven't had as busy a Saturday as this in months!'

'Great!' I said and was then collared by someone wanting to buy an armful of essential oils.

'I had no idea this place was here,' she said. She was a woman of about fifty with blue hair and a nose ring. 'I'll definitely be back!'

'Amazing, thank you,' I said, offering my phone for her to dab her card. I heard a mental *kerching* go off in my brain. 'And don't forget to pop up the hallway to Sacred Aura – I think you'd like her stuff too.'

She nodded and hurried out of the door, and I was pleased to see her turn left up the passage rather than right out into the street. As I watched her go, I noticed Jake leave the building. He gave me a brief wave through the shop window then thrust his hands into his jacket pockets and walked down the road. He'd been quiet with me since I'd awkwardly declined his offer of a date, which was understandable, but I hoped things might thaw between us eventually.

Christa came in and rushed up to me, squealing.

'This is incredible!' she said, hugging me tightly. 'And thank you for sending some people my way – you're a doll.'

'That's okay. Share the wealth, as they say.'

'And how's mardy bum taking it?' She nodded towards Penn, who was showing a band poster to a man in a donkey jacket and a flat cap.

'Silently and as supercilious as ever. I never can tell, since he has a face like he's sucking a lemon most of the time anyway.'

Christa cocked her head to one side, regarding him. 'It's a shame he's so bloody handsome. What a terrible waste.'

'Agreed. He's the human equivalent of a bad avocado. Looks lovely from the outside but has a disappointingly grim interior.'

'Ha. That's exactly it. Ooh, I didn't know you had these!' She ran her hand over the essential oils and Himalayan salt lamps. 'These are *really* popular in my shop too.'

'Oh, right. They've been selling well, so that makes sense.' I bit my lip. 'I hope I'm not treading too much on your turf.'

'Don't be silly,' she said, giving me a squeeze. 'It's fine, honestly.'

'I had no idea what was in the boxes, so every one is a bit of a surprise. I'm not doing it intentionally, I promise!'

'I know you aren't, and like I said, you've sent enough customers my way today, I won't hold it against you. Christmas has come early to Sacred Aura.' She winked and looked around the store. 'This is something else, Annie. Well done.'

I grinned at her.

'I had another reason to come and see you. What are you doing on Monday?'

'Um, nothing.' On Sundays and Mondays, the arcade was

closed, and in my free time, I'd been mostly engaged in watching Netflix and cleaning Neo's dirty dishes in our grotty kitchen.

'Do you want to come to Northumberland with me? I'm going to a rally with some friends – we're protesting against pheasant shooting. You said you were into that kind of stuff, so...?'

'Yeah! I've never been to a protest before, but I'd love to come.' I'd trade cleaning Neo's plates of dried microwave lasagne juice quite happily. Plus, sticking it to people killing birds for fun would be right up my street.

'Great! I'll pick you up at seven a.m.'

I shuddered but decided the early start would be worth it.

'We'll make an animal rights warrior of you yet. And then we'll start work on your carbon footprint.' She patted a pile of plastic boxes and gave me a mock-stern look and a wave as she left.

I spent the next hour circling the room, meeting new customers and trying to steer them to any products that they might be interested in, as well as throwing in some curveballs in case I got lucky. I managed to persuade a young mum to buy some children's books alongside her cheese grater, but crashed and burned with an attempt to get an elderly man to supplement his soup canister purchase with a selection of herbal teabags. You couldn't win them all.

What I was winning at was the accrual of wads of cash. I stared in disbelief at my bulging cash tin and at the building figure on my card payment app. I'd smashed all of my goals. Buoyed up beyond measure, I noticed that another of my tables had started to grow empty, so I heaved another box out of the store room.

I ripped it open and looked inside... and started laughing. *Oh my God.* Inside were a selection of novelty musical items. A pizza cutter with a wheel that looked like a vinyl record, some guitar ice-lolly moulds, and sets of spoons with treble clefs on the end. This was just perfect. I looked over at Penn, who was apologising loudly to one of his customers about the Adele-heavy soundtrack to my event, and began to relish my impending revenge.

I merrily stacked up everything out of the box and retired to the chair behind my cash desk to field more sales. My mam continued to hobnob, and I was glad she was there – I was starting to get exhausted with the busyness of the day, but despite her condition, she seemed to be thriving off it. It was only a shame that Dad hadn't wanted to come.

He'd cried off at the last minute, saying that his leg was hurting, and of course that was likely to be true, but I couldn't help wondering if Penn had something to do with it. I'd tentatively asked Dad again what had happened, but he'd brushed it off and changed the subject. I leaned my elbows on the desk, feeling a slight dip in my mood, and this invited in thoughts of the social media comments I'd read earlier that week.

There had been more. *Seems like a bargain basement but more expensive. Tin opener broke after one use – I won't be back.* I'd replied to this one offering a refund or replacement and had no response. But my mind always went back to that one particular comment. *It wouldn't be so bad if it wasn't for the owner.* It still stung, and I wondered what on earth I could have done to have earned it.

I remembered being too pushy on my first day. Was that it? If so, I couldn't imagine someone would be bothered enough to take to social media about it. Then I considered that it might be more personal than that. My stomach twisted when I thought about how distant Jake had been since I'd turned him down. Surely he wouldn't do this though... It seemed so extreme. I shook my head. Of course he wouldn't; I was being ridiculous.

More customers came up to make their purchases, which took my mind off things. Gratifyingly, the novelty music items were selling really well, and I dared a look over at Penn to see how he was taking it. He was deep in conversation with one of his own customers and annoyingly hadn't seemed to notice. But when the customer left, he glanced over. I was just bagging up one of the vinyl-themed pizza cutters, so I waved it at him with a triumphant smirk. He narrowed his eyes at it, then they widened in surprise. He jumped off his stool and marched over.

'What the fuck are you playing at?' he whispered as the customer said thank you and left.

'Making a ton of cash and encouraging repeat custom. How about you?'

'How droll. I think you need to explain yourself, don't you?' He gestured at the table, which was now only half full of musical products, since they'd been selling so well.

'I can't help it if my rock and roll merchandise is selling better than yours,' I said with a sassy little head wiggle. I had to admit, I was enjoying this more than I'd envisioned.

'Well, that's the problem, isn't it?' he said, crossing his arms over his slim chest. 'It *is* my merchandise.'

'Whatever,' I said, flicking my hand towards him dismissively. 'You don't have the monopoly on *all* music-related paraphernalia. Although I'm sure you think you do.'

He ran a hand over his face. 'You don't seem to get it. They're mine. As in, they literally belong to me. You've taken one of my boxes from the stock cupboard.'

I blinked at him, my jubilant mood faltering. 'No. I don't think so. It was on my side of the shop.'

He sighed. 'I admit, it might have ended up there while I was sorting stuff out. But it is mine. I mean, what possessed you to think it was meant for your shop?'

'I... I...' My stomach had tied itself in a knot that Bear Grylls would have been proud of. 'They're novelty products. I *sell* novelty products.' I pointed at a row of ketchup bottles in the shape of tomatoes.

'And the music theme didn't give you a clue?'

I paused. 'Hang on a minute... Were you actually going to sell this stuff in your shop?' A laugh escaped me. 'Music buff Penn, with your *achingly* cool albums and T-shirts. Selling *pizza cutters?*'

His nostrils flared, and his eyes glittered ominously. 'I ordered them by mistake – I must have added them to my cart by accident. I was about to send them back, but clearly that's not happening now.'

I breathed heavily, realising that I'd run out of options to keep my dignity. My face started to get very hot.

'Fine,' I snapped, opening my cash tin. 'How much do I owe you?'

He quickly tallied what I'd sold and how much for, and I handed over the money, roughly thrusting my hand at him. Mortification was making me more belligerent than I should have been. His eyes met mine, and I was surprised to see them soften; the indignation with which he'd approached me seemed to seep out of him, and he looked almost reluctant to take the cash from my hand. I felt a flicker of hesitation too but kept my chin raised, wanting to salvage some respectability out of the whole situation. Then he gently took the money, his finger grazing mine, a tiny warm touch that reminded me that perhaps he didn't really have ice running through his veins.

The babble of conversation around us seemed quieter to my ears as we briefly held each other's gaze, and for a moment, I wished we could just start again. Then he picked up an empty box, went to the table and swept all that was left into it, his jaw twitching.

He started to walk over to his side of the shop, and I felt a new pulse of frustration. Just when I'd felt like I might be able to build a bridge, he'd withdrawn again.

'Let's call this justice for upsetting my dad,' I called after him, knowing how petty I sounded but unable to help myself.

He froze, his back muscles growing taut under his T-shirt. He turned around slowly, his eyes now looking tired. 'I still have no idea what you're talking about.'

'I think you do.'

He stared at me for a moment, his Adam's apple rippling as he swallowed.

'That's another thing we'll have to agree to disagree on,' he said and turned his back again.

I sat there, my eyes stinging. I willed myself not to cry – despite my bravado, I hated confrontation. And now the frost between us had turned into an ice age; all hope of a thaw in this millennium was dashed.

Then something occurred to me. I watched him stuffing the box under his desk then sitting down, his face stony and glaring into the middle distance. I'd made a true nemesis today, but what if he'd always been more of an enemy than I'd thought?

It wouldn't be so bad if it wasn't for the owner.

What if Penn had been trying to bring me down all this time?

TEN

The sky was dove grey and cloudy when we arrived in Northumberland early on Monday morning. Christa had driven us in her Mini through towns and villages with buildings of buff stone and quaint marketplaces that already looked like a picture on a Christmas card even though the festive season was not quite upon us. Eventually, we arrived on the edges of Northumberland National Park. Here, the grass on the fields and hills lay in shades of green, orange and brown, and the peaks in the distance were highlighted with white snow. I was glad I'd worn my puffa jacket.

'It should be just down this road,' said Linda from the back seat, leaning forward with her phone in hand, double-checking her map. I'd met her that morning when we'd picked her up on the way. I'd been expecting someone with a septum piercing and dungarees, but she was a woman in her fifties wearing a bright pink fleece and stripy wellies. Her brassy blonde hair was scooped up into a ponytail.

Christa rounded the bend, and we were greeted by a cluster of cars in a lay-by. Hovering around them a gaggle of assorted protesters. They were wrapped up in thick coats, scarves and bobble hats, brandishing placards and steely expressions.

'Let's get some animal-killer scalps, eh?' said Linda, rubbing her hands together.

I wasn't sure who would be more bloodthirsty today – the people with the shotguns or her.

We got out, and Christa introduced me to everyone she knew, which was about half of the fifteen-strong pack, and she briefed everyone on the plan of attack. A friend of a friend of a friend had leaked the plans for a private shoot that day, organised by Lord Ashcliffe for his wealthy cronies.

'They're shooting on his estate, so we can't go onto his land. But the roads next to them are fair game. No pun intended.'

There was a smattering of laughter.

'So, they'll be moving in vehicles between their first and second drives in about' – she checked her watch – 'half an hour. We'll let them get settled and then make our appearance. Remember, placards, shouting, but no damage to property. We're meant to be taking the upper hand here, okay?'

There were nods and murmurs of agreement all round, and we all stood in wait, leaning on cars and chatting.

'This your first time?' asked Linda.

'Yeah,' I said. 'I don't know why it's taken me so long though. Every time I read an article or see a picture of pheasant shooting, it makes me feel ill.'

'Me an' all,' she said gruffly. 'Bunch of bastards the lot of them. I'd love to see how they'd like being peppered with shotgun pellets, let me tell you.'

'Right...' I said, edging slightly away from her. Linda really meant business, but I hoped she was speaking metaphorically. I glanced at her large rucksack uneasily.

Then there was the rumble of vehicles, just out of sight, followed by distant voices and dogs barking. Christa gave everyone a nod and held her hand up like the leader of an armed response team signalling for us all to hold back. After about ten minutes, the sound of gunfire began, and the assembled group reacted like they were cracks of a whip. Linda's mouth was a thin white line.

I tried not to imagine the beautiful birds tumbling from the sky and being carried around like rags in dogs' mouths. In the distance, I could hear the yells of the beaters and thought angrily about how frightened the pheasants must feel once they took flight. Then the rally of shots petered out, and we could hear muted conversation again.

'Let's go,' said Christa, and we marched after her, banners high in the air.

'Come on, you sadistic fuckers,' yelled Linda as the field came into sight. 'Let's have you!'

The entrance to the field was cluttered with mud-spattered cars and trucks, Defenders and Discoveries in greens and blacks, most of them parked on the grass verge by the road. A group of tweed-clad men and women had their backs to us far off in the field, and they turned towards us, peering under their flat caps from the distance. A few people clustered around the vehicles shook their heads with murmurs of, 'Bloody hell' and 'Not the "Woke Warriors" again.'

'Bugger off,' yelled one ruddy-faced man, squaring up to us. His wax jacket was bulging at the stomach, maybe because of all the pheasant dinners he'd had.

'*You* bugger off!' shouted Christa, to cries of agreement from the protestors, myself included. In the back of a truck, I could see the brown-and-jewel-coloured bodies of dozens of beautiful birds, making my throat fill with bile. 'Who do you think you are, killing innocent creatures?'

'We breed them for it, my dear,' said the man in a patronising, plummy tone. 'It's what they're *for*.'

'You "breed" your dogs too,' she said loudly, 'but you don't go chasing them around with guns, do you?'

'You don't know what you're talking about. Now, clear off, or we'll call the police.'

'I already have,' piped a tall woman with honey-coloured hair, waving her mobile. She was strikingly pretty, with long legs in jodhpurs, and she wore a brown felt hat with a spray of pheasant feathers tucked into the hat band. 'They'll be here any minute.'

'We aren't trespassing, and we have a right to protest,' said Christa calmly.

'I told them we felt threatened,' replied the woman, her plump pink lips breaking into a triumphant smirk. 'You're all being extremely aggressive.'

I heard an abrupt snort from Linda beside me.

'I'll show you aggressive,' she said under her breath.

I glanced at her sharply. If I thought she was pumped up before, she was now positively frothing at the mouth.

'So, if you'll kindly fuck off, we can all get on with our days without any time behind bars,' said the Amazonian blonde sweetly.

The people who'd been shooting in the field were wandering closer now and approached the gate, faces like thunder.

'Where's Perry?' asked the woman. 'We need to get in the cars and on to the next drive once this lot have cleared off.'

A short man wearing a checked shirt and waistcoat under his brown coat gestured up to the field. 'Hendrix has run off. He's gone with Gus to find him. What's all this?'

'Can you not read, pal?' said Christa, wiggling her placard. 'We're here to let you know you can't just kill innocent animals without consequences.'

'I should say we ruddy well can,' said the round, older man, growing redder in the face. 'This is my estate, and I can do whatever the hell I want. Now get out of here, or I'll press charges against the lot of you.'

Christa stalked towards him, her voice low and menacing. 'This road is public. So we can do whatever the hell *we* want. Try and press charges and make them stick – I dare you.'

Just then, there was a rustle behind me, and I turned to see Linda rummaging in her backpack. My stomach plummeted, remembering how vitriolic she'd sounded all morning. She reached inside and... Surely not. Surely she wouldn't. But instead of some kind of weapon, she produced a tin of red paint and ripped the top off.

'Let's see if I can make *this* stick,' she roared.

There were gasps all round as she reared back, and then time started to slow down. Christa, who was standing in front of a khaki Land Rover, was directly in Linda's line of fire. Without thinking, I ran the few feet between us and shoved her out of the way. Milliseconds later, I felt the slap of paint hit the side of my body, face included, and froze in shock.

At first there was stunned silence, which then broke into an almighty uproar. Tweedy people pushed past me to look at the red paint spattering the car, wholly neglecting the fact I had paint in my left eye, earhole and hair. Some had started to trickle down my neck and under my collar.

'What have you done?' seethed Christa to Linda. 'We said no damage to property.'

Linda shrugged and crossed her arms, a satisfied smile on her face. Christa scowled then came over to me and started swiping at my face with her gloved hand.

'Are you okay?' she asked, her brow furrowed.

'I'm alright,' I said but then moaned as a police car glided smoothly around the bend.

Linda grabbed her rucksack and started to run down the road, but after the landowner shouted who the culprit was, she was swiftly apprehended.

'I'll be back!' she screamed over her shoulder as she was led off to the police car.

The assembled protestors started to drift away, muttering angrily, and Christa took my arm.

'Come on,' she said, rolling her eyes. 'We'd better follow her to the station. I've got to give her a lift home after all.'

'Okay. But I'd better turn this coat inside out or your Mini is going to look like the inside of an abattoir.'

I started to unzip my coat, trying to ignore the continued outrage around me. The blonde horsey woman's voice stood out above them all as she called us every name under the sun. But then her voice softened.

'Perry, darling, look at the state of Haz's car. Fucking animals.'

'Christ,' he replied. 'What's going on?'

I stopped mid-zip. I'd heard that voice before.

I turned around slowly to find a familiar face staring at me from under a tweed cap. Dressed in full shooting gear; breeks, waistcoat, with a black Labrador sitting obediently at his heel, was my arch-enemy, Penn.

ELEVEN

When Christa and I arrived at the police station, we were told by the desk sergeant, in no uncertain terms, that Linda wouldn't be out for a number of hours. She would be charged with a variety of offences, including but not limited to criminal damage, and it would take a bit of time to sort it all out before she was bailed. Her shouting was a bit more subdued as we left, although we could just about hear her castigating a bored-sounding officer about him wearing leather shoes.

Christa went to debrief the other protestors after dropping me into town to sort out my clothes. We'd be spending more time in the area than we'd bargained for, due to Lairy Linda, and I wasn't going to sit around all day looking like an extra from *Texas Chainsaw Massacre*.

While I searched for a public loo to rinse the paint off my hair and face, I replayed the moment I saw Penn in my head. If I'd looked shocked, he'd looked like his soul had departed his body. We'd stared at each other for a long moment, paint dripping from my chin, until Christa had said, in an incredulous voice: 'Penn?'

The people around him had looked at each other, puzzled,

and then continued fussing over the ruined paintwork on the car.

Then, as Penn's face grew redder, and when he was just about to speak, the Glamazon had taken him by the arm.

'Come on. Let's get to the next drive. The birds aren't going to fall out of the sky of their own accord.' Then she'd given us a smug look and dragged him away to a black Range Rover.

I'd watched them speed away, my head spinning, thinking, *What did I just see?* Seeing Penn there, divested of his muso uniform and looking like an extra from *Downton Abbey*, made me feel as if I was going mad. I couldn't conjure both versions of him in my mind at the same time; the two images were like opposing magnets that I couldn't push together no matter how hard I tried. Who *was* he?

I tried to focus on something else, like getting rid of my ruined clothes, so went into a charity shop and got myself some leggings and an unseasonal pink sweatshirt with a palm tree embroidered on the front. I finished up with the warmest-looking coat I could find – a khaki military-style felt affair with gold buttons. The overall effect was as if a World War Two army officer had wandered into the 'Club Tropicana' video.

Christa met me outside and burst out laughing. 'Come on, General Coconuts – I'm starving.'

'Me too. An early morning brush with the law sure builds up an appetite.'

We hopped in the Mini and drove out into the country lanes until we found a nice-looking pub, and settled in by the fire. We ordered vegan burgers and chips and munched quietly for a while.

'What the fuck was Penn doing there?' she asked through a mouthful of chips. 'And what the fuck was he wearing? And why the *fuck* was he shooting pheasants?'

'I don't know,' I said wearily, wiping my mouth with a napkin. 'You think you know somebody...'

But really, I didn't know him at all. We'd barely said a civil word to each other since becoming shop-mates, and all I knew of his supposed home life was that he lived in a flatshare in a dodgy area. It just didn't add up with this new image of a country gent with a shotgun crooked over his arm.

'I mean... who *is* he?' breathed Christa. 'How can he go from *that* to *that*?' She separated her hands wide apart.

'I know. It's so weird. And that woman he was with; do you think that was his girlfriend?'

'Probably. She seemed to be pretty attached to him.' She suddenly exploded with laughter. 'The flat cap! And the little knee-length pantaloons! I can't believe it.'

A ripple of mirth shot through me too. 'And his fancy-looking boots. He looked pretty comfortable with that shotgun too.'

Christa abruptly stopped laughing, her features growing stern. 'The nasty piece of work.'

I nodded. 'Just when I thought he couldn't get any worse. He's not just a music snob; it turns out he's an elitist, tweed-wearing posho too. I bet he rides a pony and has a trust fund.'

'Worse – I bet he's a fucking Tory.'

I shuddered. Then Christa's phone rang and she looked at the screen. 'It's Poundshop Banksy; I'd better take this.' She went outside, mobile clamped to her ear, and I continued eating my burger.

She came back moments later.

'She's been bailed and she's starving. I said I'd run over to get her and bring her back for some food. Are you alright waiting here? Save the table?'

The place was filling up with a recent surge of customers so I agreed – I could finish up my food too. Christa left, and I ordered a half pint of cider to drink with the rest of my meal.

I gazed over the bar area as I ate the last of my chips, and noticed that there were quite a few people wearing tweeds and wax jackets. Par for the course in rural Northumberland, but I had an uneasy feeling nonetheless. I noticed a few of them giving me funny looks, but then remembered that one side of my face and hair was stained lightly pink from the paint. One particular man was looking at me more intently, and he got up and walked over.

I involuntarily shrank away from him as he stood over my table, dressed in a shirt and tweed breeks and waistcoat. He had auburn hair and a matching short beard, and his blue eyes twinkled enough that my heart rate slowed a little.

'I almost didn't recognise you without the coat of emulsion,' he said in an accent that I vaguely identified as from the Borders – a blended lilt of Geordie and Scottish. 'I'm Gus.'

I shook his proffered hand. 'Annie,' I said, still guarded. 'I don't remember you from this morning.'

'I was just coming down the hill when you left. I'd been retrieving one of the retrievers.' He grinned. 'So, do you make a habit of slinging paint around, or is it just on special occasions?'

'It wasn't me who slung it. And, if anything, the owner should be thanking me for taking the brunt of it. I just about halved the damage to their car.' I started to relax – it didn't appear that he was about to give me any grief. Gus gestured to the stool next to me; I nodded, and he sat down, placing his pint of stout on the table.

'I don't think Haz will be too worried – he's got another four of them at home.'

'Wow. You guys must be made of money.'

'Not me,' he said with a shrug. 'I'm just the lowly gamekeeper. I look after Lord Ashcliffe's land.'

'And organise the shoot.' I gave him an appraising look.

He held up his hands. 'Guilty. But that's the way of it out here. Besides, they all get eaten – it's not as if they're killed just for sport.'

I grimaced. That was just as bad in my opinion.

'I think we'll have to agree to disagree on that,' I said.

'So I won't be able to convert you to country pursuits then?'

I shook my head but found myself smiling. Despite his barbaric proclivities, there was something disarming about him.

He took a drink and regarded me over the rim of the pint glass. 'I wondered if you're familiar with Perry.'

'Oh?' I felt my face heat up.

'You two looked like you'd seen a ghost when you clocked each other.'

I shrugged, deciding to remain vague. 'We've seen each other around. Although I didn't know his name was *Perry*.'

'That's the Honourable Peregrine Burton-Edwards to the likes of you and me,' he said with a wink.

My jaw dropped like it was attached to a bag of shotgun pellets. The Honourable *what*? And *Peregrine*? I was literally lost for words but was unable to contain a snort of laughter.

'Right. Good to know,' I said, playing with a beer mat, trying to compose myself.

'So do you live in Newcastle then?' he asked. 'I guess that's where you know him from. He's been trying his hand at being a city boy for a few years now.'

'Yeah. Newcastle born and bred.'

'I'm down there sometimes. We should meet up – you could show me the best places for a night out.' He smiled, holding my gaze. I didn't know where to look – I hadn't had any of this on my bingo card for today; the inexplicable Peregrine, or being hit on by the gamekeeper whose shoot I'd just taken part in ruining.

'Yeah, maybe.' To be fair, he seemed nice enough. 'Listen... why are you being so nice to me? You should be tearing a strip off me for spoiling your day. Plus, you should know we're at polar odds when it comes to our stance on bird slaying.'

He nodded. 'Agreed. But I make an exception for pretty girls who'd take a face full of paint for their friend and their principles.'

Just then, the pub door swung open, and who should it be but the Honourable Penn himself. He saw me and Gus immediately, and his brow furrowed. He marched directly over to us, ignoring anyone who tried to greet him.

'What are you doing here?' he asked, as blunt as ever.

'I could ask you the same thing, *Peregrine*,' I replied, my voice dripping with sarcasm.

A flush spread over his chiselled cheekbones, then he turned his attention to Gus.

'I'm surprised to see you here too,' Penn said to him.

'Fraternising with the enemy,' said Gus, raising a wry eyebrow.

'Yes.' Penn glared at me, and I gave him an innocent, butter-wouldn't-melt look.

'I'm discovering that Annie here is one of the good ones.'

Penn gave him a chilly look. 'I was coming to find you actually. Dad wants to see you. Now.' I noticed that his normally pseudo-Geordie accent was now even more refined.

'What about?' asked Gus, clearly reluctant to leave.

'He didn't say.'

Gus sighed and sank the last of his pint. He then scribbled his number down on a beer mat and handed it to me. 'Give me a call, city girl. We'll make a date.'

Penn stared at the ground, his jaw tense, as Gus passed by him and left.

'What an enlightening day,' I said, unable to keep the amusement out of my voice.

'I don't have to tell you anything about my personal life.'

'I'm not surprised you didn't!' I cackled unbecomingly. This was delicious. 'I never imagined in all my wildest nightmares that I'd see Newcastle's answer to Brandon Flowers dressed up in tweeds and a flat cap.'

'Like I said, it's none of your business.'

'And an animal killer too.' Any mirth I was feeling sapped

away as I remembered the shotgun draped over his arm. A coldness rippled through me. 'I don't know how you can live with yourself.'

'You don't know what you're talking about.'

'Really? I thought you were bad enough in the shop, but now I think I've got the measure of you. This sabotage I've been going through – now I know how dodgy your moral code is, my suspicions might be right.'

We stared at each other stonily for a moment.

'Again, I have no idea what you mean. Sabotage?'

'Sabotage. The horrible comments on my social media posts?'

His expression was difficult to read, but he looked slightly troubled.

'I haven't left any comments on your social media. I don't even use social media all that much. At least not nowadays.'

My nostrils flared. 'You want me out of the shop though. You've got a hell of a motive.'

He sighed and rubbed his forehead. 'Listen, I can't be bothered with all this. I need to go back to my family. But before I do, I'll give you some advice. Throw that beer mat away.'

'This? I might take Gus up on it. He seems alright.'

'He's not for you.'

The absolute gall. 'Not for me? Because I'm not posh enough for him, is that it?'

He shook his head, took a step back and turned away.

'Get rid of that number. You'll thank me later.' And he stalked off.

I sat there, grinding my teeth, twirling the beer mat around between my fingers. With a degree of satisfaction, I tucked it into my bag.

A gust of cold wind blew through the door as it opened, and Christa came in, staring daggers at the beaters as she walked over to me.

'Come on – we're going.'

'What about Linda? I thought she was wanting to eat.'

'She made me stop for a chickpea pasty from the petrol station on the way through.'

I gathered my things, and we made for the door.

Christa clocked Penn as we walked by their group. 'I'll see you tomorrow, you sadistic weirdo,' she said, shaking her head.

He gave her a cold shoulder.

Just then, the door swung open, and Linda's head poked around it. She saw us and then noticed the pack of green-and-brown-clad beaters.

'I hope you choke on your pints!' she yelled, sticking up double Vs. 'You remorseless fuckers!'

We left before the barman could eject us.

TWELVE

The next day at Palmer's Arcade was chillier than the winter wind howling outside. Penn and I kept to our own sides of the shop, and Christa drifted by the doorway at intervals, glaring at him through the glass. He paid her no attention and tended to his stock. He was wearing a beanie hat and a hoodie, in sharp contrast to his dapper countrywear of the day before. I marvelled at the juxtaposition – yesterday he was lord of the manor (or at least son of the lord of the manor), and today he looked like he'd had a trolley dash at Urban Outfitters.

I'd arrived that morning, washed clean of the last of the red paint, ready for a deluge of customers after the roaring success of my Christmas do. But it was as if it had never happened. It was more of a trickle than a flood, and the footfall dried up altogether every now and then. It had been an hour since the last person had come in, for either me or Penn.

He sat at his cash desk, using two pens to drum a beat on the countertop – it went on for a number of minutes before I cleared my throat loudly and gave him a look. He returned my look and carried on. So I turned Harry Styles up a notch.

Luckily, the shop party had made enough money in one day that I'd at least got my parents out of strife this month, with a bit left over to boost my bank account. But if things continued to dwindle, then the surplus wouldn't last long. Neo had the month's rent I owed him, but the next one was still all to play for.

The pen-drumming continued but was slightly muffled by the increased volume of The Smiths from Penn's side in retaliation. I sighed and kicked my music up a bit too. Not this bullshit again.

I'd popped into Mam and Dad's on my way in that morning and they were in good spirits. Dad was propped on the sofa eating a bowl of Coco Pops, and Mam was bustling around him like a mother hen, at the same time wearing her call-centre headset. When she'd said, 'I understand you're frustrated,' I wasn't sure if she was talking to the caller or my dad, who was struggling to reach the telly remote. He was still insistent he'd be back at work in weeks rather than months, and although I knew he was talking nonsense, I couldn't help but hope he made such a miraculous recovery. Despite all my ambitions, the shop didn't seem like it could sustain the three of us for all that time.

Worryingly, I'd seen another red-topped mortgage bill on the kitchen counter alongside an estate agent's business card. Anxiety had rippled through me – could they be closer to complete financial collapse than I'd imagined?

My eardrums prickled as Penn turned up his music yet again, and he seemed to be going harder on the pen drumming too. I was just about to reach for my speaker to outdo him once more when Arthur appeared at the door.

'I wonder if you'd mind...' he said in such a sweet voice that we both turned our speakers down immediately.

'Sorry, Arthur,' we said in unison, like we'd been admon-

ished by our favourite schoolteacher. He smiled kindly and
went back to the bookshop. There was near silence as Fleetwood Mac and Peter Andre whispered at each other from
across the room.

'Did you enjoy eating your pheasant and chips last night
then?' I asked archly.

'You need to hang them for twenty-four hours before you
eat them.' His tone was bored, and he didn't bother to look
at me.

'Gross. So will you be back next weekend then? To shoot
some more?'

'No. I've got a gig.'

An image of Penn standing on stage, guitar against his hip,
flashing that seductive smile drifted into my head. The memory
of how I'd been drawn to his confidence as well as his looks
stirred uncomfortably somewhere deep inside me, but then
almost as quickly, I was back in the room. He wasn't the person
I'd imagined he was.

'Do your family know you're a secret rock star, or does the
deception only go one way?'

'It's none of your business.'

'Aha. I'll take that as a no then.' I sat back on my stool, satisfied. I rearranged some receipts, then curiosity got the better
of me.

'Did you go to boarding school?'

He didn't answer.

'Do you have any hobbies other than shooting? Like fencing,
or falconry?'

His jaw twitched, and he looked out of the window. Then
he laughed lightly, rolling his eyes. 'I'm not going to entertain
any of this with an answer.'

'I suppose us proles wouldn't understand.'

He shot me a look, any hint of amusement gone. 'You know,

prejudice goes both ways. Just because I happen to come from a... wealthy family' – his face looked pained as he said it – 'it doesn't mean you can take some kind of moral high ground about it. You don't see me calling you...'

'Calling me what?' My voice was icy.

His mouth worked as he seemed to try and find a suitable answer. But he was saved by a jingle at the door, and his wild-haired, leather-clad mates walked in.

'Don't worry – I won't tell...' I mouthed at him, and he turned his back on me coldly.

The door opened again, and I looked at it hopefully in case it was a customer for me, but it was Melissa, bearing a neat baby-pink bag from her shop.

'Hi, Annie. How are you today?' she said with a wide smile.

'Great! How are you doing?'

'*Really* well. Rushed off my feet, as ever. You know how it is.' She laughed gaily, and I joined in, very aware that I didn't actually know how it was.

She glanced around at the empty shop. 'I'm glad I caught you in a quiet moment. I just wanted to give you these.' She handed over the little glossy bag.

Inside was a selection of sample-sized products from her shop – creams and serums and fragrances.

'Thanks!' I said. 'But you didn't have to.'

'I know, darling, but I like to take care of my friends.' She put her hand on mine.

'That's so kind. Really, I appreciate it.'

I was already imagining scrubbing the tidemark off Neo's bath and pouring in the bath oil. It was such a lovely gesture.

Melissa walked over to my small array of natural beauty products, running her manicured fingertips over the packaging. 'You know, I think I'll give these a try. I do love sandalwood and bergamot. There's a lot to be said for essential oils in a beauty routine.'

She scooped up several containers and handed over some crisp bank notes. I wavered – it seemed wrong to let her pay the full amount when she'd just given me such a nice present. But when I tried to give her some money back, she flat-out refused.

'We local businesses need to support each other,' she said, waving goodbye as she glided out.

I made a mental note to pop round and buy one of her least expensive sheet masks in return.

Mercifully, I made a few sales throughout the rest of the morning, and then Christa came in to ask me out to lunch. I had to say no – I'd brought a sandwich as I couldn't justify spending money eating out.

She noticed the bag from Visage Unique on the counter and sniffed. 'I didn't know you shopped next door.'

'Oh. I don't. Melissa dropped them in.'

'You do know some of her products aren't ethical, don't you? This mascara' – she said, plucking a sample-sized tube from the bag – 'has carnauba wax in it.'

I blinked. For all I was on the side of sustainability, I wasn't too clear on what the implication of that was.

'Its production has been associated with modern slavery and deforestation?'

'Ew,' I said, taking it from her and dropping it in the bin.

'Sadly, when it comes to business, some people are happy to deal in blood money. Success at any cost – and she's raking it in.'

'Yeah, she must be.' I thought of her slick, exclusive shop and imagined its tills brimming with cash. Then I looked at mine, with its pitiful scattering of notes and coins. Despite all that, I knew I couldn't trade my principles for financial gain.

'I tried talking to her about it, and she said she'd look into it, but it seems she's still selling this stuff.' Christa frowned. 'Do you know, she's doing so well she wants to expand? She offered to buy this building from Mike.'

'Really? I had no idea.'

'He won't sell it though. He loves this place, and he wouldn't let it go for any money. Not unless...'

She gave me a pointed look, and I understood that she'd also heard of Mike's woes. I wondered then if that was the reason for the strained atmosphere between Melissa and Mike at the party – maybe she was holding it against him.

'Well, we need to make this place a success then,' I said stoically. 'Mike can rely on us.'

'That's the spirit! Anyway, I'd better dash. There's a vegan cheese panini with my name on it.' She cut Penn a glacial stare and left the shop.

That night, I lay in the bath, having checked that the bath oil was environmentally friendly before pouring it in. I'd done the same with the clay mask before slathering it onto my face too. As I floated there, trying to ignore Neo's greying bath towel hanging from a hook on the door, I dreamed again of getting my own place. I'd have a cosy bathroom that had pillar candles dotted about and smelled fragrant. My living room would be decorated with pot plants and scatter cushions rather than posters for the director's cut of *Lord of the Rings* and half-empty Pot Noodle cups. It felt so close but so far away – the shop had so much potential, but I couldn't find a way to tap into it.

My mind was drawn back to those horrible messages on social media. There had been more that day, all along the same lines. My shop was garnering a very negative reputation, and I still couldn't shake the idea that Penn might have something to do with it.

I had a restless night, with dreams of holes in my pockets, money falling through. Then I woke up and decided I just needed to stick at it. If my family had taught me anything, it was that hard work pays off, and to stick two fingers up at anyone who tried to wear me down. I got dressed with a renewed sense

of purpose and started to feel more positive on the bus ride over
to Pilgrim Street.

I arrived outside the shop, and my breath was knocked right
out of me. Across the window was a jagged black bolt of graffiti.
A single menacing scrawl.

SHITHOLE.

THIRTEEN

I don't know how long I stood there, my hands weaved into my hair, just staring at it. *What the hell?* Tears stung my eyes. I'd been unsettled by the spiteful social media comments, but now I felt like I was spinning out, my heart pounding and my breath ragged. It brought back unwelcome memories of school, when my days had been peppered with spikes of adrenaline, not knowing when the tide would turn against me next.

I was early, the first to arrive, so the only other onlookers were passers-by who tutted disapprovingly at the window but paid me little attention. I was transfixed – the graffiti was disturbingly intermingled with the reflection of the street behind me, plastic Santa Clauses hung on the lamp posts. *Ho bloody Ho.* Then footsteps approached from behind me, slowing gradually until I felt a presence just behind my shoulder.

'Fuck,' he said softly, his tone almost awestruck. I turned to see Penn looking pale.

'Ditto,' I said, my lip trembling. I bit it. I wouldn't weaken and let him see that side of me.

His eyes scanned my face, troubled, but then he looked back

at the window, running a hand over his stubble. 'Do you believe me now?' he asked.

My jaw tightened. He had a point – why would he do this to his shop too? The graffiti was scrawled purposefully across both sides of the window, Uncle Al's side reading *SHIT* and mine reading *HOLE*.

'I suppose I ought to.'

We stood there in stunned silence for a while, until the others started to arrive, with varying expressions of dismay.

'Whoever would do such a thing?' asked Sven in consternation.

'Proper shady that, like,' fumed Jake, who offered to speak to a mate of a mate who 'knew some people who could sort it out'. I didn't think he meant window cleaners.

But business needed to go on. After we declined offers of help in cleaning up from all of them, not wanting to rob them of a day's sales too, they went into their respective shops, and we set to the laborious task of getting rid of the spray paint. Without speaking, we took washing-up bowls and sponges from my selection of kitchenware and filled them with warm soapy water in the arcade loos.

We scrubbed in silence for a while, my wet hands stinging from the cold November air. Penn worked away at the paint, his jaw tense. I had to force myself not to notice how the tight muscle gave his angular face a certain attractive masculinity. He became even harder to ignore when he wordlessly moved to my side of the window, his height giving him easy access to the paint I couldn't reach. He smelled of soap and something more botanical, maybe an oil that he polished his guitar with? I pictured his hands working over the smooth burnished wood and swallowed – how were my thoughts straying in this direction when I had so much to worry about?

'I've had comments too. On Instagram,' he said after a while.

'What?'

He nodded. 'Started a few days ago.'

'What kind of thing?'

'Just... negative stuff. Records were scratched, memorabilia not legit. That one really pissed me off. As if I would...'

'Right. Well at least they weren't attacking your character,' I said. That comment about me still stung.

At first, he said nothing and continued scrubbing at a stubborn corner of the letter E.

'They did actually. They said I was "insufferably arrogant".'

'Are you sure that one wasn't genuine?' I asked, the corners of my mouth twitching.

He rolled his eyes. 'Very funny. Although, if it wasn't for your shop getting the same treatment, I'd have wondered if it wasn't you. And you aren't the only one whose business needs the money.'

I shrugged and reloaded my sponge with water. Interesting that his shop wasn't doing as well as it appeared.

'It couldn't have been me anyway,' I said. 'I'd never have thought to look you up on Instagram – you said you didn't do social media. I assume it's too mainstream.'

'Well, you assume wrong. I don't *do* social media for fun. At least not anymore. I needed to promote the shop somewhere.'

'Just Instagram? Or are you on Facebook too?'

He pulled a face.

'Thought not,' I said smugly.

'Look, I'm not the person you seem to think I am,' he said wearily.

I laughed. 'You've got that right, the Honourable Cholmondeley-Warner, or whatever it is you're really called.'

'Give it a rest,' he said, sighing. 'It's getting boring now. And it's Burton-Edwards.'

'That's it. And *Peregrine*... I mean, wow.'

'It's a family name.' He studiously focused on his scrubbing.

'Okay. So what makes you Honourable?'

'My dad's a lord.' He made it sound casual, like it was the most pedestrian, inconsequential thing in the world.

I shook my head. 'That is *mad*. I've never met the son of a lord before. Ooh, will you be a lord one day then?'

'No.'

'Why not?'

'I have an older brother. And even if I didn't, I wouldn't want it anyway.'

I imagined a stately pile that his family lived in and felt a burst of indignation. 'That seems ungrateful.'

He turned to look at me, his expression serious. 'You have no idea what you're talking about. I have other things I want to do with my life other than live off my parents. My background isn't as much of a golden ticket as you think it is.'

I thought of my parents at home, my mam doing all she could to keep them afloat while my dad was laid up. The way I was having to help them out, even if I didn't begrudge a penny of it.

'Really? Because I'm sure that if your business needs the money as much as you say it does, they could probably bail you out.'

He glared at me for a long moment and then threw his sponge into the bowl of water. Without saying anything else, he stalked past me and went back into the shop.

It reached the afternoon and we still hadn't said a word to each other since the pavement showdown. We'd come to a silent arrangement where we'd taken shifts, alternately scrubbing the window or tending to the shop, until the glass was clean again. We were now sitting quietly at each end of the room, after the last smattering of customers had drifted away.

I'd immediately felt guilty after he'd stormed away from our conversation that morning. I still stood by my opinion that he was basically complaining about the boot of his Ferrari being too small for his collection of Louis Vuitton luggage, but I regretted being so strident about it. Whatever my feelings were towards his privilege and snobbery, I felt I'd maybe gone too far.

I sat, tapping my foot nervously against the leg of my stool, and then leaped up and went into the back room. Before I could change my mind, I boiled the kettle, made two cups of instant coffee and took one to him. He said a gruff thank you and took a sip, courteously stifling a wince at the taste of it. I went back to my desk and rested my chin on my hand, thinking.

Who was behind this targeting of my shop? *Our* shop, I reminded myself. It seemed that Penn was as much a victim as me. But now he'd been eliminated as the likely culprit, I had no idea who would be motivated to do this.

The rest of the arcade tenants were so nice – surely it couldn't be one of them. Sven and Arthur were among the sweetest, most gentle people I'd ever met. Jake was a decent person and had seemed as outraged as everyone else at the graffiti. But I had turned him down for a date... I shook my head; that would be a ridiculous reason to hurt someone's business. And Christa – it was true that we shared similar products and were in extremely mild competition with one another, but I knew she would never do anything like this. She was my friend.

Then there was Melissa – she'd been so supportive and kind, bringing gifts and inviting us to her party. And Mike wouldn't do anything to harm his already struggling arcade. It didn't make sense. But as I thought of Mike and his business woes, my mind drifted to Neil, the aggrieved former tenant of mine and Penn's unit. He'd been so aggressive and bitter, and I'd seen him outside the shop, looking in at us. I shivered. What if he had some kind of vendetta?

I was brought back into the room by the sound of Penn stepping down from his stool. He put his closed sign on his desk and headed for the door.

He muttered, 'Back in a bit,' and left.

I needed something to do to keep busy or I would drive myself mad with conspiracy theories about our saboteur, so I decided to move some stock around and put some new stuff out. I busied around the shop, consolidating certain product lines and making space for more. I'd just brought out an unopened box from the back room when Christa came in.

'I've just heard what happened,' she said, rushing over to me. 'Are you okay?'

Christa had arrived after lunchtime and we hadn't had a chance to speak until now.

'I'm fine,' I said. 'It creeped me out a bit though.'

She drew me into a hug. 'What utter bastards. Do you have any idea who it could be? Or might it just be some arsehole kids messing about?'

I sighed and told her the story of how Penn and I had both been on the receiving end of some unsavoury messages online.

'You should call the police,' she said, her mouth a thin line.

'What's the point?' I said. 'There aren't any CCTV cameras outside the building – we checked. And it was through the night, so it's unlikely anyone saw anything.'

'Give me a look at these messages,' she said, holding out her hand.

I gave her my phone, and she scrolled through.

'These are all fake accounts,' she said. 'Look. They've not posted anything themselves; they've been set up to troll you.' She looked at Penn's page too and saw that there were matching accounts that had targeted us both. 'Maybe they're doing this to lots of businesses, just stirring up trouble?'

'Have they done it to yours?'

She grimaced. 'No.'

'Good,' I said bracingly. 'I'm glad they haven't. And anyway,

I'm not going to let them get to me. The best way I can tell them
to go fuck themselves is to make this shop a success. I just have
to figure out how.'

'Another promo event?'

'Maybe. This afternoon I'm just going to get the shop in
order, then I'll start afresh tomorrow. Onwards.'

'Too right. Do you want a hand?'

'Sure.' I smiled, feeling a bit better now that someone had
my back.

I picked up the box I'd brought from the back room.

Premium sensual lifestyle products, it read on the side of the
box. Interesting. I liked the sound of the word 'premium'. My
shop could do with an injection of good quality. I wondered
what was inside. Fancy candles? Luxury wool throw blankets?
Maybe not – when I shook the box, it rattled a bit.

I thumped it down onto the counter, and it started to make
a buzzing noise. Christa and I exchanged a puzzled look. I took
a box-cutter, sliced open the tape and looked inside. What I
saw took the wind out of my sails for the second time that day,
but for a very different reason. The box was filled to the brim
with packages of various sex toys, one of which was vibrating
furiously. I quickly picked up the eye-wateringly large phallus
and fumbled around with it until I found the button to switch
it off.

I turned to Christa who had her hand clamped over her
mouth and was laughing her head off.

'Go, Denise,' she cackled. 'The sly fox!'

'Bloody hell,' I breathed, throwing the vibrator back in the
box like it was radioactive. 'I had no idea...'

'That your mam was peddling dildos?' She shook her head
gleefully. 'What a legend.'

'Ewww!' I squealed, the enormity of what I'd discovered
starting to sink in. 'I can't believe it.'

Christa was now doubled over laughing.

'It's not funny!' I said, although I'd started to giggle myself. 'Christa, what am I going to do with it all?'

'Sell it, of course!'

'I can't.'

'Of course you can. Don't be such a prude.' She looked into the box and prodded around, then her expression grew serious. 'Hang on a minute...'

'What?'

She lifted out a set of small silver balls in a neat white box with black lettering. The packaging was startlingly similar to some of Melissa's tasteful products next door.

'Annie, these are worth a fortune,' she breathed. 'Liaison Secrète. It's a French brand of sex toys that you can't get in the UK for love nor money. They're like the saucy version of a Play-Station 5 on release day.'

'You're kidding me?'

She shook her head. 'No joke. These can go for multiples of their retail price.'

'Oh my God...' I breathed.

'That's what your customers will say, according to the company's satisfaction guarantee,' she said with a smirk.

'I can't sell these,' I said. 'I mean... how would it look?'

'You have to! These babies *cannot* go to waste.'

Just then, Penn walked back into the shop. Immediately, Christa and I leaped in front of the box, shielding it from view. He gave us a look of irritated confusion and went to his side of the shop.

Christa nodded towards the back room, so I gathered up the box and followed her in there.

'Listen to me,' she whispered. 'You've just been talking about how you're going to stick it to whoever's been trying to sabotage your business.' She foraged into the box and produced a large, intimidating rubber penis. 'And what better way to do it than with this.'

I nodded. Maybe this could work, if I could pluck up the courage to become Pilgrim Street's answer to Ann Summers. I was just about to say so, when Christa's eyes strayed to the boxes behind me and widened. She pushed past me and started rearranging them to reveal box upon box with the same *sensual lifestyle* wording.

'Annie,' she said, her voice quivering. 'You're sitting on an X-rated goldmine.'

FOURTEEN

'Don't tell your dad,' whispered Mam down the phone the next day.

'Of course I won't!' I said, not just because she'd asked, but because the prospect of discussing strawberry-flavoured lube and love eggs with Dad made me shudder. 'Why is there so much of this stuff though?'

'I'd just signed up for all that, and then I went through a bad spell with my MS. If I'm honest, when I got better, I'd lost the nerve to sell it. I felt a bit out of my depth. I mean, what do *I* know about strap-ons and what-not?'

Just hearing my mam utter the word 'strap-on' took a year off my life. I braced myself to plough on.

'So, before you lost your bottle, how were you going to sell it?'

'I was going to do parties. Private soirées for groups of friends: wine, nibbles, pin the willy on the swimwear model, that kind of thing.'

'Right. Well, I'm not sure I can do that kind of thing in the shop. Not unless I do it in the dead of night and hang up sheets over the window.' I chewed my nail. 'I need to figure this out.'

'What about a secret sale? Under the counter, like in the war.'

I nodded, cogs starting to whir. 'Black market ball gags,' I murmured.

Mam tutted. 'There's nothing of that sort in there. The leaflets said nothing about sadomasochism.'

There went another year of my life.

'So, I could advertise them discreetly... Christa said they're desirable products, so people should know what I'm on about with a thinly veiled description. Then there's no risk of alien-ating other customers.'

'That's very sensible,' agreed Mam. 'I can help if you like?'

I declined. The last thing I needed was my mother coming up with creative puns about how to pleasure oneself.

I hung up and immediately set to work on my plans. There was no time like the present; I needed an injection of cash, and fast. I'd received my latest rent invoice from Mike, and it was due any day.

I took some arty, obscure pictures of the packaging with my phone, using the dim lighting of the back room to create a sensual atmosphere. I made sure the exact titles and contents of the boxes weren't in plain sight. I just had to hope that the design was recognisable enough that those in the know would pick up on it, and that my stock of Liaison Secrète would also then spread by word of mouth.

I added the caption, *If you know, you know...* then hit 'post' and almost immediately there were some likes. All I could do now was sit back and wait – I would post more through the day to drip-feed some more teasers. I *literally* sat back and waited; the shop was quiet so I sat on a box and rested back against the wall, closing my eyes. This had to work. *It had to.*

I'd been sitting there for ten minutes when Penn came out back. He looked at me askance before foraging through some of the boxes on his side.

'I'm just resting my eyes,' I said, getting up.

'Mmhm,' he replied, taking out a stack of albums and starting to sort through them. 'I saw your Instagram post.'

'Really? I only added it ten minutes ago.'

'It came up on my notifications.'

'You follow me?'

'Yeah,' he said begrudgingly. 'I thought I ought to. So I know what kind of vibe it's giving. To check it's in keeping.'

My nostrils flared. 'Maybe I should follow *you*. To make sure you're 'in keeping' with *my* shop.'

He shrugged. I went to go back into the shop when he spoke again.

'What is it you're posting about? It looks very cryptic.'

'That's for me to know.'

'I haven't seen any of that packaging in your shop. What's the big secret?'

'None of your business,' I said, my cheeks starting to warm. I didn't think he'd be delighted to know that our premises was about to become a den of iniquity. 'And there's no need for you to know, but don't worry. I won't be flogging any more squeegee mops that might cramp your style.' I flounced off into the shop with him staring after me.

The afternoon passed without incident, other than Christa coming in and whispering excitedly to me about my treasure trove. Penn looked on with suspicion. I posted a few more mysterious pictures with captions like, *I have a little Secrète...* and *Make a Liaison with Everything Must Go*.

Then just as I was about to close up for the evening, a woman came in, looking furtively around. She hurried up to the counter, wrapping her wool coat around her.

'Hi,' she said. 'Um, is this the right place for...?' She glanced uneasily at Penn, who was looking on with unbridled interest.

She lowered her voice so he couldn't hear and turned her face away. 'For Liaison Secrète?'

I beamed. 'You've come to the right place.' I'd bought a nice-looking hardback folder from the stationery shop down the road and inserted all of the literature for the product lines inside. I handed it over and tactfully left her at the desk to peruse it. She spent five minutes leafing through and then coughed twice. I presented myself behind the counter again, like a porn-peddling Mr Benn.

She pointed to a small selection of items and I said, 'Coming right up.' After a brief forage in the stock room and placement of the goods in a discreet paper bag, I exchanged her swag for a cool £120. She didn't bat an eyelid and left with a very satisfied smile on her face, promising me that she would tell all her friends.

Penn eyed me once more as he swung his jacket over his shoulder. His gaze roved over me questioningly, and for a moment my brain released a little dopamine hit from the attention.

'That was... weird,' he said.

'Nothing to worry about,' I said, beaming widely as I buried the flicker of chemistry I'd just imagined. 'Have a good night. See you in the morning!'

He scowled and left, while I cashed up, £120 the richer.

That night, I lay on my bed. Neo had gone out with some hairy friends to the pub, so the flat was devoid of battle cries and farts drifting from under his bedroom door.

I scrolled through Instagram and Facebook, smiling at the build-up of likes and comments. The comments were as cryptic as my posts, with emojis such as love hearts, side eyes, and the occasional aubergine; it was reaching my target audience and spreading faster than I'd dared hope.

I'd been scrolling for a while when my eyes fell on the stream of 'follow suggestions'. There, on my Insta feed, was a box suggesting I follow back an account called *penn_be*. The Honourable Mr Burton-Edwards himself. Curious, I clicked on his profile, feeling as intrusive as if I was digging through his underwear drawer, mildly embarrassed in spite of there being no witnesses.

It mostly comprised of grainy pictures of him and his band, none of which were recent. This seemed to be an old personal account rather than one for his shop. There were snapshots of dark venues lit with reddish lights, or some with a bright white glare highlighting the stage. Penn was in most of them, a guitar against his hip, dark hair hanging down over his face. A memory of seeing him for the first time flashed into my mind. I then noticed that I was unconsciously biting my lip, and a strange warmth radiated through the lower half of my body. I shook my head abruptly. *Musician Penn is* not *Shop Penn.*

Other photos showed him relaxing with some of the guys, bottles of whisky and beer dotted around shabby living rooms, smoke clouding the ceiling. In a few of these, he was laughing, his eyes screwed up and his mouth open wide. I'd never seen him do that. *Not with me...* The realisation that I wanted him to was as disconcerting as it was tantalising.

I scrolled further, starting to delve into the deeper past, my thumbs flicking and flicking. Eventually I paused on a photo that stood out from the rest. It was a picture of a wedding – a summer outdoor affair with a festival theme. The bride was shoeless and had a ring of flowers around her strawberry blonde head; the groom was wearing a mint-coloured suit with a white T-shirt underneath. I struggled to see the context until I spotted Penn in the background. He was wearing a slim-cut suit and trainers and was pulling a blonde woman in close to his side, his hand resting on her waist – she was wearing a soft pink dress that showed a lot of boob, and was pouting and holding her fingers up in a peace sign. I squinted. I recognised her; it was the snooty one from the pheasant shoot – the one who'd branded us all 'animals'. The proprietorial way she'd spoken to him that day now made complete sense. She was his girlfriend.

A strange feeling trickled through me. He'd never mentioned her either before or after the day of the shoot, and she'd certainly never visited the shop as far as I was aware. It hit me, with surprise, that I felt affronted. Not *jealous* – the man was an arse after all – but something more subtle. It made me feel like the rift between us was deeper than I'd thought; not only did he have a secret upper-class identity, but he didn't deem me worthy of knowing he was in a relationship, or anything at all about his life other than the most superficial veneer of it. I was working alongside a misanthropic enigma.

Sighing, I went to shut down my phone but fumbled it. It slipped around in my hand as I tried to regain a hold, and in doing so my fingers mashed the screen. I turned it over, knowing the danger I was now in, being two years deep in Penn's profile. With a sickening lurch, I saw the bright red heart under the picture of him and his girlfriend, signifying that I had indeed accidentally 'liked' the photo. With a whimper, I pressed it again to 'unlike'. But I knew it was too late. If he had notifications turned on, he'd now be reading hard evidence that I'd stalked him good and proper.

For the next hour, I lay on my bed and stared at the damp patch on my ceiling.

FIFTEEN

If Penn knew I'd been sniffing around his social media, then he didn't show it. I'd arrived at the shop the next day summoning every shred of nonchalance I could muster, in spite of my mortification still giving me the shakes. But the atmosphere was the same as ever, in terms of our distant relationship, although a completely different ballgame when it came to the footfall through my shop.

The day started with me hiding for as long as I could in the back room to avoid him bringing it up, only coming out when I heard the door jingle. The first few customers were for Penn, as usual, but then someone came in and sidled up to the desk.

A woman of about twenty-five wearing smart workwear smiled conspiratorially and said, 'I'm looking for Jean-Luc?'

'I think you'll find this to your *satisfaction*,' I said, producing my hardback menu of products and placing it on the desk. She grabbed the book and started to flick through it with interest.

I'd added a few more social media posts yesterday and that morning, thinking about the awkward, whispered conversation I'd had with my first customer. I'd given people the option of 'asking for Jean-Luc' as code for doing their smutty shopping. I imagined Jean-Luc to be the bronzed, stubble-chinned god of all these women's fantasies, which seemed appropriate to accompany their purchases.

She made her selection, I provided the goods and she went out happily. But not as happy as me, as I now had another 150 quid in the till and two more customers coming through the door, hand in hand.

'Is Jean-Luc here?' asked one of the women, older with steel-coloured hair, alongside a woman I guessed was her wife or partner, judging by their body language. I presented the book again, and they pored over it together, oohing and aahing over all the possibilities.

Penn, who was now at a loose end, was staring at my side of the shop again, his brow knitted. 'Who's Jean-Luc?' he asked as I wandered near the no-man's land at the border of our floor-spaces.

'He's my new silent business partner,' I said, smiling sweetly.

He observed the two women, who were now nodding enthusiastically at each other and seemed to be writing a list on a piece of paper.

'A silent partner? Right. And what's that book all about?'

I rearranged a stack of paperbacks. 'Jean-Luc is... supplying extra stock. It's an inventory.'

'Uh-huh.' He crossed his arms and narrowed his eyes at me. 'I've seen your mysterious Insta posts. What are you really up to?'

The mention of Instagram after last night made my hackles rise. I turned away before he could see the look on my face.

'Running a highly successful business,' I said over my shoulder and scurried away to start loading a carrier bag full of vibrators.

. . .

Over the next few days, my custom grew and grew. Christa kept coming to gawp at the stream of people – single women, couples, some men, young and old – coming in and out of the shop, discreet packages in hand. Even Sven and Arthur came in to congratulate me on the sudden upturn in my fortunes.

'Bravo, my girl,' said Arthur, giving me an avuncular squeeze.

'Yes, very well done,' agreed Sven. 'Half of your customers have paid our shop a visit too. The same for Christa and Jake. So thank you.'

I grinned. It was all working out. My shop was doing well, I was raking in money and the other tenants were benefiting too. I prayed this would be enough to help Mike keep the place going, and to attract new tenants once Sven, Arthur and Jake vacated their units. The only person who didn't seem to be reaping the rewards was Penn, although I suspected his moody, petulant expression at the busyness of my shop might have been putting off any potential customers crossing onto his side.

Arthur coughed politely and gave me a shy smile. 'Now, would you mind if we made the acquaintance of your friend, Jean-Luc?' Sven hovered by his shoulder expectantly.

'Of course!' I said and produced the famous book.

Five minutes later, I handed over a bag of assorted penis paraphernalia at a healthy staff discount. They went back to their shop happily, and for once I welcomed a reprieve from the flow of trade through Everything Must Go, going out back to make myself a much-needed cup of tea.

When I came out, Penn was thumbing through Jean-Luc's brochure, his mouth hanging open.

'What are you doing?' I yelped, grabbing it off him.

'I could ask you the same thing!' His eyes glittered with poorly concealed amusement. He shook his head with mock disapproval, but there was also a hint of curiosity. Looking down, I could see the pages had flopped open to reveal a selection of multicoloured phalluses. I snapped it shut.

'What the hell were you doing rifling through my stuff?'

'I figured it was fair game since half of Newcastle has had a look already,' he countered, but he had the good grace to look a little ashamed of himself.

'I didn't hear you ask for Jean-Luc!' I yelled, immediately aware of how ridiculous I sounded but too angry to stop myself. And embarrassed too. There was something too close for comfort in talking about anything sexual with Penn, especially when his dark eyes were on me, trying to figure me out.

He grimaced. 'Alright. I'm sorry for looking, but it's been driving me mad not knowing what was going on. You can't expect me to share a shop with you and not have any clue what kind of stuff you're selling.'

I breathed heavily, like a dragon with smoke coming from its nostrils. 'You had no right...'

'I know. Like I said, I'm sorry.' He held up his hands. 'But I didn't expect this. Annie, I'd never have imagined you were into all this stuff.'

'I'm not! I mean, even if I was, that would be up to me. I'm a progressive, sex-positive woman, after all.' I did consider myself this way, although it was irrelevant since I hadn't had a boyfriend for ages and hadn't dared pilfer any of my own stock as it was too valuable. 'You don't know anything about me.'

'I know more than you realise,' he said, holding my gaze, and I remembered my Instagram gaffe again. If he was implying what I thought he might be, I needed to cut that conversation off at the pass.

'Anyway, what I sell in my shop is a business decision, not just a personal one. I can't help it if my side is busier than yours.'

He paused for a moment then laughed. 'Listen, I'm sure you *are* a sex-positive woman.'

My eyes widened and my cheeks flamed, despite my loudly proclaimed progressiveness.

'And...' he continued in a surprisingly light-hearted tone, 'I don't begrudge you doing well, even if it does mean I'm being overlooked by the parade of perverts trooping through your shop.' He smirked, shaking his head. 'But when it comes to the whole vibe of the shop, it's not...'

'*In keeping*?' I finished. I was lost for words for a moment. In spite of his attempt at levity, yet again the deeper meaning won out. It always seemed to come back to me being the lesser of us.

Instead of trying to find a snappy response, all the energy seemed to seep out of me.

'Penn, I'm tired of this,' I said, my shoulders sagging. 'I don't think we're ever going to see eye to eye. So can we just agree to stick to our own side of the shop and sell our own stuff without speaking to each other unless strictly necessary?'

He tensed, any vague attempt at humour fading. 'Fine with me,' he said quietly and turned his back on me, the muscles in his shoulders tensing against the fabric of his T-shirt.

I sat down, shaking, and tucked Jean-Luc away. Arguments always made me want to cry with frustration, not just anger, and that set-to had already made my throat start to feel thick. For some reason, out of all the rows we'd had, this one had burrowed deeper under my skin.

Why did it have to be *him* working here? Snooty, snobby, sexually-stunted Peregrine, looking down on my shop and *me*. I'd rarely felt so judged. But there was a small part of me that felt I could never just accept complete annihilation of a relationship, of any kind. All my bravado, telling him to stay out of my way, had come out of my embarrassment and exhaustion with this ongoing tension. But I hated feeling this divide coming down between our shops, like a flotilla of ice across the water.

A customer came in, and out of the corner of my eye, I saw

Penn look up hopefully. But he slumped back onto his chair when the well-dressed woman in her forties made a beeline for my desk, already reaching for her purse. I felt an involuntary pang of guilt. I was pained to realise he had a point when he said that his customers were being put off by the hoopla in my shop.

As I rang up the woman's purchases – some very fine fluffy handcuffs and three pairs of crotchless knickers – I paused, biting my lip.

'You know,' I said, while handing over her change, 'I think the guy in the music section over there has a few Barry White albums... to set the mood?'

She nodded then walked over to speak to Penn. I heard her say that her husband was into vinyl and he had a player, so he talked her into buying a Barry White as well as a Fleetwood Mac for her husband's collection. She went out smiling, and the door clicked shut, leaving us in silence.

After a moment, Penn spoke. 'I know I'm not supposed to talk to you. But thank you.'

I gave him one nod, my face as poker straight as his, then we both picked up our phones and pretended to be busy.

Later that day, after a steady, almost exhausting stream of Jean-Luc's callers, I stood at the desk counting my cash again. I could hardly believe the difference since those first days where the cash tin looked like a five-year-old's piggy bank. Even the sales on the day of my special event couldn't compare to the pile of money I had now, as well as the healthy sum that glowed on my banking app screen.

I was just about to close up when a customer came through the door, a girl who looked to be in her early twenties with swingy auburn hair and horn-rimmed glasses. She gave me a brief smile and then looked around, picking up various things,

examining them and putting them back. Hovering over the
romantic novels, she thumbed through a few of them, seeming
uncertain.

'Can I help at all?' I asked. 'I can recommend some books if
you're after anything in particular.'

She looked uncertainly at the paperbacks again and whispered, 'Actually... do you have anything a bit... spicier?' She
giggled nervously.

'Of course! In fact, I've a copy of something you might
enjoy very much over here.' I gave her a reassuring smile and led
her to the counter, then handed her the book. She seemed to
loosen up a little and smiled meekly as she turned the pages. I
gave her some privacy. She seemed sweet, like a kid in the old
days, walking up to the chemist's counter for condoms then
bailing and asking for toothpaste instead.

She took her time, and I was starting to wonder if she'd be
here all night when she coughed to get my attention.

'Would you recommend this one?' she asked, pointing to a
demure-looking cylindrical vibrator.

'Absolutely. It comes with a lovely storage case that actually
looks like something you'd keep your glasses in. Very discreet.'

She visibly relaxed. 'I'll take one, please.'

I went to the back room and packaged it up in the usual
unmarked bag and brought it out to her. She was looking across
at Penn, who was throwing his messenger bag over his shoulder.
He nodded at us both as he left.

'It's funny,' she said. 'Having a record shop in the same
room as... well, one of these kinds of shops. How did you end up
with this arrangement?'

'Pure chance,' I said. Then, feeling the strain of mine and
Penn's constant bickering, I found myself adding, 'And sometimes it does feel like a funny arrangement. We don't have a lot
in common.'

'I can imagine. At university, I live with a girl who keeps

birds in her room. Cages full of them. I don't know what's worse, the noise or the smell.'

'*That* I can identify with too,' I said, grinning. 'Where are you studying?'

'Warwick. I'm home for Christmas.'

'A nice break from the menagerie then. Well, I hope you have a lovely Christmas.'

She picked up her package. 'You too! Although I'd imagine you'll be very busy until then, with this stuff being so popular.'

'Like you wouldn't believe. The shop's been heaving with people wanting to give themselves a festive treat.'

'You're like a smutty Santa,' she said, laughing, and I did the same, feeling a little surprised at the change in how comfortable she was with all this. 'Anyway, I'll let you get on,' she said.

I smiled. 'Lovely to meet you, and enjoy the rest of your holidays.'

'Thanks, I will, although I'll likely be bored to tears. Most of my friends are away.' She shrugged and headed for the door, pausing to look at the selection of gardening equipment. I had masses of the stuff, enough boxes to rival the Liaison range, but what I knew about gardening you could write on the surface of a love egg.

'Is this seed propagator fully electric, or does it come with a heat mat?' she asked.

I grimaced, knowing I would be of little help.

'Sorry,' she said, slightly flustered. 'You're closing up; I'll come back another day.'

'No!' I said, deciding a later finish would be worth a bird in the hand. 'Not at all. But, to be honest, I've no idea. Gardening isn't my strong suit.'

'Oh, I love gardening,' she said, upturning the box. 'It *is* fully electric. I'll take it, if that's okay?' She then grabbed up some seeds, twine and an unidentifiable gadget that looked like a miniature scythe. 'These too, please.'

'Of course!' I rang up her purchases.

'You know, you should really charge more for these,' she said, holding up the little scythe. 'It's a Japanese razor hoe – they normally go for ten pounds more than this.'

'Really? Well, thanks for the tip.'

'No problem. I feel like I should give you more money for it.'

'Don't worry about it,' I said, grinning. Then something occurred to me. I knew absolutely nothing about the gardening stock and was clearly undercharging. What if I could get a little help with that, not to mention lightening my load in general? Now the shop was doing so well I could afford it, and it sounded like this woman was at a loose end for the holidays...

'What's your name?' I asked.

'Olivia.'

'Okay, Olivia. I could probably do with some help on my busier days. I could definitely do with someone who knows their stuff about the gardening gear, and as long as you don't mind wrapping up the odd pair of edible knickers, I could offer you a part-time job?'

She looked at me with her mouth slightly open and then smiled. 'Of course I don't mind! I'd be a kind of Erotica Elf to your Smutty Santa. When can I start?'

SIXTEEN

The days passed by in a whirlwind of Kegel exercisers and lube as Christmas approached and the footfall through town increased. Outside, Pilgrim Street was glowing with Christmas lights, the people walking below wrapped up in thick coats and hats, arms weighed down with bags full of gifts.

The cash in my account was stacking up at a rate I'd never dared dream of. And I still had about half my stock left, along with a promise from my mam that she could try to get her hands on more if needed. What was more, my Liaison Secrète customers very often picked up a veg peeler or one of the steamier paperbacks I'd discovered amongst the collection and placed prominently near the desk. Olivia was doing really well, too. She buzzed up to the shop in her Fiat 500 every day I needed her and was an absolute godsend for selling the gardening gear, not to mention becoming gradually more comfortable with presenting the ever-popular book.

I'd continued to send customers Penn's way. Each person who asked for Jean-Luc was given the nod towards his side of the shop. Before long, I noticed that he'd been in receipt of some more Barry White albums in various formats. He'd also added some copies of Marvin Gaye's *Let's Get It On*, as well as albums featuring 'Je t'aime... moi non plus', perhaps in homage to our French benefactor.

We still weren't really speaking – this ceasefire was purely of a professional nature, which seemed to suit us both. I was very popular with the other tenants though, as they continued to benefit from my erotic wares. Even Melissa popped her head in to congratulate me and left with a bulging package under her arm, pun intended. However, Penn continued to irritate the life out of me.

I winced whenever his mates came in, tinkering with guitars and drinking beers, and he struggled to suppress his disdain whenever I vibed along to Taylor Swift while tending to my merchandise. He'd developed some more annoying habits too, such as leaving half-eaten sandwiches in the back room, usually in inconspicuous places so that the first clue they were there was the pungent odour of rotting ham. He left the toilet seat up in the staff loos, chewed gum loudly and called other men 'bro' or 'my guy' when making a sale. All in all, I was nettled at least twenty-five per cent of the time.

One day, about a week into December, it was near to closing time and we were restocking for the following day. Olivia and I were arranging some cheese graters on a shelf when I spotted a familiar face through the window, barely visible in the dark. It was Neil, the previous tenant of the shop, who'd behaved so weirdly in the cafe that time. He was staring at the glass where I'd added another message under the main sign in green and red swirly print. It said *All I Want For Christmas Is Jean-Luc*, to promote my illicit spicy goods. *A little gift for the one you love... or just for yourself*, I'd added below, in smaller writing.

Neil clamped his lips between his teeth so that the edges grew white, and marched towards the door. He clattered through it, the door slamming off the wall as he entered.

'I'd like to see this Jean-Luc,' he said, white patches blooming on his florid cheeks.

Olivia beamed and leaped behind the desk, reaching for the book. 'Coming right up,' she said with a cheeky wink. At twenty-one, she was of such a guileless, sweet nature that it hadn't seemed to occur to her that he wasn't in the best of moods.

Neil stood there, pausing for a moment, but then strode up, flicked open the cover and winced at its contents.

'I knew it,' he said. 'I thought that's what it was after seeing those posts you've been splashing around the internet.'

I laughed nervously. 'What's the problem, Neil? Are you not here to make a purchase?'

He glared at me, and the smile fell from my face.

'Am I hell. How are you getting away with selling this stuff?'

I blinked. 'I'm not sure what you're getting at. It's really none of your business, to be honest, and I can't understand what you're objecting to. Are you part of some kind of chastity movement, or is this on religious grounds?' Bolstered by sudden indignation, I'd stalked a few paces closer to him, squaring my shoulders. I glanced at Olivia, who'd frozen in place, her face now pale.

He chuckled nastily. 'It's nothing to do with *chastity*. It's to do with principles. Mike seems to be happy with all sorts under this roof now, when he gave me the heave-ho for a few swimwear pics. Which were advertising the swimwear I was selling!'

I hesitated. He seemed, at this point, to be making a fair argument. If that was the reason Mike had turfed him out, then my stuff should have raised an eyebrow too.

'That's, of course, if he knows what it is you're up to. Mike!' he yelled, looking around, then hulked towards the door, poking his head into the passage. '*Mike*! I want a word.' His voice was like icy gravel and didn't extend a friendly invitation to our landlord.

Penn walked over. 'Mike's not here, pal.'

'And who the bloody hell are you, *pal*?' Neil said, rounding on him, his tone now dripping with sarcasm. 'Jean-Luc?'

'Jean-Luc is a silent partner,' replied Penn smoothly. 'Now clear off. Whatever beef you've got with Mike has nothing to do with us.'

'I'd say it does, if you're breaking the same "rules" as me.' He mimed quote marks. 'If he doesn't already know, then I'll tell him and make sure he upholds his precious principles. And if he *does* know, and you're getting special treatment for some reason, then we'll be having more than just words.' He ground his fist into his palm.

My heart started to thump as I realised how unhinged he was.

Olivia let out a soft whimper, and I felt a flash of anger. How dare Neil come in here and upset my staff? I walked closer, looking stonily up at his looming figure, trying not to let my legs shake.

'I don't know if you heard my friend the first time,' I said, tipping my head towards Penn, 'but I believe he told you to clear off. And I'd second that by telling you to fuck off, and go fuck yourself while you're at it. And never come back.'

'What did you just say to me?' he leered, his voice dropping dangerously low. He narrowed his eyes, his fists flexing, and took a step towards me.

He never got to take a second step. There was a rush of air beside me as Penn hurried to stand between us. He held one hand behind his back to steer me away, at the same time pointing a finger in Neil's face.

'You stay away from her, you nasty piece of shit,' Penn seethed through gritted teeth. 'Leave her the fuck alone.'

Neil flinched and stumbled back, his sturdy back crunching

into my shelves, which clattered off their supports, spilling their contents onto the floor. His arms pinwheeled, and he landed on his arse in amongst the wreckage.

Then the door crashed open and Jake ran in, looking at the scene with horror. He immediately got the brief and helped Penn drag Neil out onto the street like two terriers mauling a Dobermann. They sent him flying onto the pavement.

'You haven't heard the last of this,' he said, getting up and dusting himself down, practically frothing at the mouth.

Jake ran at him, and Neil, thinking better of it, turned on his heel and raged off into the darkness. The four of us stood on the pavement, all breathing heavily.

'Are you okay?' Penn asked me.

'I'm fine.' I turned to Olivia, who looked on the verge of tears. 'Come here. I'm so sorry.' I went to her side, pulling her into a hug. She was shaking like a leaf.

Christa then ran outside. 'What the...?'

'Don't worry,' said Jake, his chest puffing up. 'It's sorted. Man won't show his face here again.'

Christa stared down the road. 'Is that... Neil?'

'Unfortunately,' I said, rubbing at my chest, trying to soothe the ache of the adrenaline rush to my heart. 'He's a lunatic. He seems to think he was thrown out for putting up swimwear adverts and that I'm now getting away with far worse.'

Jake shook his head. 'Nah. They were more than just swimwear pics. Well, they *were* of women in swimwear, but each time he put up a new one, it edged closer and closer to *Readers' Wives*.'

'I had no idea,' breathed Christa. 'He only lasted a few weeks after I moved in, and let's just say I wasn't interested in frequenting his shop. He was always a bit weird.'

'Aye, weird and creepy. That's why Mike gave him the boot,' said Jake.

He looked at Olivia, who was still cowering under my arm. 'Is she alright?' he asked me.

'I'm okay,' she said, her voice trembling.

'Let's get you home,' I said. 'I'll call us a taxi, and I'll take you myself. I can bring your car over later.'

She shook her head. 'No. You don't need to do that. I got the bus in today; I'll be fine.'

'I can't let you go alone. Just give me a minute to shut up the shop,' I said.

'It's fine!' she protested.

'Listen, I'm on the same bus I think,' said Christa. 'I left my car at home. It's the 33 you'd be getting, isn't it?' Olivia nodded. 'Right. That's settled then.' Christa took her inside to get their coats, and they left. Jake followed shortly after, fist-bumping Penn on the way.

I stood in the shop, looking at the mess Neil had made with the cheese graters. The shelf supports were askew too – I'd have to sort it out in the morning. Meanwhile, I got a box and started filling it with the graters to clear them from the floor.

Penn had been standing in the street, his back against the window, presumably composing himself. But now he came inside; I heard the door snicking shut behind me as I gathered the remaining kitchenware. He kneeled beside me and helped put the last ones in the box.

'Are *you* alright?' I asked.

He laughed softly. 'It's not my first time wrestling someone out of a room when they're not wanted. I have a brother, remember?'

'I didn't think posh people were into brawling.' A smile tugged at the corner of my lips.

'I didn't think you were into sex toys, but we all have our hidden depths.'

We locked eyes and then started to laugh, a little uncomfortably. This was uncharted territory, a World War One Christmas football game for the modern age.

I watched him reach for a rogue grater that had scattered almost out of reach, his T-shirt riding up just enough that I caught a glimpse of his lithe waist. Just above his hip was a ripple of muscle that sloped towards his belt buckle... something tingled in a similar area of my body. I gritted my teeth, frustrated at another of these intrusive thoughts. *I don't think of Penn that way.* It was just because of seeing him stand up to Neil, that was all. A simple animal response to being defended and protected. Or Stockholm syndrome. One of the two.

He sighed and stood up, brushing dust off his knees, and I followed suit, turning my face away to hide the flush I could feel across my cheeks.

'Thanks,' I said quietly. 'For doing that.'

He shrugged. 'He deserved it. And I think we might have uncovered the saboteur.'

'God. I think you're right.'

It all made sense. The stalking around outside, taking umbrage at me for having the audacity to rent what he thought of as his space. He'd clearly been looking at the shop's Instagram if he'd suspected what I was selling, so he could easily have left those nasty comments.

'I can absolutely picture him wielding a spray can at the window of our shop,' I agreed. 'He's not the most stable of people.' I shivered.

'Well, I don't think he'll be back,' Penn said, looking at me with mild concern. He noticed the way I'd shuddered and put his hands on my upper arms. His dark eyes didn't quite blaze, but there were embers there. 'I'm *sure* he won't be back.'

For a moment, I couldn't tear my gaze away from him. But then I remembered I was meant to be a strong, independent woman and stood back. 'Too right,' I said with an awkward cough. 'I don't think he'd run the risk of tearing the arse out of his jeans with my cheese graters again.'

He went off to sort out his side of the shop, and I finished up on mine. After getting my coat from the back room, I came out to find he was still there, jacket on and keys in hand.

'How are you getting home?' he asked.

'Just on the bus. Like normal.'

He glanced out of the window. 'Look, I don't *think* Neil will come back, but he was pretty amped-up. Can I help you get home safe?'

Inside, I recoiled. Penn and I weren't really friends. Despite our united front over that loser Neil, I wasn't used to feeling congenial towards him. But there was something else. That tingle I'd felt as I saw his bare skin had unnerved me – even as I looked at him now, the image flashed into my head, and what was worse, my mind was peeling back his T-shirt even further... I tried to keep my expression neutral.

'There's no need. It's only a short bus ride away and at the completely opposite end of town to you. I'll see you next week, eh?' I shrugged my handbag over my shoulder and walked out the door.

Then, as I hit the pavement, I stopped. Standing there alone in the dark, all I could see in my imagination was Neil, his wild eyes boring a hole right through me, the veins in his forehead popping. My bus stop was a few streets away and, despite my bravado, my paranoid brain conjured Neil appearing from a side alley ready for round two. I hovered there indecisively, just long enough for Penn to come out, locking the door behind him.

I turned around. 'Have a good weekend,' I said, forcing a smile. 'See ya.' I turned away again and took a few hesitant steps towards the junction at the end of the road.

'Wait.' Penn was still there, rubbing the bristles on his cheek. 'I wasn't actually planning on going home just yet. I was going to see a film.' He nodded to the small independent cinema up the road. 'You could come with me.'

'Why?' I blurted. The moment felt so similar to being asked on a date, I immediately balked at it. Then, just as quickly, I reminded myself he was only offering to keep me company.

He looked amused, and I wondered if he'd read my thoughts. 'Just to give Neil a chance to cool off, or at least get bored of waiting. If he's out there at all,' he hastened to add, noticing my alarmed expression.

'Right,' I said, composing myself and standing a little straighter. 'Well. That's a thought. I mean, it's good of you to offer.'

I wavered. Beyond Penn was a warm, safe space, and behind me were the mean streets of Newcastle, with one especially mean citizen who bore a grudge.

'Okay. I'll come.'

We sat in the darkness with a box of popcorn each. A shared bucket I'd thought was a little bit too intimate, and Penn seemed to be of the same mind. Also, I liked sweet and he liked salty, which seemed to be the perfect metaphor for our relationship thus far. I took a handful of mine and stuffed it into my mouth, savouring the buttery taste – it was exactly the comfort food I needed.

The film was an arty, highbrow one, with an indecipherable plot and lots of long scenes where people said nothing while haunting violin music played in the background. A woman appeared to think she'd grown a tail, which I think was some kind of symbolism, and the man she was in love with occasionally disappeared into a hole in the ground, an equally obscure metaphor. At least I hoped they were metaphors, or I was starting to dissociate.

It was crap, in all honesty. Penn was watching it, rapt and

barely blinking, but I'd much rather have been watching *Fast and Furious 27* (or whichever number they were up to), or anything with Channing Tatum in it. However, the dark, closeted atmosphere was doing wonders for the knots in my neck. With every minute and every handful of popcorn, I relaxed a little more until my eyes started to blink more heavily and I sank deeper into my seat. The scene in front of me – a statue of a Roman soldier with a single tear rolling down its cheek – seemed to blur and then disappeared altogether.

The next time I opened my eyes, the credits were rolling. Then, under my right cheek, something stirred. It was Penn's shoulder. With an unfeminine snort, I sat up straight, wiping a little drool from the corner of my mouth.

'Shit,' I said, cringing to my core. My eyes flicked to his shoulder, which was mercifully free of saliva.

He gave me a wry smile. 'Morning.'

'Ha. Um, sorry about that. I think today took it out of me.'

He shrugged. 'It's fine. I wondered if you'd just got bored of the film.'

'No. It was... absolutely fine.'

'They should put that endorsement on the poster. Anyway, we should probably head out.'

We walked out into the street, and I felt like I'd been ejected from the womb into the freezing-cold world. I pulled my coat tightly around me. Penn shoved his hands into his pockets, and we looked at each other then quickly away. Now that we were out of the cinema, we were back to the stilted politeness of before.

'Night then,' I said.

'Night,' he replied.

I turned and walked off down the street, until I heard footsteps behind me.

'I don't need you to shepherd me home,' I said with a note of impatience.

'Um. My car's parked down this way.'

My face flamed, and I lifted my chin. 'Right. Well. I guess we'll walk together then.'

He fell in step beside me, and we headed down the road and through the next two streets in complete silence. We'd reached my bus stop before he'd arrived at his car. There was no one else there, Neil or otherwise, so I took a seat.

Penn stood there for a moment and then sat beside me, but a good few feet away down the bench.

'What are you doing?' I asked, giving him a sideways glance and shrugging my handbag further onto my shoulder. He tapped his foot and seemed to be thinking very hard.

'Can I ask you something?' he asked.

'Like what?'

He took a deep breath. 'What are you doing next weekend?'

I whipped my head round, goggling at him. 'Eh? You don't mean...?'

'No! No. I don't mean...' He held his hands up in front of him. 'I... I need a favour.' He looked so anxious, I wondered if he was about to ask me for a kidney rather than a date.

'Go on,' I said with caution.

'It's my parents. They're having a Christmas ball, and I'm expected to be there.'

The way he said this gave away his suppressed poshness. He was *expected to be there*, rather than he needed to go. And a *ball*, of all things. No Noddy Holder and a bottle of Bucks Fizz for this family's Christmas celebrations.

'The thing is, they keep trying to fix me up with someone. They want me to come home and settle down, and they think if I settle down with *her*, then I'll never fly the roost again.'

'I thought you already had a girlfriend,' I blurted then immediately realised my mistake. I looked away, cringing.

'I can imagine why you'd think that.' I could hear the smile in his voice, although he had the good grace not to say how he knew. 'But Sophia, the girl in *that* photo, is my ex. My family want me to get back together with her. She's a "good match" apparently.'

'Wow. Your life really *is* like *Downton Abbey*. How archaic.'

'Tell me about it,' he said, without a hint of amusement.

'So what does this have to do with me?'

He swallowed and screwed up his face. 'I need you to pretend to be my girlfriend.'

'*Excuse me?*' I stood up abruptly and looked down at him. 'Are you kidding me?'

'I'm really not.' He shook his head, looking thoroughly mortified. 'I've tried everything. Bargaining, pleading, blackmail – nothing works. I've decided the only thing that will get it through their head is if I turn up with someone else. Make them, and her, see that I'm not available.'

I stared at him for a long while and then shook my head, trying to expel the shock from it. 'Why me? Don't you know any other women? Your actual friends?'

He winced at the implication that we were, in fact, not friends. 'I do. But you know my mates that come into the shop? Think the female version of that. If I want my parents to take me seriously, it needs to be someone more... normal.'

'You mean boring.'

'I mean polite, inoffensive, able to hold an adult conversation. Minimal tattoos and hair that isn't blue.' Hope was starting to bleed through his embarrassed expression.

'I don't understand. You... *hate* me. And surely your dad and Sophia will recognise me from the protest.'

'Given that you spent most of your time there drenched in red paint, I'd be surprised if they did.' He paused, taking a breath. He looked me straight in the eye. 'And I don't hate you.'

I stood there for a moment, breathing almost as deeply as after our altercation with Neil. This was ludicrous. Literal madness. The thought of me cutting around rural Northumberland, hobnobbing with landed gentry and swishing about in a ball gown made my head hurt. I had to tell him no. No way.

'It's not going to happen, Penn. Sorry about your... predicament, but I'm not the answer.'

'I'll do anything you want.' He looked up at me, looking suddenly much younger and less arrogant than ever before. 'Please.'

His face was pained enough that a treacherous part of me started to genuinely feel sorry for him. Despite all of our enmity, I could feel myself being suckered into my usual inclination to do a good deed. But it was a ridiculous thing to ask me to do, even if I did feel bad for him. Not knowing what to say, I stared in the other direction.

'Annie,' he said from behind me, his voice a little hoarse. 'Really, I know it's a strange request, and I'm mortified to even ask. But you're... perfect.'

I turned slowly.

'You're the perfect person to do this. You tick all the boxes – social skills, confidence, no visible piercings...' I rolled my eyes, and he gave me a hopeful smile. 'Listen, I can... compensate you.'

'I am *not* taking money for some kind of parental pantomime,' I snapped, crossing my arms tightly across my chest.

'I don't necessarily mean money. Like I said, I'll do anything you want.'

'Anything?' I said with a disbelieving laugh. 'Like hoovering my side of the shop? Or being a model for my range of latex thongs? Or I could go all out and ask you to put a "ban shooting and hunting" sign in your front window.'

'I would do all of those things. Maybe not the thong, but the rest of it.'

'Penn, I'm joking. And besides, you'd never be able to pull

off the anti-shooting poster. Not with all that blood on your hands.'

He looked at me for a long moment. 'I can assure you, there isn't a drop of blood on my hands.'

I sighed. 'Yeah, I get it. Bird blood doesn't count.'

'I've never shot a bird in my life. I always miss. On purpose.'

My jaw dropped, and I just stared at him.

He shrugged. 'It's true. I hate it all, but I'm expected to do it, just like I'm *expected* to turn up this weekend. So I'd put up a poster – gladly.'

Eventually, my shock dissipated enough for me to speak. 'You would?'

'Of course I would. Annie, I don't think I'm the person you think I am. Not the whole deal, at least.'

I stood there, my mind racing. This was so unexpected, I didn't know what to think at all. This new information about Penn had thrown every preconception I had about him into the air. *He was against shooting?* The stone-cold opposition I'd had to him started to feel like it was on shaky ground. If I'd misunderstood this about him, then what other things had I got wrong?

Then I thought of how he'd defended me and how a delicate stitch of trust had been woven between us. I opened my mouth to say no again, but it caught in my throat. Maybe it was the mental whiplash I'd just experienced, but I found myself considering it. He was sitting in front of me looking... vulnerable. What I said next was almost like a reflex – against my will but as natural as breathing in and out. 'Okay,' I said softly, and he sat up straighter, his eyes widening. I raised my hand. 'Not so fast. There would need to be ground rules. I'd want my own bedroom.'

He was stock-still, seeming as shocked at my U-turn as I'd been about his hidden principles. 'Of course. My parents are *beyond* traditional. Not until the wedding night and all that.'

'I'd need regular breaks. Time off for good behaviour, if you will. I don't think I could put up with the pretence twenty-four-seven.'

'Done.'

'And then I'd need to be repaid.'

He now looked cautious.

'Not money. First the posters. Then no more jam sessions in the shop.' I held up my fingers and started counting them off. 'No more music battles with the speakers – I get to choose the music we play. The rotten sandwiches have to go, and you need to put the toilet seat down. Every time.'

'Done, done and done,' he said, jumping up and running a hand through his hair. 'Whatever it takes. I will owe you big time.'

'You will.'

Just then, my bus rounded the corner.

'Thanks, Annie,' he said. 'Really. I can't thank you enough.'

'You can thank me once it's done. For now, we'll just concentrate on pulling off the best acting of our lives. See you next week, *boyfriend*.' I stuck out my hand to hail the driver.

He grinned. 'Have a nice weekend, *girlfriend*. But seriously, you're a good mate for doing this.'

My eyebrows rose.

'Oh come on, we can call each other mates. You even said to Neil... what was it? Oh yeah – "I don't know if you heard my friend". You said it first.' He smirked smugly.

'Don't get ahead of yourself,' I said, giving him a withering look as I stepped onto the bus. But when the doors closed and it pulled away, I found I was smiling.

SEVENTEEN

The following Friday evening, my train pulled into Corbridge station in darkness, though I could see through the window the quaint stone-built station with white columns and a portico over the platform. It was quiet, except for a few tired-looking commuters coming home from the city, trudging underneath the Christmas garlands strung across the platform roof.

I'd spent the forty-minute train journey wondering what the hell I was doing. Each station stop felt like an opportunity to bail, but every time the doors opened with a hiss, I couldn't seem to get up from my seat. Instead, the train pulled away and I was driven another step closer to what might be the oddest weekend of my life. I questioned myself over and over again, wondering whether this was worth the fairly flimsy list of conditions I wanted Penn to adhere to. But that little do-good bit of me that had felt sorry for him kept nagging. I couldn't turn my back on someone clearly having a hard time.

It was odd though. After all the prickliness and bickering, I never would have imagined myself trundling across the North East towards his home – a home where his tweedy, blood-sport-loving family lived. Could I really overlook that, let alone give the impression I was happy to be there? Not to mention convince them I was there with the love of my life? It all felt very precarious.

I heaved my wheelie suitcase onto the platform and looked around for the exit. Penn had said he'd meet me in the car park, and that I should look out for a muddy Land Rover Defender, the make of which came as no surprise. What *was* a surprise was the excitable black Labrador leaping around in the back – after Penn took my case and I sat in the passenger seat, it poked its head between the headrests and licked my cheek enthusiastically, as though I'd moisturised with pork pie jelly.

'Sorry about him,' said Penn, swinging himself into the driver's seat. 'Get down, Henno,' he said. His voice had that gilt edge of plumminess again.

'It's fine,' I said, wiping my cheek with my sleeve. 'That's a funny name.'

Penn pulled out of the station onto a country road, dark fields on either side. 'Hendrix. Henno for short. Beelzebub when he's being a pain in the arse.'

I remembered how he'd been off searching for the dog at the shoot, and suspected Hendrix might be a pain in the arse a lot of the time. But he seemed nice enough right now, settling comfortably on my suitcase.

'All okay at the shop?' Penn asked. He'd left earlier that day at the request of his family, so I'd minded his place for the afternoon. I noticed he wasn't in his regulation band T-shirt and ripped jeans combo, and had on some smarter jeans and a soft blue shirt, a few buttons undone despite the cold weather. Dark hair smattered his chest. The ensemble was finished off with a navy gilet. If Dr Jekyll had his Mr Hyde, then this was Penn's alter ego, based on early 2000s Prince William.

'Fine,' I replied.

I'd told everyone that I was going to a trade convention to look at new lines for the shop. Nobody had batted an eyelid.

Between them, Olivia and Sven had agreed to cover both mine and Penn's shops for the busy Saturday. Olivia had been with me long enough to know the ropes, and Sven was, of course, a seasoned shop owner. The place was in safe hands.

'So, what's the itinerary?' I asked. 'I assume tonight's mainly eating roast swan, followed by brandies and billiards.'

He shook his head, a smile twitching the corner of his lips. 'When are you going to give up on the piss-taking?'

'I can't help it. It comes out of me like a fountain.'

'Well, try, please. You're meant to be undercover, remember?'

'Of course. I will try. I've watched *Downton Abbey* on repeat all week, and I'm going to base my persona on the Dowager Countess.'

'Maggie Smith?' He glanced over, frowning.

'Joking. No, really. I'm just going to be myself but more refined.'

Even as I said it, a ripple of apprehension ran down my back. I still had no idea how to present myself. I suddenly thought it mightn't have been a bad idea to read an etiquette book or pay better attention to how the Crawley family behaved.

'Listen,' Penn said, 'you don't have to "posh it up" at all. They're not expecting anything – they know I met you in Newcastle, not at some debutante ball. Just be yourself, but with less taking the mick.'

'Will do. But seriously, what's on the timetable?'

'Dinner tonight with the family, and then the rest is a mystery even to me, except for the ball. I'm not always in the inner circle.'

'Right.' How to read into this I didn't know. Was the double-sided Penn some kind of black sheep of the family?

We eventually arrived at the opening to a driveway flanked by curved stone walls, and I could just make out a sign saying

'Ashcliffe Hall' in the moonlight. Penn turned in, and we rumbled down a long, gravelled driveway, through dense trees, then emerged onto a vast courtyard. In front of me was the biggest house I'd ever seen, and I mean *huge*. It was three times as wide as it was tall and had a large wooden door in the centre, framed by a lamplit porch. It looked like a hotel.

'Holy shit...' I breathed.

Penn sat awkwardly beside me, saying nothing. To be fair, there wasn't much he *could* say. The house spoke for itself – this was wealth like I'd never encountered before.

'Come on then,' he said at last. He stared through the wind-screen gloomily. 'Come and meet the family.'

We got out, Hendrix skittering on the tiny driveway stones, and I felt a flash of terror. The door loomed like a portal to another world. But now I was here, and Penn was walking towards it with my suitcase, I didn't have a choice but to cross to the other side.

I sat in a large, tastefully decorated bedroom, drumming the fingers of one hand on the arm of an antique wingback chair and chewing a nail on the other. Hanging on the front of the wardrobe were two dresses. I'd told the same lie to my parents about the convention and added that there would be a fancy drinks event on the evening, one that was a bit classier than a stumble down the Quayside in Newcastle. Thanks to my cousin Kelly, who bought a lot of stuff from Vinted, I'd been furnished with a selection of outfits 'to suit every occasion'. But now, I wasn't sure what kind of occasion dinner with the family counted as.

The massive hallway had been deserted when we walked in. No family members, not even a liveried footman to greet us, as I'd foolishly imagined from my most recent *Downton* binge, and Penn told me that they would all be up in their rooms dressing for dinner. But when he'd delivered me to the guest room, he'd neglected to tell me what the dress code was.

I looked around at the sage damask curtains, the crisp white bed linen with a heavy, expensive-looking quilt folded at the end, the lacquered antique wardrobe and chest of drawers. Whatever the dress code was, it had to be quite fancy. I'd short-listed a black velvet number that finished above the knee and was rather figure-hugging, and a slightly more forgiving teal midi dress with sheer sleeves and a deep, wide V-neck that skimmed the shoulders. I ceased the nervous tapping of my foot and pulled the teal dress on. I bundled my hair up into a loose chignon and finished the look with some knock-off designer jewellery that Kelly had bought from a street vendor in Magaluf. The necklace had a pendant of cubic zirconia on it that could have rivalled the Koh-i-Noor diamond if it weren't for the slightly visible bubbles of glue around the setting. I slashed on some lipstick, popped an Accessorize clutch under my arm and headed for the stairs.

As I descended into the empty entrance hall, I had a chance to take in my surroundings. The double staircase curved around each side of the hall, and in between stood an enormous Christmas tree, tastefully decorated with warm white lights. It was laden with red bows and antique festive figurines, interspersed with bunches of cinnamon sticks, and the heady scent of them provoked a wave of seasonal nostalgia. It made me think of Christmases at home, and my throat grew thick at the thought of those red-topped bills. *What if they can't be paid? Could this Christmas be the last one in my childhood home?* I shook my head, forcing myself to focus on the here and now. It wouldn't come to that. It couldn't.

I could hear the sound of soft music and muted conversation and headed towards it. There was warm light emanating from a doorway, and I rounded it to find Penn and his family lounging on armchairs and sofas. All wearing clothes that you might see in a country casuals catalogue.

I froze in the doorway, a rigid smile on my face. A man I recognised from the shoot as Penn's father was wearing chinos and a white shirt, an older woman who was likely his mother wore navy slacks and a sweater, and Penn himself hadn't got changed at all, other than taking off his gilet. They all stared at me for a moment then snapped their mouths shut, clearly mustering their manners. Penn jumped up and came over to me, taking me gently by the arm to bring me into the room.

'Hiii,' I said to the assembled group as I sat down on a sofa in a puff of skirts. In addition to Penn's mam and dad, there was a man slightly older than Penn, who looked similar enough to him that I guessed he was his brother. He also wore smart jeans, and had on a pink shirt, the sleeves rolled up to the elbow.

'Welcome to Ashcliffe,' said Penn's father, extending a hand, which I shook limply. He was being considerably friendlier and was less red in the face than he had been on our last encounter. He didn't seem to recognise me at all. 'I'm Hugh, and this here is Bunny.'

'How do you do?' said Bunny, Penn's presumed mother, a brittle smile cracking her mouth. She had a helmet of bouffed blonde hair and wore pearls at her mildly wattled neck.

'I'm good, thanks,' I replied, just before remembering that posh people used that phrase to say hello rather than expecting a response about your well-being. My face was starting to grow hot.

'And I'm Bertie. Perry's brother – since he's neglecting to make introductions himself.'

I shook Bertie's hand too, noting the glitter of a gold watch and a whiff of expensive cologne.

They all looked at Penn expectantly, and he said, 'This is Annie. My girlfriend,' he added unnecessarily.

My face flamed as if I was thirteen. In that moment, I'd

never regretted something as much in my life as deciding to be there. It surely couldn't get any more awkward.

Just then there was the clatter of heels down the hall and the honey-blonde woman from the shoot and Penn's Instagram appeared in the doorway. She took one look at me and a hoot of laughter escaped before she rapidly composed herself. Her mouth twitched in suppressed amusement as she introduced herself as Sophia, simultaneously looking me up and down. She was wearing leggings and an oversized black cashmere jumper, and smelled of fresh winter air.

Penn's eyes opened in surprise at her arrival, but he recovered quickly. After he said hello to her, he surreptitiously raised his eyebrows at me. Between that and a satisfied look that I caught from Bunny, the reason for Sophia's presence was clear – she was here to remind Penn of where he was 'better off'. Well, I was here to give a clear message too. Game on.

'Annie, darling,' Sophia said. 'Perry's told me all about you; I'm simply dying to get to know you this weekend. Gorge dress by the way. Love it.' She plucked at the chiffon sleeve and smiled guilelessly.

'Um, thanks,' I said.

I was just trying to formulate a further response when a noise emanated from somewhere nearby – it sounded like an old-fashioned school bell.

'Ah, grub's up,' said Hugh, slapping his knees and getting up. 'It's a kitchen supper tonight, Annie dear. I hope you don't mind roughing it with us until the big shebang tomorrow.'

'Of course not,' I said, trying for a bright smile.

The assembled party all got up and left the room, giving me the opportunity to grab Penn by the arm.

'Did you know she was going to be here?' I hissed, glancing at the door to make sure we were alone.

'Of course not! I would have warned you.'

'Just like you filled me in on what to wear? And what the fuck is a "kitchen supper"?'

'I'm so sorry,' he said, his face stricken. 'I didn't think.'

'You said everyone was getting dressed for dinner. I thought...'

'I just meant they were getting changed out of their muddy walking gear. Fuck... I'm an idiot.'

'Yes. You are,' I said coldly. 'So I'm going to be sitting in the kitchen looking like I'm going to my sixth-form prom?'

He winced. 'Kitchen supper isn't actually served in the kitchen... It just means a slightly less formal dinner.'

I shook my head, stomping towards the door. 'Never mind. What even are you people?'

Penn didn't reply, so I turned and mock graciously gestured to the door. 'Come on then. This swan isn't going to eat itself.'

'It's spag bol actually,' he muttered, walking past me.

I rolled my eyes. Great. Not only was I about to face the Spanish Inquisition, I was about to do it with tomato sauce all over my face.

Thankfully, Penn had briefed his family that I was vegetarian and my version of spag bol was made with meat-free mince. It was poles apart from the bolognese I usually concocted from a jar, and was fragrant with fresh herbs and curls of parmesan. There was also an exquisitely dressed salad on the table and an artisan loaf. I delicately wrapped spaghetti around my fork and looked around the dining room. It was painted in deep red and had sumptuous velvet curtains tied back with woven gold ropes with tassels. You could have fit my parents' entire house into the floor-space.

'So, Annie, Perry tells us you're working in his funny little shop,' said Bunny, nibbling a piece of cucumber from the end of her fork.

'It's not *my* shop,' Penn interjected. 'It's both of ours.'

'Marvellous,' she said without enthusiasm. 'And what is it you're selling?'

'Uh. Mainly lifestyle products. Self-care items, that sort of thing.'

Penn gave me a warning stare. Perhaps I should stay clear of the 'self-care' angle.

'How charming. And who are your people?'

I looked at her blankly.

'Your family, dear.'

I remembered Penn's instruction to just be myself. 'Oh! Well, my dad, Keith, is in the building trade, and my mam is a telephone customer services operative. She's called Denise.'

'Good salt-of-the-earth people,' said Hugh bracingly. 'The world needs people who keep things moving after all.'

Bunny dabbed at the corner of her mouth with a napkin and gave an almost imperceptible shudder.

'Oh, yes,' agreed Sophia. 'I don't know what I'd do without car mechanics and delivery drivers. Good for you,' she said, patting my hand.

I wasn't sure how I was responsible for my parents' choice of career, but I nodded and smiled anyway.

'So, did your eyes meet across the shop floor then?' asked Bertie. 'Romance blossomed from a staff meeting?'

'Something like that,' I said, taking a sip of wine.

'Oh, Bertie, you *are* naughty,' said Sophia with a light laugh. 'Perry and Angie don't need grilling about their relationship. Give the girl a moment to get her bearings.'

'It's Annie,' I said.

Penn's face clouded. The implication that I wasn't accustomed to this lifestyle was as subtle as the decor in this room.

'Absolutely,' Sophia said, wagging her beautiful head from side to side. 'Silly me.'

'And are you a *musician* as well?' Bunny asked me, handling the word 'musician' like it was a rather nasty virus.

Despite all the attention being on me, I felt a flash of indignation for Penn that he'd been patronised more than once during this meal. I remembered what he'd said about not being in the inner circle.

'I'm not actually. I haven't the talent, but Penn— sorry, *Perry*, is just incredible. You must be very proud of him.'

Penn's eyes opened wider with surprise.

'Oh, we are, we are,' said Hugh unconvincingly. 'Although you're getting on a bit now, m'boy. Time for the flight of fancy to come to an end, eh?'

Although the words were encouraging, his tone was slightly steely. I was pretty sure the aforementioned flight of fancy wasn't just referring to the shop, but to me too.

Penn bristled. 'I'm happy as I am, Pops. You know that.'

'Quite so.' Hugh frowned and tucked into his spaghetti with renewed vigour, while Bunny shot him a look. I wondered if he'd been tasked with bringing it up and was now deemed a failure.

'You have a lovely home,' I said after a short silence, the only sound a ticking clock in the background. 'Really spectacular.'

'Thank you,' said Bunny. 'It's been in Hugh's family for generations, of course. And the boys will be next to carry the mantle.'

Bertie looked very satisfied at this, while Penn stared at his plate.

'And then there's the next generation too,' said Hugh. 'Tell me, Bert, will Catherine and the boys make it back from St Moritz in time for the do?'

'Skiing,' whispered Sophia to me with a little smile.

'She wouldn't miss it for the world. Flying in tomorrow morning.'

'Splendid,' said Bunny with the most genuine warmth I'd

encountered from her since I'd arrived. 'I've missed my little poppets.'

'They're little tyrants really,' said Bertie in my direction. 'Although Mummy won't hear a word said against them.'

'Barney and Rufus are no such thing,' countered Bunny. 'And it's a grandmother's right to spoil her grandsons.'

'Too right, Buns,' agreed Sophia. 'And the more grandchildren the merrier, I say.' She cut a look at Penn, who remained impassive.

'Oh, indeed,' said Bunny. 'I expect we'll hear the patter of tiny feet again one day.' Then she smiled generously at Sophia and sipped her drink. Bunny avoided looking at me at all.

The god-awful meal continued for a short while longer, with mostly banal chit-chat and gossip about people I didn't know. After only one minor wine spillage from me, it was thankfully over.

The family were decamping to the sitting room once again to round off the night when I was hit with a wave of complete exhaustion. It was borne from a week of fretting about this assignment, several bad nights' sleep and the draining kitchen-supper experience. I caught Penn's arm and let him know I wanted to cry off.

'Time off for good behaviour, like we agreed,' I whispered as we hovered outside the sitting-room door.

He nodded, since I had him bang to rights on our contract, then we popped our heads into the room where Sophia and Bunny were sitting close together, whispering to each other, and Bertie was flicking through *Horse and Hound* magazine.

'Annie's going to have an early night,' Penn announced.

'I'm bushed,' I said. 'Long day, and the travelling. You know.'

Although we were all well aware of the mere forty-minute train ride I'd endured, they all politely said goodnight. Penn offered to take me to my room, but I demurred.

We stood there in the doorway, the family now looking at us expectantly, and then Penn put his hand at the back of my head and kissed the top of it. As his lips touched me, I felt a jolt in my stomach that wasn't just nerves. *What the hell?*

'Goodnight, beautiful,' he said, and I looked up at him. For a moment, I almost believed him but then shook it off. He was acting his socks off, and the flicker I'd felt was only because of the sterling job he was doing. I needed to play my part too.

'Night, babe,' I said and gave him a brisk hug. Then I left and stood just outside the door for a second to compose myself. This was all so weird.

The last I heard was Sophia saying to Penn, 'Come and sit by me, trouble. Tell me more about lovely Amy.'

I was headed for the stairs when Hugh emerged from a side room, whisky glass in hand.

'Ah, off to Bedfordshire already?'

'Yes,' I said. 'I hope nobody minds – I don't want to be a party pooper.'

'Not at all, m'girl. All the better rested for tomorrow night.' He tapped the side of his nose and winked. 'I just hope we haven't worn you out.'

'Oh, no! It's just been a long day. You've all been wonderful,' I lied.

He smiled ruefully. 'Now, now. I know we're a bit of a handful. Like a swarm of Labradors around a bowl of kibble when there's a new person to get to know.'

I smiled, although when I thought of Sophia and Bunny, a pack of wolves came to mind. However, judging by his friendly attitude right now, I wondered if Hugh was warming to me after all.

'I'm glad you're here,' he continued in an avuncular tone, but then his expression turned more serious, his eyes becoming flinty. 'It gives me the chance to speak to you properly. Maybe you can knock some sense into Peregrine about this *lifestyle* of his. He's always been... difficult, and his mother and I have tried and tried to set him on the right path. But while he turns a deaf ear to us, he might listen to you. I'm sure you understand, he won't stay in the city forever – his place is here.'

He gave me a meaningful look that made it very clear that Penn should – and *would* – leave me behind when that time came, and I should disabuse myself of any notion that I would be welcome to follow 'It's all very well carousing around the city when you're a young buck, but he's almost thirty now. Time's a' ticking.' He tapped at his heirloom watch.

Just then, Sophia's tinkling laugh carried down the hallway, and mine and Hugh's eyes locked. Time was a' ticking indeed, almost as loudly as their preferred daughter-in-law's biological clock and the cultured offspring that Penn and Sophia would produce.

I set my jaw. I might have been there under false pretences, but I still felt the sting of rejection. 'Uh-huh. I hear what you're saying. I'll... bear all that in mind.'

'That's a girl,' he said, suddenly brightening, the jovial host once more 'We'll all be up bright and early for a spot of wild swimming in the lake before breakfast.'

'In December?' I yelped. 'I'll have to sit that out, I'm afraid. I haven't brought my cossie.' Thank God.

'Nonsense. I'm sure Sophia can get you rigged out, and we've some spare wetsuits in the boathouse. It's a family tradition.'

'Right. Well, I'll look forward to it,' I murmured. 'Night then.'

He gave me a cheerful salute, and I trudged up the stairs, wondering how many of their Egyptian cotton bedsheets I would need to tie together to abseil out of my bedroom window and make my escape.

EIGHTEEN

The landscape out of my window the following morning looked as if it had been popped into a freezer overnight. The horizon was dove grey, meeting snow-topped hills, and the foreground was crusted with a thin white layer of frost. I cursed the traditional country pursuit of wild swimming, especially since this family were mad enough to want to do it in the depths of December. Health benefits of ice-cold water be damned; I was about to run the risk of hypothermia in order to keep up this façade.

My first (hopeful) thought was that the lake might be frozen over, but judging from the clattering about and buoyant voices from beyond my door, the morning's plans hadn't changed. My stomach rumbled in protest when I remembered that this was a pre-breakfast activity.

I edged out into the hallway, still in my pyjamas, with the reluctant intention of finding Sophia and the promised swimwear. But I didn't need to go far. Hanging on the doorknob outside was a bright yellow bikini that looked like it had shrunk in the wash. In the middle of the spaghetti string ties, there were tiny bits of fabric, no bigger than a Toblerone triangle, that would barely cover a nipple. The bottoms were also string tied, G-string at the back with a marginally larger triangle at the front, but not by much. I held it up, thinking that this wouldn't look out of place in the Liaison Secrète range. And then I remembered it had been a very long time since I'd tended to my lady garden and bile rose in my throat. I hadn't brought a razor so the overall look was going to resemble a bearded man eating a tortilla chip.

Penn came down the corridor, dressed in a stripy dressing gown, and I quickly held the bikini behind my back. The fewer people party to my shame, the better – after all, this was going to eventually be concealed under a wetsuit.

'Morning,' he said. 'Did you sleep okay?'

'Mm. This morning's activity came as a bit of a surprise though.'

'Same for me.' He looked pained. 'I had no idea, I'm sorry. Did Soph give you something to wear?'

I nodded, my sweaty palm gripping the coat hanger more tightly. 'So, where are the wetsuits?'

'In the boathouse. Don't worry, there's a little room to change in. Just pop a dressing gown and a coat over your swimmers and I'll take you over.'

There then came a shout from downstairs. It sounded like Bertie. 'Come on, you two. Last one in's a mangy badger.'

I ducked back into the bedroom and wrestled on the offensive swimwear, tying the long straggly elastic strings at either side of my hips. I then pulled on the dressing gown that had been left for me on the back of the door, and finally added my thick coat and Chelsea boots. Penn and I hurried downstairs and out the back of the house, Penn grabbing a wax jacket on the way. I could see a large lake in the distance with a wooden hut on the shore. As we walked towards it, the frozen grass crunched under our feet.

'You owe me big time for this, Peregrine,' I said, already shivering.

'You never know – you might like it,' he said, grinning.

I just rolled my eyes.

Inside the boathouse, the family hovered expectantly, dressed in their wetsuits, wet shoes, gloves and swimming caps. All were there except for Sophia, and I wondered if she wasn't coming after all.

In the middle of the boathouse, flanked by two boarded walkways, was a channel of water where a small rowing boat and another with a petrol engine were tethered. To the rear of the hut was a door leading to a small storage room.

'This will warm the cockles,' said Hugh, rubbing his gloved hands together.

'It will when we're finally in and out,' said Bunny. 'Chop chop, you two.'

'Ladies first,' said Penn, gesturing towards the door, and I went inside, shutting it firmly behind me.

Inside was an array of boating paraphernalia, engine fuel and a selection of swimming outfits, lit up by harsh strip lighting overhead. I pulled on a swim cap then rummaged for a wetsuit of about my size, putting it to one side for the moment. I then squatted down to inspect a large wicker box of wet shoes and gloves, combing through it for something that would fit.

Suddenly, I heard Sophia's braying voice from the boathouse and murmurs of good morning from the others. A brief muffled conversation ensued, then her voice drifted closer to the store-room door.

'Perry, you naughty boy!' she purred from very nearby. 'But you're right – I'd be late to my own funeral.'

There were some cries of warning, and then suddenly the door was yanked fully open. In a panic, I leaped up, clutching some swim gloves to my scantily covered boobs. A split second later, I felt the firm tug of the string tie at my left hip being stretched to breaking point – it had caught in the weaving of the wicker basket. It pulled the knot loose and the elastic string pinged like a rubber band, the already indecent triangle of fabric flung to my right hip. My unkempt private area was fully on display to the assembled family outside for at least two seconds before I covered myself with one of the gloves, hence revealing a good proportion of my left boob.

I screamed and pulled the door closed, in the last moments seeing Penn's parents' horrified faces and Penn himself, both hands pressed to the lower half of his face, eyes wide.

Oh God. Ohgod, ohgod, ohgod.

I rested my forehead against the door, my heart thumping. Not only had my fake boyfriend seen more of me than he ever should, but I'd just done an impromptu striptease for Lord and Lady Ashcliffe.

'I'm so sorry,' came Sophia's voice from the other side. 'I thought I'd lost one of my swim gloves and came looking for another one. But it's just here, on the floor. Oopsie!'

'No worries!' I trilled. 'It's fine!' I'd never felt so British in my attempt to console a person who'd shamed me, and shamed me hard.

'We'll just be on the shore, m'dear,' came Hugh's traumatised voice. 'Meet you out there.'

It took me a solid ten minutes of dragging on wet gear and giving myself a pep talk before I slunk out of the boathouse and down to the shore. I couldn't even look at Penn.

Bunny smiled at me coldly, and Hugh coughed and looked anywhere but in my direction. Penn came over and put an arm around me, and for a moment I felt a rush of vulnerability. I looked up at him gratefully, realising that for the first time, in this place, he was the closest thing I had to a friend. His eyes flickered with an indecipherable expression – a beat of solidarity? Then I glanced away to see Sophia's nostrils flaring. She quickly rearranged her features then pouted and made her fingers into a heart shape at her chest.

'Sorry,' she mouthed.

Penn went to get changed, then we were off. Bertie and Penn were the first to step into the shallows, moving quickly and determinedly and making manly, gritty noises. Sophia bounded in next, squeaking coquettishly. Then Hugh took Bunny by the hand, and they followed on.

'Come on, Annie,' yelled Bertie, who was now shoulder deep and shivering. 'The quicker we get going, the quicker we'll warm up.'

There was nothing for it. I either got in or I'd be responsible for two generations of English gentry succumbing to hypothermia (although in my current mood, that mightn't have been a terrible thing). I speed-walked into the water, my breath freezing in my lungs as I waded out to chest height. It was like walking into a frozen margarita, if the margarita was sludge grey and had leaves floating in it. Screwing my eyes shut, I dropped my shoulders under the surface and pushed off into a glide. I swam in the direction of the group, seeing that Penn had hung back, treading water to wait for me.

'You're doing fine,' he said, his teeth gritted together from the cold.

'Really?' I gasped. 'Because swimming in ice-cold water wasn't on the itinerary I expected.'

'Not just this. Everything.'

We paddled along beside each other, trying to keep pace with the seasoned strokes of the family ahead.

'I don't think I'm doing okay at all. Your mam clearly hates me, and she and Sophia seem thick as thieves.'

Penn nodded stiffly. 'I know. But we've got to put on a good show. The more we can convince them that we're in love, and you aren't going anywhere, the sooner they'll get the message.'

'And you think... this one weekend... is going to solve... all of your... problems?' I had to keep stopping every few words to deal with the cold taking my breath away.

'Not all of them. But one of the biggest ones. I don't want to get married to Sophia.'

'The... man's not for taming?'

He swam on, saying nothing for a moment.

'The man's not for settling.'

Then he ploughed on, forcing me to redouble my efforts to keep up.

Back in the house an hour later, after a hot shower and wrapping myself in a dry dressing gown and fluffy socks, I had to admit that the wild swim had felt good. After the initial sting of cold, the strenuous swimming had got my blood pumping and the heat building in my body. Then, after the hot shower made my skin tingle all over again, I'd felt a rush of endorphins normally reserved for my sensual product range.

I texted Olivia to ask how everything was going.

We're three vibrators and a mini-chopper down already! she replied, swiftly followed by: *Mini-chopper as in kitchenware, not a new Liaison product.* She signed off with winky face and aubergine emojis.

Fab, I typed. *Thanks for holding the fort.*

That's okay! Hope the convention is going alright.

I sent her a thumbs up and lay back on my pillow. The smell of fried eggs drifted up the stairs. I pulled on some clothes, wondering if I'd be expected to use a special egg knife from the selection of cutlery at the breakfast table, or if I'd embarrass myself yet again by using a regular one.

NINETEEN

Later that day, I took refuge in the library after asking Bunny if
there was anything I could do to help with the preparations for
the ball. She'd looked at me as if I was insane.

'Of course not, dear,' she'd said in a patient tone. 'We have
people for that.'

I'd smiled and backed off, then watched as vans pulled up,
spilling out event planners with clipboards, people lugging
poles, banners and all sorts of decorative items, followed by
caterers with huge trays and tureens. As I observed them
through the window, I'd been struck by the notion that if I
hadn't been here as a visitor, I would likely be classed as one of
the 'people' Bunny had referred to.

Now, sitting in the quiet of the library, I was glad of the
reprieve. I was completely alone, since Penn had been whisked
off after breakfast to collect a new dinner jacket from the family's preferred tailor. I thumbed through a copy of *Lady Chatterley's Lover*, feeling a kinship with Oliver Mellors, the
gamekeeper. Then I came to the part when he ravishes Lady
Chatterley in the woods of her country estate, and an image of

Penn and I doing the same flashed into my mind. Heat flooded into my cheeks and, surprisingly, between my thighs, and I squeezed my eyes closed, willing the thought away. Just because we were pretend lovers didn't mean I ought to put in overtime in my imagination.

'Darling,' came a smooth, husky voice from the doorway, making me jump. Sophia stood there in a pair of khaki chinos and a navy sweater that draped just nicely on her statuesque frame. 'I hoped I'd find you here.'

'Oh. Yes, I'm just entertaining myself while things are quiet,' I said, waving the book, trying to steady my voice.

'One of my favourites,' she said, coming to sit on the armchair beside mine. 'Every schoolgirl's dream, being ravished by the gamekeeper. At least at my school anyway. Not a boy in sight until I went to university, and then I was like a woman possessed.'

I raised an eyebrow.

'I wasn't a complete trollop,' she clarified with good humour. 'But I made up for lost time.'

'Right.' I searched for something to say. 'So. Um, did you and Perry meet at university?' I remembered at the last minute to use the name she would expect.

'God, no. Mummy and Daddy have known Hugh and Buns forever. Perry and I used to chase each other around the gardens with the hosepipe in summer and torture our older siblings. No, we had a little teenage thing, and then we got together properly in our early twenties.' She suddenly placed a hand on mine. 'But you mustn't think I have any issue with you, Annie. Far from it; Perry and I are *completely* over.'

Her eyes bored into me intensely. They were a little steely, and despite her protestations, there was a definite undertone of ownership over Penn. Tales of a history that I was supposed to hear loud and clear.

'Anyway,' she said more breezily. 'I just wanted to apologise for this morning. I feel like an absolute dunce, opening the door on you like that.'

I blushed, wishing she hadn't brought it up again. 'It's fine – don't worry about it.'

'You are *such* a brick. And you should be way more cross with me. I mean, the string coming loose, your... *area* on display. You must be mortified.'

I mustered a stiff smile. 'Really, it's okay. It isn't the most embarrassing thing to ever happen to me.' *No, that would be liking a historic photo of you and your ex-boyfriend on Instagram.*

'Oh, bless your heart,' she said, patting my hand again. 'Now, I just wanted to say, I can give you the details of the woman who does my Brazilian. She's really very good, even with more challenging cases.'

I opened my mouth to politely decline when the door swung open again. It was Penn, holding a swanky-looking suit bag over his arm.

'Am I interrupting?' he asked, hovering in the doorway.

'Not at all,' said Sophia, beckoning him in. 'Annie and I were just having a little girls' chat.' She nudged my arm in a chummy way.

Penn shot me a discreet look that said, 'Really?' and I gave a subtle shrug in return. He hung the suit bag by its hanger on one of the bookshelves and took a seat on the small sofa opposite the pair of us.

'I was telling lovely Annie about the perils of boarding school. Rampant teens all cooped up together. Hormones going off like a hunting horn.'

'Yeah,' agreed Penn. 'A boys-only school when you're a girl-obsessed sixteen-year-old is pretty frustrating.'

'Of course, it must have been easier for you, going to a state school,' said Sophia to me. 'I mean, you must have been beating off boys with a stick. Being so... pretty. She's very pretty, Perry. Isn't she?'

'Uh-huh,' he replied, looking suddenly wrong-footed.

'Come on – you can do better than that,' baited Sophia, her voice dripping with charm. 'She's your girlfriend after all.'

'She is. And *in private* I tell her all the time.' He looked at me and hesitated, his eyes holding mine. 'She's beautiful.'

I stared at him for a second then broke his gaze. I felt an unexpected flutter under my breastbone, but I breathed it away. That steamy passage from *Lady Chatterley's Lover* had done a number on me, and I needed to stay focused on the con.

'Awww,' Sophia said, cocking her head to one side. 'You two are adorable. Right, I'll leave you both to it. Oh, and Hugh asked me to tell you both, it's Silly Sunday tomorrow, so make sure you don't get too squiffed tonight in case one of you is doing the driving.'

She swept out, and we waited until the door was closed before looking at each other. We both exhaled deeply.

'It's going okay, I think. Well done on the whole "she's beautiful" schtick,' I said. 'Top marks for that.'

He paused, his eyes roving over my face, and for a moment, his gaze softened. But almost as quickly, he was all business again. 'We've got to do what we've got to do.'

'Right. And what the hell is Silly Sunday?'

He groaned. 'It's this tradition. We sometimes do it the day after these kind of events – family and close friends. It's a sort of treasure hunt by car. Following clues and seeing who gets back first.'

'Well... that actually sounds quite fun.'

'It's okay. Everyone gets very competitive though. And the winner gets to keep the trophy until the next one. It's our grandad's old welly boot with every winner's name on in biro.'

'Sounds *lovely*.'

'It's weird, I know. But it's tradition, like I said.'

It *was* weird. And it made any prizes I'd won in the past, like gift vouchers or booze hampers, seem very gauche. I was reminded of the Royal Family's custom of exchanging joke presents at Christmas, because after all, what do you get for someone else who has everything they need? I looked around the wood-panelled room, with its silk curtains and rows of anti-quated books, and then laid eyes on Penn, who was wearing chinos similar to Sophia's and a rugby shirt.

'Why do you wear that stuff?' I asked quietly. 'I mean, it's the complete opposite to what you wear in Newcastle. Which one is the real you?'

'They're both the real me,' he said, shifting uncomfortably. 'Well, sort of. I guess the city clothes are more the real me. But here... these clothes are easier.'

'Because it helps you fit in?'

He looked at me sharply. 'No. I don't fit in anyway. This place is a round hole and I'm very much the square peg. But wearing this stuff causes less of a fuss.'

I nodded, saying nothing for a moment. 'I just never imag-ined. You're so... *particular* about your image at work. It's come as a bit of a shock to see how easily you leave it behind.'

He stood up. 'Is that what you think of me? First I'm arro-gant, and then I'm a pushover?'

'No. I... I didn't mean... I'm just trying to understand.'

His jaw tensed, and he seemed to be internally counting to ten. When he finally spoke, his tone was quiet but brittle. 'You know, Annie, I could tell you a thing or two about yourself, since you appear to think you know it all. You seem to take great pleasure in baiting me, here and in the shop. You make a perfor-mance of being "humble" as if it somehow makes you a better person than me.' He paused, breathing heavily, then continued with added frustration. 'And while you look like butter wouldn't melt, you're out there selling fucking sex toys! Talk about having a split personality.'

He took a breath to continue but then stopped, his outburst collapsing into weariness. 'Let's just get this weekend over with and go back to our own sides of the shop on Tuesday. I'll see you tonight.' He yanked the door open and went out.

I got up and tore after him into the hallway.

'Where do you get off with the character assassination? I was asking genuine questions, and you've just reeled off insult after insult. Don't forget, I'm here doing you a favour.'

He wheeled around, his face like thunder. 'You can't say you don't have an opinion about me. Whether it's veiled or not, you're still insulting *me*. My life isn't as charmed as you think it is.'

I snorted. 'I see. The poor little rich boy, complaining about his diamond Doc Martens being too tight? You have no idea what the real world is like.'

He ran a hand down his face. 'You're unbelievable. Annie, I mean it. Let's get tonight over with and go our separate ways.'

'Fine by me.' I crossed my arms, trying to control the tremble in them, and stared him down.

Just then, there were footsteps and someone came around the corner. It was Gus, the gamekeeper, wearing a checked shirt and moss-green trousers. His eyes flickered with interest, and I wondered how much he'd heard.

I hastily stepped to Penn's side and linked arms with him. Then, as if I'd had a bucket of cold water thrown over me, I remembered that Gus would know exactly who I was after our conversation after the protest. From the sudden tightening of Penn's grip, I assumed he'd reached the same realisation.

'Annie?' he asked, narrowing his eyes as he walked towards us. 'What are you doing here?' His eyes scanned us both, falling finally on our entwined arms. He blinked in surprise.

'Oh. I... I'm here with Penn. I mean Perry.'

Gus's face creased with confusion, but he recovered. 'I can see that. I thought you two just knew each other in passing.'

'Oh, we did,' Penn said. 'But after getting to know each other better, what can I say? Sparks flew.'

'Ah. That explains why you never called me,' he said to me, grinning. His eyes twinkled like I remembered – the cheerful antithesis to Penn's brooding nature. I remembered Penn chasing him off in the pub and felt a flicker of indignation.

'That's right,' I said. 'Sorry about that, but once Perry and I spent more time together, we just... knew.'

He looked at us for a long moment, a fixed smile on his face. His expression looked like he was trying to figure something out. I wondered how he'd interpreted the overheard row.

'Ha,' he breathed. 'Well, I'm happy for you. But I'm surprised. With your feelings about shooting, I thought you wouldn't give Perry the time of day.'

'Mmhm,' I murmured, floundering. I didn't know if Gus knew about Penn's secret stance on their country pursuits. 'Er...'

'We've come to an arrangement,' Penn swooped in. 'Annie's a vegetarian, so we agreed if I go veggie too, then the books will balance. Anyway, babe, I need to catch Bertie before he goes to the airport for Catherine and the boys. I'll see you in a bit. Catch you later, Gus,' he said, giving me a dry kiss on the cheek and disappearing down the corridor.

Gus watched him go then turned back to me, shaking his head in amusement.

'You and Perry. Interesting.'

'Yes.' I cleared my throat. 'Listen, Gus. Perry's parents don't remember me from the protest, and I'd prefer it to stay that way. I think it would only upset them.'

'Of course, of course,' he said. 'Your secret's safe with me.'

'Thanks,' I said. 'So, will you be at the ball tonight?'

'I will. Lord and Lady Ashcliffe have been decent enough to ask me along. So I'll see you there.'

'Great. Bye for now then.' I smiled and headed down the hall.

'Oh, Annie,' called Gus from behind me. I looked back. 'You needn't worry about Perry shooting pheasants anyway. He's terrible at it. Always bloody misses.' He chuckled and raised a hand as he walked in the other direction.

I made my way back to my bedroom, meandering through the many corridors and staircases, silently fuming. Who did Penn think he was, accusing me of performative poverty? I was reminded of that Pulp song, 'Common People'. If his business failed, then Mummy and Daddy would be able to bail him out with ease. His shop was a plaything, whereas mine was the last frontier before financial annihilation.

I'd spoken to Dad that morning, and he'd asked cheerful questions about the imaginary convention I was at. I'd provided vague answers, feeling guilty about the deception, while noticing that his happiness seemed a little forced. It was gradually breaking my heart, the memory of that mortgage letter and the knowledge that our home was slipping through their fingers as each day passed. When I got back to the shop, I'd find a way to step up my game. I wouldn't— no, I *couldn't* let them lose the house.

I entered my room and stopped in surprise. Bunny was sitting on the edge of my bed, her legs crossed.

'Hi,' I said, straightening my face.

'Hello, dear. I hope you don't mind. I just popped in to check you have everything you need.'

'Yes, thank you.' I recalled the little soaps in the en suite, wrapped in thick paper, and the soft, sweet-smelling towels. 'You really have thought of everything.'

'Marvellous. Although that's not quite what I meant. Do

you have everything you need for *tonight*?' Her smile was patient yet cold.

'I think so. I've brought some dresses, shoes, a bag.' Inside the wardrobe were three options to choose from: one from Monsoon, another from Coast and, lastly, a ten-year-old custom-made dress from Kelly's leavers' prom that happened to fit me. I'd brought them all since I couldn't decide which was best at the time, and I'd hoped to get some flash of inspiration from just being in Ashcliffe Hall. But last night's fashion disaster had left me in serious doubt of my own judgement.

'I'd like to help you assemble the outfit,' said Bunny. 'If you'll indulge me. Having two boys gave me little opportunity.'

'Oh. Okay. Thanks, Bunny.'

Without further invitation, Bunny went to the wardrobe and opened it, swiftly removing the three garments. She laid each one on the bed and stepped back, surveying them. Then she approached the bed again and picked at the fabrics, which in the cold light of day looked cheap and garish compared to even Bunny's casual outfit of navy slacks and a crisp white blouse.

'I'm afraid this one won't do,' she said, picking up the one from Coast – a black slip dress, ruched at the side, the satin looking shinier and more plasticky than I remembered. She put it back in the wardrobe.

'And this...' She regarded the Monsoon dress; a baby pink fifties-style gown, with a flared skirt and halterneck. 'It's a little out of season.'

On reflection, she was right. What was I thinking wearing light pink this close to Christmas? This was also returned to the closet, before she surveyed the prom frock.

'I suppose this will have to be the one.' She held it up and fiddled with the fabric. It was a warm ruby-red, floor length, off-the-shoulder number, with a trail of sequins from left breast to right hip. Up the sides of the bodice were several cut-out slashes where skin would be seen. Bunny grimaced at these, and I did too. Kelly had convinced me they were fashionable, but it was clear to me now that they weren't *elegant*.

She flopped it over her arm. 'Leave it with me. My seamstress is here this afternoon, so I'll ask her to take a look at it. Smarten it up a bit.'

'Well. Thanks,' I said, flustered. 'But you really don't have to.'

'I think I do,' she replied with a prim smile, her claw-like fingers gripping the material.

Message received.

She made for the door but paused. Turning back to me, her eyes flicked briefly up and down my frame before she looked me dead in the eye. 'It's been really very nice to meet you, Annie. We don't often meet friends of his from the city, so it's quite the novelty. Of course, when he comes back home for good, I'm sure he'll keep in touch.'

Then she dusted some invisible lint off my dress, straightened her back and left.

I flumped down on the bedspread. *What a bitch.* If I'd really been here as Penn's actual girlfriend, I would have been crushed. Whoever Bunny thought I was, I was of no consequence to her, no threat to her precious family and heirs. I'd been firmly put in my place, make no mistake.

I pulled my knees up to my chest, seething at how snooty she'd been about my clothes, handling them as if she'd pulled them out of a dumpster rather than a Louis XVI wardrobe. Who did she think she was, making me feel like I would embarrass myself wearing what I'd brought? Like I wouldn't be *in keeping*. And why had I just... succumbed to her will? I normally had much more backbone, but she'd manipulated me so deftly I'd barely noticed until she was halfway out of the room.

Then the penny dropped. I thought about Penn and his

country casual chinos and gilets. How he'd insisted that he only wore them to make his own life easier, at which I'd practically laughed in his face. Well, who was laughing now?

An uneasy feeling rumbled in my guts. If Bunny could cow me into submission in one day, then how must Penn feel after twenty-nine years?

TWENTY

In the early evening, I stood under the shower, scrubbing my skin pink and washing my hair. I gathered it up in a soapy pile on top of my head, massaging the bubbles while thinking what Kelly would say when she saw her dress had been altered. I was now feeling very guilty about allowing Bunny to waltz off with a dress which wasn't even mine.

I got out, towel-dried my hair and wrapped myself in a fresh white robe – which had been provided to replace the one covered in lake juices and leaves. Standing in front of the mirror, I gave myself a stern look.

'You can do this. You are a strong, confident woman. You've had a French manicure, you have Christa's curling tongs with you and your make-up skills are surprisingly good for a beauty heathen.'

When I went back to the bedroom, I saw that the dress had been returned and was hanging from a hook on the door. My breath caught in my throat as I walked up and touched it. The open panels had been filled with a sheer material, the sequins had been removed and the folds of fabric on the bodice had been overlaid with a spray of the same sheer crimson fabric, making a semi-circle of tulle above the neckline. It looked like something from a catwalk; a work of art that I never would have pictured myself wearing.

After I'd blow-dried my hair to perfection and applied my make-up – smoky eyes and a neutral lipstick – I slipped on the dress and stood in front of the full-length mirror. I almost didn't recognise myself. I looked like Gisele Bündchen in a fairground mirror, which was good enough for me. I would take that and run. Hearing the noise building from downstairs, I took a deep breath and headed out.

I reached the top of the stairs and paused, steeling myself to join the throng below. I would have to throw everything I had into convincing Penn's family that our relationship was real. I would need to put our spat that afternoon to one side for now. After my encounter with Bunny, I had a renewed sense of indignation on Penn's behalf, as well as the need to recover my own dignity. She wasn't going to get the better of either of us.

Just then, Penn appeared at the bottom of the stairs, dressed in a black dinner suit and bow tie. His hair looked glossier and sat in waves near his shoulders. He looked up and stopped dead, his eyes meeting mine. A stunned expression crossed his face, and I presumed it was because he didn't think I would scrub up too well.

'Evening, darling,' I said in a mock fancy voice when I reached the bottom.

He said nothing for a moment, his eyes roaming my upgraded face, his lips slightly parted. Then he blinked and said, 'Evening. You look nice.' He offered me his arm, and we walked into the crowd.

I was introduced to so many people, I couldn't possibly keep up. There were members of Penn's extended family, local digni- taries, mayors, business owners and property investors. I made the brief acquaintance of Penn's sister-in-law, Catherine, as well as her two little boys on their way up to bed, narrowly avoiding being covered in the contents of their mugs of hot chocolate as they jumped about. Bunny passed by and gave me a brief, approving nod when she saw how her sartorial plans had turned out.

Penn never left my side, eager as he was to make sure there were enough eyes on us to cement our deception. We wandered from room to room, every one decorated with tasteful Christmas decorations, the cinnamon scent of mulled wine drifting through the air.

We came across Gus, who did a double take when he saw me.

'You look amazing,' he said into my ear, while Penn was engaged in conversation with someone from a previous shoot day. 'Really pretty.'

I blushed and thanked him, not sure what to do with myself. I thought back to his phone number on the beer mat back at home and wondered if, after all this, I should make use of it. He looked handsome in his dinner jacket and tartan kilt, his auburn beard neatly clipped.

Just then, Sophia slunk through the bevy of guests and put a hand on my shoulder.

'Swit swoo!' she exclaimed. 'Good God, Annie, you look an absolute dream. Bunny told me she'd gussied you up a bit, but I wasn't expecting *this*.'

'Thank you,' I said. 'You look lovely too.'

She really did. Her dress was an emerald green velvet, long-sleeved with a deep V-neck, where a diamond necklace nestled into her peachy décolletage. Her blonde hair was swept up in a chignon, emphasising her graceful neck.

'Oh, this old thing,' she said, smoothing down the fabric. 'It's *so* last year, but I just didn't have time to shop for something new. Disgusting of me really. But, honestly, Annie, you look absolutely *gorgeous*. That red dress – it reminds me of that dress that Julia Roberts wore in *Pretty Woman*. Not that I'm implying you're dressed like a sex worker, of course.' She stood back and appraised me once more. 'No. It's very chic.'

Another woman came over and took Sophia's arm, so she made her excuses and left me. The mere mention of the phrase sex worker in her running down of my outfit made me feel suddenly very self-conscious, and I wrapped one arm across my middle while slugging a healthy dose of champagne with my free hand.

Then Hugh barrelled over with another man in tow, making a beeline for Penn.

'Perry, old chap,' said Hugh, gregarious with fine wine and festivity. 'You remember Nathaniel Jackson?' Nathaniel, a man who looked to be in his late forties, with salt-and-pepper hair and an easy smile, shook Penn's hand and gave me a polite nod.

'I do. Nice to see you again,' said Penn smoothly. He was clearly practiced with schmoozing. 'How are Harriet and the kids?'

'Oh, doing well. Laurie's going up to Oxford next year, and Jen started at the Royal Ballet School in September.'

'Perry,' interjected Hugh, 'I thought you might like to know that we've become patrons of Nathaniel's newest venture. What with your music hobby.'

'Yes, your parents have very kindly made a rather substantial donation to my project, Northern Creatives. Bringing the arts to rural Northumberland. We're sourcing funds for galleries, educational facilities, a music centre.'

'Wow. That sounds great,' said Penn.

'It's going *very* well. The plan is to bring opportunities that you'd normally find in a big city out into the rural hubs,' Nathaniel said.

'A very worthy endeavour,' said Hugh, directed at Penn, before turning to Nathaniel. 'Did you know our Perry has been doing a project of his own in Newcastle? A record stall in a little market.'

'It's a pop-up shop,' said Penn, bristling. 'Not a market stall.'

'Of course, of course,' soothed Hugh. 'My mistake.'

Nathaniel smiled politely. 'Well, I must make a point of dropping in on you when I'm in town.' Then Hugh took him off to mingle some more.

The evening wore on, and Penn continued to grip me to his side as a constant beacon, signalling that he was in a committed relationship. The only break we had from each other was at the buffet table, when I needed to cut loose for the vegetarian dishes at the opposite end to the mini beef and horseradish Yorkshire puddings that he was hungry for. When I reminded him he was now meant to be a fellow vegetarian, he threw the remains onto an empty tray nearby.

Eventually, after hobnobbing with what seemed like half the population of Northumberland, we arrived at Ashcliffe Hall's palatial ballroom. It was high-ceilinged with a huge chandelier, parquet flooring underfoot and heavy embroidered curtains swathed across the tall windows. All of Penn's family were there, either dancing to the swing band, who were assembled in the corner of the vast room, or mingling at the edges, holding champagne flutes.

'I think we need to take this to the next level,' he murmured, steering me onto the dance floor and checking that his family knew we were there. He placed his hand at the small of my back, gently guiding me towards him. My stomach and chest met his with a small bump, making me stagger a little. His hand stiffened at the base of my spine, steadying me.

'Thanks,' I whispered. 'It's a while since I wore heels.'

'No problem. Just follow my lead.'

He moved effortlessly, tracing across the floor with simple yet confident steps, making it easy for me to be drawn along with him. It wasn't such a traditional set of movements as a waltz or a quickstep, more of a loose swaying and gliding, keeping me close throughout.

'You've done this before,' I said.

'Ballroom lessons at school. Against my will, but it kind of stuck.'

'I learn something new about you every day. How did I not know you could give Bruno Tonioli a run for his money?'

He rolled his eyes.

'Maybe it's because you're such a music buff. Rhythm just flows in your veins,' I teased. 'Or maybe you're just one of those people who are good at everything. That's why you're so... self-assured.'

'By that, I presume you're having a dig again? Reminding me that you think I'm an arrogant arsehole.'

I said nothing, glancing around the room. Bunny and Sophia were standing together, watching us intently.

'You could at least try and give me a break,' he said, and he sounded slightly wounded. 'Just while we're here. If we're giving off tense vibes, then it might not be easy to hide.'

I sighed. 'I know.'

'Can... can you just... hold me a bit closer? I feel like I'm dancing with a robot.'

'I'll try.' I shook my shoulders to ease my taut muscles and tried to relax into his arms. My chest fell closer to his, and I spread my palm across his back. He smelled of mint and a woody aftershave – I breathed it in and felt light-headed, a little weak at the nearness of him.

His arms gripped me a little tighter, his jaw grazing my hair. I could feel his breath on my bare shoulder. It sounded stilted, which was unsurprising; he must have been making as much effort as me to appear composed. The music switched to a slower number, and we swayed at a gentler pace.

'Are they still looking?' he asked.

'Yeah. In fact, I feel like I've got a sniper laser hovering on my forehead.'

'Okay. Listen, we've got to make this loud and clear to them. Like... what most couples would do when a slow song comes on.'

'Right.'

'I'm going to have to kiss you. Is that okay?'

'Uh-huh.' My pulse ticked up a notch. I hadn't been expecting this, although in this moment, it made complete sense.

'I'm sorry in advance. But it's now or never.'

'Okay. Go for it. I'm braced and ready.'

He pulled back slightly, so he could look into my eyes – a note of panic flashed in his, but he covered it immediately. Then he ran his hand up my arm, skirted my neck and lifted my chin. Slowly, with an intensity that could have won him a place at drama school, he bent towards me and pressed his lips to mine.

I could hardly breathe. This felt so weird. Weirder than my first kiss with Spotty Kev at school, when our braces mashed together. I tried to keep my eyes closed without squeezing them too tight.

But then Penn's lips moved gently, grazing mine, catching my upper lip softly between his. His tongue brushed against it, then he kissed me more deeply; this time our tongues met, and I started to respond, like a reflex. It must have only lasted for five seconds, but when he pulled away from me, it felt like I'd been underwater and had come up for air. For a moment, it seemed the band had stopped playing and the lights had dimmed – in my dumbstruck mind, it felt like the room had faded away and we were standing in a single spotlight.

He looked at me for a long while, and then we resumed dancing. I laid my head on his shoulder uncomfortably. My heart was pounding. This whole thing felt like it was getting out of hand. Jollying along with his family was one thing, but now I had to perform in a physical sense I was starting to feel like it was becoming too much. My shoulders tightened again, and I pulled away, just enough to look up at him.

'Nobody said anything about tongues,' I joked, trying to break the tension.

He shrugged. 'It needed to look authentic.'

I swallowed dryly. *It had felt authentic.* 'I need a break, if that's okay. I'm going for a bit of fresh air.'

He let me go, and I made my way out of the ballroom, feeling like I could breathe again. I pushed through the shoals of guests, allowing the physical distance between me and Penn to break the spell of that kiss. Like Penn said, the authenticity was purely a pretence, and every step cleared my mind enough to remind myself of that.

Walking outside onto the terrace, I took a lungful of country air, which was lightly laced with tobacco smoke. I looked across to see Gus sitting on a low wall, stubbing out a cigarette on a nearby ashtray.

I went over. 'Room for a little one?' I asked.

He looked up in surprise then patted the wall beside him. 'Annie, it's five degrees out here – you'll freeze.' Before I could protest, he took off his dinner jacket and put it over my shoulders.

'Thanks,' I said, genuinely grateful. Those sheer panels did, after all, let in the cold air.

'Needed a break too?' he asked, his faintly Scottish accent coming through.

'Yeah. It's... intense in there.'

He nodded. 'Especially if it's your first time.'

Somehow, when Gus reminded me that I was a fish out of water, it didn't seem like such a criticism. It came across like he understood how I felt.

'I've been there myself,' he continued. 'I'm originally from a little village near Jedburgh, where there's nothing much but sheep and their shit. I was raised on a farm, but my dad got to know Lord Ashcliffe from the country shows, and he introduced me to some of the lads from the estate. And the rest, as they say, is history.' He smiled in a self-effacing way. 'How about you? What's your story?'

'Oh, nothing flash. Brought up in a Newcastle suburb, comprehensive school, then a succession of not very highbrow jobs. I'm working in the same place as Penn now. Sorry... *Perry*.'

'Oh yeah? And you don't need to correct yourself. I know he goes by his cooler alter ego when he's not here. So what kind of thing do you sell in your shop?'

'Just odds and ends. Homewares, books, cosmetics.' Then, feeling buoyed up by the fresh air and escape, I had a sudden burst of devil-may-care abandon. 'And I'm doing a roaring trade in a line of sex toys.'

Gus let out a burst of laughter. 'Bloody hell! I wasn't expecting that. And you look so innocent.' He looked at me as if he was trying to figure me out.

I shrugged. 'Sex sells.'

'I bet it does.' I thought I could hear a tinge of flirtiness to his tone. 'So, do you have a favourite product?'

I laughed. 'That would be telling.'

He grinned, and I held his gaze for a moment. It was so refreshing just to have a laugh with someone – someone who wasn't constantly judging me or asking something of me. For the first time that weekend, I felt something approaching my normal self. We sat for a bit, looking out at the dark, velvet night, until I felt the creep of cold chilling me, despite Gus's jacket. I pulled it tighter around me, and when he noticed, he moved up the wall to sit closer.

'Fancy Perry letting you come and freeze out here,' he said. 'Where is he anyway?'

'I'm not sure,' I answered honestly.

'He's a fool,' Gus said, looking into the middle distance, pausing for a moment. 'I couldn't help overhearing earlier...'

'Oh, that. That was nothing.' My shoulders tensed, and this time it was nothing to do with the cold. Was I about to find out our cover had been blown?

'It didn't sound like nothing,' he said softly. 'I could gather what was going on. You've broken up, haven't you? He said you should just ride out the weekend and go your separate ways.'

'That wasn't quite...' I began to protest, but he carried on, putting a hand over mine. It felt callused and work-worn, a departure from Penn's smoother palm.

'You don't have to keep up a pretence with me,' he said. 'This family... they're all about appearances. But people like you and me, we're *real*. We shouldn't have to carry the burden for them.'

'I don't...'

'Shh.' He put a finger to my lips and moved closer. 'He isn't worth it. You know, he doesn't have respect for you. You said he was going vegetarian to support you, right? Well I saw him eating meat barely an hour ago. So much for solidarity.'

I blinked at him, not sure what to say. But then, before I could come up with anything, he lunged forward and kissed me, his big hands pulling me towards him. His mouth tasted like cigarettes and booze. Stunned, I froze for a moment before grabbing his arms and pushing him off me.

'Come on, Annie. People like us need to stick together.' His eyes grew dark, and he groaned. 'God, you're so sexy.' He pulled at my waist, going in for another kiss, and I wrenched myself away from him, turning my head away and squeezing my eyes shut. And then he was gone, and fresh, cold air rushed into my open palms.

Opening my eyes, I saw Penn pinning Gus down on the flagstones, Gus's shirt scrunched up in one hand, Penn's other fist drawn back, ready to land a punch.

I leaped up. 'No!' I screamed. 'Leave him, Penn. Don't do it.'

Penn hesitated, breathing heavily, then stood, dragging Gus up by the collar. He leaned his face in to Gus's until they were almost nose to nose.

'If you ever... if you *ever* so much as look at her again, I swear to God I will tear you to fucking pieces.' Penn's voice was ragged and reedy as his jaw was clenched so tight. He let go of Gus's collar and shoved him. Gus staggered backwards, and it was only then that I gathered how drunk he was. He ran a hand down his face and looked at me, a mocking smile spreading across his lips.

'You're welcome to her, mate. She's a fucking prick-tease.'

Penn lunged at him again, but I grabbed his arm, holding him back. Gus just laughed and held up his palms before stumbling inside the building.

We stood there, panting, Penn with his hands on his hips. He noticed I was still wearing Gus's dinner jacket, and he took it off me, balled it up and volleyed it into the garden beyond. It disappeared into the darkness.

Shoving a hand into his hair, he paced away from me, his back turned. His shoulders flexed through his jacket and he gave a muted yell. 'Fuck!' Whipping round, he strode towards me again. 'Fuck, Annie, didn't I tell you he was bad news? In the pub?' He shook his head in frustration. 'This is exactly what I meant.'

'I... I...' I faltered, a memory of him saying that Gus wasn't for me, that I would thank him later. I'd thought he was telling me that I wasn't posh enough for people from his estate. Now I realised it had been a warning of a different kind. 'I'm sorry... I didn't understand.'

'Don't say sorry. The man's got a reputation worse than Donald Trump when it comes to grabbing women by the...' He stopped and groaned. 'It's my fault. I should have explained better.'

He seemed torn between contrition and frustration, but despite that, I was now starting to feel foolish. I bristled and wrapped my arms around myself. 'You don't have to labour the point. I get it, he's trouble. Let's just leave it and get back to our performance.'

'I'm just looking out for you. I can't expect you to know how it is around here.'

My nostrils flared, embarrassment morphing into indignation. 'Here we go again. Poor little Annie and her proletarian ways. How could she *possibly* know how to handle herself in polite society?'

'You know that's not what I meant,' he said with bald irritation.

'I don't need you to always be the hero,' I snapped, remembering how he'd scared Neil off too, back in the shop. 'I can take care of myself.'

Scowling at him, I turned on my heel, but before I could take two steps, he called out.

'Annie, wait.'

I whirled round. 'What is it? What else do you need to explain to me?'

He stared at me, breathing heavily. Then the blaze in his eyes seemed to be snuffed out by the look on my face. A little part of me knew I was digging my heels in, pushing back at him out of mortification, but I couldn't seem to let go. As I waited to hear him snap back at me, the moment was filled by only a stilted silence, and eventually he looked at the ground.

'Nothing. It's nothing. I'm sorry,' he said defeatedly. Then, without looking at me, he walked back into the house.

TWENTY-ONE

Sunday dawned with a deep blanket of snow. I'd had a restless night, befuddled by champagne and confusion; after Penn had stalked away, I hadn't seen him for the rest of the night. When I asked Sophia where he was, she told me he'd complained of a headache and gone up early to bed. I strongly suspected the headache in question was me.

I decided not to go to breakfast, and instead stayed under the covers, eating a bag of Quavers that I'd found in the depths of my handbag. I stared out the window, sprinkling the mangled crisp crumbs into my mouth.

What had happened last night? The reaction I'd had to Penn defending me started to seem excessive in the cold light of day. While I still believed I could have handled it myself, I remembered the intense way he'd looked at me before I'd stared him down, and how I'd never know what he'd wanted to say when he called me back. And a memory kept swimming back into my mind, one which should have been an unpleasant reminder of Gus. But when I thought back to Penn tearing Gus's jacket from my body, all I could picture was the sensation of being undressed by him. Unexpected fantasies that merged the kiss we'd had in the ballroom with the idea of him taking off the jacket then slipping the straps of my dress from my shoulders... I couldn't stop thinking about him.

Later in the morning, there was a soft tap at the door.

'Annie?' It was Bertie.

I sat up abruptly, Quaver bits scattering down my chest.

'Yes?' I replied, my voice gravelly.

'Are you coming to Silly Sunday? It's just we'll be off in half an hour and nobody's seen you.'

Was I going? Or did I just want to hide in here until it was time to go home? Sadly, I had no more ancient foodstuffs in my bag, and I did have a purpose here after all. No matter what had happened the previous night, I wasn't one to welch on a deal. And I hoped there would be lunch.

'Yeah,' I shouted. 'I'll be along as soon as I can.'

'Righto. See you out front.' Footsteps padded away down the corridor.

After a super-quick shower, I dressed in warm clothes and headed downstairs. The whole party was assembled on the snowy courtyard, where several vehicles were waiting, engines rumbling. Penn's entire family appeared to be taking part, as well as Sophia and some of last night's guests. Thankfully, Gus was nowhere in sight.

Penn was standing by one of the Defenders, an envelope in hand, just like some of the other participants. The sight of him caused ripples in my stomach that were definitely not because I'd skipped breakfast. He gave me a nod and then focused on Hugh, who'd called for everyone's attention.

'Listen in, listen in!' he said. 'Now, we're going to press ahead with the treasure hunt as planned, in spite of the appalling weather. That's what these are built for after all.' He patted the bonnet of a nearby Land Rover. 'Inside your envelopes is the first clue. Each location will give you a clue to the following one, and so on. Everyone's due back by four thirty, and there will be penalties for late returners. So, let's see who the honoured recipient of Papa's welly boot will be this year!'

Everyone coupled up, two per car, and, of course, Penn and I were assigned as team-mates. I hoisted myself into the car and we waited our turn to depart, sitting in silence. Clearly, he was as preoccupied with last night as me, but I didn't imagine it was for the same reason. When it was our time to go, Penn instructed me to open the envelope.

'It says, *If you need to spend a penny, here's as good a place as any; don't forget to turn the lock, or you might give the town a shock.*'

'Public loos in the village,' said Penn lazily. 'They did the same clue two years ago. Seems Dad's getting a bit slack.'

'Right. Well, it's a good job you're here to figure these out. I'm not going to be a lot of use.'

'Mmhm.' Penn seemed to be in complete agreement.

'Shouldn't I drive if you're solving the clues?'

'It's fine,' he said.

'Okay.' I sat back in the seat and said nothing else, feeling like I was with a monosyllabic taxi driver, for all the cama-raderie in the vehicle. Thankfully, beyond the grounds of the hall, the roads were gritted and the snow was thinner and easier to traverse.

We shortly arrived in the village to see Sophia's car speeding off. She blew a cheeky kiss from the passenger window. Penn pulled up at the public conveniences, I got out and took a picture of the next clue with my phone and we headed out again in the same direction as Sophia.

'*Where poppies lie for fallen men, you'll find yourself on course again; an ecclesiastic name is sure to help you win the game.* I'm guessing this is a war memorial?'

'Top marks. There's one in the next village. Let's go.'

We trundled off again, winding through lanes until we came to a square with a monolith in the centre, names carved onto all four sides. We both roamed its perimeter, searching for inspiration.

'Ha!' I said, pointing to one of the carvings. 'What about this one? A soldier called *A. Church. Northumberland Fusiliers.* A. Church – that's an ecclesiastical name if I ever heard one. So I'm guessing the next destination is exactly that – a church.'

Penn nodded, looking gratifyingly impressed. 'I think you've got it. Question is, which one.'

'One in every village, I presume?'

'Yep. Come on then – we'll check this one first.'

The church in the village where we'd solved the riddle had no sign of a clue, so we hopped back in the car and set off again. Eventually, three villages later, we found a church with another clue taped to the door and carried on the hunt. Before long, I was eagerly jumping out of the vehicle at each stop like a woman possessed.

'You're enjoying this then?' asked Penn as we drove away from an old pub bearing a clue in the form of a blue plaque, stating that a semi-famous playwright had been born there.

'I want that welly boot more than I thought I would,' I said, grinning. The uncomfortable silences from earlier seemed to have eased off now. Whatever had passed between us the night before felt of less consequence, and we'd resumed our usual near-tolerance of one another.

His eyebrows lifted. 'I did *not* predict that when we headed out. You're way more competitive than I realised.'

'Really? Do you not work in the same shop as me? I thought you'd have seen my ambitious side by now.'

'That's a fair point.' A smile tugged at the corner of his lips.

We drove on, racking up the correct guesses, until we stopped for a very late lunch. We'd been so absorbed in the game that we'd almost forgotten the packed lunch on the back seat of the car. There was a flask of hot coffee back there too, so we clinked our enamelled cups together and chewed cheese-and-pickle sandwiches in amiable silence.

'Do you think we're winning?' I asked. Since seeing Sophia, we hadn't bumped into any of the other cars on our route.

'It's hard to say. Like I said, everyone takes it pretty seriously, so we'll find out when we get back.'

'Do you think there'll be many more clues?'

'Not too many more, I don't think.' He looked at his watch. 'We've done well, and it's nearly three p.m. I think we're nearly there – let's crack on.'

I clapped my hands then flicked on the radio. We'd driven in silence up until then, but I was now feeling more buoyed up with excitement, caffeine and food. Britney Spears drifted out of the speakers. Penn rolled his eyes and reached for the dial to switch to another station, but I put my hand over his. He glanced at me, smiled and shook his head patiently, and we drove on to the sweet sounds of '... Baby One More Time'. And that's when things began to go wrong.

'Well, that's the deadline come and gone,' grumbled Penn as we trundled down a country lane in near darkness. Hours had gone by since we'd found our last clue, and having no idea what it meant, we'd been driving aimlessly around the wilds of Northumberland.

'Are you sure you don't have an Uncle Eustace somewhere back in your family tree? Is an Uncle Eustace a type of plant? Or is it an upper-class euphemism for something?'

Penn grimaced. 'If it's any of those things, I've got no idea. And I'm fairly sure it's not a euphemism. This clue makes no sense.'

'Uncle Eustace, Uncle Eustace. Wasn't there a Eustace in *The Lion, the Witch and the Wardrobe*? Ooh, could it be Turkish delight?'

'Can you see any sweet shops around here?' said Penn, gesturing to the barren landscape, the snowy fields pale grey in the gathering moonlight.

'I suppose not. I was just making a suggestion.' I didn't bother to hide my huffiness. We'd clearly strayed well off the trail and neither of us had any idea how to get back on it.

'Listen,' Penn said, pulling into a passing place, 'I think we should just go back to the house. We've lost anyway, so there's no point in flogging a dead horse.'

'Absolutely not!' I snapped. 'We've come this far. This could be the very last clue for all we know. I'm not going to give up this easily – if we're going to miss the deadline, then we should at least go back with our heads held high.'

'Annie, it doesn't matter. It's just a stupid game.'

'It matters to me.' I crossed my arms and stared out the window, my teeth gritted together. Penn's family already thought I was an outsider – an unwelcome one to some of them. I refused to give them another reason to think I'd failed at fitting in. The Ashcliffe Hall Silly Sunday tradition wouldn't better me.

He sighed. 'Okay. But I'll need you to drive. My parents will be starting to worry, so I'd best give them a call.'

'Fine.' We got out and switched seats. As I walked around the Defender, I noticed that the snow had become thicker underfoot. More had begun to fall, dusting the windscreen with crisp flakes. I turned on the wipers and pulled out of the passing place.

'Just head on the way we're going for now,' said Penn, tapping at his phone. 'There's one place out here we haven't tried. It's a holiday rental of ours – not that I can imagine what Uncle Eustace would have to do with it, but we might as well check it out while we're up here.'

'Okay. Maybe Uncle Eustace was the company that fitted the bathrooms?'

'God willing,' he murmured. 'The sooner we find out, the sooner we can get home. Ugh. I can't get a signal.' He dropped his phone into his lap and stared out front.

We drove on for ten minutes more, until we came to a farm-style gate. Penn hopped out and unlatched it – the sign on the gate read 'Upland Lodge', and in the near distance, I could see the dark outline of a squat building. He got back in, and we rumbled over a cattle grid and up the long lane. About halfway up, the snow on the ground had started to bank up, narrowing the already small single-track road.

'Steady,' said Penn as I slowed down to a tentative crawl. 'But not too slow, or we'll lose traction.'

I put my foot to the accelerator again.

'Not that fast!' he yelled.

'Fuck's sake, Penn!' I said, whipping round to speak to him. 'Which of those do you want?'

'Careful!' he shouted, and I turned back to see that I'd veered off course and was heading towards the edge of the lane. I grabbed the wheel tighter and swerved back, but the wheels skidded and bounced over the grass verge into the edge of the field. With a crump, the Defender wedged nose-first into a massive drift of snow.

Both of us were speechless for a second. Then Penn well and truly found his voice.

'Annie! I told you to be careful!' he yelled.

'I *was* being careful until you started distracting me with all your "instructions".'

'Which you didn't listen to.'

'I did! And they were ridiculous.'

He rounded on me. 'No, *this* is ridiculous! It's an off-road vehicle, but this isn't what the manufacturer meant.'

'Ha bloody ha. Just be quiet and let me sort it.'

I shoved the gearstick into reverse and tried to back out,

wheels spinning. The car wouldn't budge, despite all my determination to prove Penn wrong.

'Let me try,' said Penn impatiently, and I reluctantly got out and let him have a go. All that achieved was another spray of snow from the back wheels and a faint whiff of burned clutch. He crossed his arms over the top of the steering wheel, bent his forehead to them and gave a groan of frustration.

'The front wheels are too wedged in, and the back ones aren't getting enough traction. It's going to need to be dug out. Or hauled out by a tractor.'

'Okay, well let's just ring...'

'No signal, remember?' He waved his useless phone.

I checked mine too – nothing.

'What about the cottage?' I asked, pointing to the stone building a few hundred yards down the lane. 'Can we get on the Wi-Fi?'

He shook his head. 'Unfortunately for us, this place is billed as a digital-detox getaway. The guests get an old Nokia for emergencies when they arrive, but it's unoccupied, as you can probably tell. The phone will be back at Ashcliffe.'

The cottage was as dark as the night sky, but standing in the freezing snow, cold water trickling into my boots, I wanted to be inside it. Penn seemed to read my mind.

'Come on. Let's get ourselves warm. I think we'll have to stay here tonight and then we could maybe walk out and try and get a phone signal when it's light tomorrow.'

We trudged up to the door, where Penn tapped a code into a small lockbox to retrieve the key, and we went inside.

'Let's hope Uncle Eustace isn't the resident ghost,' I said as I crossed the threshold.

TWENTY-TWO

Penn flicked on the light, revealing an open-plan living room so cosy and stylish it wouldn't have looked out of place in an interiors magazine. For all it appeared to be a tumbledown old farm building from the outside, it had been modernised inside, with comfortable squashy couches, fur rugs and rustic wood furniture. There was a small farmhouse kitchen area, an inglenook fireplace and on the far wall were floor-to-ceiling bi-fold doors that I imagined would frame a spectacular view in the daylight. But however welcoming it was, it was bloody freezing. I shivered and rubbed my hands on my arms.

'I'll light a fire,' said Penn. 'It'll take ages if I put the central heating on.'

He set to work, gathering old newspaper, kindling and logs from a basket on the hearth, and built an impressive-looking pile. Then he poked a match into the kindling and it caught, flames licking through until it started burning nicely. Meanwhile, I wandered around the cottage, looking in the cupboards and drawers, poking my head into the bathroom – Molton Brown toiletries, very nice – and opened the last remaining door to find one double bedroom.

'Is this...?'

'The only bedroom? Yep.' We exchanged a glance, then Penn coughed. 'I'll sleep on the sofa – don't worry. There are plenty of spare blankets in the cupboard.'

'Right. Well, thank you. So, there's no telly, no Wi-Fi... what do people do for fun here?'

He shrugged. 'Read books, look at the view.'

'I like reading as much as the next person, but my concentration span wouldn't stretch to a solid weekend of it.'

'People go walking, have bubble baths... I don't know, I guess they just entertain themselves.'

I nodded, suddenly becoming aware that without any distractions, Penn and I might have to actually have a conversation that lasted longer than five minutes. Then my belly filled the awkward silence by rumbling loudly.

'You know, there should be something to eat in here. Mum and Dad keep a supply of stuff for the welcome packs.' He felt on top of the kitchen cupboards and produced a small key, which opened a locked store cupboard. Inside were packets of local shortbread, fruitcake and some boxes of eggs. Alongside were several bottles of wine.

'Take your pick,' he said, and I chose a bottle of wine and some cake. 'Good choice – that might thaw us out a bit.'

He poured us a glass each, and we sat on the sofa sipping it in between mouthfuls of cake. The rush of sugar and alcohol settled my jitters following the car accident, and the heat from the fire warmed me so well that I needed to take off my sweater. As I pulled it over my head, I caught Penn stealing a glance, and I flushed, remembering the daydreams I'd had about him undressing me.

'I guess your folks are going to worry,' I said, banishing any intrusive thoughts and relaxing back into the plump cushions.

'I suppose they will, but there's not a lot I can do about it. In the morning, I'll walk out into the fields and see if I can get some signal. If not, we might be saved by a passing shepherd.' His eyes crinkled at the side. I noticed again how they drew me in and tore my gaze away to look into the fire.

'At least there's a decent stock of biscuits to keep us going,' I said. 'I'm a dab hand at an omelette too. We'll just have to pretend we're in a zombie apocalypse and ration our provisions.'

'Between the two of us, we should manage.'

'True – I just hope we don't run short of Molton Brown shower gel, or we might have to improvise with dish detergent.'

He laughed, but I was distracted by the sudden image of him in the shower, soap bubbles running down his torso, down his hips, and... I felt my face go hot and slugged a large amount of wine. These intrusive thoughts about Penn were getting out of hand.

'Anyway,' I said, trying to push the image from my mind in case it revealed itself on my face. 'Do you think we'll be saved in time to open up on Tuesday?'

'I hope so. What's Newcastle going to do without its premier purveyor of sex toys?' Interestingly, he said this with a smile on his face.

'You've changed your tune. Whenever it's mentioned, you sound like I'm committing a mortal sin.'

He shook his head. 'I didn't mean it like that. I think what I was getting at was that you sometimes surprise me.'

'I didn't think you paid me that much attention. Other than being irritated with me.'

'You get irritated by me too.'

'I can't disagree. Although, you are growing on me a tiny bit.' His eyebrows rose. 'Just a pea-sized amount, like the label on that fancy shampoo in the bathroom says.'

'A little goes a long way.' He looked at me, an unreadable expression on his face. 'It's funny, with all the bickering and cold shoulders in the shop, we've never really got to know each other.'

'What do you want to know?'

He leaned back, crossing his arms behind his head. He mulled this over for a moment.

'Tell me about your family,' he said. 'I've only met your mum and dad in passing.'

'Okay. Like I said at the kitchen supper, my dad's a builder, although as you can tell by the wheelchair, he's out of action for a bit. Mam's tried her hand at being an entrepreneur, but she tends to flit from one thing to the next, so that's why I've got what I'd call an eclectic range of items in the shop. Er, they still live in the house where I grew up.' At this I felt that flutter of worry again but squashed it down. 'And my grandparents all live in Dunhall. Have done all their lives.'

'Coincidence... that's where I live.' Then, suddenly, his face fell. 'Does that mean your mum and dad both grew up there?'

'Uh-huh.'

He groaned and rubbed his forehead. 'Fuck. Now I know how I upset your dad. The lads and I were talking to him about where we live, and they were taking the piss out of it for being a shithole, as usual. Since I didn't disagree, I'd assume your dad was rightly offended.'

That explained it. My dad wheeling his way out of the shop, pink in the face and making haste to get away. I sighed.

'That's not... ideal,' I said. 'But to be honest, I thought it might have been something much worse. It usually takes a fair bit to wind up my dad. He might have just been having a bad day.' Penn's pained expression eased a bit. 'Honestly, I wouldn't worry. He won't even remember it now.'

I really did hope my dad would have brushed it off by now, and was very relieved that it was a simple misunderstanding rather than Penn wilfully making him feel like shit.

'Well, tell him I'm really sorry,' he said. 'They both seemed nice.'

'Your parents are nice too,' I said politely, looking away as I did.

'I think you're being very diplomatic. Dad's not such hard work, but I know my mum can be a bit prickly.'

I thought of her judging my clothing choices and giving me a clear message that I wasn't good enough for her son, and struggled to disagree.

'I'd imagine she just wants the best for you.'

He shook his head. 'I think she wants what's best for *her*, to be completely honest. Me back at home, dressed head to toe in tweed with a specially selected wife on my arm.'

'Sophia,' I said.

He grimaced and looked at his lap. 'Yes. She's still pushing that agenda. I'm sorry you're having to deal with Sophia.'

'She's very full on,' I agreed. 'But I can handle her. And beyond the passive-aggressive comments and baring my arse to your entire family in the boathouse, she seems charming.'

He laughed heartily then, and I felt a flush of pleasure at making it happen.

'But seriously, do you think you'll give in? I mean, your mam is pretty skilled at masterminding the clothing situation.' He pulled a face. 'No judgement! She got me too.'

'She won't win this one. Absolutely not.'

We sat quietly for a moment, sipping wine, until I felt emboldened enough to ask, 'Why did you and Sophia split up?'

He puffed out his cheeks. 'Let's just say we weren't as compatible as we thought. We started seeing each other properly after graduating, and after that I moved to Newcastle. I wanted to get something going with the band – me and the lads met at uni – and Sophia seemed to like tagging along. One of the "band groupies" – and I say this lightly as we aren't exactly big time enough to have actual groupies. She enjoyed the parties and the kudos of being involved in everything. I think she wanted to stick two fingers up at her own mum. Think Bunny on steroids, when it comes to micro-managing her kids' lives.'

'Uh-huh. So where did it all go wrong?'

'I think Sophia thought it would just be a short-term thing – the band, the lifestyle. She always wanted to go back home after having a wild year or two. And when I wouldn't come with her, she walked away.'

'And broke your heart?' I asked with a small smile.

'No. It had run its course. We'd outgrown each other long before. And I hated how I wasn't good enough because I had no money of my own. I didn't want to live off my parents anymore. So because I lived in a shitty flat, and didn't want to go to all the best restaurants and schmoozing events, she was the one who called it a day. But I didn't object.'

I sat thinking. All this time I'd believed that he was living a pretence at being the struggling musician. It seemed to be more of the real deal than I'd imagined.

'Anyway,' he said. 'That's enough about me. I've wanted to say something all day – about last night.'

I tensed. I'd tried to keep last night out of my mind all day long, burying the horrible event under my enthusiasm for the treasure hunt.

'I'm sorry,' he continued, sitting forward with his elbows resting on his knees. 'I'm really sorry for losing my rag so badly. I should never have been so worked up. I have no regrets about dragging him off you, but I came pretty close to punching him, and that was too far.'

'It's okay. I was stupid not to listen to you when you warned me off. The guy's a monster.'

'He is. He's got terrible form for being handsy at the very least. God only knows how he's still working at the estate – he manages to fly just under the radar. When I saw him all over you, I just saw red. Like I said, I'm sorry.'

'You don't need to apologise. If anything, I should say thank you. And I'm sorry too for giving you a hard time about it.'

Then the memory of him taking off the jacket swam into my mind again. My breath caught, and I tried to level myself.

'He's an idiot,' I said, trying for a light laugh. 'He even tried to run you down in front of me – he was quite pleased to tell me what I already know about your shooting record.'

'Ha! Well, trust Gus to try and win you over by outing me as a terrible sportsman. If only he knew the whole story.'

'God forbid Lord Ashcliffe's son be revealed as a secret animal rights supporter,' I said with a grin.

He smirked. 'That isn't even the half of it.'

'What do you mean?'

'Who do you think tipped off your protest group?'

My mouth fell open. 'You didn't...'

'I did. A friend of mine from one of the places we gig is one of Christa's lot. He promised not to out me.'

'You're outing yourself now.'

He held my gaze. 'I think I can trust you,' he said softly.

I swallowed. There were those eyes again. All the times I'd looked into them scathingly in the shop – they seemed very far away. The Penn I knew, the one who took himself so seriously and seemed to have the world at his feet... who seemed to find me such a thorn in his side... had changed in the glow of the fire-light. He didn't break eye contact with me, and we were inches away from each other, leaning on the back of the couch.

Almost unthinking, I leaned towards him, and he responded. Our lips touched, and my pulse quickened as his hand grazed the side of my neck, holding me to him. I sensed an urgency in him, and he kissed me harder, his tongue flicking against mine. Then, suddenly, he pulled away, still holding the nape of my neck, his forehead against mine. He was breathing heavily.

'Annie, I can't,' he said.

I sprang back, peeling his hands away. My eyes started to sting with the immediate effects of the mood change. He wouldn't look at me.

'What do you mean?'

He let out an exasperated breath. 'I just... It's not the right...' He ran out of words and looked at me with a bleak expression on his face.

I got up abruptly and walked to the door, unsure of what I was planning to do, then on a whim I stuck my feet into my boots and strode outside into the snow. I heard Penn shout after me as I walked as fast as I could, the snow hampering me from breaking into a run.

My head was spinning as white flurries whirled around me. I hadn't even thought to put on a coat. I was mortified. I'd opened myself up to him, let my long-held defences down and all I'd got was another knock-back. How many more ways could we fail to meet in the middle?

I'd reached the snow-banked car by the time he caught up with me, calling my name. I stopped by the tail lights and whirled round, cold tears clinging to my eyelashes.

'What do you want?'

'You,' he said, panting.

'You don't. You just said so.'

'I didn't mean... God, Annie, you're so hard to...'

'Hard to what?' I snapped. 'Hard to like? Hard to help fit in here?'

He stepped towards me. 'You're so hard to understand!'

'What the hell does that mean?' I shouted, momentarily glad we were so isolated. My voice rang into the frigid air.

He was close enough now to touch me. I could feel his breath warming my face.

'I can't work you out,' he replied, almost as loudly as me. 'One minute we're fighting; the next we're kissing. You're not the only one who's confused.'

I stared at him then pushed him hard in the chest. 'I'm not confused. I didn't like you, but now I do. It's as simple as that. Is this because you still don't like *me*? Or is it something else?'

'Like what?'

'Like, I'm just here to do a job, and we'll go back to our own separate lives, like you said yesterday?'

'No.' His tone was firm even through his ragged breaths, and he looked almost furious. 'It's the opposite. I knew when I kissed you on the dance floor last night that if I ever kissed you again, then there'd be no going back. If I ever kissed you for real, I'd not be able to stop.'

I shook my head, barely able to make sense of it. That surge that had gone through me when we'd kissed at the ball, the undeniable connection that began at our lips and had spread right to my fingertips – it hadn't been only me that felt it. I reached up and pulled his head to mine and kissed him hard.

Penn let out a brief gasp and then returned the kiss with even more force. Our tongues sought each other; our hands roamed over each other's bodies. Neither of us was wearing a coat, but I hardly noticed the cold.

He guided me quickly towards the back of the car and pressed against me, his hands running down my back until they cupped my backside, pulling me towards him. His hips ground against me, and I felt him growing hard through his cords. He moaned quietly and lifted me just a little, so he was almost carrying me. Then he kissed down the side of my neck and to my chest, where my shirt had grown damp in the snow and was clinging to me. He nudged it with his nose to find the skin underneath then paused, breathing heavily against me.

'You're freezing,' he said. 'Come back to the house.'

Instead of letting go of me, he hitched me higher so my legs wrapped around his waist, kissing me over and over as he carried me up the path. In spite of the snow, each step was sure and full of purpose, until he gently let go of me to open the door. We stumbled through and fell into each other again, my wet shirt colliding with his T-shirt, which was also soaked. He pushed back my damp hair and looked into my eyes with a tenderness I could never have pictured, then it clouded with clear desire. He started to unbutton my shirt, and I ran my hands up under the back of his, feeling the muscles of his back grow taut under my touch.

He peeled away the fabric sticking to my skin, then unclasped my bra and bent his head to my breasts, his tongue circling my nipple. Goosebumps broke out all over me, nothing to do with the cold. I pulled off his top, and we pressed together, naked from the waist up. The feel of his skin on mine was a pleasant shock, making me tingle right down my body and in between my legs. I'd gone from not wanting Penn anywhere near me to needing him so badly it hurt. I pulled him to the kitchen table, and he hoisted me up, pulling at my trousers while I unbuckled his.

'I want you, Annie. Do you want me?' he asked.

I nodded, unable to speak.

He went to retrieve a condom from his wallet, leaving me perched on the edge of the table trying to steady my breath until he returned. Then he lay me back and kissed me down the length of my torso, his lips skirting my curves, his hand between my thighs, making my breath come in sharp bursts. His mouth caught up with his hand and replaced it, and his tongue moved in time with the moans escaping from me. Every time I came close to the edge, he held back. I felt light-headed with wanting him, dizzy with the sudden crystal clear realisation that I'd wanted him for so long.

Finally, he stood up and pushed himself between my legs, one hand massaging my breast. I gasped and sat up, holding on to his shoulders, kissing him feverishly as the movement of his hips nudged me against the edge of the table. I shifted myself forward, and this new position made me go weak from the stimulation. He gripped my back tighter as I shuddered, holding me close, and I watched as those beautiful brown eyes hazed over with his building urgency. Then he stiffened, his mouth against the side of my head, a ragged gasp escaping from it.

Breathing heavily, we stayed there, not moving away from each other for a long time.

TWENTY-THREE

We slept very little that night, having moved to the bedroom, warming ourselves under the blankets and against each other's skin. Every time I felt close to drifting off, we started to kiss again, sleepily, and then before long, he was on top of me, underneath me, to the side of me. It was as if we needed to make up for every argument we'd ever had in that one night, and by the morning, my body had a pleasant soreness that would keep me thinking of this all day.

As the sun came up, I lay on his chest, turning his dark hair between my fingers. His hand stroked down the side of my waist. I don't know if it was tiredness or the light of day creeping in, but I suddenly realised how strange this felt. Amazing but strange. I started to laugh.

'What?' he asked, and I could hear the smile in his voice.

'After all this time, I never imagined I'd be lying in bed with you without any clothes on.'

'Really? I thought about it loads. Maybe I should be offended.'

'You didn't,' I said, propping myself up to look at him.

'Of course I did. You might have been a pain in the arse, but you're a beautiful pain in the arse.'

I dug him in the ribs. 'I had no idea. And if you really do feel offended, you should know I thought you were handsome too. I just never thought we'd be able to bear being in the same room long enough to get naked.'

He laughed. 'All it took was being trapped together in a snowdrift. You've been forced to put up with me.'

I pressed my lips to his chest and lay on it again. 'I can't be forced to do anything – you know that.'

'So it's real? All this.'

I said nothing for a moment, running my hands through his light smattering of chest hair. 'I think so.' His arm gripped me a little tighter.

I lay with my eyes closed for some time, enjoying the feeling of him stroking my back.

'Are you asleep?' he asked.

'No. I can't. Too many thoughts.'

'Me too,' he said.

'Tell me,' I murmured.

'I keep thinking about the shop. How I'm not going to be able to concentrate. With you there.'

'Even more distracted than with a music volume battle?'

'Even more than that. Watching you going about your day, thinking about how I'd like to unbutton your top isn't going to help my sales figures.'

I smiled against his chest. 'I'm sure you'll manage. I'll try and stick to wearing nun-like garb to keep your mind focused on work.'

'Mm, that might just make me even more interested in what's underneath.'

'Anyway, you'll be too busy to notice me. You've been selling loads lately.'

He shifted a little and made a doubtful 'hmm' sound. 'I'm

doing better than I was. Especially thanks to a certain novelty music range.'

'You're welcome,' I said.

'Much obliged. But, to be honest, things are still tight. That's why I was open to the shop-share, to keep the rent down, not because I had too much space. It wasn't as affordable as I'd hoped.'

'Well that makes more sense now... It explains why you had to tolerate me.' I paused. 'Why did you pick me in the first place? To share the shop.'

'Oh, I just flipped a coin. Anyone to cut my rent in half.'

I gasped, and he burst into laughter. 'I'm joking.' Then he went quiet, twirling a lock of my hair around his finger. 'There was something about you. I'd noticed you in the bar – you're hard not to notice. Then when I saw the spark in you when we talked to Mike... I liked it.'

A warm feeling flooded through me, but my urge to make a quip won out, as ever. 'I bet that didn't last for long. Did you wonder if you'd bitten off more than you could chew?'

He smiled. 'Yeah. But I'm glad I stuck it out.'

'Me too.' I held him tighter. 'So, how did you end up opening a pop-up shop in the first place?'

He took a deep, hesitant breath. 'When I left uni, my parents were bankrolling me. I had an allowance. I'm cringing even telling you this, since I know you think I'm a spoiled little rich boy. But when I moved in with the lads and told them I wasn't coming back, my parents cut me off.'

I'll admit, I found the fact that he'd been financially supported unsurprising. And even though it didn't sit well with me, I could imagine how it must have hurt, knowing his parents disapproved of his choices so much.

'So now, the savings I had have run out, and I'm relying 100 per cent on Uncle Al's. Well, that and the odd fifty quid I get from gigs every now and then. I'm embarrassed to say I'm unqualified to do anything else, and even more mortified that when I was younger, I took my family's money for granted. I always had this notion that one day I'd be independent, but my degree hasn't helped much.'

'Right,' I murmured. 'So, what's your degree in?'

'Music. Naturally. I'd hoped to go into teaching, but it never worked out.' He sighed. 'So I'm not going to be able to find a side hustle as a hedge-fund manager or a brain surgeon.'

'What will happen if you do run out of money?'

'I don't know. Worst case scenario I would actually have to come back to Ashcliffe. Which is exactly what my parents want.'

We said nothing for a while, and a question needled at my brain.

'Can I ask...?' I said tentatively. 'Why did you want to leave home so badly? I mean, I think it's great that you did, but what happened?'

His fingers stroked my back more rapidly, as if he was building up momentum to reply.

'When I said that my parents cut me off, it makes it sound like I was being punished. Which I suppose I was, but really I didn't want their money anymore. I... I wanted to be independent on my own terms, rather than them calling the shots. To my parents, money solves everything; if they kept throwing it at me, then I was still theirs.'

'And you don't want to be?'

He shook his head. 'I love my parents. And I know they love me too. But being brought up by a nanny and then a school houseparent doesn't exactly make you close with your mum and dad. And even in the holidays, they were often away with friends – skiing and so on.'

He paused, seemingly lost in his thoughts.

'Christmas was the worst. One time, when I was about ten, I asked for this robot dog toy. I'd been desperate for it for ages.

Then a parcel appeared under the tree, and every time Dad walked past, he'd give me a little wink – I was sure they'd got it for me, and I was so excited to open it in front of them. When I woke up on Christmas morning, they were gone. Hadn't even told me they'd planned to go to St Barts for the holidays. I sat with the nanny and opened the parcel – I'd got the robot dog but not what I really wanted. They could give me all the ponies and fencing tutors in the world, but they could never give me themselves.'

I squeezed him tight, my chest aching with pain for him. He let me hold him while his breathing slowed. Then he coughed and squeezed me back. 'Anyway, enough about me. I'm glad Everything Must Go's doing well for you.'

'Thanks.' I hesitated. His honesty made me open up in return. 'I'm helping my parents out while trying to get out of my own flatshare. My flatmate is, how can I put it...? Socially incompetent. He lives in his room with the curtains shut – it's like a hotbox of farts and Chinese takeaway in there – and he only comes out to add some more dirty plates to the pile in the sink.'

'He sounds lovely. But what's going on with your parents?'

'They... they've had a hard time lately. And if things don't improve, they won't be able to manage the mortgage, might even have to sell the house. Which would be up to them I suppose, but they love that house, and it's where I grew up. I can't bear the thought of it.'

'I can imagine. So you're trying to keep both your head and theirs above water. Annie, I had no idea.'

I bit my lip hard. 'Mmhm,' I managed. 'It's just... such a shitty time for this all to be happening. We've never been flush for cash, and Christmases have been up and down for us too. But they always tried their best. One year, when I was about ten too, they hadn't been able to afford much more than a few small gifts so they made it into a treasure hunt to find them – they just wanted me to have an amazing day. I feel bad saying it – at least they gave me their time – but I always felt guilty about them spending money they didn't have, and it took the shine off the day. I guess what I'm saying is, I know how you feel. It might be for different reasons, but I get it.'

He kissed the top of my head, and we stayed there for a while, his lips against my hair, my hand draped against his neck. He swallowed thickly a few times, and I sensed we'd unlocked some buried emotions. Eventually, he shifted under my weight.

'We need to get up soon,' he said. 'Or at least I will – I'm going to have a wander out to try and call home. If I can get up a bit higher, I might get a better signal.'

'Good idea.'

He rolled onto his side and pulled me towards him. 'For now, I've got an even better idea.' Then he kissed me and, with his musically trained fingers, demonstrated just how skilled he could be.

I was cooking an omelette at the stove wearing just pants and a shirt when he came back in, kicking the snow off his boots. He kissed my neck, his cold lips making me shiver in more ways than one.

'I got hold of Sophia,' he said. 'I finally got the phone to work out in the top field and tried everyone, but nobody answered except for her. She's going to send help.'

My heart sank a bit at the mention of Sophia, in light of how we'd spent the night, but I shook it off. Then I picked up a bit of omelette with a fork and fed some to Penn.

'You weren't joking when you said you were a mean omelette maker. That's delicious.'

We sat together and picked at our breakfast, chatting and, in my head, making the most of this time on our own. I thought of a rescuer on their way from Ashcliffe Hall and almost wished they weren't coming. Going back there would be like going back to reality, but with the snowy terrain, I imagined it might be a while yet.

After we'd eaten, we sat on the sofa together. He pulled me onto his lap, my shirt hanging loosely over my backside, bare legs straddling him. I bent my head, kissing him over and over again even though my lips felt bruised from overuse. We paused, and he held my face in his hands, looking deep into my eyes, stroking my hair back from my face. He looked at me like he was taking a long drink from an oasis in the middle of the desert, as if he'd walked for miles before finding what he needed. He was drinking me in.

Suddenly, there was a loud rap on the bi-fold door. We both jumped and turned to see Sophia and Gus standing outside the huge pane of glass, looking in at us with undisguised discomfort.

I dismounted Penn, and he went to unlock the door. I hovered awkwardly in my state of partial dress as they sidled in, looking anywhere but at my bare legs.

'Thank goodness you had your accident so near to the lodge,' said Sophia bracingly. Her privileged upbringing had clearly given her the ability to navigate a delicate situation. 'You'd have frozen to death otherwise.'

Gus stood with his arms crossed, glaring at the floor, making no effort to cover the duress he was under in our rescue. Penn wouldn't look at him either.

'Yes, it was very lucky.' Penn gave me a secret smile. 'Thanks for coming. Listen, just give us a minute and we'll tidy up and meet you outside. What did you come in?'

'Tractor,' said Gus and walked out into the snow.

'See you outside, guys,' said Sophia, following, giving me a last flickering glance.

Penn and I hurried around, pulling on any discarded clothes and tidying away any mess we'd left. When we went outside, Gus had already hauled the car out of the snow bank and was detaching the chain.

'Thanks,' said Penn as we made to climb in. 'We'll see you back at the house.'

Without giving a reply, Gus hoisted himself back into the cab of the tractor, looking expectantly at Sophia.

'No problem,' she said and gave us a curious look before climbing in herself. For a second, she let the mask slip, and a sad expression seeped through. I felt a pang of guilt – she'd walked in on a scene that had truly rubbed her face in it when it came to Penn.

We got in the car and followed the tractor until there was space to overtake, leaving our little cocoon behind.

After a brief dressing-down from Hugh regarding Penn's lack of care when driving, Penn and I went off to our separate rooms. Penn had very kindly chosen not to out me as the actual driver, so I was merely a bystander to the telling-off. Neither of us had the energy to ask what the Uncle Eustace clue had actually been referring to, and I doubted we would ever know.

It was time to go. The shop needed to open the next day, a more exciting prospect now that Penn and I could be together all day and do the exact opposite of pissing each other off. I slung my belongings into my bag with abandon and made my way downstairs to say my thank yous and goodbyes. Penn was going to drive me home, or rather to my mam and dad's since I needed to drop Kelly's clothes back.

I left my bag near the front door and walked through the ground floor of Ashcliffe Hall, looking for Penn's parents. I heard voices from the sitting room and headed for it, pausing at the slightly ajar door to make sure it was an opportune moment to interrupt.

'And you won't be convinced?' came Bunny's cut-glass voice.

'No. I told you, I'm happy with my life in Newcastle.' It was Penn, sounding exhausted. I wondered how long this conversation had been going on.

'Come on, old man,' said Hugh. 'You've had your fun. It's time to grow up – take some real responsibility.'

'Your idea of responsibility isn't the same as mine. Look, I love you both, and I'm grateful for the start you gave me. I've never wanted for anything. But I want to make my own way. And being independent *is* a responsibility, just not the one you had in mind for me. Can't you just be proud of me for being myself?'

Bunny tutted. 'You're an heir to Ashcliffe Hall. *That* is who you are. There are no two ways about it.'

'Bertie will inherit, not me.'

His parents said nothing for a while, and I heard the sounds of pacing. I was just considering walking in, under the pretence that I hadn't been lingering outside the door, when Bunny spoke again.

'I don't know why you won't reconcile with Sophia. You and she could have one of the cottages on the estate; we'll make sure your finances are taken care of again.'

'I don't want your money,' Penn said carefully. 'And I have a girlfriend.'

Bunny let out a bitter laugh, and Hugh piped up, 'Now, she's a lovely girl, but—'

'But what?' snapped Penn.

'She's not for you,' Bunny said.

'She is for me.'

She sighed. 'Peregrine, girls like that... I'm sure she's a lot of fun. And she no doubt suits your devil-may-care lifestyle in the city. But she isn't marriage material, not by any means.'

My breath caught in my throat. I already knew what Bunny

thought of me, but hearing her say it out loud was like a dagger to the chest. Especially now mine and Penn's relationship was no longer just for show.

Then, before I had a chance to even let it fully sink in, steps came towards the door. I ducked into a nearby room and held my breath. The three of them walked down the hall, conversation clearly over.

When I thought my appearance would look better timed, I went through to the entrance hall where Penn was now talking in hushed tones with his parents. I pasted on a bright smile.

'I've been looking for you all everywhere. Are we ready for the off?' I asked Penn.

'Ready if you are,' he replied, his expression not giving any hint of the discussion I'd just overheard.

'Bunny, Hugh. Thank you so much for having me.' I tensed, noticing how I'd automatically curbed my strong accent just as a result of standing in front of them. I carried on, rectifying it, speaking as I'd been born and raised. 'I hope you guys can come and see us in Newcastle – visit the shop.'

Bunny gave me a weak smile and offered me her hand to shake, which I did. 'I'm sure we will,' she said unconvincingly.

Hugh patted my arm. 'All the best, Annie. You take care now.' The way he said it sounded like a final goodbye to someone he wasn't expecting to see ever again.

We went out to Penn's car as his parents remained inside. Perhaps waving people off at the door was deemed common, as only Hendrix the Labrador was there to say a last goodbye with licks and barks. Penn sent him back inside, and we got in the car and set off down the long driveway.

'Back to normality,' murmured Penn, switching on some music by a band I'd never heard of. It was another reminder of all the ways we were so different, and I didn't say anything for a long while.

'You okay?' he asked, resting a hand on my thigh. I felt a brief stir of arousal, but it was damped down by my worries.

'I'm fine. Just a bit tired. We didn't sleep much last night.'

'Too right we didn't.' He flicked a look at me that told me exactly what he meant, and I couldn't help but smile back. 'So, what are we going to say to the others at the shop? I mean, are we going to keep this to ourselves for now?'

'I think we should,' I replied. 'I mean, it would seem very out of the blue; they don't even know what we were up to this weekend. Plus it might be quite fun, to have a little secret.'

He grinned. 'I like the sound of that.'

'Maybe we can meet up in the stock cupboard.'

'Or send each other dirty texts across the room.'

'What if I was to distract you from a sale by flashing you my boobs?'

'I don't think you'd dare, considering the massive window to the street.'

'Fair.'

We sat for a while, listening to the music. I looked out at the white winter sky and felt that I was leaving Bunny and Hugh's comments behind me like puffs of air from the exhaust pipe. When Penn and I were back in Newcastle, it wouldn't matter what they thought. I squeezed the top of his thigh, and he covered my hand with his, linking our fingers.

'Here's to a good week in the shop anyway,' he said. 'It's only a week 'til Christmas, so we need to get it while we can.'

'Yeah, we can do it. I'm going to double up the number of fairy lights, and I got a dancing Santa decoration from eBay to put in the window. So maybe it might attract some more people in.'

He winced, and I extracted my hand from his and batted him on the arm.

'I thought we'd agreed to be nice to each other.'

'I have my limits. But you're right. I should probably make my side a bit more festive too.'

'It's not too late to get a few Slade records in, or maybe *That's What I Call Christmas*?'

'I'll think about that,' he said with a reluctant smile.

'Or maybe you could finally sell your Pink Floyd album. I'm guessing it's worth a bit if you keep turning down offers. Someone might come in and make you an offer you can't refuse.'

He shook his head. 'Not going to happen. And yes, it's worth a lot, in more ways than one.'

'Do you want to tell me?'

'It's worth a few thousand. Nobody that's made me an offer has even come close,' he said, keeping his eyes on the road. My jaw dropped. 'But it's also of huge sentimental value. My godfather, my dad's younger brother, gave it to me when I was a teenager. He was part of the reason I got so into music, but he died a few years ago. I couldn't part with it.'

'I'm so sorry,' I said. 'And I totally get it. But why do you display it in the shop?'

'It reminds me of him. His name was Alexander. Uncle Al.'

'You named the shop after him,' I said softly.

He nodded, his mouth a tight line. 'He would probably be the only one in my family who was happy for me.'

'He must have meant a lot to you.'

'He really did. He was... incredible. Nothing like the rest of my family. He always carved his own path too, working for a living, having a million hobbies that didn't include horses or art collections. He was a gifted musician, and he was the one who bought me my first guitar, taught me how to play it. He even brightened up some of those crappy Christmases by having me and Bertie over to his place. But it was me he spent most time with – maybe because we were both the younger brother, he felt I was a kindred spirit. I think I felt that way too. I miss him.'

He changed gear, and I put my hand over his. We drove on in silence.

The country roads widened into dual carriageway then narrowed again, buildings starting to become more and more densely arranged at the sides of the road, until we entered the city. Penn navigated through the busy streets, coming through the other side to Heaton, my parents' little suburban locale. I gave him directions, and we swung into the street.

When I saw my parents' house, I didn't breathe from the moment we turned the corner until we came to a stop outside. Inside the front garden, looking every bit like an enemy flag, was a 'For Sale' sign.

TWENTY-FOUR

'But why? I thought things were getting better, with the money from the shop.'

My parents just looked at each other; they were sitting on the sofa like two naughty schoolchildren while I loomed over them. Immediately, I felt terrible and sat down on the footstool nearby.

Penn had tactfully dropped me off after checking I was okay, and I'd lied as best I could to make sure he didn't feel any more obligation. He'd driven off, giving me an uncertain look, promising to talk the following morning when we opened up shop.

'We're sorry, pet,' said Mam in a soothing tone that made me feel even worse.

'No, I'm sorry,' I said, sagging in my seat. 'I shouldn't be giving you a hard time. But what's changed since I saw you last?'

'Nothing's changed,' said Dad, his hand reaching for Mam's. 'It's just... we've still struggled to make the books balance, even with the income from the shop. We know you've done everything you can, and we're still blown away with how hard you've worked for us as a family. But... it's just not enough.'

I looked around at the living room – the wallpaper that they put up when I was seventeen, the door frame that still had marks from where they'd measured me growing. Through the patio doors lay the garden where I'd done my first cartwheel and had water balloon fights with the neighbours' kids. It couldn't become someone else's – it just couldn't.

'There has to be something else I can do. I'll try harder to sell more. I'll move back home – that'll save my rent payments, and if I can just have a little bit for my phone and some odds and ends, then you can have the rest...'

Dad held up his hand. 'Annie, that's enough,' he said gently. 'You've done more for us than a child should ever have to do for their parents. I'm... I'm embarrassed that you've had to be involved at all.'

His lip quivered, and the sight of it was like a hand wrapped around my throat. My eyes prickled, and I didn't dare speak; I knew my voice would crack, and I had to be strong.

'We're so grateful, sweetheart,' said Mam. 'And we're so proud of you.'

Then that was it. The sadness and frustration rose up through my body like a tidal wave and I burst into tears. My mam kneeled beside me and rubbed my back as I cried, while Dad sat helplessly on the sofa, his injured leg holding him back once again.

Back in the shop the next day, I'd shed all the tears I was going to and was filled once again with a vicious determination to succeed. The previous night, when I got back to the flat, Neo had heard me crying through the wall and brought me a cup of tea and some Hobnobs, which made me momentarily have fewer regrets about choosing to be his lodger. But then, as he left, he scratched his armpit, sniffed it and rubbed his fingers on his already grubby T-shirt, and I was reassured that my goal to get out of this flat was still the right path to be on. I would sell and sell and sell until I came up with enough to get that house back off the market, and then I would sort my own life out.

Penn was already there when I arrived and, as promised, had hung a 'ban hunting' sign in his shop window. I grinned seeing it, reminded of the purpose of our weekend, and then the events that had followed after... But as soon as I made steps to go and kiss him, Olivia entered the shop, stopping me in my tracks. Penn gave me a slow, knowing smile and turned away to get his shop ready for the day. Seeing him again boosted both my mood and my loins; now that I knew what lay underneath that oversized band T-shirt, I could never unsee it or stop wanting it.

'How was the convention?' asked Olivia, bounding over. I'd asked her to come in for some half-days during the last week before Christmas. If we were going to be as busy as I hoped, two salespeople were better than one.

'Oh. It was very enlightening. I learned a few new tricks, and I think I've come away with a fresh perspective on things.'

Penn's back tensed, and he shook his head just a little. I could picture the smile on his face even if I couldn't see it.

'Amazing,' said Olivia. 'Well, things went brilliant here. I sold at least a dozen vibrators and almost all of the salad spinners. Oh, and the remote-controlled clitoral stimulators are all gone!' Then she shot Penn a troubled look and lowered her voice. 'Sorry. I know he gets moody if we talk too much about the sex stuff. Such a prude.'

I just smiled and remembered him between my legs as I lay on the kitchen table. 'I know. A complete puritan.'

We spent the morning drumming up trade, Olivia serving customers while I redoubled my efforts with the shop's online presence and researching marketing strategies. I needed to make Everything Must Go into a thriving concern, rather than just a short-term means to an end. In a bid for a last-minute surge of sales before Christmas, I advertised another party day with nibbles and wine. I never stood still, pacing back and forth, trying to come up with any possible way of making more money.

Christa came in at lunchtime and needled me about working through lunch. 'You need a break!' she insisted, pulling at my hand.

I smiled and pulled it back. 'I can rest when I'm dead. I might make five more sales in this hour – you never know. So what did you get up to this weekend?' I asked, changing the subject.

'Oh, nothing. Just normal stuff. Bought some Christmas presents.'

For some reason, she'd gone a bit cagey.

I narrowed my eyes at her and smiled. 'Is that all?'

'Yep. Oh, and I got a new delivery of crystal jewellery just in time for Christmas.'

'Brilliant. I'll remember to send people along.' I noticed some lovely new earrings hanging from her ears – they were a white pearly stone in a silver setting. 'Those are nice. Are they from your new collection?'

She flicked one with her finger. 'They are. Moonstone, the stone of new beginnings. I'm manifesting a better year to come.'

'I know how you feel. Even though Liaison Secrète's doing well, I've got to start next year with a bang. So, on that note, I need to make a lunchtime sale.' I nodded towards a hesitant-looking lady who was now lingering by the till.

Olivia knocked off at 2 p.m., and I met Penn in the stock room. He kissed me like he hadn't seen me for weeks, and after all that had happened with my mam and dad since yesterday, it felt like that to me too. I weaved my hands into his hair and let out a groan of relief.

'You need to be meaner to me,' he said, holding my face.

'You're ugly and you smell,' I said.

'Ha ha.' His face broke into a wide grin, his eyes crinkling at the sides. 'I mean when other people are around, if we're going to avoid blowing our cover.'

'I'll try. I'm finding it hard to muster it though. Could you try and be more irritating? Start leaving ham sandwiches to rot under the tea towel again?'

'If that gets you going, then yes, I'll try.'

'Don't talk about getting me going,' I said, feeling my body melt under his firm hands against my back. He ran his hands down further, and I pulled his head closer so he could kiss me. We carried on like that, casting furtive looks at the door every now and then. The shop was quiet, and for the first time that day, I was glad.

Before long, he'd hitched me up onto a pile of boxes, running his hands under my long skirt until it was bunched up around my waist. His thumb ran down the front of my pants, making me squirm in anticipation.

His eyes were burning with desire and mischief, and he broke away for a moment, rummaging in one of my Liaison Secrète boxes to find what he needed. I couldn't even think about the loss in profit as he held me by the hip and made excellent use of it.

After what seemed like an eternity but was probably only ten minutes, we were still clinging together, his T-shirt ruched up above his chest, my bra undone. There then came a polite cough from outside, and we sprang apart, hastily putting ourselves right, buttoning, zipping and straightening. I held a finger to my lips and slipped through the door, closing it behind me. Arthur was standing by the cash desk, his cheeks a little pink.

'Ah. Annie. There you are. Hope I'm not interrupting you.'

My face flamed. 'Not at all! Absolutely not. I've been...
sorting through some stock.'

'I see. That explains the crashing around.'

'Uh, yep. I dropped some of my "products". Butterfingers!'

'Just so.' He coughed uncomfortably. 'Now, I dropped over
to tell you that our lovely neighbour, Melissa, has invited us all
to a New Year's Eve shindig in her shop. She asked me to spread
the word. I'll let her know if you can make it, shall I?'

'Oh. Yeah, that sounds really good. Count me in.'

'Marvellous. And how about our rock and roll friend? Do
you think he'd like to come along?'

'Um, I'll ask him when I next see him. I'm not sure what
he's doing.'

Arthur glanced at the stock-room door, a little smile flickering across his lips.

'Very good. I shall leave you to it then.' He paused as he
headed for the door and turned back. 'Oh, and just so you know,
your buttons are misaligned.' He chuckled and left, shaking his
head with amusement.

My face now almost purple, I looked down at my shirt
buttons, which looked like a three-year-old had done them up. I
went back through to the stock cupboard, where Penn was
laughing to himself, and re-buttoned myself.

'I don't know what you're laughing about,' I scolded but
laughing myself. 'He knows you're back here, leaving me to face
the music.'

'I'm sorry. Come on – let's get back to work before we get
disturbed by an actual customer.'

We went back outside, and I asked him about the New
Year's party.

'I don't think I'll be able to,' he said. 'I'll be at Ashcliffe for
the Christmas week. Unfortunately.'

Unfortunately indeed, I thought, trying not to show it on
my face. The prospect of not seeing him for a week was

strangely disappointing considering just a few days ago I'd have been counting down the hours to be rid of him.

'Will you be at home?' he asked lightly.

'Yeah. I will.'

'How are things?'

I sighed, my shoulders bunching up. 'Not great. They're pushing on with the sale. My mam texted me this morning to tell me they've got a viewing tomorrow.'

'Already?'

I nodded. 'But not if I have anything to do with it. I just need to try harder.'

'What if selling is what they want?' he asked, his tone careful. 'I mean, they can't rely on you forever. And they shouldn't have to really.'

My hackles rose instantly. 'Of course they shouldn't have to. I *want* to help them. It's my home too, and I can tell you they *don't* want to sell. Not at all.'

'Okay, I didn't mean to upset you. I just wondered... what would happen to *your* life if you end up supporting them long term?'

'It won't be long term. Dad will get back to work when he's better, and Mam... well, who knows. It depends on her health. But if I can just get them back on their feet, then I can concentrate on myself later.'

He bit his lip. 'Okay. Fair enough.' He said nothing for a moment, seeming to be deep in thought. 'Is there anything I can do to help?'

'No. And if you mean financially then, A – you're mad, and B – you haven't the means. You told me you're on a knife-edge too.'

'I know. I just hate seeing you wringing yourself dry with the responsibility.'

'And that's so good of you,' I said, wishing I dared give him a hug. 'Really. We'll be fine. If I can just bridge the gap until my dad can get back to work, then they won't need to go through with the sale.'

'You're a good daughter, Annie,' he said. 'They must feel very lucky.'

Then a customer came in, and he turned his attention to selling some records.

The afternoon continued at a steady pace, a stream of sales when what I really needed was a deluge. Penn was busier than me and yet again turned down an offer on the Pink Floyd album, shaking his head derisively at the woman who'd asked. After that, he sat at his desk, drumming lightly on it with his fingers, seemingly lost in thought.

He was quiet for the rest of the afternoon, then, once it was closing time, we tidied up and turned off the lights. Penn still seemed a little distracted but pulled me out of sight of the window and kissed me.

'Listen,' I said. 'I could do with a bit of fun tonight. Do you want to go and get a drink? We could go somewhere out of the way, so people don't see us.'

'I can't,' he said. 'I've got a gig tonight. I can't get out of it.'

'Not to worry. It's fine.' I smiled brightly, hoping the dim light might hide my disappointment. Another night in with Neo it would have to be.

We headed for the door, but then I realised I'd forgotten my scarf.

'I'll see you tomorrow,' I said. 'I'll lock up. Good luck tonight.'

'Thanks. See you tomorrow.' He kissed me on the forehead and left.

I grabbed my scarf from the stock cupboard and followed shortly after, to find that he was lingering by Melissa's door, phone to his ear. His back was to me, and he didn't notice my footsteps.

'Yeah. I'm free tonight. Where do you want to meet?'

I froze, pulling back quietly, my stomach turning over.

'Okay. I'll meet you at nine tonight at the Black Horse. Yep. See you there.' He rang off and continued down the road away from me.

Why had he just said he was free tonight when he'd told me he had a gig? My heart started to pound. Taking out my phone, I hesitated before opening Instagram. I was being silly, not to mention a teeny bit paranoid – not a trait I could usually be accused of. I was easy-going, trusting and a good judge of character. So why was I tapping in the name of Penn's band and scrolling to see the post with their gig dates on it?

I stopped at the square image with a list of dates and venues. There was no Black Horse on the page, and there was no gig that night.

TWENTY-FIVE

It seemed unlikely to me that I could feel much worse. I'd lain in bed that night, tossing and turning, running different scenarios over in my head. Maybe there was a secret gig that wasn't on their social media? He could have some kind of emergency that he didn't feel comfortable talking to me about – after all, we'd barely been friends, never mind sleeping with each other for long. But my mind kept being distracted by a pulsing beacon of suspicion. He was gorgeous, in a band and lived a pretty rootless lifestyle – the opportunities to have more than one woman on the go were immeasurable. Had I been naive to think that I could completely trust him, or that we were exclusive? Eventually I drifted into a fitful sleep.

When I woke up the next morning, I thought again – with my parents' problems and my new worries about Penn, I wasn't quite at rock bottom, but I was slipping down the slope. Then I arrived into Pilgrim Street to see Arthur, Sven, Jake and Penn clustered outside the shop, having a frantic discussion. Penn gestured at the shop and rubbed his forehead in exasperation.

Fuck. Had Neil been back and sprayed offensive graffiti over the window again? I picked up my pace and stopped in

front of the shop. The windows were clean, but the main door
to the arcade was splintered and broken.

'What's happened?'

Penn looked at me, his eyes pained. 'We've been burgled.'

'What?'

'We're very sorry, dear,' said Arthur. 'If there's anything we
can do to help...'

I stared more closely at the window and then noticed that
the shop was in more disarray than I'd first realised. Not
trashed, but things looked out of place and chaotic. Several of
my tables were empty.

'Is it just us?'

'I'm afraid so,' said Sven. 'Maybe they tried the other doors
and couldn't get in, or got disturbed, but... it seems to be just
yours.'

*Neil. He failed to make an impact last time, so he's gone a
step further.* I gave Penn a stricken look.

Just then, Mike pulled up in his car and clambered out, his
hair sticking up and shirt untucked. He groaned when he saw
what had happened.

'Bloody hell. I've called the police – they should be here any
minute. Have you had a look at what's gone?'

'Not yet. Come on – let's go and see the damage.' Penn led
on, and we all followed.

The door to our shop had been forced open, and inside
there were empty spaces where some of mine and Penn's stock
had been. I noted it was the more expensive items that were
missing. I went to the back room, already knowing what I'd see.
Inside, where my Liaison Secrète boxes had been were simply
bare floorboards and dust motes. A couple of my other boxes
were left behind in the corner, mostly empty except for random
bits and pieces of little value. Penn's side had been similarly
plundered.

I walked back into the shop in a daze to find the police had arrived and were speaking to Mike.

'What about your CCTV?' a tall red-haired police officer asked.

Mike shook his head, grimacing. 'I don't have any.'

The officer raised his eyebrows and looked out into the street. 'Unfortunate. The shopfront's in a black spot where the security cameras are placed along the street. Unless we can find eyewitnesses, then we're going to struggle.'

I considered how quiet this road would be in the dead of night and didn't hold out much hope. I approached the officers.

'I have an idea who could have done it. We've been getting threats and abuse from the previous shop owner. His name's Neil.'

Mike's eyebrows rose – presumably this was the first he'd heard of it. 'Neil Crosby,' he added, then frowned, seeming to process this revelation. 'I've got his last address if you want to go and speak to him. It sounds like he could possibly be responsible. He was a bit of a livewire after all.'

The policemen exchanged an amused glance. 'You don't say.'

'You know him?' I asked.

'Know him?' said the other officer, a beefy-looking man with a shaved head. 'He's one of our best customers.'

'What?'

'He's a bit of a *livewire* wherever he goes, love. Must be once a month we have him in for drunk and disorderly, affray, breach of the peace. He's on first-name terms with the custody officer.'

Mike rolled his eyes and muttered something indecipherable, the only recognisable words being 'background checks'. I guessed he hadn't done one.

'So, are you going to go and see him?' I pressed. 'With his

history and what he's been putting us through, it looks like he could be bang to rights.'

The taller police officer chuckled. 'He'd have had a hard job breaking in here last night. He spent the night in his usual cell down at our station. I think he must enjoy the breakfast.'

I gaped at him and then at Penn. So it wasn't Neil. Then who the hell could it be? It seemed too much of a coincidence that the sabotage wasn't linked. Maybe we had it all wrong. Penn just shook his head and ran his hand down his face.

The officers went out into the street, promising someone would be over soon to dust for prints and so on, leaving me, Penn and Mike standing in a state of shock and exhaustion.

'Please tell me the two of you took out some insurance. Mine will cover the damage to the building but not your contents.'

Penn nodded, but I stood there, the question sinking in. No, I hadn't taken out insurance. Since it was such a short-term arrangement, it hadn't crossed my mind. Now I felt incredibly stupid.

Mike left, and I sat down heavily on my chair. Any hopes I'd had of helping Mam and Dad had been thoroughly dashed. Everything was gone. My most valuable commodity, Liaison Secrète, had been a lifeline, and now it had been cut off. My heart felt like it had been put through a mangle.

Penn came over and pulled me to standing, enveloping me in a hug, stroking my hair.

'What if someone sees?' I whispered into his neck.

'I don't care.'

I relaxed a little, trying not to think about that phone call the previous night. He still seemed so into me, so attentive. Meeting another woman last night seemed so unlikely now I was in his arms, but the idea still hovered over me like a rain-filled cloud. I rested my chin on his shoulder, trying not to cry, and then saw the empty glass cabinet on his side of the shop. I gasped.

'Penn. The Pink Floyd.'

He flinched and squeezed me tighter. 'I know. It's okay.'

I pulled back to look him in the eye. He avoided my gaze.

'It's not okay. You said it was worth thousands.'

He sighed. 'The insurance will cover it.'

'But your godfather... Uncle Al.'

The muscle at his temple twitched, and he stared out of the window. Then, like he'd flicked a switch, his expression cleared and he shrugged. 'It is what it is.'

I reached for him, but he gave me an apologetic look. 'I'm going to get a coffee. Do you want one?'

'I'll come with you.'

'Is it okay if I go alone? I just need a minute.'

I nodded and watched him go, his black Converse treading towards the door as if it were gallows. I felt a rush of sympathy for him, which made a strange bedfellow with the confused feelings I had about that phone call. After a minute, in a flash of mania, I followed him out, deciding if I didn't ask him about last night right then, I would drive myself mad. I couldn't cope with more than one dilemma that day.

By the time I'd made it down the street, he was just about to turn into the door of the coffee shop, but stopped and took out his mobile, leaning against the shop wall. Before he could see me, I ducked into the doorway just yards away, immediately feeling guilty and, frankly, like Columbo going through a break-down. But the overheard call the previous night had made me cautious and ill-at-ease – I had to hear if my suspicions might be right before I confronted him.

'Phil. Hi,' he said, and my belly turned over with relief. It wasn't another woman at least. I waited where I was, not wanting him to know I'd been listening in, then he carried on.

'Yeah, the upfront money's cleared. Where shall I meet you?'

There was a muffled, tinny sound as 'Phil' replied.

'Okay. I'll see you there, and you can transfer the rest when I hand it over... Of course you can check it. Fair enough, you've seen it's the 1973 version on the photos last night, but I told you – it's in mint condition... Right. See you later.' He rang off, and I heard him go into the coffee shop.

I stood there, my mind racing. The relief of finding out it hadn't been another woman had been solidly trumped by the sickening feeling that replaced it. *The rare Pink Floyd.* Missing from its case, presumed stolen in the burglary. But he still had it. He'd arranged to sell it last night, and then the shop was robbed. Cogs turned in the most disturbing way. Penn had told me he'd claim on his insurance for it... but he was also about to sell it to someone else. My brain scrambled to make sense of it.

Despite all my best efforts to find a rational explanation, one thought kept pushing through the rest. What if he'd... staged the burglary so he could sell the album then claim the insurance too? No, he wouldn't. The Penn I knew wouldn't do that. But the Penn I thought I knew had lied to me last night. I needed it not to be true, but I couldn't completely discount the awful possibility. Then I remembered that my things had been stolen too, and it was like a punch in the gut.

What if he'd staged the burglary to make money? And then taken me down with him?

TWENTY-SIX

I'd watched *The Muppet Christmas Carol* twice that day, appreciating the distraction of the festive puppets and Michael Caine's deadpan performance. The Ghost of Christmas Past loomed large in my parents' house, from the slightly tired-looking fake Christmas tree that I'd helped drag down from the loft (decorated with lolly-stick angels and a toilet-roll-middle reindeer that I'd made in primary school), along with the annual bottle of Advocaat and wedges of Christmas cake that I'd been making good use of. The Ghost of Christmas Yet to Come hovered in the wings in the form of packing boxes. An offer had been accepted from a cash buyer who wanted to move quickly, so my mam and dad were set to move out in February. As I observed Kermit the Frog mourning Tiny Tim, I took another deep slug of Advocaat.

Mam had popped out to see her parents, and Dad was having a nap upstairs, so I was having a rare moment alone since I'd arrived with my bags a few days ago. In the end, after weighing up my feelings about Penn alongside the pointlessness of trying to sort out the shop in the wake of the burglary, I'd decamped to my childhood home earlier than planned for

Christmas. Carrying on and trying to use what little money I had to start restocking the shop was even more fruitless now that the house sale was a done deal, for all but the exchange of contracts. The ship hadn't quite sailed, but it was sitting at the docks waiting to go, and any meagre amount of money I could still plough into their funds was too little too late.

I hadn't seen Penn before I left, and hadn't answered his calls or responded to his worried messages. I hadn't answered *anyone's* messages, to be fair, since I was in no mood to talk. After a while, I'd blocked Penn's number. I had no way to prove that he'd done what I thought he'd done, but I just didn't know what to say to him. I couldn't even bring myself to ask the question. Thankfully, he hadn't made an attempt to turn up here, but every time the doorbell went, I flinched. Anyway, now that it was the day before Christmas Eve, I assumed he was ensconced in the splendour of Northumberland with his awful family, probably drinking champagne or the blood of a freshly slaughtered stag, or whatever their festive tradition was. Now that I'd distanced myself from Penn, I had, to some degree, rekindled my disdain for his background.

I'd just plunged my hand into the tin of Twiglets, withdrawing a Marmite version of a Freddy Krueger hand, when the doorbell rang, making me jump. Dropping my snack, I headed cautiously to the door, only daring to breathe when I saw a familiar shape through the frosted glass.

'I thought you might need this,' said Christa, waving a bottle of Sauvignon Blanc at me. She was wearing a 'Save the Turkeys' sweatshirt. 'Plus, I'd like to know what the fuck has happened. Season's greetings by the way.'

I let her in and retrieved two glasses, each of us taking a substantial swig before I asked her how she'd found me.

'Penn, of course. He didn't want to arrive unannounced, since he's quite sure he's upset you. He doesn't know why though. So he asked me to check if you're okay. Plus you weren't answering my messages.'

'I'm fine,' I said, pulling my lightly stained dressing gown over my Grinch pyjamas.

Christa's unconvinced gaze swept over me. 'Come on, Annie, you're not fine. What happened? Was it the burglary?'

'You could say that.'

'I'm sorry I wasn't there. But by the time I got to the arcade, you'd already cleared off. Penn was frantically calling you and nobody knew where you were. Then Mike said you'd shut up shop for the holidays and wanted to be left alone. But why?'

My shoulders rose. 'I just... I couldn't see the point anymore. The stock is all gone; Mam and Dad have sold the house. It's over.'

'But you were doing so well. I thought you wanted to get out of your flatshare too – isn't that a good enough reason to carry on?'

'It's complicated.'

She regarded me for a moment. 'Is this something to do with Penn? I know you don't like each other, but has he done something?'

I made a brief exasperated noise and ground my fists into my eyes. 'Like I said, it's complicated. But yes, that's part of the reason I want out of the shop.'

'Tell me, Annie. I'm your friend. I want to help you.'

Pausing for a moment, my heart pounding, I made a wild decision to just tell her the truth.

'I didn't like him before, and I don't like him anymore. But there was a brief period where I liked him too much. And it seemed to be reciprocated.' As I said it, I was aware that my eyes must have looked as haunted as Christa's looked surprised.

'Bloody hell,' she breathed. 'Wow.' She sat back on the sofa, looking at the TV. Miss Piggy bustled around a snow-covered street wearing a bonnet and shawl.

'I'm not sure what came over me,' I said.

'I still don't get it. Are you upset about the burglary? Or have you and Penn broken up? If that's what you'd call it – like, did you just hook up, or...?'

'I don't really know anymore.' I explained in as simple terms as possible what had happened in Northumberland. Christa listened, rapt.

'So you had a falling-out? Was it because you remembered he's a known bird murderer?' She shuddered.

I hesitated, deciding I hadn't the energy to explain Penn's real views on shooting, or the fact he'd orchestrated the protest. Plus, if I told her my suspicions about the insurance fraud, I could sound like a tinfoil-hat-wearing lunatic. After all, I had no proof. And worse, she could shop him to the insurance company or the police. I might have been disgusted with Penn, but I wanted no part in initiating criminal proceedings.

'We... had a disagreement. I overheard a phone conversation, and I think he's seeing someone else.' A blatant lie, but at least it was vaguely close to my earlier suspicions. I needed Christa to understand why I didn't want to see Penn ever again.

'The dirty bastard,' she whispered. 'If I'd known that, I wouldn't have come on his account. I mean, I was going to check on you anyway, but still... he kept insisting that I report back to him.'

'Why did you agree to help him anyway?' I asked. 'I thought you hated him.'

'I do. But he looked so cut-up. Now I know it was his guilty conscience rather than genuine concern.' She noticed my face crumple. 'Sorry. I didn't mean to be so blunt. But it sounds like you're well rid of him.'

I raised my chin and gave a decisive nod that didn't necessarily match the turmoil in my head. 'That's right. I'm going to sell the odds and ends the burglars left behind, then I'll hand back the shop. I'll never have to see him again.'

'I'm so sorry,' said Christa, squeezing my arm, her eyes misting. 'I can't believe it's come to this. I feel like I've only known you for five minutes, but you're my friend now, and I don't want to see you leave. I'll miss you.'

'It doesn't mean we can't stay in touch. We can still be friends even if I'm working somewhere else, you dafty.'

She smiled. 'Yeah. We can.'

She topped up our wine glasses, and we settled back onto the sofa, watching the Muppets' Christmassy celebrations. I sighed. After Christmas was over, I'd have to find myself another job, or even Neo's place would be financially out of my league.

The next day was Christmas Eve, and despite my miserable mood in previous days, I felt slightly more buoyed up by the festivities. Auntie Pat and my cousin Kelly came over in the morning to drop off presents, both dressed like they were going on to a club. Kelly took one look at my tracksuit bottoms and patted the envelope she'd sellotaped to a box of chocolates, assuring me the enclosed New Look gift card would see me right in the New Year. Then, once they'd left, Mam put some party food in the oven, and we settled in front of the TV once more.

We watched *The Holiday*, against my dad's will, although he seemed happy enough with a can of Fosters and a bowl of peanuts rested on his outstretched cast. I buried the momentary flicker of pain at the sight of Kate Winslet's snow-dusted cottage, which sparked the memory of mine and Penn's night alone in the lodge. Everything seemed to remind me of him; I'd even had to abandon a knitting project as the little black dog I was stitching started to look too much like Hendrix.

'Ah, I love this film,' said Mam. 'I think I'd rather go to Los Angeles for Christmas than stay in the freezing cold.'

'Me too,' I agreed. 'There's a lot to be said for a change of scenery.'

'Aye. Well, if you keep on with the shop, you'll be earning the big bucks in no time and you can book yourself a nice holiday.' Dad grinned at me, and I smiled back with as much enthusiasm as I could muster.

I hadn't been able to bear telling them the truth yet. They had enough to deal with without hearing about the burglary, and the less they knew about me and Penn, the better. I'd just said I wanted a longer Christmas break – the perks of being self-employed – and decided I'd tell them after they'd moved house that I was giving up the shop.

'Yep,' I murmured. 'Next stop, the Maldives.'

'That's a girl,' he said, patting my knee.

We finished watching the film, played a round of Monopoly then settled back down with some mince pies to watch Mam's favourite soap's Christmas special. Someone had kidnapped someone else and had answered the door to carol singers while their captive was tied up in the background. So far, so festive.

The doorbell rang.

'Ooh, I wonder if that's carol singers for us,' said Mam, starting to get up.

'It'd be a bloody good coincidence, since I feel like I'm being held hostage watching this rubbish,' said Dad.

'Sit down, Mam – I'll get it,' I said, and she rested back on the sofa.

'Give us another mince pie,' she said to Dad as I went to the hall, and I heard him rustling in the box. I smoothed my tatty hair and switched on the flashing red nose of my Rudolph sweatshirt before I opened the door, deciding a Christmas Eve visitor should be greeted with just a little bit of cheer.

Outside stood Penn, in his trademark trendy clothes, fairly ill-suited to the cold weather except for an artfully slouched beanie on his head. As if by reflex, I started to close the door.

'Annie, please!' he said, not quite jamming his foot in the door but coming close enough to make me pause.

'What are you doing here?' I hissed through the gap.

'I needed to see you.'

'I thought your emissary would have reported back. I'm fine, and I don't want to see you.'

'She did. And for some reason she seems to think I've cheated on you. Which is complete, utter bollocks.'

I hesitated. For a moment, my curiosity to hear him explain everything superseded my wish for him to bugger off. I opened the door just a little more, wide enough for him to see my furious expression.

'Glad to hear it. But, unfortunately for you, I already know that. I just needed to make an excuse to Christa without potentially getting you in trouble.'

His brow creased. 'What do you mean?'

'I know about the Pink Floyd album, Penn.'

He was still looking confused. 'What...?'

'I know it wasn't stolen. And I heard you selling it to someone else. Now, would you just leave? There's nothing more to say.' And I slammed the door, my heart thudding against my ribs. I turned and leaned against the wall, taking deep breaths.

'Who was that?' shouted Dad from the living room.

'Jehovah's Witnesses,' I said. 'I'm just going upstairs.'

I stumbled up towards my bedroom, just hearing my mam as I went.

'Jehovah's? On Christmas Eve?'

I lay on my bed feeling like the little wall of happiness I'd started to build up inside me had been knocked down again into a pile of bricks. What the hell did Penn think he was doing turning up here? I didn't doubt that Christa had put the fear of God in him when she'd reported back, even if Penn and I both knew that another woman wasn't the real reason I'd run off. But I was surprised that he'd had the gall to come over when I'd made it very clear he was persona non grata. What exactly had he intended to say?

For the last few days, over and over in my head, I'd tried to piece it all together. If Penn had staged the break-in, then it made sense that he would set the scene – graffiti, online trolling... If he could pretend that we had a common enemy, then he could deflect suspicion away from himself, and by robbing my stock, it made everything seem more plausible. But part of my brain insisted that it wasn't plausible at all, that he couldn't do this to me. It was a dizzying cycle of emotions that I couldn't break free of.

I put a pillow over my face and screamed into it, wishing I'd never even met him. Some time passed while I lay on my side, staring at the magnolia wall. I could hear Mam and Dad laughing at something on the telly, and the crack and hiss of Dad opening another can. I pictured the cosy scene as I lay in the semi-darkness.

Then the doorbell rang again. I heard my mam get up to answer it, and then the sound of several voices singing 'O Little Town of Bethlehem'. I allowed myself a small smile – they'd got their carol singers after all.

After half a minute, my mam's voice drifted up the stairs. 'Annie, pet. Can you fetch me down a pound? I've left my purse in the bedroom.'

I got up, retrieved a coin for her and went downstairs. In the doorway was a small crowd of people wrapped in padded jackets, gloves and hats, their breath clouding the air white as they sang. As they segued into 'Silent Night', I saw Penn standing at the back, not even pretending to join in. Instead, he locked feverish eyes with me and mouthed the word 'Please'.

TWENTY-SEVEN

The thin crust of frozen sleet and grit crunched under our feet as we walked; I stared at the white blooms of frost on the path ahead instead of looking at Penn. We hadn't spoken since I'd pulled on my coat and boots and hustled him away from the doorstep, my mam looking bewildered until she remembered Penn from the shop. The last thing I wanted was to have a conversation in our house with its thin walls and curious parents.

We came to the park, which was deserted, and trudged through the gate and down the winding lane under the trees. There were street lights interspersed between them, casting a dim light under the canopy.

'Talk to me,' said Penn finally.

'Are you sure you want to have this conversation?' I snapped. 'Because it could go very badly for you.'

'Annie, you've got it all wrong. Yes, I've sold the Pink Floyd, but that's all. I swear.'

'So you're telling me it's just a coincidence that the shop was burgled the very night you sold it to some guy down the pub?'

'I know it's hard to fathom, but yes!' he said, his voice suddenly heated. 'I couldn't believe it when I arrived at the shop. And I almost couldn't believe my luck.'

'I bet you couldn't.'

He groaned, exasperated. 'That's not what I mean. Annie, please, will you just hear me out?' He tried to take my arm, but I shook it off and walked on, my hands shoved into my pockets. He jogged to catch up with me.

'I did sell the album to some guy down the pub, yes. He came in and made me an offer a while ago, which was the closest I'd ever got to its real value. He left me his number, so I called him up the day after we got back from Ashcliffe, like you overheard. We haggled... and when we agreed a fair price, he paid me some money upfront, and I made the arrangement to meet him the next day and hand it over. So I took it home with me. When I came to the shop the next morning, I couldn't believe that I'd taken it home before it would have been nicked.'

'I'm sorry, but it sounds unlikely. And even if it is true, and you then claimed it on your insurance, then that's just as bad.'

'I *didn't* claim it on my insurance!'

I whipped round to face him. 'What?'

'I only said I would because I didn't want to tell you I'd sold it. Not right then anyway. I haven't even submitted my claim yet, and when I do, I won't be putting the album on the form. Because it *wasn't there.*' He looked at me with nervous expectation, willing me to believe him.

I wrapped my arms around myself, thoughts cascading like Tetris blocks trying to fall into place but stacking up into a haphazard pile.

I looked into his eyes, trying to work him out. The closeness we'd shared in Northumberland had been damaged by these last few days, and during that time, I'd spent more and more time remembering how much we'd been at odds at first. I'd started to paint over the newer picture of him with the old colours. But now he was standing in front of me, his dark eyes looking tortured, I saw shades of him starting to shine through.

'How do I know you're telling the truth?' I said, sounding like a belligerent child, even to my own ears.

He took his phone out of his pocket and tapped it a few times before presenting it to me. A document lit up the screen.

'Here. The claim form I've started filling in.'

I scrolled through it. He'd listed estimates for the boxes of CDs and tapes, the individual values of some of the collectors' albums. Even the novelty music items we'd shared were on there – just half the value of them, since we'd agreed to share them. But there was no Pink Floyd album on there. I looked up at him, and he didn't even look triumphant. He looked distraught.

'It wasn't there, so I would never have claimed for it.'

I stood very still, my throat feeling dry and thick. My brain was catching up with my misunderstanding of the situation, and with that came the first twinges of regret.

'You said the shop was struggling for money.'

'It is. But I would never lie, or steal, or cheat.'

'You also said you would never sell the album. That it was precious to you.'

He said nothing for a moment, his expression unreadable, then he glanced away. 'I'm starting to reconsider what's precious and what's not.'

'What does that mean?' I asked, genuinely puzzled.

'It means...' He paused, searching for words. 'It means that even though I've never valued money that much – or at least I thought there was more to life than wealth – I've got a deeper understanding now of what makes me happy. Living away from Ashcliffe, making my own choices, has made me a better person... I think.' He faltered momentarily, eyes flickering from side to side. 'I guess what I'm trying to say is that I've learned enough these past few years to not place value on *things*. They don't make me as happy as... people do.'

'People?'

'You.'

I stared at him, watching his Adam's apple bob up and down, his eyes holding mine but still uncertain. I didn't know what to say.

After what felt like a long time, I said, 'I'm so confused.'

'About me?'

'Yes.' I sighed. 'I just... don't get what this has to do with the Pink Floyd album.'

'I sold it for you.'

'*What?*' I blinked at him, my jaw slackening.

'I saw how much you were struggling. You said you were trying everything you could to help your family. I wanted to help *you*.'

'Excuse me? You sold the album... to give money to *me*?'

He nodded.

My breath started to come in sharper bursts, and I turned away, my eyes stinging. Without a backwards glance, I stormed away, further into the passage of trees.

'Annie, wait!' he shouted and ran up behind me again.

'This is ridiculous,' I said as he caught up with me. 'Utterly ridiculous. And offensive! I don't want *charity*, Penn! God, what must you think of me? Poor little working-class Annie, trying to save her parents' poky little house. I know, I'll swoop in and sort out all her problems with a wodge of cash.'

'I know you're an independent person,' he said, striding to keep up with me. 'And I'm sure your parents are too. But I couldn't stand to see you working yourself into the ground, wearing yourself out. You were grafting enough before we went to Ashcliffe, and now with the burglary and the money you've lost by closing...' He sounded so pained that I slowed down to a stop again.

'I can't believe you did this,' I said, a rogue tear now trickling down my cheek. I couldn't admit my stupid mistake to not take insurance. Not right now, or he'd feel even more motivated to help me. 'It's just so bloody patronising. I get it, you're rich; thousands of pounds is pocket money to you.'

'It isn't. I told you: my parents might be rich, but I'm not.'

'So you're saying you'd get yourself into more financial strife to help me out? It doesn't make sense.'

'None of this makes sense! I spent weeks thinking we couldn't stand the sight of each other, and now I think I... I think I...' He ran out of air and plunged his hand into his hair.

'You think you what? Penn, what could make you imagine that this was a solution?'

His eyes blazed as he walked closer to me. He stood chest to chest with me, breathing heavily. 'I know. I've fucked up. I should have realised that it would come across like this, and I'm sorry, I really am. But when it comes to you, I can't think straight anymore. When it comes to us, I'm spinning out.'

Then his eyes darkened, and he cupped the back of my head and kissed me hard. I held my breath for a moment, surprised and confused and... exhilarated. My anger short-circuited into passion and a strange sense of relief at his touch. Although I'd spent the last few days pushing him away, I melted into him; even in that short time, I hadn't realised how much I'd missed his lips against mine. I felt all of his feelings in that kiss, and I knew then that I was spinning out too.

Later, we sat on a park bench, close together against the cold. I shivered a little, and he wrapped his arm around me and kissed my forehead.

'I'm sorry,' he said for the third time. 'I'm an idiot, and I deserved all of that.'

'You are, and you did. But it doesn't matter now. I just feel awful that you sold something that meant so much to you.'

'It's just a thing. I've still got my memories of my godfather, and that's what counts.'

'I hope you'll use it for something good.' He shifted against me and opened his mouth to speak. 'Not me, before you say anything. I'm touched that you did this, but I won't accept it, Penn. I can't.'

'I wish I could persuade you.'

'You won't.' I shook my head with finality.

'I should have remembered how stubborn you can be from our early days in the shop,' he murmured.

'Takes one to know one,' I said.

'Fair enough. You know, although I'm frustrated that you won't take the money, I love that about you. You're a strong, proud person.'

My stomach fluttered at the word 'love'. Even in that context, I felt a ripple of affection, wondering if we might ever say it to each other in a different way. But the idea of it struck a strange chord within me. That evening, my heart was full, but my head was scrambled; I filed my thoughts away for the time being. 'Pride doesn't always come from a good place.' The moment I said it, I regretted it. I didn't want to spoil this.

'What do you mean?'

I hesitated. Did I really want to ruin this by opening up old wounds? 'Nothing,' I said, cuddling closer to him, nudging my head under his chin. His neck was warm and smelled of a woody scent that was starting to become familiar.

'Annie... I want to know everything about you. Whatever that might be.'

I turned my head even closer to him, the bristles under his chin skimming my forehead. I didn't speak for a while.

'I got bullied at school. Because my parents didn't have much money.'

His arm tightened around me almost imperceptibly and he stayed quiet, allowing me to carry on.

'I didn't go to a fancy school, not by any means, but it was a mixed bag when it came to the other kids' backgrounds. There were people like me, who didn't have much, and others whose parents had their own businesses or were lawyers and doctors, and some of them looked down on us. I always had a hand-me-down jacket, knock-off designer sweatshirts from the market. The richer kids would pull the label out the back of my top to prove it wasn't really Juicy Couture, that it was a cheap fake. It was embarrassing and demoralising. I hated school because of it.'

I could feel him breathing steadily. 'I'm sorry that happened to you. It sounds horrible.'

'It was. And back then I was so desperate to impress, to make them see that I was a worthwhile person by having the same things as them.'

I stopped. This was more painful than I'd thought, reliving these memories. And if I continued, Penn might think less of me, but with his arms around me, I felt safe. My voice shook as I continued.

'I started stealing things. Just little bits, like nice make-up or jewellery that looked a bit more expensive than the necklaces I already had that made my neck turn green. But one day, after they'd taken the piss out of me for having supermarket trainers, I aimed higher. I stole a pair of Nikes from a shop, and unsurprisingly got caught. They didn't press charges, but my parents got hauled in, and I got a vicious dressing-down from them and the security guard. I'd never felt so ashamed.

'Then, not long after that, I left school and decided I'd never lower myself to try and impress anyone ever again. I would be proud of being myself, and I wouldn't allow anyone to make me feel "less than" for not being rich.'

Penn stiffened. 'I'm so sorry, Annie. Now you've told me, I

understand completely how I've offended you. I know I can't take it back, but can you forgive me?'

'Yes. I know you've done it out of kindness. But I'm not sure I can ever forgive *myself* for being the reason you sold your pride and joy.'

'I told you. It was just a thing.' He sighed gently. 'At least you know I'm not playing away with another woman.' His voice wavered with amusement.

I elbowed him in the side. 'You can imagine how I might have thought that.'

'Mmhm. But I hope you can see now that it's never going to happen.' I started to relax into his side again, but he raised my chin and kissed me softly. 'There is no one else.'

He looked deep into my eyes as he said it, and it felt loaded with meaning. It didn't just sound like there was no other woman in his life; it felt like he was saying there was no other woman in the world. I kissed him so intensely I lost my breath.

When I pulled away, something occurred to me.

'Penn, how did Christa get the chance to see you after she came here? Why aren't you in Northumberland?'

'I didn't fancy it after all. To tell you the truth, when we left Ashcliffe, my parents and I'd had a... disagreement.'

My stomach twisted, remembering the conversation I'd overheard. 'But it's Christmas Eve.'

He shrugged. 'Like I said. I've worked out what's more important to me.'

'But... your family... Were you just planning to stay in you flat alone? I mean, what if I'd refused to see you?'

'You didn't though. And I still intend to stay in my flat, although I won't be alone. Sam makes a mean turkey curry.'

I shook my head. 'That doesn't sound... great.'

'It's fine. Really. And I'm just happy I came to see you. And that you let me kiss you, even though you wouldn't take the money. Without sounding like a Hallmark movie, that's the best Christmas present I could have asked for.'

I thought for a moment.

'No,' I said firmly. 'You're not going to spend Christmas in your flat. I bet you haven't even got a Christmas tree.'

'Does a string of tinsel across the top of the telly count?'

'No, it doesn't. I know this will sound ironic since I've just refused to let you take care of me. But I'm taking no arguments. You're coming home with me.'

TWENTY-EIGHT

'Merry Christmas,' I said, shuffling into the living room in my dressing gown and fluffy slippers. Dad was sitting on the sofa, his leg outstretched as ever, the crutches he'd just started to use propped beside him. He stopped mid-slurp of a spoonful of Frosties and blinked up at me.

Swallowing, he replied, 'Happy Christmas, pet. Where's lover boy?'

I blushed a deep red. 'He's not...' Well, he kind of was, but I didn't want to get too far into it. 'He's just getting ready. And he's very grateful for our hospitality, so please don't give him a hard time.'

I'd awkwardly presented Penn to my parents last night, tactfully explaining his need for a room at the inn and, in their usual generous way, they'd agreed that he should stay. It was offered with much more enthusiasm from my mam, while the reception from Dad was a little on the cooler side. I suspected his last encounter with Penn was still on his mind.

'I won't. It's Christmas after all. But I had no idea you were... stepping out with him.'

I sighed. 'It's complicated – it's early days. And I hope you get a book on updated slang in your stocking later.'

'Well, I don't know what else to call it. Is he your boyfriend then, or are we just fetching any old waifs and strays to sleep in our spare room now?'

'Yes, he is.' I cringed. We hadn't got far enough to put a label on it yet. 'I think. But you know I wouldn't bring him here otherwise.'

Dad nodded stiffly. 'I suppose. You've always been choosy. I just hope he's a decent lad.' His brow knitted briefly. 'Where's he from originally? He doesn't sound local.'

I opened my mouth, unsure what was going to come out of it – I didn't know if I should tell him about Penn's background or not, given that Penn seemed to prefer his Newcastle alter ego. But I was saved from making that split-second decision by a call from the kitchen.

'Happy Christmas, darl. Do you want a cup of coffee?'

'Yes, please,' I replied and skipped off to the kitchen, leaving my dad to the distraction of itching under his cast.

I plonked myself down on one of the kitchen counter stools and accepted a mug from my mam. She leaned against the fridge, arms crossed, mug in hand, an amused expression on her face.

'Care to explain yourself?' she asked with a glint in her eye.

I shrugged and took a sip of my coffee. 'Like I said, it was either this or him spending Christmas in his grotty flat with his grotty flatmate.'

'You didn't seem very happy to see him when he arrived. I saw the look on your face when he was with the carol singers.'

'We'd had words. Back at the shop.'

'Mmhm. Well, I had no idea you were courting him.' Another worthy recipient of an updated slang phrasebook. 'I did say he was dishy.' Strike three on the lingo. She wiggled her eyebrows.

'Stop it. Ugh. This isn't how I would have wanted to tell you. But it's not like we're headed up the aisle or anything. Like I said to Dad, it's early days.'

'And you've already had a falling-out?'

More often than I'd care to tell you. 'It's fine. It was just a misunderstanding.'

'And why's he got nowhere else to go? What about his family? Is he not wanting to spend Christmas with them?'

I hesitated. 'He... It's complicated.' This seemed to be my stock answer *du jour*, and I wasn't sure how long I could get away with it.

'How so? I mean, not being at home for Christmas – I can't imagine it. What kind of people...?' She shook her head, perplexed.

'Mam, don't stress. He's not upset about it; it's his choice. And we'll make him feel as welcome here as he would be at Ash —' I stopped myself just in time, or so I thought.

'*Ash* what? Is he from Ashington? I thought his accent sounded a bit peculiar.'

I grimaced and propped my elbows on the counter, pushing my eyes against my palms, then let out an exasperated moan. If I didn't give in now, then my mam certainly wouldn't – not when she was sniffing for information. 'I didn't want to go down this rabbit hole. Not yet.'

She said nothing, giving me just enough rope to hang myself.

I looked up at her, cringing. 'He lives— his *family* live at Ashcliffe Hall. In Northumberland.'

Her eyes widened. 'Ashcliffe Hall? You don't need to tell me where it is – I'd be hard pressed not to have heard of it. So what do they do there? Do they work on the estate?'

'They *own* the estate.' The silence that fell after I spoke felt like it lasted forever. 'His parents are Lord and Lady Ashcliffe.'

'I beg your pardon?' she asked, and her jaw dropped. 'Are you telling me he's...?'

'He's not rich, before you start. He's financially independent.'

'I meant to say, are you telling me he's an aristocrat? What kind of aristocrats call their son *Penn*?'

I took a deep breath, both for my nerves and so I had enough air in the tank to get through the length of his real name. 'He's called Peregrine Burton-Edwards. Uh, the *Honourable* Peregrine Burton-Edwards. Actually.'

Mam started to laugh. 'Behave. No he isn't.'

'He is,' I said, squirming. 'But don't go talking to him about it, and *please* just call him Penn. He doesn't like fuss.'

'I can't believe it,' she said, smiling and shaking her head. But then she suddenly froze, her face falling. 'Bloody hell,' she said. 'I didn't get the cloth napkins out. We've got paper serviettes for the dinner table! Oh, and I've only got Aunt Bessie's roasties. What's he going to think?' She looked stricken.

'Calm down! He's not like that. He lives in a little flat that's probably overflowing with ready meals and beer cans. Plus, he's nice.'

I remembered how much I used to loathe him, how awful he seemed when we first met, and felt a little glow in the pit of my stomach, knowing what I knew now.

'Okay,' she said with a little sigh. 'But you'd better skedaddle. I've got a turkey *and* a nut roast to cook, and I'd better dust off the good wine glasses. These ones from Home Bargains won't do.' She cast a worried glance at some perfectly nice-looking glassware.

'I mean it, Mam. Just forget I said anything and act normal.'

I left her frantically opening cupboards and went back to the living room, where Penn was sitting in an armchair by the window. Dad was sitting where I'd left him, looking even more uncomfortable than usual, which was something, considering his current physical state.

Penn briefly raised his eyebrows. He had on last night's clothes, naturally, but had tied his hair up in a neat man-bun, his perennial stubble looking not too out of place. After sleeping in his arms all night, I'd got kind of used to him being in my bed, but seeing him in the living room was a different thing altogether.

'You alright?' I asked, giving him an encouraging smile.

'Yeah. We were just talking about the match.'

My dad nodded tightly. I knew he wasn't into football, and I didn't think Penn was either. I'd clearly walked in on a standard-issue male chat where there was nothing else to say. My heart sank, and I wondered if Dad would ever forgive Penn. Then I had an idea.

'Right. Listen, I'm just popping upstairs, but I wanted to give you one of your presents first,' I said to Dad. I rustled under the tree and produced a small package. 'Go on – open it.'

He grinned and ripped open the paper to reveal an electronic guitar tuner.

'You said yours was broken, so I got you a new one.'

'That's smashing. Come here, kidda.' He pulled me in for a hug. 'Thank you very much.'

'Why don't you give it a try – make sure it's working? Maybe Penn could come and see your guitars?' I suggested.

'Alright then, I will.'

I helped him up onto his crutches and steered him towards the garage. Penn stood up, and I gave him a meaningful look – he understood and followed Dad into the guitar cave. Crossing my fingers, I ran upstairs to throw on some make-up and Christmas tree earrings.

Twenty minutes later, I came back down and hovered near the garage door. From the other side, I could hear the strum of two guitars, murmured conversation then a salvo of loud laughter. Smiling to myself, I left them to it and went to help my mam peel some sprouts.

A few hours later, we were all assembled at the table, my dad and Penn still chuckling at a shared joke. I was very relieved to see that all seemed to be forgiven. Earlier, before she and I laid food on the table, Mam had excused herself and returned to the room wearing a smart blouse and a pearl necklace that she'd got from Next. She flicked a nervous glance at Penn, and I kicked her under the table.

We started to eat, and Penn enthusiastically complimented Mam on the turkey and stuffing, saying it was the best he'd ever tasted. She blushed and said that was surely not true.

'So, what kind of Christmas Day do you usually have at home?' she asked.

I gave her a warning glance, and she avoided my eye.

'Oh, quite similar to this really,' he said. 'We have lunch, then presents, and then play games and what-have-you. Just normal stuff.'

'That *does* sound normal,' said Mam in a relieved tone. Dad screwed up his face at her, confused. 'I hope you don't mind the Aunt Bessie's. I expect you have a professional at home.'

'Mam,' I whispered through gritted teeth.

'What on earth are you talking about, Denise? Professional what?' asked Dad.

Penn bit his lip and looked at me across the table, a patient smile hovering at the edge of his lips. I mouthed 'Sorry' and winced.

'I think Annie's been giving you all the gory details,' said Penn gamely. 'But yes. We do have a professional. Although I really do mean it – this is miles better.' He took a big scoop of red cabbage and stuffed it into his mouth.

Mam seemed to glow with pride.

'Have I missed something?' pushed Dad, glancing at each of us in turn.

'Penn's family own a fair proportion of Northumberland,' I muttered. 'But we weren't supposed to be making a big thing out of it.' I threw Mam a scathing look.

'It's fine. Honestly!' Penn said. 'I did grow up at Ashcliffe Hall, but I have my own life too. I prefer it here in Newcastle.'

'Oh, but it must be lovely, pet,' said Mam. 'If I lived in Downton Abbey, I wouldn't be looking to move to Coronation Street.'

He smiled politely. 'I think you're doing Coronation Street a disservice.'

'Mam, Penn has his own life now. Leave it, would you.' I rubbed my forehead, wishing I could slither under the table.

'I'm just curious,' she said. 'I've never met an *Honourable* before.'

'Hang on. Are you telling me you're some kind of lord?' Dad asked Penn, incredulous. 'Have I just been jamming to Def Leppard with an aristocrat?'

Penn made a nervous noise, halfway between a sigh and a laugh. 'I'm definitely not a lord, and I identify a lot more with rock guitarists than landowners. It's not a big deal – really.'

Dad shrugged, seeming to take this at face value, and popped another sprout in his mouth. Mam looked disappointed but then changed the subject to what we might watch on TV that afternoon.

'Well, as long as we watch the King's Speech,' said Dad. 'I'm still getting used to seeing Charlie instead of Liz, mind you.'

I noticed Mam out the corner of my eye, suddenly emitting excitement like static electricity. She sat up straighter, and I met her eye, shaking my head.

'No,' I mouthed. 'Don't you dare.'

Her smile turned stiff, and it was like watching someone

trying not to lick their lips while eating a donut. I watched in real time as the temptation overwhelmed her.

'Have you ever met him?' she blurted in Penn's direction. 'King Charles?'

I put my head in my hands and sighed.

That afternoon, and into the early evening, we watched Christmas telly, my mam ticking off the programmes from her *Radio Times* shortlist. *Call the Midwife* came on, and Penn showed no sign that this wasn't his cup of tea, even though my dad made efforts to get him onside in complaining about it. Penn was the picture of diplomacy.

As I snuggled into him, my legs curled up on the sofa, his arm around my shoulders, I couldn't help but draw comparisons with the weekend I'd spent with his family. He was so good at fitting in here, from complimenting my mother to bonding with my dad – he made it look so easy. I imagined it was a product of his upbringing, that despite his family's overt snobbery, there was a cultured, polite side to their nature that always sought to make a social event run smoothly. He'd been raised to schmooze.

My stomach turned over at the memory of my many faux pas at Ashcliffe Hall, realising that it would never work both ways. I was simply not equipped to slot seamlessly into his family life like he'd done here. But I was reassured in the knowledge that this was where he wanted to be. In Newcastle, living his own life... with me.

The roiling in my belly settled as he squeezed me just a little, and I took another Kettle Chip from the bowl, my body sinking comfortably against his. This felt so right, as if he'd always been here, like part of the furniture.

Finally, the programme ended, and Penn went to the kitchen to get himself and my dad another beer. Mam and I were still nursing a glass of Baileys apiece. He handed my dad his can and sat back down.

'So, when are you back in the shop? Day after Boxing Day?' asked Mam.

Before I could head him off at the pass, Penn said, 'Yeah. There's still a bit of cleaning up to do, but I think we can shift some of the stock they left behind before the new stuff arrives.'

I wilted. I'd forgotten to warn him I'd decided not to tell my parents about the burglary.

'Eh? What do you mean "left behind"?' said Dad, turning to look at me.

'Um... I was going to tell you, after Christmas. The shop got burgled.'

Mam and Dad sat up straight, both clamouring to ask questions. Penn gave me an apologetic look.

'It's fine,' I said, holding up my hands. 'I can sell the rest of what I've got before I shut up shop, and I'll pay you back for everything I've lost.'

Now it was Penn's turn to look shocked. 'Shut up shop? What do you mean?'

I put my hand on his. 'I'm done, Penn. I'm not going to order any more stock. Once the last few bits are sold, I'm finished.'

His expression was a mix of confused and crestfallen. 'I don't understand. You can build the business back up again when you get your insurance payout, especially if you get some more Liaison Secrète gear.'

'What's Liaison Secrète?' asked Dad.

'Never mind,' said Mam and I in unison, exchanging a furtive glance.

'Listen,' I said to them all. 'I... I feel idiotic, but I didn't take out an insurance policy. So that's that. And it's pointless now anyway. I thought I'd be in with a chance of making enough to stop you having to sell the house, but now I can't.' I stopped then suddenly. My voice had choked at the end of the sentence, and I felt my eyes grow wet.

I looked at the fireplace, the Christmas tree and all of our family's belongings, and my heart hurt to think that this would be the last time we would spend Christmas here. My lip trembled, and a tear escaped and ran down my cheek. Penn caught it with his finger and caressed the side of my cheek.

'Annie,' said Mam. 'You need to stop worrying about the house – that's for us to sort out. You shouldn't give up on the shop; you should be doing it for yourself.'

I gave her a watery smile. 'Thanks. But I don't think I'm quite so popular at the arcade anyway.' Reluctantly, I explained the problems we'd had with the mysterious saboteur, whose identity was once again unknown. They looked shocked at first, but then Dad gripped my hand hard.

'I'll tell you what.' His voice was fierce. 'I didn't raise a quitter. And I thought you'd learned not to give in to bullies.' He gave me a stern stare.

'I know, but...'

'No buts,' he said. 'You've already shown how good you are at this job. You were meant to be a business owner; you've found the career you've been looking for all this time. Don't give up, pet.'

'He's right,' agreed Mam. 'This time the shop will be all for you. You've taken care of us – it's high time you took care of yourself. And I'll try my best to get some more Liaison stuff...'

'I still don't know what you're on about,' grumbled Dad.

There was a moment, then Mam and I burst out laughing, my tears already starting to dry. Penn grinned conspiratorially, although I wondered if he'd fill in his new best mate with the details later on. Maybe they were all right. Maybe I shouldn't give up so easily.

. . .

Later, in the darkness of the spare bedroom, Penn and I lay entwined together. Mam and Dad had turned in an hour ago, and I could hear gentle snores beyond the wall. After the bizarre and emotional day, I couldn't fall asleep.

Penn and I had talked as we settled into bed. He told me that his parents had called that morning, to say Merry Christmas and to ask again why he'd refused to come home to Ashcliffe. He'd declined to comment. I asked him if he had any regrets, and he'd just kissed me hard and with feeling, which seemed to settle the matter.

The clock on the wall ticked, and Penn's heartbeat thrummed against my chest; an alternating rhythm that soothed me. After the stressful conversation that evening, I felt like my anxiety was being dialled down with every beat. Things didn't seem so bad, lying there with him.

The rise and fall of his chest, which I'd thought was deep and regular enough to suggest he was asleep, started to become more erratic. Against my leg, I felt his arousal. I shifted slightly, letting my hand fall between us, stroking him.

He gave a muted gasp and ran his hand down my back, pulling my thigh over his.

'What about...?'

'We'll be quiet,' I said, meeting his mouth with mine, gently biting his lower lip. He groaned. 'I thought I told you to be quiet,' I whispered, my voice more husky than reproachful.

He tried to push me onto my back, kissing my neck and running his hands all over me, but I pushed towards him instead, pressing his shoulders back so he was flat on the bed. Starting at his neck, I trailed a path of kisses down his chest, each kiss a stepping stone further down his body. I reached the achingly beautiful V-shape near his hip and paused there, running my lips across the softer skin and holding off on my travels just long enough to hear him make another quiet noise of frustration. As my mouth found its final destination, one of his hands gripped the bedsheets, the other weaving into my hair. I stayed there just long enough to leave him wanting more, and as he frantically reached for me, I knew how much he really did.

He drew me back up to face him, pulling me in for a deep kiss, smoothing my hair back from my face as it draped down over him. His hand snaked down between us to slide between my legs, and when he felt how ready I was, he smiled against my lips. In one movement, he guided my hips over his and thrust into me, taking my breath away.

'Shh,' he warned, one hand holding my buttock, taking control of my rhythm, the other tracing over my mouth to quiet me. I bit his thumb and tried to contain my ragged breaths against his palm. The feeling of pleasure deep in my body was already building, and he met me with the same urgency, like we were striking a match and both of us were starting to burn at the same time. His breaths began to shorten, and his hand squeezed my hip almost painfully, until he took my arm, pressing his mouth against it, his lips making a silent moan against my skin. In that same moment, my body answered his with sweet, nearly unbearable pulses, my back arching. We stopped together, almost frozen in place, panting and gripping each other. After a moment, he sat up between my legs, holding me to him, his hand cupping the back of my head.

'How did you do this to me?' he murmured, his lips against my cheek.

'Do what?' I answered, my voice lazy and spent.

'Made me need you so much, so fast.'

TWENTY-NINE

Penn and I stayed at Mam and Dad's on Boxing Day and went back to Palmer's Arcade the day after. It seemed that all of the other shops were opening between Christmas and New Year, so we did the rounds, wishing everyone belated season's greetings.

I barrelled into Christa's shop, where she was setting up for the day.

'I've got news. I'm going to try and give the shop another go. So you're stuck with me for the foreseeable future,' I said with a grin.

After my parents and Penn had pressed me to carry on, I'd decided to try. Even though the house sale was going ahead, and it broke my heart that I'd have to give up on my dream to intervene, it now meant I had no time pressure. It would be a struggle, but I was willing to give it another go.

A look of surprise flashed over her face. 'Amazing! That's really great.' She squeezed my arm.

'Thanks. If I can sell the stuff left behind, I might be able to slowly build back up again. Plus my mam found some more boxes of the sustainable beauty products in the garage, so that's a bonus.'

Her smile faltered. With a sinking feeling, I realised my mistake.

'I promise I'm not trying to step on your patch. I'll be back to salad spinners and shoe polish in no time.'

'I know you aren't. It's fine – really. But what about the Liaison stuff?'

Mam had been pained to tell me that her supplier had nothing else to give her. 'I don't think there's going to be any more,' I said morosely.

She frowned and was just about to reply when Jake popped his head round the door. When he saw me, he did a brief double take.

'Had a good Christmas, Annie? I wasn't expecting to see you here.'

'Let's just say I don't give up easily. And yes, it was good, thanks. You?'

'Aye, it was canny. I was out on the lash for most of it.'

'Well, I haven't got any homeopathy stuff for liver failure,' said Christa.

'Ha ha,' he replied. It was then that I noticed a very prominent love bite on his neck.

'Ooh, you really *did* have a good time,' I said, laughing.

He touched his neck as if he'd forgotten it was there then grinned. 'Aye... a very good time was had by all.'

Christa stared at him then turned to me – her expression still seemed a bit guarded. 'Anyway, Annie, I'll catch you later, okay?'

I nodded, and she looked away, busying herself with some pieces of rose quartz. As I left the shop, Jake took my place and closed the door. I stood there for a moment, stung. I wished I hadn't mentioned the beauty products. A horrible feeling that I'd upset my friend prickled my skin – the fact that Jake, who Christa normally couldn't bear the company of, was still welcome made it feel even worse.

'Hey,' Penn said, seeing my face as I went back into the shop. He pulled me in for a hug and kissed the top of my head. 'We're here to start again, remember. You're amazing at this – you've overcome other stuff with the shop, and you can do this too.'

'I know. It's just...'

'It's just nothing. We can do it together. Now, come into the back room, we'll make some coffee and figure out what we need to do next.'

I sighed but then remembered some of our encounters in the back room and smiled wickedly.

'You can't be serious. Just a second ago, you looked like you were ready to cry, and now you look like you want to...' His expression was wry and then playful.

I raised an eyebrow. 'What can I say? You have that effect on me.'

He pulled me towards him, his hand cupping my bum, his eyes narrowed with lust. But before I could drag him off to the stock cupboard, something through the window caught my eye. I flinched and pulled away, my gaze drawn to the street outside like it was magnetised.

'Is that...?' I breathed, my heart skipping a beat.

Penn turned his head to look and abruptly let go of me. 'What...?'

'What is *she* doing here?'

Outside, in roughly the same place across the road that we'd seen Neil before, Sophia stood, arms crossed, studying the shop intensely. From the lack of self-consciousness on her face, I assumed she couldn't make us out clearly through the signs on the window.

'I have no idea,' Penn murmured, scratching his head.

'Should we go out and see her?' I asked, although I didn't really want to.

Just then, Arthur bustled in with an armful of paperbacks.

'Annie, dear. These were donated to us this morning. Christmas regifting, I'd imagine. I wondered if you'd like them for the shop?'

I blinked at him distractedly. 'Um, that's so kind, thank you,' I mustered. Then I couldn't overcome the urge to look back out the window. Penn was still staring too. Arthur put down the books and trotted over, curious.

'Back again?' he said. 'I think she's rather a fan of your shop.'

'Huh?' Penn and I exchanged a glance and looked at Arthur.

'I said she must be keen on the shop. I've seen her round and about a few times lately. The day before the burglary, in fact.'

'What do you mean?' Penn asked.

'I mean exactly that. She was standing outside the shop, just like she is now. Didn't she come in to buy anything?'

I shook my head. 'No. She didn't,' I said softly. 'And I'm about to ask her why.' I made for the door, my back ramrod straight, and Penn called after me.

'What are you doing?'

'I'll be back in a minute,' I said over my shoulder. 'I just want to know what Sophia's doing, lurking around like a certain other person who meant us harm.'

I went out onto the street, but Sophia had already left her post. She was now walking quickly down Pilgrim Street, her stylish trench coat swishing behind her. I strode after, and a moment later, Penn caught up with me.

'Annie, what's wrong?'

'Why is she here?' I asked, shriller than I would have liked. 'She was here before the break-in; now she's sniffing around again. What if she had something to do with it? What if *she's* the saboteur come back to make sure her work is done?'

'That's crazy,' said Penn, with a tinge of unease.

'Is it? She hates me, she wants to be with you, and if the

shop was to fail, you'd have to go back to Ashcliffe. Which is exactly what she and your mam want.'

Penn shook his head. 'That's a real stretch. A really big one.' He made an exasperated sound. 'You don't mean to tell me you think she organised a *burglary?*'

'I don't know, but I'm going to ask her some very probing questions.'

Sophia rounded the corner, and I picked up my pace.

'Annie, please. Just stop. Sophia's not like that. She would never...'

'How do you know for sure? Look, I'm just going to talk to her, and see what she says.'

We turned the corner just in time to see Sophia cross the road and enter a smart bistro. Penn tried again to discourage me, but I continued towards the zebra crossing that Sophia had just used. Then, as I stood waiting to cross, I saw Sophia sit down at a table in the window. Across from her was Bunny, teacup in hand.

I felt Penn tense beside me, and in my surprise, I allowed him to pull me gently by the arm, out of sight of the bistro. Once we were round the corner again, he stood back against a wall and closed his eyes.

'Penn, I...'

He shook his head. 'Just give me a minute. I need to think.'

I stood beside him, unsure what to do. My sudden and, admittedly, crackpot suspicions of Sophia now felt like they had actual substance and, as a result, a genuine impact on Penn. I waited for him to speak, and eventually he looked at me.

'I don't know what's going on. But she couldn't have. She *wouldn't* have. And my mother...'

I swallowed dryly. Bunny had every reason to want Penn's shop to fold. And seeing her and Sophia in Newcastle, surveying the aftermath of the burglary, was compelling food for thought, even if it was circumstantial. But now that Penn was trying to process it, I almost wished we hadn't noticed Sophia at all.

'You're right,' I said. 'We can't jump to conclusions. I was being dramatic – just ignore me. Maybe they're here to visit you. Do you want to go in and see them?'

He looked at the crossroads for a long moment. 'No. Let's just go back to the shop.'

We spent the next half hour in the shop, Penn sorting through his remaining stock while I rearranged mine to make it look more abundant than it actually was. Olivia sent me a selfie from her holiday in Dubai, standing in what looked like the lobby of a beautiful hotel.

I hadn't actually seen her since the burglary, when she'd arrived in amongst all the chaos and I'd sent her away. Over Christmas, when I'd been sure I was going to give up the shop, I'd held off on telling her so, wanting to break the news face to face. But when I changed my mind and messaged to say I was looking forward to seeing her when we reopened, she eventually replied to say she wouldn't be coming back.

The holiday had been a surprise Christmas gift from her parents, and although she was apologetic about it, she would be going back to university straight after they returned. I was sad to see her go, but she looked like she was having the time of her life.

She was doing the hallmark pose of the younger end of the Gen-Z spectrum – a peace sign and her tongue sticking out. It made me smile, and I texted her back with a selfie of my own – a sad face with thumbs down. This resulted in a reply with a heart and a cry-laughing face, and she disappeared to resume her holiday. It made me feel like I could do with one too.

Every now and then, Penn flicked a glance at the door, but neither Sophia nor his mother made an appearance. Despite that, I decided against making another case for their involvement.

And besides, what could I say? There was no CCTV footage, no clear prints that the police could discern, and just because Sophia was seen in the area didn't mean anything really. And why would she come back to the scene of the crime? The more I thought about it, the more I talked myself out of that particular theory.

'Here,' I said, handing Penn one of my specialty instant coffees. 'Listen, I'm sorry for jumping to conclusions about Sophia and your mam. The more I've thought about it, the more I think I've got it all out of proportion.'

'It's okay. I can see why you thought what you did. But I know them.'

'I know you do. And I'm sorry. Are we okay?'

'Of course we are. Don't be silly.' He bent his head to kiss me, and I forgot all about his family for a moment. I also forgot about the cup in my hand and let it tip to the side, spilling hot coffee over his trainers.

'Oops,' I said, pulling back reluctantly. 'We can't have you looking as dishevelled as this place. I'll get a paper towel – hopefully the burglars didn't steal those too.'

I went to the stock room and checked the remaining crumpled cardboard in the corner, imagining that a burglar wouldn't bother to weigh themselves down with paper products. I was right – one of the boxes still housed a few reams of recycled paper towels. As I put the box back, another tumbled over away from the wall. Something was glinting on the floor behind it.

I fished the object out of the dusty corner and looked at it. An earring. White pearly stones hanging from a silver setting. *Moonstone*, I remembered.

I remembered because Christa had told me so, when I'd last seen this earring dangling from her ear.

THIRTY

I paced the living-room floor in the flat, wearing a trail on the flammable carpet. Penn sat on the sofa, his elbows on his knees, hands steepled across his mouth. We'd decamped to my place after my discovery, not daring to have a conversation in earshot of Christa, never mind speak to her directly. At least not until I'd tried to make sense of it all.

'Have you ever taken her back into the stock room?' he asked.

'Yes, I have. When we discovered the Liaison stuff. But I've seen her wearing the earrings since.'

'And you're absolutely sure it's hers?'

It sat on the coffee table, gleaming even in the dim light.

'Yes. I think so... It's pretty distinctive. Plus it would be a mighty big coincidence, don't you think?'

He sighed and rubbed his eyes. 'Yeah. It would.'

'She has a unique style. The gemstones, her evil-eye coat... it's not as if she buys her accessories from Claire's.'

'But I just can't figure out *why*.'

My shoulders tensed, and my voice was quiet. 'I don't know. She's my friend. Or at least I thought she was.' The sting of potential betrayal was an unhappy reminder of my school days, and I felt like I was fifteen again, trying to hold my head up high in the face of rejection.

Penn looked at me, sympathy softening the indignant look in his eyes. 'We can't know for sure. I mean, couldn't we just ask her?'

'I suppose so. But if we're wrong, that would be the end of our friendship forever. And I can't imagine trying to make the shop work when I have a mortal enemy down the corridor.'

He nodded. 'I know what you mean. We need to think about this really carefully – throwing around accusations without any proof would be a bit of a dick move. Can you think of *any* reason why she would want to hurt us? Or why she'd want the shop to fail?'

I stopped pacing and chewed my fingernail, remembering how she'd been so cagey with me that morning. 'There is one thing. I've been in a bit of competition with her for the sustainable beauty products – only a little bit, so I thought. But she seemed to be in a funny mood when I told her I had some more left to sell. She's always said it was okay before.'

'How was she when she came to see you before Christmas?'

'She was fine! Her normal lovely self. We ate Twiglets and drank wine, and she tried to cheer me up. That's when I told her I was giving up the shop.'

'And did she try to talk you out of it?'

'No,' I said miserably. 'She didn't. I just assumed she didn't want to pressure me. Then when I told her I'd changed my mind, she had a weird look on her face.'

'So let's look at the whole picture. One, she thinks you're competition. Two, she didn't strongly object to you shutting up shop.'

I sat down heavily next to him and groaned. 'Three, she isn't very fond of you either – she can't stand the whole shooting thing, and I never got round to telling her you don't really take part. Or that you were the one who leaked the shoot location.'

'This is becoming a bit of a list.'

I nodded sadly. It really was.

We gave up talking for a while, and Penn kept me occupied with kisses. Luckily, Neo had gone out, or I'd have worried he'd come out of his room and embarrass us, or worse, save the mental image for later. After a while, Penn's lips became such an absorbing distraction that I started to relax and put aside my worries, just a little.

Then the doorbell rang. When I opened the door, my jaw dropped, and I shrank back. On the step stood Sophia and Bunny, handbags over their arms, looking for all the world like they were dropping in on another lady-who-lunches.

'H-hello?' I said, trying to unscramble my thoughts.

'Hello,' said Bunny in her cut-glass tone.

I stared at her, time seeming to stand still.

'Annie, dear, the done thing is to invite us in.'

Since meeting Penn and his family, I never thought I'd see the day when Bunny Burton-Edwards would be sitting on my sofa drinking tea out of a Sports Direct mug.

'Mum, how did you find me?' asked Penn, still looking as shocked as when I'd ushered his mother and Sophia in.

'Well, it was rather easy actually. We came to see if you were in your funny little shop, and you were just driving off in your car. So we followed you.'

'I got a nifty little Audi for Christmas,' said Sophia, jingling a set of keys. 'So I don't suppose you would have recognised us on your tail. We've been waiting outside before we ambushed you.'

'And you're ambushing me... why?'

'My dear, if you weren't going to answer any more of my

phone calls beyond our terse little chat on Christmas Day, then I thought the mountain ought to come to Mohammed.'

'And I was just dying to see your romantic little bolthole with Annie,' said Sophia, sounding surprisingly sincere. 'It's really rather lovely,' she said, slightly less convincingly.

She and Bunny glanced around at the scuffed magnolia walls, the telly with cables sprawled out of it in each direction and Neo's many, many figurines, both of the women looking as out of place as they would being held hostage in an abandoned multi-storey car park.

'But mostly, we wanted to see if you both were alright,' said Bunny, placing her mug on the coffee table. 'After the burglary.'

'How the hell did you find out about that?' asked Penn, sitting back in surprise.

'When Buns couldn't get in touch with you, I rang Sam at your flat. He told me all about it,' said Sophia.

'Great,' said Penn, grimacing.

'I can't understand why you didn't tell us,' said Bunny in a tone that suggested both concern and resentment.

'I didn't realise my "funny little shop" was of any interest to you,' he replied lightly.

'*You* are of interest to me. Despite what you think, I love you and would never want to see you in trouble.'

There was a beat of silence as Penn considered this unexpected olive branch.

'I can handle this myself, Mum. But thank you for your concern.'

'Perry, don't be such a cold fish,' scolded Sophia. 'Buns and Hugh were *appalled* when we found out. I don't know why you're so surprised we've come to see you.'

'I *was* surprised,' he said. 'When we saw you outside the shop earlier, we couldn't believe it.'

'Why didn't either of you come in?' I asked.

'I asked Sophia to go to the shop first and confirm what

Peregrine's friend had told her about the burglary. Then, as I said, after a spot of lunch, we came to see you and you were driving off. So, here we are.'

'You were seen before,' I said to Sophia. 'One of the other shopkeepers saw you the day before the burglary. What was that all about?'

She smiled, at first tentatively, but it then spread into a wicked grin. 'A little bird told me that you had some very exclusive items in stock. I was looking to... add to my collection.'

My mouth opened in shock. 'You what?'

'The only Liaison Secrète purveyor for miles around,' she said with a sly wink in my direction.

Bunny rolled her eyes at Sophia. 'If you think I don't know what Liaison Secrète is, then think again. It was the talk of the under-thirties last polo season. Young women nowadays; I don't know when it became so fashionable to talk about the secrets of the bedroom.'

Penn winced at the insinuation that his mother had 'secrets of the bedroom' herself, and I covered a smile with my mug of tea.

'Well, I'm sorry, but it's all gone.'

Sophia turned her pink face away from Bunny, looking both mortified and disappointed.

'Now,' said Bunny, patting her knees. 'Down to proper business. What can we do to help?'

Penn gave a wry smile. 'Well, the locksmith and joiner have already been and fixed the door, so I think we're sorted.'

'You know very well what I mean. You've both been through a terrible time. Can we help with any tidying up? Your father has some contacts in the wholesale industry, not to mention his associate, Nathaniel, from the arts project if you need some contacts on the music front. We can assist you with recovering your business. And yours too, Annie.'

I was stunned. From our pre-Christmas frostiness, this thaw

was as unexpected as it was abrupt. What had changed in Bunny's perception of the shop, let alone me?

'What's brought this on?' asked Penn. 'You've never approved of all this before.'

Bunny raised her chin. 'I can't say I'm thrilled about it. But when you chose not to come home for Christmas, I realised how deep the cracks were in our relationship. I don't want the cracks to become crevices.'

Penn looked at his mother for a long time, and I was surprised to see Bunny's eyes glitter with emotion.

'Thank you,' said Penn eventually, his voice a little hoarse. Sophia caught my eye and made a soppy face, fingers making a heart shape over her chest. I couldn't help but smile. She then turned her full attention to Penn.

'You *must* let us help in some way. There has to be something we can do. For you, and for the other shops. God knows, small businesses need every boost they can – my friend Fenella's silver jewellery business went down the pan, and she ended up working for an accountants' firm.' She shuddered. 'All that maths, so bloody dull.'

'Actually, the other shops weren't burgled,' said Penn. 'It was just us.'

'How dreadful,' said Bunny. 'Not for them, of course, but isn't that a little odd?'

Penn and I exchanged a look.

'We thought it was strange too,' I said. 'In fact, we're not sure, but we think there might be an enemy in the ranks.'

'Well, that's simply awful,' breathed Bunny. 'How did you come to this conclusion?'

We explained our thinking about Christa, showing Bunny and Sophia the earring.

'I think that's rather damning,' said Sophia. 'What a nasty cow.'

I raised my palms. 'Like we said, we can't be sure. We just

need to find a way to prove it, and then we can inform the authorities.'

'Then I think we've hit upon a way in which we can help,' said Bunny decisively. She retrieved a small notepad and pen from her handbag. 'We need to brainstorm ideas.'

'Ideas for what?' I asked.

She met my eye, a steely expression in hers. 'A sting operation, my dear. It won't be my first. I've had plenty of supposed friends over the years who've attempted to undermine me at charity events and galas, and I never let one of them slip through my net.'

'Oh God,' said Penn, burying his head in his hands. 'Mum, this is mad.'

'It is not. I won't allow some jumped-up hippie to ruin your livelihood. Besides, it just isn't good PR to show weakness. Now, I presume you haven't any security cameras, since she hasn't already been apprehended.'

Penn and I shook our heads.

'Right. That is job number one.' She scribbled on her pad. 'You need it to be very discreet so you'll know if this Christa character tries anything else.'

'But why would she?' Penn asked. 'If it *is* her, then there's nothing else to take.'

'That's true,' I said. 'But I've told Christa we're restocking and we're refusing to close.'

'Then you must restock – and quickly. We need bait. I can help you there, since I assume your suppliers won't be delivering for a while yet. But how can we tempt her further?' She drummed her pen on the paper.

'Ooh!' squealed Sophia. 'We could make up some kind of event. A promotional thing... one which she might want to sabotage.'

I remembered how rammed the shop had been when I'd staged something similar and nodded slowly. 'That could work.

If she thinks we're bouncing back so quickly, she might feel like she needs to try again.'

We sat in silence for a while, all of us thinking hard.

'I've got an idea,' said Penn. 'What is it that's been driving the sabotage so far? Other than her hating me for the shooting.'

'Competition,' I said. 'Her business is struggling too, and if we open again, it might get worse for her.'

'Exactly. So what if we create something that pits us against each other even more? A small business award. If all of us at the arcade are "nominated", then that might be the motivation to spoil things for us again.'

'Bravo, Perry,' said Sophia. 'That's bloody brilliant.'

'It is,' I agreed. 'I think it could work. We'll create a "prestigious award" that's being judged soon. Maybe straight after New Year?'

'But, dear, isn't that very short notice?' asked Bunny.

'It doesn't have to be. We could pretend that Mike entered everyone and forgot to tell us with all the burglary hoo-ha. Besides, I don't think we should let this go on a minute longer than it needs to.'

Sophia sat up straighter. 'I have some friends in the media who could share it around on socials, make it seem like a big deal.'

'And I know someone who could create us a legit-looking website and ads.' I glanced at Neo's door, knowing he'd love an opportunity to flex his considerable IT muscles.

'Then we set up a hidden camera in your shop and see what happens,' said Bunny. 'I'll help you restock your shops quickly, so you are ready for the "judging".'

'And I can give you some interior design tips to make the shop look stunning,' said Sophia, clapping her hands.

Penn shook his head. 'That's Annie's job. She's amazing at that stuff.'

I grinned at him. 'Are you going to let me do your side too?'

He laughed. 'Don't get ahead of yourself. No fairy lights. But I might agree to a couple of balloons.'

'Do you think we can really do this?' I asked, feeling a spark of excitement in my belly.

'I do,' he said, squeezing my hand.

'Of course you can,' said Bunny brusquely. 'You're a Burton-Edwards – you can do anything you set your mind to. And you, dear.' She looked at me. 'I had you down as a determined little thing, and I think I'm right.'

My smile froze. I remembered our conversation in the bedroom about my position in Penn's life. The suggestion I was a passing phase and shouldn't get ideas above my station. The effervescent feeling of planning the sting together began to grow flat.

I jumped to my feet, my cheeks scalding, and gathered up the empty cups. 'I'll, er... I'll just see to these.'

I stood at the kitchen sink, scrubbing at the cups, my hands as agitated as my mind. Bunny's words still stung. Even though she seemed to have meant 'determined' as a compliment today, the implication that she'd noticed my boldness before struck a chord. I'd been perceived as a 'hanger-on' and I still imagined I wasn't what she'd envisaged for her son. After a minute, the kitchen door opened. I turned to see if it was Penn, but it was Bunny herself.

'Let me help you,' she said, reaching for a tea towel. Her perfectly manicured hands looked like they'd never seen a drop of dish detergent in their lives.

'It's fine!' I said with all the brightness I could muster.

She ignored me and started drying a mug.

'I stand by what I said. You are determined.'

My shoulders tensed. Had she come in here to have another private conversation where she warned me off?

'But you're also more than that. I can see now why Perry cares for you so much.'

I turned to her, shocked.

'You make a good team,' she continued, rubbing at the ceramic. 'And he is *different* around you. My son has, in the past, kept girlfriends at arm's length. A commitment-phobe, I suppose you could call it. Even with Sophia.'

'I'm sorry...?' My voice was barely audible.

'Maybe I was wrong to want to bring him home. It seems he's perfectly at home here, with you.' She glanced around at the shabby kitchen, with its one missing cupboard door and grubby gas hob. 'Although, it could stand to have a bit of a spruce-up.'

I was still too stunned to explain that I wasn't fond of my living arrangements either. After a moment, I found my voice again.

'I thought you hated me.'

She regarded me for a few seconds, her eyes appraising me. 'I never hated you. I was unsure of you, I'll admit. But even before we came here, I'd learned a little more about you, and you went up in my estimation.'

'Oh?'

'A certain gamekeeper came to me with some "intel", as he called it. He was very pleased to tell me that Peregrine's new girlfriend was an animal rights fanatic and had been one of the paint-throwing rabble at our last shoot.'

'I was,' I said, pushing back my shoulders. 'And I'm proud of it. I can't imagine where this is going though – I thought you said I'd gone up in your estimation.'

'Mm. Gus certainly thought it would have the opposite effect. He went to great pains to run you down, and knowing his attitudes to women, I suspect I can guess why. And I'm sure he was quick to tell you about Peregrine's poor shooting record, in order to puff up his own chest.'

I nodded. 'He did. But... it didn't win him any favour with me. I... I know how Penn really feels about shooting.'

She smiled. 'So do I. And I'll let you into a little secret, dear. On the rare occasion I'm pushed into attending a shoot, I make sure I "miss" every time too. Now hand me that Newcastle United mug. Football's a very proletarian sport – you should consider watching rugby; far more of a gentleman's game.'

I handed her the black-and-white mug, shaking my head in wonder. I guessed that Bunny might always give with one hand yet take with the other. But the unexpected gift she'd just given me was a step in the right direction.

THIRTY-ONE

We had no time to waste, so that evening was a flurry of activity. Bunny set to work, calling some contacts, ordering goods that I'd insisted on paying her back for. Thanks to Bunny's formidable influence, they would be delivered the very next day. In order to spur Christa on, we made sure to source as many ethical, natural, homeopathic and sustainable products as we could.

Penn arranged a meeting with Nathaniel, the arts project guy, who promised to meet him the following day at a music contact's warehouse, where he could literally load a van with gear to sell on his side.

Sophia called in some friends to create an aesthetic for the logos and paperwork, claiming to offer a £1500 cash prize, which would be printed within twenty-four hours. Then we enlisted Mike, who was appalled when we told him what we suspected. He agreed to approach the rest of the tenants and apologise for 'forgetting to tell them about the award'.

Then, when I asked Neo to help with the fake website, he immediately sat down at his desk and cracked his knuckles. Within an hour, we had a classy-looking site that appeared to have existed, to the untrained eye, for months.

As for me, I wrote a list of things I would get to decorate the shop and began the process of steeling myself to act natural with Christa when the time came to move our final chess piece. I would need to convince her that the business award would be make-or-break for us.

We kept a low profile the next day at the arcade, pretending that the shop was on hiatus until the New Year. Then, in the dead of night, all of us worked to set the scene for our plan, stocking the shelves with brand-new products, decorating the room to within an inch of its life and making sure it looked as enviable as possible. The pièce de résistance was a small collection of disturbingly realistic faux-fur items from Bunny's collection, which we hoped would rattle Christa enough to spur her on.

After a few hours' sleep, Penn and I turned up as if nothing was amiss. As soon as we opened up, the shop full to the brim with new stock and decorated like a carnival, we saw Christa through the front window, her mouth hanging open. She came in and looked around, and, recovering from the surprise, wished us good luck, saying that she and the other tenants would have to up their game. Then, after narrowing her eyes at the fur items, she left.

Penn and I let out deep breaths. Then he came over and rubbed my shoulders.

'You did so well,' he said. 'I don't think she suspected a thing.'

'This is horrible. She's supposed to be my friend, and now I'm having to treat her as an enemy. I never thought I'd be standing there lying to her face and being so fake.'

'Christa's the fake one,' he said, pulling me in for a hug. 'We just need to get the evidence on camera and then we can carry on with our lives.'

I nodded, my head rubbing against his shoulder, then a light cough came from behind us. We whipped round, my heart spiking. Melissa stood in the doorway looking awkward.

'I'm so sorry. I didn't mean to overhear... I was just popping in to let you know the dress code for New Year's Eve. It's black and white.'

Penn and I looked at each other and then back to Melissa.

'What exactly is going on?' she asked. 'What do you mean by evidence?'

I sighed. We had no choice but to tell her now.

'Please, Melissa. I'll explain, but can you promise to keep this to yourself?'

'Of *course*, darling. Discretion is my middle name.' She mimed zipping her lips.

'Okay. We think that Christa might have been trying to shut us down.' I explained about the repeated targeting of the shop and the earring. Then I admitted that the business award was a fake, and that we planned to place a hidden camera to see if she tried anything before the judging.

'I can't believe it...' she said. 'I mean, I know that Christa can be rather militant, and she seems to be quite unpleasant when it comes to standing up for her opinions. But a *criminal*? I'd never have imagined it.'

'We still don't know for sure,' Penn interjected. 'That's why we need the proof. The "judging" is supposed to take place on the second of January, so if she does want to sabotage the shop, we think it might happen during your party. The coast will be clear, and everyone will be distracted.'

Melissa nodded slowly. 'I see. Goodness. Well, if there's anything I can do, I'd like to help.'

'Actually, you probably can,' I said. 'We'll all keep a watch on her, but if you see her leave the party, could you let us know? The camera is there as backup, but if we can catch her in the act, that would be even better.'

'Absolutely. You can depend on me.' She came to us and took our hands. 'You poor things. Something like this should never happen to such lovely people. We'll get to the bottom of it, I'm sure.'

She gave us a look of deep sympathy and left again.

'Well, there's one plus point,' I said. 'At least everyone else doesn't hate us.'

Penn shook his head and laughed. 'You know, I don't really care either way. As long as you don't hate me anymore, then that'll do for me.'

In the spirit of keeping ourselves distracted, Penn had reluctantly agreed to come ice skating with me. Even with everything going on, I was still very amused at the sight of him staggering and slipping around the ice rink like Bambi, if Bambi had a penchant for oversized sweatshirts and beanie hats.

The night sky was black and clear, stars twinkling above, our breath like puffs of smoke against the dark backdrop. Even though the rink was in the centre of Newcastle and was busy, the traditional lantern lighting and a nearby brass band playing a belated round of Christmas songs gave it the air of a jolly Victorian pastime.

Penn clambered out of the rink to get us a giant pretzel each, and I leaned against the fence, enjoying the atmosphere.

My phone buzzed, and a text popped up; it was Olivia with another selfie from Dubai. This time she was standing on a bridge with skyscraper hotels in the background.

I heard about the business award... OMG.

I smiled. She was such a pet, keeping in touch. But then something occurred to me. Sophia's social media campaign hadn't started yet, so beyond Pilgrim Street and Neo's little-known website, our fake competition currently didn't exist.

I know, exciting! But how did you find out?

Christa! We swapped numbers when she helped me home. After mad Neil kicked off.

I paused, my heart rate ticking up a notch. What was Christa doing texting Olivia?

Great! I replied, careful to sound casual. *I bet she's as excited as we are.*

Yeah, she is. I just wanted to ask... she said not to say anything, but...

I waited, my mouth dry as the three dots flickered on my screen.

She said you're going to close down. Even if you win. She offered me a holiday job when I'm back for Easter.

An awful tingling chill spread through me. The conniving, back-stabbing...

She's made a mistake, I typed, my fingers trembling. *I'm not going anywhere, and I'd love to have you back with me!*

Oh! That's great.

I hope I see you at Easter then. Have a great holiday!

I ended with a smiley emoji and stared into space until Penn came back. I told him what Olivia had said.

'Well, at least we know for sure it's Christa,' he said, taking a bit of his pretzel.

I looked glumly at my skates.

'I know it sounds difficult,' he said, 'but you need to harden your heart to her. If she's doing this to you, she's no loss.'

I nodded. He was right – but it was more difficult than he could imagine. My heart was resistant to hardening when it was so occupied with my feelings for him. Despite all the problems we were dealing with, I felt closer to Penn every minute. We were a team in the shop, and in our mission to find the truth, but most of all, we were bonding on a deeper level. I looked up into his dark, soulful eyes, and he held my gaze as if the city was fading away around us. I was falling for him so hard, which terrified me. I was feeling things I'd never felt before and, with everything else going on, I couldn't process my emotions enough to keep up with the breakneck speed at which they were developing.

He raised my chin and kissed me deeply, until a gang of teenagers shouted at us to get a room. We broke away, foreheads pressed together, smiling.

'Come to Ashcliffe with me tomorrow,' he said.

'I didn't know you were going,' I said.

'I felt like I should. After not going up for Christmas, and being here for New Year, I thought I'd better show my face. Especially now Mum seems to have had a personality transplant. But I'd still rather have your face to look at while I'm there,' he said, breaking into a grin.

'Very suave,' I said. 'And very persuasive too. Are you sure they would want me tagging along though?'

'Of course. Now that you're my mum's anti-shooting ally, she'll be laying down the red carpet.'

I laughed. 'And what about your dad? He'll be less than impressed now he knows I took part in ruining his day.'

He shook his head. 'What Bunny says goes in our family. Dad wouldn't dare disagree, even if you *are* a meddling townie. Besides, I think he likes you.'

I raised an eyebrow, thinking Penn was being a little optimistic with that opinion. But the more I considered it, the more I thought getting out of the city altogether would be good for taking my mind off things. 'Okay,' I said. 'But please, for the love of God, give me very specific instructions on the dress code this time.'

'Shall we go shopping for a lunch outfit before we go? Get you some jodhpurs and a riding crop?'

'Even I've read enough Jilly Cooper to know you don't wear jodhpurs to lunch.'

'I tried. You could have made another bold style move. But no, it'll be casual. Jeans and a nice jumper.'

'That I can do. Well, count me in.'

We stood back against the fence, finishing our pretzels and looking at the sky beyond the imposing sandstone buildings around us. The smell of hot chocolate and cinnamon drifted from nearby cafes, making me feel like the cosiness of Christmas hadn't faded away just yet.

'There is another reason I'm going home,' he said, and I noted the word 'home'. He'd always been at pains to keep Ashcliffe Hall at arm's length until now. 'Yesterday, Nathaniel offered me a job. The arts foundation are opening up a new music centre in Northumberland – he mentioned it in passing at the ball – and he wants me to consider being the director. I'd run the place, hiring music teachers, booking music acts, getting the community involved.'

'Wow,' I breathed. 'That's incredible. Penn, I'm so happy for you.' I meant it entirely, but in the moment it left my lips, I considered the implication of what he'd just told me. Penn would move back to Northumberland and out of our shop. He wouldn't be worlds away, but he and I would be leading very different lives.

'I'm not going to take it,' he said abruptly.

'What? Why not? It sounds amazing.'

'I...' His brow creased. 'I don't want it. I'm happy where I am, in the shop, with you. When Nathaniel comes for lunch tomorrow, I'm going to say thanks for the opportunity, but no thanks.'

He smiled, but I thought I saw a glimmer of uncertainty in it.

'Are you sure?' I asked, my heart sinking. The little pulse of happiness that he wanted to stay with me was fading with the realisation he was giving up his dream.

'I'm sure. Now, come on. Let's do another lap of the rink. I'm not going to make it unless you hold my arm.'

He gently pulled me from the fence and linked his arm through mine. As we made our way unsteadily across the rink, my heart sank at the symbolism. Every time I felt like we were on a steady course, something else came along to shake the ground beneath us.

THIRTY-TWO

As I crunched up the gravel drive for the second time in the last few weeks, Ashcliffe Hall looked imposing, but now not so intimidating. Having Penn walking beside me as my actual boyfriend rather than my pretend one, and knowing now that his parents didn't despise me, gave me the little boost of confidence I needed. That and the fact I was wearing jeans and my nicest jumper instead of being packed into a mortifying confection of satin and lace.

This time, Bunny and Hugh greeted us with hugs and smiles, making me wonder if Penn was right about Hugh warming to me after all. Bunny asked for an update on the goings-on at the shop, seemingly fizzing with excitement about it. We appeared to have unleashed British nobility's answer to Hercule Poirot.

'You must hold your nerve,' she said as she delivered us to our bedroom; a shared one this time. 'When I exposed Tiggy Archibald as a cheat at polo, I made sure to keep my enemy close. Do the same with Christa and she'll fall right into the trap. Now, lunch is at one. I'll see you at table.'

When we went down, everyone else was assembled with

aperitifs, chatting quietly. The table was set with a crisp white cloth, gleaming cutlery and crystal glassware, and had candles burning to offset the slightly gloomy sky outside. The room still made me cringe at the memory of my first awkward meal here, but everyone was casually dressed as promised, and there was the smell of a roast dinner emanating from somewhere beyond that was reminiscent of Sunday dinners back home. As I took my seat at the table, I felt a little more like I belonged.

As well as the family, there was Nathaniel and other friends of the Burton-Edwardses, including Sophia. She gave me a wink and tipped her glass towards me across the table. I smiled back – I wouldn't say we were exactly friends, but we were more relaxed around each other now.

As the starters were brought out – smoked salmon for everyone else, a cheese soufflé for me – the conversation immediately turned to the subject of the arts project. Within moments, I realised that this wasn't just a lunch; it was an intervention. Nathaniel pressed hard to persuade Penn, stressing how valuable he would be with his music-teaching abilities, as well as dangling a carrot in the form of an on-site apartment he could live in.

Bunny and Hugh extolled Penn's virtues in both music and ambition, and Sophia regaled the table with stories of how incredible he was in live performances.

I felt a wave of unease wash over me. Bunny had seemed to accept Penn's choice to live in Newcastle and to help us save our businesses, but this would also be an irresistible opportunity to lure him back to Northumberland at the same time as indulging his preference for a musical career. As everybody eagerly supported Penn's appointment to the job, I felt like I was disappearing both from the conversation and the big picture. I forced an encouraging smile onto my face.

'I think it sounds great,' I said. 'You'd be incredible.'

Penn looked down at his plate and turned over his fork restlessly. The atmosphere between his chair and mine felt heavy with conflict.

'Thank you,' he said to Nathaniel eventually. 'Like I said before, I'm flattered that you're considering me. But I want to keep my shop. I want to stay in Newcastle.' His hand dropped under the table and reached for mine, squeezing as he found it.

Hugh's nostrils flared, and he flicked an apologetic glance at Nathaniel. I strongly suspected they'd imagined it would be a done deal.

Nathaniel coughed uncomfortably. 'Well. I appreciate your candour. But since the centre is yet to be built, we have time yet, in case you change your mind. Unless another suitable candidate comes along, of course.'

'Of course,' said Penn. 'I hope you find the right person.'

Hugh sighed, but it was clear that continuing the discussion would create more discomfort. Good manners dictated that a change of subject was in order, so we spent the rest of the lunch talking about horses.

After, Penn and I put on our coats and went for a walk in the gardens with Hendrix. The sky was leaden and cloudy, but the frost had melted and the grass underfoot was soft and damp. We kicked along quietly, Hendrix running in rings, his feet churning up sprays of water as he went.

'You can't turn it down,' I said softly.

'I can. I don't want it.'

'I don't believe you.'

'Why not?'

I took his hand. 'Because *nobody* would turn this down. A well-paid job, an apartment. Being able to have... what-do-you-call-it... creative control? Penn, you have to take it.'

'Annie...'

'No. Please don't do this. The shop is a gamble, and one that's against the odds at the moment. If you take the job, you'll have financial security at the same time as doing what you love.'

'What if my priorities have changed?' He locked eyes with me, and his jaw muscles flexed. I tried to keep looking at him, pleading silently with him, but had to look away. My throat was starting to feel thick with frustration and sadness. I wanted this for him so much, but it might come at a cost.

Hendrix skittered up, a ball in his mouth, nudging at Penn to throw it for him. Penn kissed my forehead then wandered off, looking deep in thought as he sent the dog running back and forth. As I watched him, I felt as though I wanted to follow but didn't – I left him to it and took a seat on a stone bench in the walled garden.

Winter pansies and irises gave the ground a splash of colour, and I fixed my eyes on them, thinking hard. It all felt so confusing. I wanted him to take the job and wanted him to stay with me, but the balance was tipping in Northumberland's favour. Here, in his home, he was repairing bonds, being offered new opportunities, and the thought of him getting all of that gave me a strange feeling in the pit of my stomach. I realised that my feelings for him had become frighteningly deep. I couldn't even give those feelings a name in my head, but they were there, muted for now. No... not just for now. If I ever told him how I felt, it would only hold him back from his dream even more.

My phone rang – it was my mam. I answered it, wrapping my other arm around myself against the chill.

'Hello, darl,' she said, and I sensed trepidation.

'Hiya. Is everything okay?'

'Yes, of course. Other than your dad prowling around like a caged tiger on his crutches.' She paused. 'I just wanted to let you know. We've found somewhere to move to.'

I sucked in a breath. 'You have?'

'We've found a place to rent in Woodswell.'

'Woodswell...?' My heart sank. If Penn thought Dunhall was down at heel, then he'd have an education in Woodswell. It was well known for having a high crime rate and not much else to commend it.

'And we can move in next month. It should do nicely until we figure out what we can afford to do next.'

I couldn't speak. The thought of them living in a place where their neighbours' kids might welcome them by taking their car for a joyride made my blood run cold. Never mind the countdown to New Year – this was a countdown to disaster.

After trying my best to sound pleased for them, not wanting to make her feel any more stressed about the decision they were having to make, we hung up.

There must be something else I could do. Anything.

In my desperation, an idea that I'd thought of and previously rejected sneaked back into my mind. A bank loan. I clearly couldn't make enough from the shop in time to get them through until Dad could return to work. So what if I could quietly get a loan, not tell them about it and pretend it was still proceeds from the shop? A surprisingly successful comeback?

I'd dismissed it before as being too extreme, but now that I knew they were headed for the Wild West known as Woodswell, I decided it was as extreme a situation as it could get. Even if I had to work myself into the ground to pay it back, get myself two jobs, move back home, I would damn well get this house off the market. I had to stop the sale in its tracks before the exchange date next month, or I'd never get over it.

I searched online, scrolling through pages and pages of loan information, interest rates and terms and conditions, becoming so absorbed that I didn't hear Penn walk up behind me.

'Is everything okay?' he asked softly, his eyes fixed on my phone screen.

'Mmhm. Everything's fine.' The tension in my voice immediately gave me away.

'Annie, tell me.'

I wilted. I didn't have the energy to lie. 'I'm going to take a loan. I can't let my parents sell up – I just can't. If they go through with it, they're going to end up living in a street where every other house has boarded-up windows. So if I can just help them through the next couple of months until Dad's back at work, then they won't have to.'

His face fell. 'I thought they'd talked you out of getting involved. And how will you pay it back?'

'I'll figure that out later.'

'But the interest, and repairing the finances at the shop. It's a debt you shouldn't risk.'

I felt a flash of indignation. 'Shouldn't I? Penn, I can think for myself. And for my family, it's a risk worth taking.'

'So why can't *I* think for myself?' he asked sharply. 'You're so certain that I should take the music centre job, that it's the best thing for me, but you won't take my advice in return.'

'It's not the same. You've got a golden opportunity, and I've got to dig my family out of a hole. It's not the same at all.'

'Then let me help you. Take the album money.'

'No! We've been over this. I won't accept charity.'

'It's not charity!' He stood up and scuffed his hand through his hair impatiently. 'If you can sacrifice things for the people you love, then why can't I?'

I froze, and Penn did too. It was as if we were in slow motion for a moment as we both realised the implication of what he'd just said. Those forbidden words in my head that I'd successfully quieted before struggled for my attention again; the loaded phrase Penn let slip had galvanised them, given them strength. But I didn't dare. I'd never said I loved someone before, and this predicament wasn't the fairy-tale backdrop to my first time. And if the words reached my lips I couldn't take them back, and that would only make it harder for him to make the right decision.

I stood up. 'I can't watch you throw this opportunity away,' I said carefully.

'And I can't watch you bury yourself in debt.'

'Then maybe we shouldn't be in sight of one another.'

There was a beat as we held our breath, neither daring to speak. Then I straightened my shoulders and swallowed the lump in my throat.

'I need some time to myself. I'm going up to the room.'

I turned and walked away.

Upstairs, I sat on the bed, wiping the last of my tears. Then I repacked my bag and called a taxi to the station.

On the dressing table was a pen and some notepaper bearing the family crest. I sat down and started to write.

Penn,

These last few weeks have been amazing. Who'd have thought we would ever meet each other in the middle, never mind grow as close as we have? I've truly loved every minute of it.

But it's not right. I won't be the one who holds you back from the things you want to do. I know you said that city life and the shop are too important to leave behind, and you keep saying you don't want to leave me. Penn, I saw the look in your eyes when you turned Nathaniel down, and even though you tried to hide it, I could see the disappointment. You should stay here and be with your family, where you belong. And I'll be with mine. So I'm going to make it easy for both of us. It's over. I'd never forgive myself for stepping in the way of your dreams, or for worrying you with my problems. Once we've wrapped things up with Christa tomorrow night, promise me that you'll call Nathaniel and take the job.

I need some space, so please don't come after me. And tomorrow, to get through the business with Christa, can we just be friends?

You're an incredible person, Penn. Talented, generous and kind. I can't believe I had you so wrong in the beginning. Make the most of this chance, and enjoy it. Just promise me you won't forget that Miley Cyrus is just as good a songwriter as Stevie Nicks when you're teaching the kids.

Love, Annie

At the sound of tyres on gravel outside, I picked up my bag and left Ashcliffe Hall as quietly as I could. As the taxi pulled away, I didn't look back.

THIRTY-THREE

New Year's Eve morning began joylessly – the outlook for next year felt as bleak as my mood, with the precarious financial situation and my freshly broken heart. I sat in my pyjamas on the sofa, Neo beside me, barely paying attention to the plot of the elf-and-orc saga he'd decided to put on. The clash of steel against bronze brought me back into the room every now and then.

Penn had so far followed my instructions; I hadn't heard from him at all since my flight from Ashcliffe Hall. Even though I stood by what I'd said in the letter, I still secretly wanted him to appear at my door, to drop into my messages. But if he said what I thought he was about to say in the walled garden, I'd break. And the idea that I would lose control and reply terrified me – as long as my feelings were under lock and key, I would have the strength to be unselfish.

'Watch this bit,' said Neo through a mouthful of dry Cheerios. Crumbled hoops were scattered down his grey T-shirt, framed nicely by the wide arcs of sweat emanating from his underarms. 'See that elf there? Guess what's going to happen.'

'Well, his sword is broken so I guess he's going to either run away or surrender.' How apt.

'Wrong,' said Neo smugly.

On the screen, the ethereal long-haired character vaulted up from the ground, twirled the mangled weapon like a baton and launched it at a hulking monster before making a lithe escape. I sighed, closed my eyes and rested my head back against the sofa.

There was a brisk knock at the door. Neo made no effort to move, instead remaining enraptured by a volley of arrows heading towards the orcs, so I got up and shuffled over. My heart leaped as I realised it could be Penn, and it was with a mixture of dread and hope that I smoothed down my hair and wiped the mascara stains from under my eyes.

I opened the door to find Sophia standing there. She looked me up and down, grimaced and invited herself in.

Neo saw her, seemed uncharacteristically ashamed of his slovenly appearance and shambled off to his bedroom, brushing cereal crumbs off his T-shirt.

'What are you doing here?' I asked her, wrapping my arms around my chest.

'How charming,' she said. 'Aren't you going to offer me a cup of coffee or a sit down?'

'Penn sent you,' I said, making no move towards the kitchen.

'No. I came of my own accord. After he discovered your note, I found him in the long gallery, head in his hands.'

I felt a bolt of guilt but tried not to move my face.

'I didn't read it,' she said, 'but he gave me the summary. I hope you don't mind that he was indiscreet. He was devastated.'

Shrugging uncomfortably, I said, 'I suppose not. It's up to him who he talks to.' As I said it, I felt a ripple of jealousy. I pictured them sat together, Sophia commiserating him, maybe giving him a hug.

'What are you doing?' she asked in a gentler voice than I'd ever heard from her.

A treacherous prickle of tears stung my eyes, and I swiped at them. 'I... I just want him to be happy.'

'But he's happy with you.' There was a tiny trace of something in the way she said it – not quite begrudgery but an effort to cover some emotion.

'I know. I do know that. But if he turns down the music centre, he'll regret it. And then one day he'll resent me for it. I couldn't do that to him – or to myself.'

'I don't fully understand. It's not as if he'll be a million miles away. Why can't you make it work with a little distance to travel?'

'It's not just geography,' I said. 'It's... everything. His family – they're nice to me, but I'll never fit in. I don't know anything about fine art, or yachts, or... how to address a marchioness. And if he takes the job, he'll be back in the fold, where he really belongs.'

'Annie, you're talking a load of tosh. You fit in beautifully at the hall. Yes, you might have made a fashion faux pas, and yes, you may have exposed yourself to Lord and Lady Ashcliffe...'

I looked at her pointedly.

'Okay, that was my fault. But my point is, you're a decent, principled sort. Even if that means you're against the noble sport of game shooting, the Burton-Edwardses admire a strong-willed person. And the fact that you make Perry so happy is the main thing.'

I shook my head, deciding not to dive deeper, to stick to the class-polarity narrative. 'It would never work. We're too different. And anyway, I'm surprised you're here, making his case. I'd have thought you'd be glad I'm out of the picture.'

She said nothing for a moment, her expression conflicted. Then she looked me directly in the eye.

'I'll admit, that's what I wanted. Before. When Bunny wanted me to get back together with him, I was just as keen as she was. I was still in love with him. But after a time, when he'd resisted every advance I made, every orchestrated encounter by his mother, I started to realise it was never going to happen. If I'm honest, I was starting to cool towards him. Then, when you arrived, I felt like I had to make a last-ditch attempt. But really, my heart wasn't in it.'

I nodded, trying to absorb what she was saying. She had never been real competition at all.

'Then I saw you two,' she said hesitantly. 'Through the window of the cottage. He never looked at me like that. He's never looked at anyone like that, I don't think.'

'Like what?' I asked.

'Like he'd found everything he was looking for.'

I squeezed my eyes shut, gritting my teeth. I didn't need this; I needed there to be no confusion.

'Annie, I'm sorry about my behaviour. I really am. And it's not just because I regret everything that happened at Ashcliffe. It's because I like you.' She sighed. 'I can't make you change your mind. But you're making a mistake. Perry is a catch for many more reasons than his pedigree. Which some of us learned a little too late.'

She left, and I sat staring at my hands for a very long time.

That night, after checking that the security camera was well disguised by the side of one of Penn's wall-mounted speakers, I adjusted my borrowed white cocktail dress and headed next door to Visage Unique. I left the internal door to the shop unlocked, knowing that all Christa would have to do was unlock the main door from the street and she'd be in without any difficulty. Penn hadn't been around when I arrived to set up the camera, and I wondered whether he'd show up at all. Maybe it would be for the best if he didn't.

The party was already in full swing, and I could see the other people from the arcade clustered in small groups. Sven and Arthur were choosing canapés from a silver tray that was being circulated by a member of the catering staff. Penn was nowhere to be seen, as I'd suspected. And Christa was in the corner with Jake, tucked out of the way.

I gave Melissa a discreet nod – our plan for her to keep a close eye on Christa's comings and goings was still agreed, and I had Sophia stationed at the cafe round the corner, ready for the call if I needed her. Bracing myself, I went over to Christa and Jake – I needed Christa not to suspect a thing.

'Swit swoo!' I said, gesturing at their outfits. Christa was wearing a black silk jumpsuit and Jake had on jeans and a black polo shirt buttoned up to the chin, giving at least a nod to the black-and-white dress code. 'You two scrub up nicely. I wasn't sure if you'd come, what with your and Melissa's ethical differences.'

'What can I say? Free champagne is free champagne,' said Christa with a wide smile that could have been genuine if I didn't know better. *Champagne and an excellent opportunity to ruin me.*

'So, are you both ready for the judging?' I asked guilelessly.

'Aye,' said Jake, flexing his chest. 'I reckon I've got a pretty good chance.'

Christa rolled her eyes. 'We'll see. Anyway, I think it'll be Annie and Penn. The shop looks... well, wow is probably the word. If the award goes to any of us at the arcade, it should be you.'

I was disarmed for a moment by her effusive praise but then remembered that it was all part of the act. Covering herself by deflecting attention.

'Thanks,' I said, making every effort not to sound brittle.

Then Jake's and Christa's eyes were drawn to the door.

Christa puffed out her cheeks. 'Phwoar. If your ex-boyfriend wasn't a cheating arsehole, I'd say you're a lucky woman. Shame his heart's as black as his suit.'

I turned to see Penn walking through the door wearing a beautifully cut black suit, a white shirt underneath, open at the collar. His stubbled jaw was taut and his brow knitted, accentuating his handsome features. He looked so incredible, my stomach felt like it was doing backflips then crashing to the floor as I reminded myself we were done. But I had to stick to the plan. As far as Christa was aware, Penn and I never made up after Christmas, but if we wanted this to work, it would be better if she believed we were stronger than ever. It was important that she didn't think we were capable of sabotaging ourselves without her help.

'Actually, we're back together. It turned out it was a misunderstanding. When he made that phone call, he was meeting his brother; I got it all wrong.'

Her eyebrows rose.

'Anyway, I'd better go and give my boyfriend a New Year's kiss.'

I went over to Penn and saw the look in his eyes as he noticed me. He gazed at my dress, the shape as it curved across my chest and down my hips. His expression was a mix of longing and hurt.

'I know this sounds inappropriate right now,' I said stiffly. 'And I'm so sorry. But I need you to kiss me – Christa's watching so we need to keep up the pretence.'

The look of pain on his face deepened, and I almost reached out to him. But then he bent and gave me a chaste kiss on the lips, which lasted a beat longer than it needed to. We broke apart and were lost in each other's gaze for a moment. It reminded me of the first time we'd shared a fake kiss, but this time it was agonising.

He glanced away, swallowing deeply. 'Remind me what we're doing,' he said.

'We're watching for Christa leaving, then we'll give her a minute before following. We need to catch her on video first as hard evidence, then confront her. Melissa's going to keep a lookout too.'

He nodded. 'Fine. So we just hover around until then? Pretend to be together.'

His tone was stoic rather than sarcastic, but I still felt like he'd stabbed me in the heart. 'Yes. That's what we need to do.'

'Well, I'm glad to be of service,' he said, his jaw tensed.

'Penn, I'm sorry. Let's just get through tonight, then we can talk. I'll explain more about how I feel; why I decided to end things.'

'Don't worry, I think your note covered the main points. I'm going to get a drink. I'll be back in a minute to maintain the *façade.*'

He turned on his heel and stalked away to the bar. He was intercepted by Melissa, who hugged him tight and stroked his lapel. She seemed to be heaping praise on his appearance – understandably. As he smiled down at her and she threw back her head and laughed, I felt a surge of jealousy. I tamped it down with a big slug of champagne as the crowd thickened and mercifully blocked my view of them.

I mingled for a few minutes, expecting my unwilling partner to come back to me any minute, but before I saw any sign of him, there was a loud crash at the door and several khaki-clad people shoved into the room.

I squinted at the sturdy blonde woman at the front of the pack, wearing a camo jacket and holding a placard that said 'Save the Chimps'.

'Linda?' I asked, the wind blown out of my sails.

'I might have known you'd be here, hunter shagger,' she said roughly. 'Is your murdering boyfriend here too?'

Christa had clearly spread the word that her two enemies had also been lovers. The room had fallen silent except for the strains of smooth acid-jazz from the speakers, and everyone was staring at the protestors, agog.

'What are you doing here?'

'Never mind. It's not you and your boyfriend we really want – it's that harridan who's peddling palm oil products out of this shop.'

'Yeah!' yelled the group behind her. Then they started to bounce their placards up and down, chanting, 'Shut it down! Shut it down!'

'Now hold on one minute,' said Arthur, squaring up to Linda. 'I don't know who you think you are—'

'I know who *you* are!' she barked. 'Talk about destroying the forests – your bookshop's filled with the corpses of trees!'

'For God's...' I rubbed my hand across my face. 'Linda, go away. Not now!'

Just then, Melissa came out of nowhere, face like thunder. Penn followed behind, surveying the scene in confusion.

'What the hell do you lot think you're doing in my shop? Clear off or I'll call the police.'

They jeered at her and started chanting again.

She raised her voice even louder. 'I said, I'm going to call the police! Penn...?'

He stood beside her, scowling. 'You heard her. It's Linda, isn't it? Unless you want to end up in a cell again, I'd suggest you get out of here.'

'I've tried telling her,' I said, throwing my hand towards Linda, who was now striding around menacingly, flicking at the rows of beauty products. I looked around for Christa, thinking that she might be able to warn Linda off. But she was nowhere to be seen, and neither was Jake. I exchanged a look with Melissa.

'I think she might have slipped the net,' she said wearily. 'But, as you can see, my hands are pretty full right now.'

'Okay.' I glanced at the door, knowing this was my chance. 'Will you be alright?'

She pushed up her sequined sleeves. 'I'll make them wish they'd never been born.'

Then one of the male protestors, a big hairy guy, started to square up to Melissa, until Penn stood between them. I didn't know what to do – if I didn't go now, with or without him, then Christa might slip through our fingers. Before Penn could stop me, I shouldered through the crowd who were now joining in with surrounding the protest group. I called Sophia as I did, putting a finger in my ear to block out the rising noise levels.

'Come quickly. Christa left the party – she could still be in the shop.'

'Okay, wait for me. Don't go inside.'

I rang off and did as she said. After a few minutes, she ran up the street.

'Come on,' she said. 'Let's bust this bitch.'

I set my shoulders, and we charged into the shop, turning on the lights. It was a mess. Stock had been thrown to the floor, shelves had been pulled from the walls. Broken glass, sprays of guitar strings and cracked vinyl were strewn all over; you could barely see the floor for the debris. But the place was empty. The tiny red light of the security camera blinked from its position by the speaker.

My heart raced as I opened the app on my phone to retrieve the recording. With trembling fingers, I scrolled through the footage until a grainy black-and-white night-vision image of a figure came through the door. She was instantly recognisable. Her coat – the one with the embroidered evil eyes – was clearly visible, though she had her hood up, maybe in case someone saw through the window. We watched as she systematically worked her way through the shop, hurling things to the floor, pulling things down from the walls. It broke my heart to watch it happen in front of my own eyes.

Just as I was about to tell Sophia so, she grabbed my arm and put a finger to her lips.

From beyond the corridor, towards the back of the arcade, came a quiet moan.

THIRTY-FOUR

The hallway wasn't lit, and Sophia and I edged down it towards the source of the sound. Light shone from around Christa's closed door, and we heard another stifled groan. It sounded male.

Sophia pulled at my arm. 'What if someone's hurt?' she whispered. 'I mean, what if this situation's more dangerous than we thought?'

I glanced at the door. 'What do you think? That she's taken Jake hostage and tied him up?'

Sophia nodded readily.

'You don't seriously...? This isn't *The Sopranos*; it's Palmer's Arcade. Come on.'

I dragged her to the door, hearing a slapping sound and another moan. Now I felt a bit more uncertain. But it was now or never. I pushed open the door, and what I saw then would scar me forever.

There was nobody tied up, but someone was certainly getting a beating. Jake was bent over the cash desk, trousers around his ankles, Christa slapping his bare arse with a bright pink cat o' nine tails which I recognised from my Liaison Secrète collection. The multi-tailed whip had left livid stripes on his skin.

Both of them spun round at the sound of our arrival, and then Jake scrambled like a cartoon character, desperately trying to drag his pants up over his maimed buttocks. Christa dropped the cat o' nine tails to the floor with a light thwack.

Sophia gave a sharp squawk of laughter and covered her mouth, murmuring, 'Bloody hell!'

'What are you doing here?' Christa asked, her face now almost as red as Jake's backside.

I blinked at her, lost for words, but Sophia took over, stifling her amusement.

'Well, we thought we'd catch you in the act of screwing over Annie's business, but we weren't expecting this.'

Christa's face crumpled. 'Annie, I'm so sorry. I know it's bad of me, and I always intended to pay you back, but I feel terrible.'

'*Pay me back?*' I snapped, my temper flaring. 'How could you ever pay me back for everything you've done? All I want to know is... why?' The wind was knocked out of my sails just as fast as it had risen, and I now felt nothing but hurt and betrayal.

'It was just a spur-of-the-moment thing,' she pleaded. 'And I was embarrassed to come into the shop and buy it from you so I... I took it. I intended to slip some money into your till, but I forgot. I'm so sorry.'

'What are you talking about?' I asked, glancing at Sophia in confusion.

Christa gestured to the S&M accessory lying splayed on the floor. 'I mean this. What are *you* talking about?'

'The shop. The sabotage, the burglary, the wreckage in there right now. Christa, I know you did it. I've got the proof.' I waved my phone. 'There's a hidden camera in the shop, and you're on it, smashing the place up.'

Her eyes almost popped out of their sockets. '*What?* I have no idea...'

Before she could carry on, she pushed past me, Jake following right behind. Sophia and I hurried after them to find Christa standing in the middle of the wreckage, looking around in an excellent imitation of innocence. Just then, Penn ran through the door and gasped at the mess.

'You,' he said baldly to Christa.

'I didn't do this...' breathed Christa. 'Annie, how could you think I would?'

Grimly, I opened the app and showed her the footage of her, in her incriminatingly unique coat, running rampage through the room. She shook her head, horrified.

'That isn't me. You have to believe me.'

'Christa, it's right there!' I stabbed at my phone. 'Plus the earring. I found it in the stock room straight after the burglary.'

She sighed. 'I *did* lose my earring. It was after I "borrowed" the cat o' nine tails. Immediately after, in fact. I thought I'd lost it while we were... using it.' She glanced at Jake, and he squirmed in mortification. 'It must have dropped out while I was looking through the boxes.'

'Still,' I said. 'Even if that's true, the video caught you red-handed. Your coat is right there on screen.'

'I haven't worn my coat since yesterday! I left it here last night; it'll still be hanging up in the shop. Come and see.'

She stormed back up the corridor, the rest of us following behind, and she looked at the empty coat peg, her mouth falling open. 'It was here. I swear it was here...' She looked at us wildly. 'But why would I wear it? Why would I wear something so identifiable? I'm not lying,' she wailed, tears now welling in her eyes.

I hesitated, seeing what looked to be genuine distress on her face. But there was more I had to confront her with.

'There's something else,' I said. 'Olivia texted me from her holiday. Said you'd messaged her and offered her a job. You told her I'd be shutting down, presumably once your plan had come off.'

Her mouth was a round O, her face almost green with shock.

'Annie, I don't even have her number.' She grabbed her phone and showed me her contacts list. There was no Olivia in there.

'You could have deleted it,' I said. Frustration started to build in my belly. I thought the video would be our trump card, but now it felt like I was clutching at straws. I showed her my own phone, pointing at the messages from Olivia. 'See! It's right here.'

'I never sent her any messages. I barely know her! I just can't understand why she'd say any of this.'

I stood there breathing heavily, my hand gripping my phone tight. A silence spread through the room as everyone seemed to take it all in. Then Sophia came to my side, her eyes fixed on my phone, which was still lit up with Olivia's text messages. Curiously, she reached out and moved the last holiday photo she'd sent me into full view on the screen.

'Give me this,' she said quietly.

I handed her the phone, wondering what the hell was going on.

She enlarged the picture, frowning. 'This is Water Canal Bridge,' she said. 'In Dubai. This is where Olivia said she'd gone on holiday?'

I nodded. 'She went a few days ago.'

Sophia shook her head. 'She can't have. I've been to Dubai loads of times. See that hotel in the background? I saw it when I holidayed there last year, but when I went to Dubai again a few months back, it had been demolished. This can't have been taken a few days ago.'

I held my breath as Penn came over and looked at it too. My mind was reeling.

'If that's true,' he said, looking me fiercely in the eye, 'then maybe Olivia never went anywhere at all.'

THIRTY-FIVE

Sophia's Audi was as full of tension as it was full of people. Jake sat up front, while Penn, Christa and I were squashed into the back.

As Sophia sped from the city centre to the outskirts, we sat mostly in silence; I, for one, had too many unanswered questions in my head to be able to coherently formulate them, so I kept my mouth shut. Just once, Penn tried to hold my hand, but I carefully pulled mine away. I didn't need that whole other box of questions to be opened right now.

I looked again at the camera footage on my phone, desperately trying to find something that proved it was Olivia. I still fretted that we'd made a mistake – hoped, even. But the only thing I achieved was complete exoneration of Christa. The time stamp was wrong – she'd still been at Visage Unique at the time it happened.

Eventually, we pulled up outside a small terraced house, the address that Olivia had given me when I took her on. One light was on downstairs, but the curtains were drawn. I took a deep breath – part of me wanted her to admit it, but another part of me wanted none of this to be true. Sweet, innocent Olivia couldn't have done this. She couldn't. But if she had, then why? The only thing I could do now was ask her.

Everyone unbuckled their seat belts, but I held up my hand.

'Guys, is it okay if I do this on my own? At least until I've got her to open the door and told her why we're here. I don't want her to think we're a lynch mob.'

There were murmurs of assent, but Penn still got out with me. I opened my mouth to tell him no, but he looked at me with his intense eyes, and I couldn't speak. Without a word, we walked up the little scrubby path to the front door and knocked.

After only a few seconds, the door opened, and a girl was framed by a bright light from the hallway. But it wasn't Olivia. And she was far too young to be Olivia's mam.

'Can we speak to Olivia, please?'

Her brow wrinkled. 'Olivia? Nobody called Olivia lives here.'

Penn and I exchanged a look, and my heart sank even lower than I thought it could go. A fake address. It seemed like any hope I had of Olivia being innocent had finally dropped away.

Then I had an idea. I showed her the photo of Olivia on holiday.

'Oh, *that* Olivia. We used to hang out when we were in sixth form. She went off to uni, but she used to live over at Rowan Park. That posh estate?'

I knew of it – an exclusive development near Forest Grange.

'Thanks,' I said. 'We'll head over. You don't happen to know the exact address, do you?'

She looked at us suspiciously. 'I don't. I'd better text her to ask and make sure she doesn't mind me passing it on.' She dashed off a message, and Penn looked at me with alarm.

'Look, don't worry about it,' he said. 'Thanks anyway.'

Penn and I both pasted on stiff smiles and headed back to the car as the girl called after us.

'Drive,' I said to Sophia. 'We need to get to Rowan Park quickly. She might know we're coming.'

Sophia roared out of the street, throwing all of us back in our seats.

'I bloody love this,' she purred. 'I feel like a younger, sexier Miss Marple.'

After a hair-raising and possibly illegal race through the streets, we ended up in a quiet, very classy cul-de-sac. Large red-brick houses surrounded a circular lane with a well-tended central island stocked with herbaceous plants. The estate was small, and as soon as we saw Olivia's little Fiat 500 in the driveway of a large double-fronted house, we knew we were in the right place. The windows of the house were pitch-dark. This time we all got out and assembled on the doorstep as I knocked.

There was no answer. I leaned on the bell, hearing it ring inside, but still Olivia didn't appear at the door.

'Olivia, I know you're in there,' I called through the letter box. 'I just want to talk to you.'

No response. I looked at everyone else, my shoulders slumped. We weren't going to get anywhere.

'I think we should call the police,' said Christa. 'She's sabotaged your shop, framed me, and stolen or damaged most of your stock!'

I pinched the bridge of my nose. 'I know... I know. I just want to hear what she has to say first.'

'Well, if you don't call them, I will,' said Jake. 'I'm not having her drag my lass into all this.'

I looked from Christa to Jake, deciding this wasn't the time to question them on their surprise relationship, but just asked them to give me a minute. I walked down the path and sat heavily on the low garden wall. After a moment, I felt Penn sit beside me.

'Are you okay?' he asked.

I shook my head. 'Are you?'

'No,' he said, sighing. 'But for many more reasons than this.'

He took my hand, just like he had in the car, trying to weave his fingers between mine. My heart throbbed as I peeled mine away.

'Annie, please. We need to talk.'

'No,' I said, my voice tight with frustration. 'Unless it's about this absolute shit-show of a situation, it's not the time.' Now that I'd sat down and let the adrenaline subside, I started to feel the cold. I shivered.

He put his arm around me, pulling me close, and this time I didn't object. The warmth of his body was so enticing, I couldn't stop myself from settling into the side of his chest. When his chin rested on top of my head, the reminder of our connection was too strong to fight against. My breathing slowed, my pounding heart throbbed a little less; I felt like I'd come home.

'I know it's not the time,' he murmured. 'But I'm right here. I'm with you, no matter what happens.'

I stiffened. I knew then that he didn't just mean tonight, and I couldn't open that door again.

'I can't...' I whispered.

'You *can.*'

I pulled away from him and looked up into his eyes. He didn't need to speak because the way he looked at me was loaded with everything that had gone unsaid at Ashcliffe. He was silently urging me to listen. All I could do was shake my head.

He let go of the breath he'd been holding and looked down. 'Okay. I won't push anymore. But promise me, once this is sorted out' – he flicked a nod at Olivia's house – 'you'll talk to me. I've got something important to tell you – about the music centre.'

I flinched. I'd got what I wanted – he was going to take the job. So why did I feel like I wanted to go back in time and tear up that letter? To let myself say the words that refused to be spoken? He'd made his decision, the one I'd hoped for, but instead of feeling triumphant, I felt empty. I needed to put some physical distance between us in case I weakened.

But before I could get up and walk away, a sleek Mercedes pulled into the street and parked outside the house. The door opened, and a slender leg appeared, followed by the hem of a sequinned, beautifully cut black dress.

'I suppose you should all come inside,' said Melissa as calmly as if we'd arrived for afternoon tea.

Inside, Olivia hovered by the kitchen island, her face white, as we all stood there amongst the glossy cabinets and soft spotlights. Olivia could barely look at me and mostly flicked nervous glances at Melissa.

'I don't understand,' I said. 'What are you both doing here?'

Melissa said nothing but tipped her head towards a photograph on the wall. She and Olivia were framed in black and white, seemingly on a cruise ship, both wearing evening gowns and holding glasses of champagne. Then I saw another smaller picture beside it – a younger-looking Melissa with a miniature version of Olivia sat on her knee, auburn curls nestled against Melissa's chest.

'She's your mum,' I breathed, and Olivia nodded.

'That's right,' said Melissa. 'And I wasn't going to let a pack of wolves surround her alone. She rang to let me know you were on your way.'

'But why?' My mind cast back to Olivia coming into my shop, ingratiating herself with me. Then day after day, listening, watching. 'You were a plant.'

'Yes. But I didn't mean... I didn't realise it would go this far.'

She looked anguished and then, as she glanced at her mother, cowed. She seemed to shrink in size under Melissa's gaze.

'Be quiet,' she said smoothly.

'You set this up,' said Penn.

'And you framed me,' barked Christa. 'What the hell is this all about?'

'Well,' said Melissa, going calmly to the fridge, extracting a bottle of white wine and pouring herself a glass. She sat at the island and sipped it. 'I suppose I should explain, since the baying mob is here.'

'Aye, you should!' shouted Jake. 'Is this some kind of fuckin' joke?'

'Far from it.' Her finger circled the edge of her glass while she regarded me and Penn. 'But it's less about you two than you'd imagine. It's Mike that I wanted to hurt. Your silly little shop just complicated things. I wanted to burn Mike to the ground, and stopping short of *actually* burning the arcade to the ground, running him out of business was the next best thing.'

'I know you wanted to buy his shop to expand, but this is a pretty extreme way of going about it,' I said.

'Yes, I wanted the shop, but he wouldn't give it up no matter what I offered. So I started an affair with him, thinking I might persuade him that way.' Her face grew pinched. 'Trouble is, I grew... fond of him. And he wouldn't leave his wife, broke up with me. So I wanted to get my own back.'

'That's... ridiculous,' said Penn.

She shrugged. 'A woman scorned... I knew that Arthur and Sven were due to retire, and Neil had been given the boot. Christa and Jake... well, neither of you were going to set the world on fire with your tin-pot shops. But when you two turned up, I could see there was potential for a successful shop at last. I needed to get rid of you.'

'You left all those awful comments on our social media,' I said.

'And the graffiti....' Penn's voice was brittle.

'Guilty,' she trilled then took a sip of wine. 'But once you started all that Jean-Luc business and people began flocking in, it didn't seem so easy. So I sent Olivia to keep an eye on things. She's been studying in America for a few years – nobody in Pilgrim Street would have had any idea she was related to me.'

'I'm sorry,' interrupted Olivia, looking at me with big, sad eyes. 'I started to like you, but she wouldn't—'

Melissa cut her off with a harsh look.

'But the burglary...' I breathed. 'You couldn't have.'

'I didn't. Some of my slightly less cultured contacts did. After that, I didn't want Olivia to be attached to the shop anymore, so I told her to pretend she'd been whisked away on a holiday. Then when you found Christa's earring, it seemed like a good opportunity to shift the blame.'

Olivia looked at me, tears streaming down her face. She looked distraught, and although I felt angry and betrayed, I could see how intimidated she was by her own mother. She was simply a pawn in Melissa's game.

'You bitch,' hissed Christa, stalking forward. 'You were willing to get me *locked up* to stick it to your ex-boyfriend?'

'Except it didn't pan out,' I said coldly. 'We figured it out straight away. We're not as stupid as you thought we were.'

'Those outdated photos of Dubai were the giveaway,' said Sophia acidly. 'You should really keep up to date with your knowledge of luxury destinations, darling.'

Melissa sighed, and I saw the first signs of exhaustion, as if by telling us the whole tale, she'd deflated, like an emptying balloon. 'So what happens now? You call the police, I'm led off in handcuffs? To be quite honest, I'm almost past caring.' She slugged the last of her glass of wine and looked at us defiantly.

'Mum...' said Olivia, her voice shaking. 'Mum, I'm scared.'

'Oh, give it up!' Melissa snapped at her before facing us

again. 'Thanks to you and your iffy choice of holiday snaps we're both fucked.'

'No,' I said, almost involuntarily. I couldn't take my eyes off Olivia. 'You're not. Or at least Olivia won't be.'

'Annie, what are you doing?' asked Penn.

'We aren't going to the police. Olivia, I'm not going to do that to you. Anyone can see what a nasty, bullying bitch your mother is. I don't think you'd have hurt a fly if she hadn't put you up to it.'

'Hold on,' said Jake. 'They've committed a crime. Quite a fuckin' few of them.'

'I know,' I said. 'But Olivia's a victim too. An idiotic victim, who should have known better, but she's been forced to do this by her mother. And we all know now how conniving Melissa is.'

She'd poured herself another glass of wine and raised it in an ironic way, which would have been funny if she wasn't such a nasty piece of work.

'I won't have your daughter's life ruined any more than it already has been. God knows she's drawn the short straw being brought up by you.' I looked at Penn; his mouth was a grim line, but he nodded. 'We won't go to the police. But you have to pay us back everything you've stolen and some compensation over and above that. Then you need to pay out your lease and get out of Pilgrim Street for good.'

Melissa sat back on her stool, holding my gaze. I bolstered mine with steel. She thought she could get the better of us, ruin our businesses, our friendships. The only thing I could thank her for was her attempts at sabotage bringing me and Penn closer together. But then thinking of Penn almost made me lose my nerve. Whatever bond we'd forged over all this mess was now a thing of the past. Although I wouldn't give Melissa the satisfaction of seeing it on my face.

Finally, she spoke.

'Fine. I'll give you what I owe you, and I'll leave. The reputation of Pilgrim Street is on its knees anyway. Gone to the dogs with all these bargain pop-up shops.' She sneered in my face.

'You know what, Melissa,' I said smoothly. 'If there's anything I've learned since starting my "bargain pop-up shop", it's that it doesn't matter how flash your shop looks, or how much cash you've got in the bank. It doesn't make you a better person than me.'

I looked at Olivia, whose cheeks were still pink from tears, but she'd stopped crying. 'Thank you,' she mouthed. I shook my head, feeling sorry for her but not ready to listen to her apologies.

'Come on,' I said to everyone else. 'I've got a shop to clear up, or I won't be ready to open up next week.'

Penn's eyes met mine, and they were full of admiration and longing. He took me by the hand, and this time I didn't let go.

THIRTY-SIX

Christa and I stood in the wreckage of the shop, looking around at the mess. We hadn't spoken in the car – she'd sat against Jake, his arm tight around her. In fact, none of us had said much at all. Penn sat in the front, feeling very far away from me again, and Sophia had driven at a much more sensible pace, delivering us back to the shop before leaving for home.

Penn and Jake were outside, Jake dragging deeply on one of his vapes while Penn gathered up discarded eco-warrior placards from the pavement. It turned out Linda had been persuaded to create a distraction, as well as send a well-timed message to Christa to leave if she didn't want to get involved. Linda's penchant for criminal damage to other 'unethical' beauty salons made her susceptible to a spot of blackmail and ensured Christa would appear to be in the right place at the right time.

'I don't think it's too bad,' said Christa, toeing the shards of a vinyl record. 'I think only a few things are actually broken; the rest is just scattered around the floor.'

I knelt down and picked up a bento box and its spilled contents. No harm done. I could put the shop back together almost as easily as putting the fork, knife and spoon back inside this box.

'She gave you the money then?' she asked.

'Mmhm. She transferred it to each of us before we left. Everything she arranged to have stolen in the burglary – those shady pals she drafted in to do it had already settled up for the goods. Plus extra for all this damage.'

'And that means you can carry on with the shop?'

'I want to.'

Despite my bravado at Melissa's, reality had crept back in. Now that I had the money she owed me, I could start again, restock the shop and keep my own head above water while paying off the loan for my parents. Just like I'd planned. But, despite the fact that I'd insisted Penn pack up and go home to Northumberland, I couldn't stand the thought of seeing his side of the shop empty, or somebody else moving in. It would take time for me to decide what to do.

I looked at Christa, who was now gathering up piles of paperback books, stacking them neatly on a table, flattening out the dog-eared corners with care. How I could ever have suspected my friend felt utterly beyond me now.

'I'm sorry,' I said quietly. 'I don't know how you can ever forgive me.'

She kept fiddling with the books, not looking at me. 'It doesn't matter. It's sorted now.'

'It does matter. I should have had more faith in you. You've never given me any other reason to doubt you.'

She laughed softly. 'Annie, I don't blame you. Really. Melissa did such a good job at setting me up, it's a miracle you didn't take a swing at me.'

'I know. I can't believe how accomplished Melissa was at all this.' I couldn't include Olivia's name. Despite everything – the fake photos, the text messages laying suspicion on Christa – I still felt sorry for her. 'Do you think I should be worried about not calling the police? What if she does something like this again?'

'I don't think she will. Not unless she finds another married man to take vengeance on. And we still have the video and the texts from Olivia in case she's stupid enough to try anything.'

I nodded. 'Do you really forgive me, Christa?'

She came over and wrapped me in a hug. 'Of course I do. Now stop apologising and help me pick up these fairy lights. It's Christmas tradition to untie the knots in them while swearing like a sailor.'

I grinned and took one end of the snaggled wire.

'So, do you want to tell me about you and Jake?' I asked, raising my eyebrow.

Her face glowed with what looked like embarrassment and affection.

'I thought you weren't keen on him. That he was cringe and a scourge on the environment with his disposable plastics.'

'Let's just say he grew on me. The night he and Penn sent Neil packing, I started to see him in a different light. Like one of those bodice-ripping alpha males on the cover of those romance novels you sell. I couldn't look at him without a little zing in the knicker area.'

It made me think of Penn again. He was different now, compared to what I thought I knew of him that first day in this shop. But he really hadn't changed at all – he'd always been a good person underneath.

I shook my head. 'Well, I suppose that explains why you were acting so shifty, having private conversations in your shop... It's going to take some getting used to seeing you two love-birding away in front of my eyes. It's cute... but weird.'

She smiled and bit her lip. 'On that subject, I've got something to tell you.'

'Please tell me you're not planning on starting an S&M club in the back of the arcade.'

'No,' she said, rolling her eyes. 'That stuff's just for me and him. The truth is, we're going away overseas. Together.'

My jaw dropped, then I remembered a conversation I'd had with Jake. 'Hold on. You're not going to be a holiday rep in Ibiza too, are you?'

She laughed, showing all of her teeth. 'Can you imagine me in a baseball cap, handing out vodka jellies to the eighteen-to-thirties?'

'Probably not.'

'No. We *are* going to Ibiza, but he's abandoned the holiday-rep idea. We're going to get jobs on the quiet side of the island then go travelling. I'm going to take him to Goa, to Machu Picchu – try and enlighten his spirit a bit. And we're going to offset our carbon footprint by planting trees in Nepal.'

'Wow. That's amazing. Good luck with getting him out of his tracksuits on the beaches though.'

'Oh, I'll have no difficulty doing that,' she said with a wicked look on her face.

'But what does that mean for your shops?'

'It means we're handing back our leases. I'm sorry I didn't tell you. When you came into my shop to tell me you were staying on and looked so pleased that we'd still get to work together, I didn't know how to say it. And I know it's exactly what Mike was worried about, losing his tenants, but we have to do what's right for us.'

I understood. Mike had always said he was worried about a few of the shops lying empty. And now that three out of the four were confirmed to be closing, there was no chance my little shop could sustain the arcade on its own. It seemed like any agonising I'd been planning to do about my future was point-less. Mam and Dad could have Melissa's money, and I'd start again, get a new job and say goodbye to Palmer's Arcade. It was almost a relief knowing I wouldn't have to cope with Penn's absence.

'I'm happy for you,' I said, meaning it. 'May your skins be as tanned as Jake's well-paddled arse.'

We burst out laughing.

'Remember, I need to pay you back for the cat o' nine tails.'

'That one's on me,' I said, tears streaming down my cheeks.

Then there was a noise behind us. Penn stood in the doorway.

'Can I borrow you?' he asked. His face was as worried as it was hopeful.

I looked at Christa.

'Go on,' she said. 'I'll see you in the New Year.'

It was approaching midnight, so as we walked closer and closer to the Quayside, the crowds of people grew more dense and rowdy. Penn held me close to his side, using his height to our advantage, seeking out spaces to weave into. It was so noisy we couldn't hear each other to speak, so I just held his hand tightly and let him guide me to wherever he wanted us to go.

Eventually, after pushing against the hordes heading towards the River Tyne for the fireworks, we arrived at the Millennium Bridge, which was equally full of people getting a good spot to see the show. We crossed over and ended up on the pavilion outside the modern art museum, which was a little quieter. The Glasshouse music centre stood opposite, its silver domes reflecting the moonlight. The significance of being outside it wasn't lost on me. In not too long, Penn would be running a music place of his own.

I stood against the railing and looked out at the river. He came up behind me, putting his arms over my shoulders, pulling me gently to him. He kissed the top of my head, and my chest throbbed with wanting him and needing to let him go. But I didn't push him away. Maybe if I had this last memory, I might be able to look back and feel it was all worth it.

'I miss you,' he said, his mouth still against my hair.

'It's only been a day. You'll miss me less soon.'

'I won't. I don't want to have to miss you at all.' I could hear him breathing unsteadily. 'Did you mean it? That it's over? You just want to be friends?'

'Yes.' *No.* 'But I'm not sure we can be friends either. It's just too hard.' Even saying this made my throat want to close up, like the words were stitching it up tighter as they came out. If I spent any more time with him, my walls would start to crumble and eventually I'd say how I really felt.

He sighed. 'I know. I don't think I can see you each day without wanting to take you home with me and lay you down in my bed.' His voice turned stiff. 'So if this is what you really want, then... I'll have to let it happen.'

'It is what I want.' I yearned to say that it was only because I couldn't bear to stand in his way, to repeat everything I'd said in the letter. But from what he was saying to me now, I could tell that he'd thought about it – and he agreed.

He let go of me. 'I just needed to ask you. I needed to be sure.' He turned me round and looked into my eyes. There was more pain there than I'd ever seen before, and I felt it myself, deep in my body like everything inside had been tied into a knot around my heart.

He kissed me gently on the cheek, rubbing the edge of my chin with his thumb, callused from years of playing guitar. 'I guess this is goodbye then. I won't bother you again, but I need you to know something. I'm meeting with your dad next week. I've got a business proposal for him. You won't have to see me. I'll tell him it's over between us.'

Then he turned and walked away, leaving me in a whirl of confusion. What did my dad have to do with this? I chased after him and tugged his arm.

'What do you mean you've got a meeting with my dad?'

'I... I wanted to tell you earlier. But I also wanted to see if you really meant what you said in your letter first. You said that we're done, so I'll take you at your word.' He stood back as if to leave again but faltered. He looked at me as if he didn't know what to do next.

'I still don't understand.'

'The job... I spoke to Nat again. I said that I'd only take it if he'd listen to my recommendation for the building work. I put forward your dad.'

I stared at him. 'What...?'

'I looked at his work online. He's good – really good. And Nathaniel thought so too. He agreed to it, for me to try and get your dad on board. I want you to know that I haven't done this to try and win you back. Well... maybe I hoped at first. But now I *know* it's final. I'm still going ahead with the deal, if your dad says yes. Building doesn't start until the spring, and there'd be an upfront payment for his services, so your parents won't need to sell the house. And you won't have to take a bank loan.'

'I'm not getting a bank loan anymore. The arcade isn't likely to stay open, so I'll give them the money I got back from Melissa and I'll have a fresh start.' Then I felt a bolt of frustration.

I walked up to him and thumped him in the chest with both fists. 'I told you, I don't need you to swoop in with money and connections to fix my family's problems, and my own. That's *my* job. It's mine!'

He held me by both arms, steadying me. 'It *isn't* your job, Annie! Your parents are grown-ups, and so are you. You need to have your own life, so now that they can keep the house without needing your help, you can actually do whatever it is you want to do. Even if there's no shop to hold on to, you can get your own place, pick a job you actually *want* rather than need.'

All the energy seemed to seep from me, and I couldn't respond.

'You won't give up,' he said. 'I know you. All those times I saw you bounce back after things went wrong. You're stronger than anyone else I know.'

'I'm not strong; I'm just stubborn.'

'So am I. So this business partnership is going to happen. Your dad will shake my hand, and everyone will get what they want. Including you.'

He gave me a sad smile and walked a few steps back, not breaking eye contact. He was just about to turn round when I called out.

'This isn't what I want!'

He stopped, as if his whole body had been locked into place.

'It isn't...' I repeated, more quietly. 'I miss you too. Already.' As soon as the words left my mouth, I wanted to take them back. They'd erupted from me like hot lava, and now I wanted to gather them up so they didn't cause him more pain.

He looked at me, breathing heavily. 'Say it again.'

I shook my head, taking a step back, forcing down the emotions that were trying to push to the surface. 'Don't listen to me. See! I'm not strong. I'm weak enough to say how I really feel, and that's really fucking selfish of me.'

'Why is it selfish? Annie, if you really *do* feel something, why didn't you tell me before? I know you understood what I meant back at Ashcliffe.'

'I did. But it was all happening so fast. I'd only just started to realise that I... that I...'

He looked at me with a glimmer of hope in his eyes. I swallowed dryly and scuffed my hand through my hair, looking away.

'If there was a right time to tell you how I felt... how I *feel*...' – my voice trembled as the wall I'd built inside threatened to crumble – 'then that wasn't it. But I'll get over you, and you'll get over me. You'll start your new life in Northumberland and make up with your family too. It's for the best.'

'I'm not moving back to Northumberland.'

'What?'

'I never planned to, but you didn't give me a chance to explain. Annie, please. Are you saying you still feel the same? Because if you are, you need to hear me out. I told Nathaniel I don't want the apartment. I meant what I said at Ashcliffe – I don't want to leave Newcastle. I'm staying in the flat, still doing gigs after hours. I'll commute to Northumberland.'

I couldn't move. I could barely breathe, never mind speak.

'If you still want me, just say the words. I'll be here, in the city, even if you don't ask me to be. I'll work with your dad, even if I have to beg him not to talk about you. But if you say you still want me, we can have it all.'

There was a tightness in my chest, a feeling that oxygen wasn't reaching my blood. My thumping heart felt like it could be heard across the river. He wasn't going anywhere. My parents wouldn't have to move. And Penn would still be reunited with his family as well as doing what he truly loved. My breath started to slow; my toes and fingertips could feel again.

'I want you,' I whispered. 'I want you so much, Penn. I want everything.'

He walked forward, that burning look in his eyes that I loved so much searing into mine.

'You *are* everything,' he said, plunging his hand into the hair at the back of my head, almost lifting me off my feet to bring my mouth to his. He kissed me so deeply, so hard, I felt like he was claiming me, telling me he'd never let me go again. And I claimed him right back, holding his face, kissing his lips, his cheeks, his stubbled chin.

He seemed to weaken as I grazed his face and neck with kisses, and when I stopped to look at him, he ran a thumb over my cheekbone.

'I love you, Annie. I don't know how you've done this to me, but I love you.'

And there it was. The words I'd willed him not to say in case they tipped me over the edge, made me give in to how I felt too. I'd tried to hold us both back from the precipice to keep him on safe ground. But now we were falling, and the rush was euphoric.

'I don't know how we got here either, but I love you too. I should have said it before. I should have told you a thousand times.'

We stood there in each other's arms, looking into each other's eyes. A wide grin spread over his lovely face.

'Did you ever think when we first met that you'd be standing on the Quayside kissing me on New Year's Eve?' he asked.

'I'd have probably pictured shoving you into the River Tyne.'

'And I might have had dark thoughts about putting you on one of those sailboats and sending you out to sea.'

'Not a yacht to St Tropez? I'd have thought that was more your style?'

He laughed. 'Very funny. You'll never give this up, will you?'

'Do you mean us, or me making fun of you for being called the Honourable Peregrine?'

'I'll never give up on us. But now and then I'd like to be *dishonourable* with you...'

'The lord of the manor and the kitchen maid?'

'No. The powerful businesswoman and the struggling musician...'

He wrapped me tightly in his arms and kissed me, more gently this time. I let myself fall into him, my whole body pressed to his as if even an inch of space between us was too far apart. I could feel every difference we'd ever had melting away, and we were matched perfectly in how we felt about each other.

Somewhere in the distance, a clock struck midnight and fireworks crackled over the Tyne Bridge, but the explosions in the sky were nothing compared to how I felt; inside, I was soaring higher than the glittering display above us. Then rain started to fall, light drops followed a deluge. Within moments, we were drenched but didn't move an inch. I remembered standing on a street months ago, soaked to the skin and dreaming of better times. And here I was now, at the start of a love story, finally getting my kiss in the rain.

THIRTY-SEVEN

ONE YEAR LATER

'I wanted to put a ribbon across the door, but Penn wouldn't let me,' I said, crossing my arms. 'I think it would have been fun.'

'I think so too,' said Mam. 'Although I might have known buggerlugs wouldn't agree to it.'

Penn put an arm around her shoulders and grinned. 'I already said yes to the balloon arch in the lobby, Denise. The ribbon was a step too far. Besides, who would have cut it?'

'Well, we do have a lord and lady here,' said Dad, nudging Hugh with his elbow.

Bunny rolled her eyes. 'When are you going to give up with that nonsense, Keith? I think we've had enough kitchen suppers to dispense with "Your Lordship" jokes.'

The six of us stood in front of the Northern Centre for Music wrapped in coats and scarves. There was a gentle flurry of snow falling around us and onto the roof of the building, a modern glass-fronted rectangle that somehow still fitted into the Northumberland landscape beyond. Inside, warm orange light burned from hanging lamps, and people buzzed around with champagne flutes admiring the local artworks that Penn had commissioned.

'Who'd have thought, eh, Den?' Dad removed Mam from under Penn's arm and slid his own around her. 'This time last year...'

I smiled, watching them. This time last year indeed.

After we'd dealt with Melissa, things had moved fast – Dad had shaken hands with Nathaniel faster than you could say 'load-bearing wall', and once the architect had designed the building, Dad had assembled his team and got to work. The upfront capital from Nat had bolstered Mam and Dad's finances enough to take the house off the market, and a new guitar or two had appeared in my dad's collection.

They'd made fast friends with Bunny and Hugh too, although they thoroughly enjoyed winding each other up. For Christmas, Bunny gave Dad a copy of *Debrett's Guide to Etiquette and Modern Manners*, and he gave her a Wickes catalogue, promising to buy her a power tool of her choice. They'd all enjoyed the traditional freezing-cold wild swim, while Penn and I watched from the boathouse, drinking hot chocolates and laughing at my dad turning the air bluer than his skin with expletives.

I squeezed Penn's arm when we walked inside the music centre. So much had changed since last Christmas, and yet many things stayed the same. Penn still gigged in Newcastle with the lads, but instead of him living in their flat, he now lived in a Quayside apartment... with me. And although I'd moved out of Neo's place, I'd been surprised that I missed him. So much so that I'd introduced him to Mike, and he now inhabited Jake's old unit at the back of Palmer's Arcade, selling movie memorabilia and telling customers how little they knew about Scorsese films. He still did a roaring trade.

The arcade hadn't gone under after all. Mike had mysteriously come into a sum of money, and I suspected it was something to do with his knowledge of what had gone down with Melissa, and his decision not to involve the police.

We walked around the lobby, stopping every now and then for Penn to shake hands with the guests. There was a huge amount of excitement about the new venture, and it was already overwhelmed with bookings, events and educators offering their services. Penn already had a long list of students wanting to learn guitar with him.

As I left Penn to it, I took a glass of champagne from a passing waiter and thought about the special event I'd hosted at Everything Must Go. It seemed a very long time ago. Looking at the elegant fixtures and tasteful party decorations here (including Mam's balloon arch, which I loved), I felt a pang of sentimentality about my little shop. It was still weird seeing someone else through the window, selling vintage clothing instead of my random collection of products. But now that Arthur and Sven had gone to Sweden, and Christa and Jake were somewhere in Polynesia, the place wasn't the same to me anyway.

There was a clatter of heels behind me, and Sophia rushed up with a bottle of champagne in hand. She slopped some into my half-empty glass and gave me a wicked grin.

'Don't tell anyone, but this is stuff from Daddy's cellar. Only the best for us, darling.'

We clinked glasses. 'If only my dad's cellar was brimming with champagne instead of bags of cement,' I said.

'Oh, there's time yet. I hear he's been signed up to work on the new rugby ground off the back of this.'

I nodded. I was so proud of my dad, and Mam too. She'd become part of Dad's business, making sure bills were paid on time, and woe betide anyone who didn't pony up.

'Now, I had an idea for launching the new range,' said Sophia, trailing a hand through the air theatrically. 'What if we hire some male models to hand out canapés wearing the jock straps and thongs? I think it would be marvellous, and if we pose a few of them by the window, we might bring in some passers-by?'

'Soph, we're running a high-end erotic boutique, not the red-light district in Amsterdam. Let's keep it classy.'

She pouted. 'But they're so gorgeous. I looked on the website, and there's one with the most amazing green eyes...'

'No!' I said, laughing. 'We want people lusting after the hand-stitched underwear and state-of-the-art sexual aids, not being distracted by other, er... packages.'

She laughed like a drain. 'God, Annie, you crack me up. But fair enough. Newcastle's exclusive rights-holders to Liaison Secrète have standards to uphold. Now, speaking of packages, I've got to dash. We've a delivery coming, and Olivia will need a hand sorting it out. *Ciao, bébé.*' She kissed me on the cheek and pressed the vintage champagne bottle into my hand before buzzing away.

After Melissa had stayed true to her word and vacated Visage Unique immediately, I'd started to eye up her building. It was larger, more conspicuous and, dare I say it, more sophisticated than my shop at the arcade. After I'd mentioned my idle thoughts to Penn, he and Sophia had come up with the idea of her investing and going into business with me. She was even able to use her contacts to secure us a meeting with Liaison Secrète in Paris and shake hands on an exclusivity deal. So Maison Jean-Luc, Newcastle's largest, most tasteful adult lifestyle product boutique was born.

We'd never seen Melissa again, hearing through the grapevine that she'd sold her house and moved away. But Olivia remained, distraught at the harm she'd caused, and after a while, and many tearful apologies, we'd taken her on to work in the shop. She was a hard worker, excellent with customers and had nothing good to say about her mother.

I was just about to go and rescue a stricken-looking Bunny

from one of Dad's building crew, who looked to be telling her a very filthy joke, when Penn walked up.

'Come on,' he said, taking my arm. 'I've got something to show you.' He led me towards the back of the building, nodding to our parents to follow along, and we turned a corner to face the bar area of the music centre.

Above the door, a space which had previously remained empty now had a sign reading 'Uncle Al's'.

I squealed and hugged him. 'Penn, this is perfect. He was such an inspiration to you.'

Hugh came to stand beside him, his eyes growing a little damp.

'Well done, m'boy,' he said after a shaky cough. 'He was always very proud of you.'

'And we are too,' said Bunny, patting Penn's arm.

Penn studied both of them, and I could see a look in his eyes that I knew was his heart growing fuller. He looked at me like that – often.

'There's something else,' he said, leading the way to the door, and he paused there. 'You all kept asking me what I was going to spend the Pink Floyd money on. It's taken me a long time to think of something that would be really important to me.'

Mam gasped. 'It's an engagement ring, isn't it? Annie...!' She bounced on the spot, tapping her hand on her chest.

'Don't be ridiculous, Denise,' said Bunny sharply.

A shocked silence fell across the group, and we all looked at her, open-mouthed. She returned the look with a steely gaze.

'Of course he hasn't spent his money on an engagement ring. It's tradition in our family to hand down their grandmothers' rings. Bertie had the first, and Peregrine will have the second. And I'm very much looking forward to seeing it on Annie's finger one day.' She smiled at me warmly, and then it was my turn to feel dewy-eyed.

'So, what *have* you spent it on, kidda?' asked Dad.

'Come and see,' said Penn, and we all followed him into the room. It was dimly lit and painted in forest green; leather armchairs were dotted around by the polished walnut bar. Immediately I noticed something new. A classic 1950s jukebox stood in between the windows, its lights glowing.

I went over and ran my hands over the glossy surface. 'It's beautiful. I'm sure Uncle Al would love it.'

'He really would,' agreed Penn. 'Now, let's test it out.'

He tapped a few buttons, and the first few bars of a very familiar song came from the speakers.

'Very clever,' I said, laughing as he pulled me into his arms to dance. 'But I thought you preferred the Manic Street Preachers' earlier work?'

'Everything Must Go' was a difficult song to slow dance to, but somehow the last year had taught us that it didn't matter what the steps were – as long as we danced them together, we'd do just fine.

A LETTER FROM LILY JOSEPH

Dear reader,

I want to say a huge, heartfelt thank you for choosing to read *Stuck Together*. To say I enjoyed writing this would be an understatement, it was such good fun. I also got a real kick out of writing about the North of England again, a place very close to my heart, inhabited by people who inspire humour and warmth in equal measure.

If you'd like to be the first to know about my latest releases, you can sign up at the following link. Your email address will never be shared, and you can unsubscribe at any time.

www.bookouture.com/lily-joseph

I first had the idea for *Stuck Together* from a Twitter/X post with a photo of a shop selling both vinyl records and tortoises. It seemed hilarious to me that you could buy a record and a very long-lasting pet under the same roof. The idea of two completely mismatched people competing to sell completely mismatched things sprang from there, and although Annie is selling her mum's 'premium sensual lifestyle products' instead of reptiles, I knew there was an enemies-to-lovers story in there somewhere!

Thank you again for reading, and, if you enjoyed it, I'd be very grateful if you could write a review. It would be great to hear what you think, and it can help others find and enjoy it too! I also love hearing from readers, so you can contact me via my website or by the social media links below.

Love from Lily

www.lilyjosephauthor.com

facebook.com/lilyjosephauthor

x.com/LilyJoWriter

instagram.com/lilyjosephwriter

ACKNOWLEDGEMENTS

Firstly, to my readers, thank you so much for reading my novels. It's an absolute joy (and also feels a bit mad) to write a story at my little desk then see it out in the world. So thanks for all the messages and social media pictures that remind me it's a *real, actual book*, and people are enjoying it.

To Nina Winters, my editor-slash-therapist, who has poured her time, expertise and passion into shaping this book – I am truly grateful for everything you do. Thank you for your patience and kindness, and also for coaxing me into a shorter deadline, which worked wonders on making me sit at my desk and actually write this thing. To my agent, Clare Coombes – thank you for being such a great cheerleader, as always. I'm so proud to be part of Team Liverpool Lit.

I'd also like to thank everyone at Bookouture for being so great to work with, especially the copy-editors and proofreaders who worked on both of my books. Special mention goes to Jess Readett for her wonderful work with publicity (even when my Wi-Fi connection lets us down!).

To all my friends in book-world and normal-world – thank you for cheering me on, listening to me whinge, cracking open the champagne and making me laugh, not necessarily in that order. Huge love and thanks to my family – Mam, Dad, Jeff and Chris, Andy, Jill, Simon, Penny, Luke, Paige and Tyler. You're all the best.

Thank you to George and Freya for being surprisingly invested in all this despite being teenagers, and for generally being the greatest kids ever. To Chris – thank you, firstly for explaining pheasant shooting to me in minute and horrifying detail, and secondly, for being the best thing that ever happened to me.

Last of all, I want to mention my great affection for the North of England. Even though I now live in North Yorkshire, my heart still belongs to the North East, and I'm thrilled I get to write books about the place I love best.

PUBLISHING TEAM

Turning a manuscript into a book requires the efforts of many people. The publishing team at Bookouture would like to acknowledge everyone who contributed to this publication.

Commercial
Lauren Morrissette
Hannah Richmond
Imogen Allport

Cover design
Beth Free

Data and analysis
Mark Alder
Mohamed Bussuri

Editorial
Nina Winters
Imogen Allport

Copyeditor
Laura Kincaid

Proofreader
Emily Boyce

Milton Keynes UK
Ingram Content Group UK Ltd.
UKHW020815231024
450026UK00004B/228

The hate is real.
So is the chemistry.

Annie is heading into the holidays alone. And as a confirmed singleton, she decides to open a shop selling the kind of treats every single woman would want to find under the tree. After all, who doesn't like to get a 'Premium Sensual Lifestyle Product' for Christmas, right?

Penn is in a bind. He needs to come home for Christmas with a girl, or his parents will set him up with someone 'suitable'. Nothing is too good for the Honourable Peregrine Burton-Edwards after all. But that's not what Penn wants. He just wants to sell vintage records in his shop and meet a nice, normal girl.

The first time Annie and Penn meet, Annie feels a flutter in her chest – he's tall, dark and handsome, with cheekbones you could sharpen a blade on. So when he offers to share the shop with her to save on rent, she gladly accepts.

Huge mistake… Annie and Penn are poles apart and butt heads at every turn. But with the holidays looming, Penn will soon need to ask for a little favour, and Annie, with no plans to speak of, is the only girl who can help. As the arguments get more heated, so do the sparks flying between them. Will they put their differences aside and come together? And could it be for more than just Christmas?

A completely addictive, utterly hilarious and totally swoonworthy romantic comedy, Stuck Together will make you fall head over heels for Annie and Penn. The perfect holiday read for fans of Catherine Walsh, Emily Henry and Mhairi McFarlane.

ƀ www.bookouture.com

ISBN 978-1-83525-350-2

90000

9 781835 253502

Designed by Beth Free, Studio Nic&Lou. Illustrations by Shutterstock.